THE
Saddler's Song

Sara Powter

Bible Quotes from the King James Version

ISBN: 9780645783353
Paperback edition

ABN 99 768 734 831
Pacific Wanderland Publications
Kincumber, Australia NSW, 2251

saragpowter@gmail.com
https://www.sarapowter.com.au

1st edition 2025 printed by Kindle, an Amazon Company;
available on Kindle Unlimited & KDP
Pacific Wanderland Publications
1st edition Large print, Amazon/Kindle

Cover
Background
West view of Parramatta,
1819 / J. Lycett | Collection - State Library of NSW
FILE NUMBER: FL20614252

Inset
'A Violinist'
by Leis Schjelderup,
1878, Bergen Kunstmuseum

In the Public Domain

Inside Cover image
Leather tanning industry, 19th-century illustration
A worker processing tanned skin. A tannery is where animal skins are
turned into leather. Chemicals are used to make the skins tough yet soft.
Further processing includes polishing and dyeing of the leather.
Artwork published in 1867.

Australian Historical Novels
(All stand-alone books)

A First Fleet Stories (1788+)
Gentle Annie Soames
The Emancipated Potter
Paternity Unknown

The Hunter to Macquarie Collection (1795-1822)
When Upon Life's Billows
The Saddler's Song
Tuppence to Pass
His Majesty's Pageboy
A Fist Full of Holey Dollars
Far From the Whispering Sheoaks (2026)
Quest for Survival (2027)
Bound Down in Iron Chains (2026)
Buddy's Promise (2027)
Linen Shirts Aplenty (2027)

Unlikely Convict Ladies Trilogy (1792-1840s)
Dancing to Her Own Tune
(co-authored by Sheila Hunter & Sara Powter)
Amelia's Tears
A Lady in Irons

The Lockleys of Parramatta (1800-1901)
Unshackled Lives - *Prequel novella - free with newsletter signup*
Hands Upon the Anvil
Out Where the Brolgas Dance
Diamonds in the Dirt
The Earl's Shadow
Once a Jolly Swagman
Jonty's Journey

The Convict Birthstain Collection (1820-1840s)
No More, My Love
The Vine Weaver
Scotch at The Rocks
Waiting at the Sliprails
Convict Shadows of the Past
In Defence of Her Honour
I Can't Stop Tomorrow
Madeline's Boy
Jam or Marmalade for Tea

Fools Gold Trilogy 1840s- 1850s
The Breeze Gently Shifts (2028)
The Silver Thimble (2028)
Knots Behind the Tapestry (2028)

Sheila Hunter's
Australian Colonial Trilogy (1840-1850s)
Mattie
Ricky
The Heather to The Hawkesbury

Historical note:-

Access to cow hides in the early colonial days was problematic, if not nigh impossible. Tanning the skins of the local animals was the obvious choice. Kangaroo skins produce a fine and extremely strong leather without the need to thin the skin.

Thanks and acknowledgements

To my husband, Steve,
Thank you for all your support in my writing.
He's my Alpha reader.

To Roby Aiken
for your patience in correcting my punctuation;
to my Beta readers
Noreen Robertson, Linda Upcroft, Lee Boehm
& Anna Marie Leffew
for doing the final read-throughs,
and Anna Marie Leffew for the advertising she does on my behalf.

And…
Rebekah Robinson for my cover.
Cover by Beckon Creative
beck@beckoncreative.biz

Table of Contents

The grammar and language in this book are
Australian English spelling

KEY

~ - Time passing in the same locality

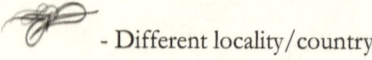 - Different locality/country

Chapter 1   The Pure Collector
Outside London, 1801

*T*he whining voice of the young boy carried over the sound of the scraper rubbing off the fur of the skin. "But, Papa, I collected a bucket full of dog poop yesterday. Have we used it already?

His father nodded. "Sorry, Georgie. I need a few more bucket loads to finish this order. I need them to soften the hides, and you know I need it to soak them in."

A massive pile of hides was fresh from the knackery, and they had spent the morning salting them. They would need to remain salted for a month and then spend a day or so in a heavy saline water bath. This meant they would be working flat out to prepare the hides over the following months. As the weather was quite hot, George knew that sometimes the skins fermented. The salt would loosen all the hair, causing it to slough off easily. It was his first time measuring out the lime for the next stage, but he was excited that he could now help his papa so much.

It was fortunate that the tannery was located on the far outskirts of town, as the entire tanning process stank. The small village would eventually grow and encircle them, but that was hopefully years in the future.

The dark-haired head nodded. "That's okay, Papa, but I cleaned all the poop yesterday from the park, so there may not be much more. I could head to the duke's pigeon house and ask if I can clean the dovecote. Would that work as well?"

Albert had not stopped working on the two-handled, curved blade; it was moved skilfully. The hair, fat, and detritus were scraped onto the workroom floor. "Get what you can, son, and be quick. Try the park again first, then swing by the duke's dovecot to see if they have cleaned the coop. Top the bucket up with *guano* or the bird or chicken poop if need be."

"Sure thing, Papa. I'll be back in a jiffy if I can."

Ten-year-old George Ellis picked up the old leather bucket and headed to the park where the rich people sent their spoiled dogs to be walked. There was usually a ready supply of the foul-smelling lumps, but he did not enjoy being a pure collector. His father, Albert, was a tanner and needed the disgusting substance to condition the leather properly. The new skins had already been salted and were soaked in a tub to remove the leftover salt before being treated with lime. Georgie liked *scudding*. That was removing the remaining hair and fur after the skins came out of the long bath. It was the next process that he didn't like. The smell of the skins was not too bad until then.

Only when the hair was gone were the skins and hides added to another vat. It was this solution that stank. It was made with dog poop and other ingredients. If they couldn't get enough doggie doo, then they had to use chicken droppings or, worse still, clean out the duke's dovecot and use the pigeon poop. The stench of this solution was nauseating, but the skins needed to go through the bating bath to become supple. This solution his father made from animal brains he bought from the butcher. Another chemical was added, it was called alum. If they skipped this step, the raw leather would be stiff and unyielding.

Ellis's tannery was renowned for producing lovely, soft hides and leathers. It was why George didn't complain much when he was sent off on this unpleasant errand.

After the skins had soaked in the bating bath, they would be removed, and the dung mix needed to be pounded into the leather. George gagged every time this was required. The smell never improved, and it often splattered everywhere. Once the skins had been treated with the poop, they would be covered in another bath, only this time it was made of bran from barley or rye. If bran was not available, they used ash bark as an alternative. This was used for longer periods and even in multiple soakings if lime was needed in the initial bath.

As George walked, he re-created the tanning process in his mind. One day, he would have to take over the business, and he would need to be familiar with every aspect of the process.

They usually paid some street children to collect the filthy excrement, but a few of them had become ill, and his papa had given them some money to buy food. The four children vanished before he realised he had run out of the required dung.

Pure collectors were some of the lowest-paid and most disgusting jobs anyone could do. The orphaned children, commonly known as street rats, were willing to earn a few pennies for a bucket of this revolting goo. Toshing was one of the few jobs that was worse. Sorting through people's poop to look for anything of value was enough to make Georgie dry retch. Even the thought of that turned his stomach.

He reached the park and saw that many dogs had visited that morning. He had brought a square of stiff leather and used that to pick up each squishy pile of doggie doo. It didn't take long before his bucket was half full.

He was about to leave and head to the nearby dovecot to top the bucket with guano when a servant appeared with six giant wolfhounds. Georgie knew that their large dumps would nearly fill his bucket. All he had to do was wait.

The servant let the dogs off their leashes, and they frolicked gleefully. The massive beasts were big enough to ride, and George was somewhat shy of the lunging hounds. The shaggy dogs eventually came towards him to sniff the contents of his bucket.

All six dogs soon surrounded Georgie. They stood at shoulder height and could easily have knocked him over and sent him flying. However, he was familiar with these animals. Each dog gave him a sniff, and then his hands were licked until the six large beasts were struggling to find some skin without a dog tongue slurping off the scent.

The footman waved to him and came over to chat. As he drew near, he said, "Hello, lad. I must admit, you kiddies who collect this filth make the park much nicer for those who have to walk the animals."

George grinned and replied, "My papa needs it. He's a tanner, and this poop is part of the process." The dogs ran off.

The servant nodded with his nose wrinkling in disgust. "Well, I'm glad I don't have to pick up after these canine horses. They may be gentle beasts, but their droppings stink."

They turned and watched one dog humping over near the fence. His large deposit made Georgie smile. "Sir, do you mind if I come and collect their droppings every day? I didn't know one dog could make such a large... um, deposit."

The footman grinned. "Be my guest. The duke, who owns these magnificent wolfhounds, requires that I pick up after them. He has walked in the vile stuff at the lodge, and trust me, it's not easy to remove from a rug once it's been walked in."

Another dog came and sniffed the steaming heap, and he made his deposit nearby. They each did their business, and Georgie collected it, then headed home with his bucket full. As he reached the park gate, he turned and waved to the footman. "Thanks, mister! That saved me a trip to the duke's dovecot. I'll be back at the same time tomorrow."

The footman nodded and waved a farewell. He produced a ball from his pocket and threw it to the other end of the park for the dogs to play with. They took off after it, not even realising that Georgie had gone.

George's early return would permit him to get his work done and do some practise on his grandfather's fiddle. This was his daily reward for finishing his work.

~

1806

For five years, George learned the trade and experimented with various techniques and treatment durations. The pure collection of the wolfhounds' excrement made the collection easy. The dogs' droppings filled half a bucket every afternoon. The local poor children were still paid to collect more as they needed the pittance they earned, but the wolfhounds' deposits met most of their requirements.

Learning the best treatments for various skin and hide types was something he came to love. Occasionally, his father would need to supply trimmed sizes, and George claimed all the off-cuts of tanned leather. He was now trying to make small items to sell to supplement their income. His older brother, Rob, lost the use of his legs, and as he aged, he became much more difficult to handle due to his frustration at feeling so useless. They didn't know what was wrong with him, but he had contracted an illness shortly before George was born, and it had all but crippled him. He could work with his hands, but his feet could not hold his weight. They were as thin as matchsticks with skin on them. He had feeling in his feet but no strength.

George realised that Rob could do very fine and fiddly work, and George had the thought of him making leather thonging from the offcuts. It was some of this that George used to finish his projects. Rob then wished to try some himself. While doing this, he asked George to play him something on their grandfather's instrument. The years of practising had paid off, and George now played the violin beautifully.

With their father's permission, the two lads used his blades, awl, and needles to make wallets, scabbards, water bags, and other small items. They also made drawstring coin purses and other assorted items from some of the soft suede inside. Rob even invented a new decorative two-needle sewing technique using waxed linen thread. Their mother would take these items to the weekend markets, and their sales would supplement the family income. The soft leather drawstring coin purses were popular, and people soon ordered these items. Scallop edges were cut into a leather circle, and holes were set half an inch in the sides. Rob could thread the thin leather thong through the holes and then pull it together to make purses. Rob could make these by himself, and soon he had a full-time job assembling these soft suede products.

The tannery no longer stood alone on the edge of the town. Other companies had built sheds near them, and there was even a brave house or two within smelling range of the tanner's shed.

George's mother, Amelia McLean, was the daughter of the tanner from a nearby town. Milly had met Albert when her father fell ill, and he needed to purchase some hides for an urgent order. Albert and his father had filled their order, but they had also shared the profits.

Albert and Milly married less than three months later, shortly before her father died. They inherited all the leather-making tools from Thomas McLean, which came rolled up in a large leather pouch. However, Milly also inherited his violin, but no longer had time to play it. Her papa started teaching her when she turned eight. She was proficient but lacked passion.

Milly had learned tanning from her father and showed her sons how to work with various kinds of leather. She took care of these tools after her mother died.

Rob was now happy as he could contribute something to the family income. Soon, Albert realised that his eldest son would sit up straighter and was happier if occupied. He started tanning hides especially for his son's use.

Previously, if a hide had a blemish, he would not bother tanning it properly. Now George and he finished them all. Rob utilised everything, making key tags from tough leather to comb pockets, sword scabbards, and knife sheaths; all the previously discarded leather was now resold as completed items.

~

George's world fell apart at the end of summer in 1807.

It was just one week after he turned sixteen. Disease ravaged the town, and Doctor Jamieson initially thought the disease was smallpox. Mr Jenner had visited their village some years before, and the entire Ellis family had been given Mr Jenner's cowpox vaccination. Hopefully, they would be safe.

The appearance of the round flat spots on some of the sick people was soon followed by high fever, chills, along with excruciating muscle aches and tiredness, to the point they were unable to rise from their beds.

These were not the symptoms of smallpox; the doctor was wrong.

It wasn't until Rob and Milly died that the diagnosis of typhus fever was made. Many in the village perished, and they were the first two fatalities in their community.

George and Albert fought against the disease as it ravaged their bodies.

Albert finally succumbed ten days after his wife and eldest son.

George survived, but at sixteen, he was utterly alone. He sat in the silent tanning shed and wept. Being sixteen is hard enough when you have a family to support you, but having those loving people ripped from his side in such a manner left him devastated and forlorn. The fact that he was still feeling weak from his illness didn't help. The villagers were still sick, so no one visited to enquire how he fared.

George was numb. He had felt ill when he contracted the disease, but an Italian friend gave him a disgusting-tasting mix he had to take daily. The oregano, garlic, and honey mix was revolting, but he had survived. However, his family refused to take the concoction, and they were now gone. They had died in agony, and he had been unable to help them. Now, his family were buried together in the local graveyard.

At his father's funeral, George overheard a conversation with his friend Bill Felton about a new life in New South Wales. A vessel was scheduled to depart in a few months, and they were willing to accommodate a few more passengers. The ship was called the *Sinclair,* and it was sailing in October.

George didn't want to stay in the village where there were so many memories. Neither of his parents had siblings or close cousins, so he had no family ties. Many of his friends had died, too. Bill was one of the few remaining.

On returning from his father's funeral, the stench of the tannery got to him. It never usually worried him, but he had not been eating properly, and he was still not well. At his front gate, he vomited until he felt dizzy. Mopps, his stray canine companion, remained by his side as he heaved up the contents of his stomach. She was the only living thing that remained at the now quiet house.

The silence was deafening. George sank onto the dirt floor in the tannery and wept.

The shaggy mutt was now his only comfort, but she was not enough to make him stay. She nuzzled at his arm, and he enfolded her and sobbed into her matted fur.

The memories of the happy times were too hard to bear. He expected one or another member of his family to appear, or he hoped to hear a laugh, or he was waiting for his name to be called for a meal. Nothing.

He decided on the spot that he would sell the business and leave. He didn't want to be alone, especially here. There were too many memories.

He wiped his eyes on his only clean shirt and took a big sniff. His mother had put up a chalkboard shingle on the front of the tannery listing leather items for sale. After gazing at the notice for some time, he rose, wiped it clean, and wrote, "Tannery for sale. Apply within."

With his eyes still stinging from his tears, he hung the sign on the front of the shed. He sniffed and wiped his wet cheeks on his sleeves.

George didn't even know how to wash his clothes or how to cook a meal for himself. His mother had always done that, and he never even thanked her. Now, she was gone, as was his beloved brother and father. He was alone, so totally and absolutely alone that he wanted to run away. He hurt. He was leaving, even if he had to walk off and leave everything there. Rather than return to work, he saw a stack of empty wooden crates. These were ready for packing the tanned hides in. Three were full of finished leather that had not been sold.

George decided to pack the necessary tools and set them aside for transport. He would set up a tannery in the New World and needed tools for his trade. There were duplicates of most necessary items, so he planned to leave the poorer quality ones from his grandfather's shop for the new owner. He carefully wrapped these sharp instruments in their leather pockets and layered them into a skin-lined crate.

All afternoon, he worked and sorted. Three more empty crates were set aside for the hides, which were currently drying on the stretching boards.

Chapter 2   Leaving It All Behind
1807

*L*ess than a week after putting up the for-sale shingle on the wall outside the shop, George had sold the tannery. He permitted the new man to start immediately, as some of the skins in the tubs needed attention. He showed Miles the stage for which each vat was used. The new tanner was a middle-aged man with a wife. Miles and Amanda Armstrong had grown children. They had recently arrived from near Liverpool and wished to start a business near his wife's family. They were currently living in the next village. Until George left, they would stay there; the new owner would travel to work.

Miles used a similar tanning process in his previous employment, but this was the first time he owned his own tannery.

George occasionally assisted if he got bored with packing. He left most of his mother's clothing for Mrs Armstrong to use, but kept some of his father's and Rob's clothing for himself. It wasn't much better than his own, but it would bulk out his possessions. His father's oilskin coat was packed along with other warm items.

Miles was instructed to let their minister have anything they didn't want to keep, and he would distribute it amongst the poor in the village.

George introduced him to the street children, and with the promise of payment, they were to maintain a steady supply of dog waste.

Miles was willing to avoid having to collect this himself. He paid them slightly more than Albert Ellis had.

George had already given Reverend Carlston two loads of old clothing plus some other household items he didn't want. These had been in storage since his parents married nearly twenty years earlier. The items had come from his grandfather, Albert Attwell's, house. George spent days going through each chest, sorting what he would take and what he would give away. He kept some of his grandmother's embroidery and a few sentimental items. After checking the pockets for forgotten coins, he repacked most of his grandfather's clothing to donate to charity. A bundle of what looked like carving tools, he shoved into his bag.

George had forgotten these cases even existed. He remembered the day when he was a child, his father showed him his grandfather's violin. He remembered the first time he had seen the instrument. They had been sorting the contents back then. Once George found the violin, he abandoned the rest of the cases and demanded to be taught how to play the instrument. His mother taught him to play 'Twinkle, Twinkle Little Star.' It was a new nursery rhyme, but easy to play.

George caressed the case. The violin was carefully put aside to be taken with his personal luggage. It was his most treasured possession. He could make it sing. His mother had told him a little about the instrument, but his grandfather had written a note of its history and tucked it in the rosin container. This instrument was made of three different timbers: spruce for the top, willow for the internal blocks and linings, and maple for the stunning single-piece back, as well as the ribs and neck. The note his grandfather had written in 1763 was still easily legible. It read that it was made in Italy by Bartolomeo Giuseppe Guarneri. He also included the original receipt of £15 from 1730. It had been given to his grandfather to clear an outstanding debt.

The violin was a deep, rich red, and although it had some scratches and wear from use, its sound was almost angelic. If George could only take one thing, it would be this instrument. His mother could play a little and taught him the rudiments. From there, he asked the minister to teach him how to read music.

George had an aptitude and played well within a year. He practised every night after dinner. He loved to feel the strings vibrate and sing, so he played whenever he got the chance. The first sounds he made were like a drowning cat. But soon, he was being asked to play at village dances. He never showed them his incredible skill with the more complicated pieces, but when other boys were given clothes for their birthday gifts, his parents purchased the most recent sheet of classical music for him. Bach, Mozart, and Beethoven were his favourites, but his last gift from his father just before the disease hit was a sheet of music from a new composer they had never heard of before. His name was Paganini, and the piece was called '*Divertimenti Carnevaleschi*, No. 1'. The frivolity of this was a delight to play, and George found that it had been first performed and written, especially with a Guarneri violin. Paganini, a lad only ten years older than George, owned one similar to George's, and this composition was perfect for him. He was already composing the most incredible masterpieces.

George played the new composition for his family only a month ago. With memories washing over him, he wiped away his tears and stowed his instrument away for safekeeping. The music sheets were stored in a leather satchel, which he kept with his instrument.

George returned to sorting his grandfather's things and found a bundle of sheet music that he had not seen before. He added that to the satchel.

Miles arrived with cases of his own tools, so George packed most of the tools he had not planned to take. He had found nearly five pounds in coins in various coats and pockets in both his grandfather's and father's clothing. He checked each item carefully before placing it in the vicar's box. Knowing he had to make his money last, the sale of the tannery had brought in twenty pounds, and with these coins and the sale of a crate of leather, he had nearly fifty pounds to his name. It was certainly enough to start a new life in the new world. He made a leather pouch and planned to attach it somewhere to keep his money safe. It had a thick thong to hang around his neck when in transit.

George left Miles working and set off to book passage on a ship to New South Wales. He didn't really care which one, but the ship he overheard some people talking about was called the *Sinclair*. The soldier who spoke about it was one of the local lads, and Bill had come to say his farewells to his parents before embarking on an adventure. It would ease the loneliness if George could travel with someone he knew. He had spoken with Bill at some length before they left the cemetery.

Bill Felton was enlisted in the 45th regiment and was travelling to reinforce the other regiments in the colony of New South Wales. He was a younger son and would inherit nothing from his family. Bill always lusted for adventure and had already journeyed to the Antipodes. He told George about the strange animals and endless sunny days. It sounded like a balm to George's hurting soul.

George didn't want to enlist; paying for a berth was the only other way to get on the ship. With money from the sale, he booked a cabin and a large section in the hold for his leather cargo. He now had twenty crates of leatherwork and one small leather luggage case his father had made for his clothing, but he needed something else. He needed a safe place for his violin and tools.

On return from the booking office, George passed a second-hand shop, and as he had time, he wandered in. He had seen an interesting item through the window. This enormous travelling case opened diagonally, and the front folded up to convert into a tallboy. When opened, it had a set of eight drawers, a desk flap with side slides, and hooks that could be inserted into the side for hanging clothing. One drawer and some leatherwork needed repair, but he purchased the damaged travelling case for only a pound. He arranged with the storekeeper for a carrier to deliver it the following day. He knew the violin would fit in one of the two large bottom drawers. George knew he had enough leather off-cuts to put on new hinges and replace the other torn or worn leatherwork. Miles was handy with the tools and may be able to help repair the broken drawer.

George could now pack more of the clothing he wished to take. He also wanted to keep his leather-working tools dry, and all his special instruments of trade could now be put in the bottom drawers. Before heading home, he also purchased some books to read on the journey and three blank journals to record his travels.

The ship was due to depart London at the end of October, and he was permitted on board ten days prior to embarkation. Miles purchased the wagon, the old nag, and the house, but George had not included his beloved shaggy dog, which he had found injured a few years earlier. Mopps would travel with him to the colony.

George was thrilled when Captain Jackson was on the dock when he booked. He had offered to show George around his ship and the cabin. The room was small, with a single box bed, but it was adequate.

The captain explained various things of interest to him. "Laddie, the ship is actually not the *Sinclair*, but *Lady Madeline Sinclair*. That's a mouthful, so we shorten it."

They discussed the cargo space and the amount he would be permitted to bring. When he explained that he was going to the colony to work as a tanner, the captain told him to bring what he liked. Captain Jackson even permitted Mopps to share George's cabin.

George knew that the shaggy mutt would eat whatever she was given. He had learnt not to feed her liver as her bowels exploded regularly with the most offensive odour. One of the old farmers had told him never to feed her onions. However, she was as happy with cold porridge as fresh chicken necks, but how she would cope on a ship for months was unknown. She had survived on the streets for some time, so she would need to survive on whatever they had. He discovered that she even ate spew. That thought disgusted him.

Over the following week, George transported his crates into the ship's cargo hold. It took three loads on his old wagon, and he had to hire dockworkers to help move the full crates up the gangplank. When he added the last big load, he was surprised to see more crates similar to his. He could see they also contained some tanned leather. The name on these crates was B. Parker. A smile tickled George's lips. He wondered who this person was, but at least he would have someone to discuss leatherwork with. He continued to lug the other items up the gangplank and stow them in the hold. He had just stacked the last crate when a young man struggling with a box of a similar size walked up the gangplank.

George grinned and went to assist. He introduced himself while they struggled with the heavy crate. "Hello, I'm George Ellis. If you are 'B Parker', I saw your stuff below. Are you a tanner?"

The young man was beaded with perspiration. While nodding, he dumped his load down and said, "I'm Ben Parker." He puffed before adding. "And no, I'm a saddler. I am moving to New South Wales to start afresh. I heard they were looking for men with skills."

George nearly shouted with joy. "Me too, Ben; moving, that is."

The two young men were more alike than they knew. Both had recently experienced family losses and decided to cut ties with the Motherland and leave. Ben worked as a saddler with his aged father. His death had left him without his teacher and best friend. He, too, had sold the business and left. Ben's crates were heavy because they contained partially made saddles.

George was thrilled. "Ben, I have crates of leather, but I've never made a saddle. Will you teach me how?"

Ben was equally pleased. "Sure thing, George. I ran out of leather to finish some, and others are half-made, so I think we could come to an agreement and finish them *en route*. This crate is the spare metal work for new saddles, stirrups, buckles and the like, but the rest are packed as kits, so this one is extra heavy."

Once the wagon was unloaded, the two young men poked their fingers through the open sides of George's crates. Ben saw one hide perfect for finishing an embossed saddle, but he had no more matching leather to make the pommel and stirrup flaps. In the darkness of the hold, it was hard to see the colours of the leather, but that could always be dyed.

Ben, at nineteen, was a little taller than George; he could reach up to feel the various tanned hides that were not fully tucked into the top crates. "You have some marvellous hides there, George. I may buy some from you *en route*."

George was thrilled. "Sure, the finished ones are on top. The lower crates are undyed hides that are ready for staining. While we have room, if you want to juggle any of the crates, we may as well do it now before we are crowded out. Apparently, the food stores will be loaded tomorrow. Other cargo will arrive once the food is on board."

With a barely perceptible nod, the two set about rearranging the crates so they could access the needed skins easily. They left the undyed hides on the bottom, as they did not want to mess up the ship with the messy stains.

George knew he had all his precious leather working tools in the bottom drawer of his travelling chest, but the top crate also contained spools of thread, suede, and thonging that they would need. They would pry that open when required, but he hoped Ben would have plenty of those.

They sorted Ben's boxes into order so that they could be finished quickly. He had nine nearly complete saddles and fifteen in various stages of construction. Ben said, "George, the bottom crates contain the wooden tree bases for English saddles. However, I also have some American stock saddle bases. I put them on the bottom as they are larger and stronger than the small English-style ones and side saddles. Sitting on top of that is the wool flocking, which I need to keep dry. I use this to stuff the bottoms of the saddles. There is a full bale of the stuffing. Can we put that on top?"

Ben tried to remember what else he had packed. "On top of that is all the metalwork for the saddles. I need stirrups, stirrup bars, rivets, buckles, and other bits and bobs. That's what was in that heavy box you helped me with. The leather used for saddle bases must be soft and supple. It doesn't matter what colour the bases are; only the feel of the leather matters. I'll teach you all about the various parts required, and we can raid your leather, and you can make your own saddle."

George was nearly jumping out of his skin with excitement. His father was only a tanner. But he now had a personal tutor for almost six months to teach him the finer art of saddlery. "Ben, I'm moving in on Monday. Are you in a cabin or steerage?"

Ben's face fell. While they talked, he saw George's cabin and how much room he had. He had a single box-frame bed, but the room was only six feet square. His steerage berth was a hardwood platform with no privacy whatsoever. "I'm only in steerage, George."

They emerged into the weak sunshine and stood at the gunnels chatting. George frowned. "My cabin only has one bed, but you could keep your valuables there if you wish. Oh, I forgot to mention that I have permission to bring my dog, such as she is. Mopps is more like an overgrown foot warmer. She's a mongrel of unknown parentage and looks like a mop. She had been my saving grace over the last month. Typhus took my entire family in just one week." He couldn't explain more as tears were not far away.

Ben's hand rested on his shoulder. "I know grief, too, George. It kicks you in the guts, and nothing can take away the hurt. Try to get through one day at a time, and you will be able to cope with it. My ma died when I was born, and my pa was nearly fifty when I came along. He died last month. So, I know what I'm talking about."

George nodded. The lump in his throat had not gone; he finally managed to say, "I don't know why or how I survived, Ben, but I'm still as weak as a blooming kitten. I'm fine for a while, then I nearly drop." The sun was filtering through gathering clouds, but it was quite warm.

Ben smiled and said, "Do you like stout? If so, bring a crate or two on board and stow them in your room. A glass a day will soon have you back on your feet. I hate the stuff, but Pa fed it to me when I was sick. It always gave me a pick-me-up when needed."

George's nose had screwed up. "I'm not a big beer drinker, Ben. I'd rather cider than the thick black stuff."

Ben chuckled. "Me too, but this is medicinal. It's like drinking black glue, but it is a good pick-me-up when recovering."

George decided to buy a couple of crates and stow them under his bed. There was plenty of room there, and they would not be too noticeable. What's more, the bottles and corks were useful for his leather dyes when he had consumed the contents.

~

Miles and his family were introduced to the minister and welcomed at George's farewell morning tea after church on Sunday. Amanda and their children moved into the house during the week and settled in. Rather than making George feel awkward, she was so sweet that her warm hugs and fabulous cooking brought a completely different atmosphere to the home. Miles was equally as friendly. George was happy the business would be in good hands. Miles and George moved the colossal travelling case to the wagon on Monday morning.

Mopps had been bathed and trimmed the evening before, and the children cuddled her, brushing and drying her in front of the fire. She was tied up, so she would stay clean. She started whining when she saw her basket and blanket loaded onto the wagon. Life had changed for her, and George was her saviour, so she would go with him wherever he led. He had wept into her matted coat when he rescued her and had bathed, fed, and nurtured her for the last two years. She would stick with him. She looked like she had some sheepdog in her, but only the Lord knew what else.

The trip to the London docks was taken at a leisurely pace. This was more so that George could absorb his surroundings than anything else. There was no hurry to board, and Ben was not due at the ship until noon. Mopps was left on the wagon on guard as the two men carried the bottom drawer of the travelling chest into George's cabin. It was full of tools and was, therefore, heavy. Mopps would guard the contents of the wagon in their absence. She liked beer, so she sat with her eyes glued to the three crates of stout that George had brought. There were also two crates of apple cider that he would share with Ben. A sheet of canvas covered these four crates.

By noon, the wagon was empty, and Mopps had sniffed her new home and had peed in the doorway only to be severely chastised by George. He bent and sopped up the puddle with a rag he kept on hand for such accidents.

Miles explained, "Lad, she is only marking her turf, only in this case, there is no grass. You will need to provide her with an area for her daily ablutions, and she will learn to use it quickly. It's a pity we didn't think of it earlier, or I could have made her a grass box." Miles needed to leave to start his new life. He was going to shake George's hand, but ended up pulling him into a bear hug. "Take care, lad. Write if you need anything. Thanks for leaving some of those old tools. If you decide you want them, let me know, and I'll send them over. Remember to write when you are settled, as everyone will wish to know where you are."

George nodded. He was pleased that Miles left his cabin first, as he could subtly wipe away his tears. Now, it came time to go; leaving was not as easy as he thought. He should have offered Miles a partnership rather than selling to him outright. George sniffed and swallowed the muck from his nose. It was too late now. He had crossed that bridge already. With a quick intake of breath, George followed Miles out on deck. Without an invitation to follow, Mopps came anyway. She was hard on his heels as he climbed the narrow staircase and exited onto the main deck.

Miles was chatting to the captain, and they beckoned him to join them.

The captain greeted him. "Laddie, when you said you were bringing your pooch on board, I took the liberty of supplying something he…" He gazed at the moving hairy canine mass, "Um… no, something she will need. It looks like she has found it already."

Mopps had found a square box filled with grass. She marked her turf, quite literally, by squatting and peeing on it. The captain continued. "I wondered how it would cope if it were a dog, but a bitch is far more accurate when doing her business."

Mopps came to George's side and sat next to him. Her tail was wagging, and her tongue lolled out the side of her almost-grinning mouth. George rewarded her with a pat and told her she was a good girl. The other two men patted her, congratulating her on her recent action. The captain dug into his pocket and pulled out some dried bones.

Miles was firing questions at the captain. "Sir, this vessel is not of the usual construction. I thought most ships were built of oak, but this is not."

Captain John Hardy Jackson chuckled. "A fine observation, Miles! No, she is built of pine. This made her much quicker to build, and her lightweight construction enables her to be quicker in the waves. That being said, on this journey, as we have no convicts on board, we are stopping in Rio de Janeiro to stock up on all manner of supplies. The last stop is Cape Town. I won't push too far south from there, as the seas are horrendous. Ice already claimed the *Guardian* in 1789. I don't expect to dock in Sydney Cove until mid-next year, sometime."

George did a quick calculation. The journey would be far longer than he was initially told. "But that's eight months, sir! Will there be enough food for that long?"

The captain shook his head. "No, laddie, hence the stops *en route*. The first port of call is Tenerife, followed by St Helena Island and Rio de Janeiro. Then, for our last stop, we will call at Cape Town and resupply. We will fill the ship with food, livestock, and goods for the colony. The *Guardian* and the *Lady Shore* were store ships that the colony desperately needed, but they never made it to Sydney Cove. George, you and Ben will also be able to stock up there, as they sell a wide range of salts, limes, and dyes for leatherwork. See if you can go on a tour of the various tanneries at each stop. I'm sure you will learn different methods of tanning. Cape Town especially uses a different way to tan." They were still talking when Ben arrived.

George told Mopps to stay, and he went to assist his new friend. Mopps sat on the captain's foot rather than beside him. She had a rope tied to her leather collar, which he bent and picked up. While carrying a small box, George introduced Ben and then assisted him with the rest of the luggage. His tools would be kept in George's cabin, and Ben's clothing was taken to the steerage compartment he had been allocated.

Chapter 3   All Aboard

Sailing day finally arrived. Much to the delight of both lads, Ben was upgraded to a small servant's cabin beside George, and his scant possessions were moved into the tiny servants' room. As he and George were the only paying passengers, moving him into a cabin meant the deck below could be left for the soldiers who had yet to arrive. The officers travelling with the military would fill the remainder of the cabins. All the enlisted men were in steerage with their families. They had left the wharf yesterday and dropped anchor in the river.

Below deck, nearly one hundred members of the 45th Regiment were under the command of Lieutenant Colonel Joseph Foveaux. With no convicts on board, they were informed that most of her cargo consisted of naval supplies and food. They overheard the captain mention that a large consignment of alcohol was also on board.

Ben, George, and Mopps were given free rein of the ship but told to stay clear of the crew's active work. They were allocated an area on the upper poop deck that was well out of the way of any rope or sail activity. From this vantage point, they watched the cabin boy pipe as the crew pulled the anchor up with the colossal capstan. Twelve long wooden bars were inserted into the capstan slots, and with two men on each handle, the anchor was slowly lifted from the bottom. This would need to be repeated every six hours or so for up to a week, as it could take that long for the ship to reach the sea.

In the Thames River, all shipping was controlled by the tide. This meant that departing vessels had to stay on the port side of the river and raise their anchor when the tide turned. The ships were permitted to raise one small sail, and they had to go with the flow of the outgoing tide. When the tide changed, they had to pull to the port side and anchor again. The incoming tide brought a new flow of water, which in turn brought the arriving watercraft.

It usually took four days to reach the open sea, but there was a breeze blowing them upstream. This quiet passage allowed the boys to settle into their new life. The captain said it would take a week.

Mopps soon realised that she also had free range of the vessel, but her favourite place was the galley. She ate everything from vegetable scraps to pan scrapings. Cook knew not to feed her onions, and he had no liver, but her love of potatoes, porridge, and burnt scraps of the stew endeared her to the typically angry and somewhat frustrated cook. He had been caught feeding her meat off-cuts and set up a small bucket of water for her under the ledge of a table.

Mopps' slovenly lolling lope soon became familiar as she raced between cuddles from the various crewmen and soldiers. She was rarely short of companionship. Someone even produced a ball, and she chased it along the lower deck corridor.

William Hustwick was the third mate on the *Sinclair*, and he offered to keep his eye on Mopps as she roamed where she wished. One of the first things he did was to have her grass box moved to the upper poop deck. This was to stop the salty water from killing the grass once the ship reached the open sea. She soon discovered he had a large packet of dried fish and chicken meat.

Mopps was as happy to shadow either William or the boys.

They reached the sea on the sixth day and started their long journey southward. William warned the boys that they might become seasick, and he wasn't wrong. The movement of the waves in the southern part of the English Channel prostrated both lads. Even Mopps seemed a little off-colour for a day or so. Eventually, the two lads and their shaggy shadow set up a work area on the top deck.

By the time they reached Tenerife, they had their sea legs, but it had taken over a month for this to occur. They didn't disembark as it was raining, and they couldn't leave the dock area, so they remained in George's cabin and worked. They did take the opportunity of the peaceful harbour to raid the crates in the hold and extract a handful of calico bags from the top of one of Ben's crates.

George also pried off the top of the crate that held the leather that Ben had chosen when they were storing the load. They unpacked four tanned hides for straps, underlining and saddle assembly before resealing everything.

At the end of the second month, the saddle they were working on neared completion. Although George knew his leather well, he wanted to learn the techniques required to turn his product into a finished saddle. There was only seawater to soak the tanned leather before embossing or carving, but this method worked well once the leather was heated in water.

George had not seen leather punched designs in the edges, only inked patterns. He was intrigued by the intricacy of the designs on leather punches Ben produced, from scallops to leaves and even heart shapes.

George soaked a scrap of leather off-cut and, one by one, tapped each punch to see how they turned out. He played with the stamp he liked best and alternated the leaf top to stem along the edge.

Ben watched and said, "You know, I've never thought of doing that. But then that's what's good about bringing fresh eyes into our work. You can also mix up the styles between decorations, which I call embossing, carving and dyeing. It gives a fabulous finished product that is three-dimensional."

Ben showed him what he meant, and with small chisels, carving tools and an Indian ink pen, the simple design that George had been fiddling with soon became a work of art.

George's friend, Bill Felton, was the first soldier to join the group on deck. He said, "How did you do that, Ben?" Bill leaned over to pick up the scrap of leather Ben had decorated. "It's incredible."

Ben shrugged and said, "Come and learn how to make some of this stuff, Bill. Not saddles, but we have enough leather to keep us all busy."

Bill moved Mopps away and sat down beside them.

Many crew members, including Lieutenant Colonel Foveaux and Captain Jackson, joined them to watch Ben ply his skills. Ben produced another roll of tools, which included additional tools for carving, punching, and stamping. So far, Ben had used pre-cut and previously embossed panels to complete his saddle. Rather than unpack his big anvil, he produced a small eight-inch one, along with a specialised hammer, to punch the even holes where he needed to sew the various sections together. Neat, evenly spaced sewing was not easy on a moving deck.

As Rob had done, Ben used two needles attached to the ends of a single, long, waxed thread. Ben pushed it through both sides of each hole to create a double-sided stitch. His movements were so quick that often George had to get him to repeat his action.

~

Two English riding saddles were complete by the time they reached St Helena Island. The third style was slightly different, with a higher pommel, thigh and knee rolls and longer calf blocks. It needed padding.

With many hands now willing to try their hand at saddlery, the finish on this one was less professional than Ben would have wished; however, everyone had learned a lot.

Most of the watchers eventually drifted away, bored. The military personnel would often play dice games with the crew or share somewhat risqué stories. The boys kept well clear of them.

George had accessed a box of off-cut leather at Tenerife, and with the tools he had with him, he set about creating practice pieces for everyone to work on rather than mess up a saleable saddle. With their four-prong diamond punch, he made rows along the edges of the leather for sewing practice. He had also dug out one of his grandfather's very old spools of thread. As it kept breaking, it was only suitable for practice.

With the stock saddle complete, Ben brought a half-finished side saddle up to work on next. At least, that is what he explained it would be when finished. The saddle was currently in numerous bits in a calico drawstring bag.

The first thing he drew out was a very odd-looking timber frame.

Ben explained each item and said, "This is called the tree. That's what you call the base frame of every saddle. All the ones we have worked on so far have a variation of this under the leather. However, this one is particularly oddly shaped as it is for a sidesaddle. Hence, the horn-like protrusions are off-centre rather than a central pommel. The lady riding hooks her legs around this. These wooden horns also require padding and then a leather coating. There are various terms for the parts, like swell, cantle, bar, seat and gullet." He pointed to each bit as he spoke. "But you don't need to know what they all mean. Each has a purpose and needs padding in a particular way, either for the rider or the horse. On a side saddle, the cantle and seat are all but flat, but the pommel is angled to hook a leg on, and there is a second lower pommel on this as well. These saddles have a wide skirt that sits off-centre from a normal saddle and a side flap where you adjust the stirrups. This must also cover the buckles, or a lady may be injured by the tongue in the buckle. I always add a leather keeper to cover the buckle prongs. The stirrups are often lighter, and I have even seen split, hinged stirrups in case the lady falls from her horse; her foot parts the stirrup, which in turn releases, should she fall, it would hopefully lessen her injury."

He then went on to describe the various straps. "These are called a girth on a lady's side saddle, and they can have up to four straps, five if you include the over girth. These have names like girth billets, Fitzwilliam girths and point straps." He said, "These girth straps should be double-checked after the rider has mounted, as often horses blow out their chest, and the saddle will be loose."

William and George gazed at each other and smiled.

George asked, "How do you know all this, Ben? Have you had to adjust a lady's saddle with her on it?"

Ben's flushed face answered his friend's enquiry. He just nodded.

As some soldiers and crew listened, he received some friendly ribbing. All was in good fun until one said, "Did she have nice ankles?"

Encouraged, another asked, "Did you take the opportunity to touch her up?"

At that, Ben's face blanched in anger, and he faced the questioner. "No, I did not; the earl's daughter was far too good for the likes of me. I would not dare to lay a hand on her."

His outburst made George realise that this was a touchy subject. However, he glared at the soldier who had voiced the question.

The conversation returned to the saddle under discussion.

~

It took over a week before they reached a stage where the saddle could be padded. Even this was a specialised technique, and special tools were needed to get into the deepest parts of the saddle. It was not good enough to shove in some wadding; it needed to be smooth underneath and adequately padded for comfort. Ben refused to permit anyone to do this. He promised

George he would teach him later.

By the time they reached Rio de Janeiro, the side saddle was all but complete. It just needed all the girth straps, but the work was stowed away for the duration of their stay in the tropical harbour.

Lieutenant Colonel Foveaux stood beside them as the ship pulled into the harbour. "Lads, I was wondering if you would be interested in coming on a sightseeing journey with us. We must head inland to source some of the fruit we need for the months ahead, and we are going in the carriage."

George was the first to respond. "Oh, yes, please, sir. Neither of us has ever stepped foot outside of England before, so this is a huge adventure for us both."

Ben was nodding his head in complete agreement. He added, "Captain Jackson told me about the fruit available here. He said I have to try something called a mango and a bent yellow fruit called a banana, not to mention a spiky fruit called a pineapple."

Lieutenant Colonel Foveaux chuckled. "Oh, never fear, boys, I shall give you the full tropical treatment of foods. Breadfruit is all right, but the fruits you mentioned are to die for. I know the apple is supposed to be the forbidden fruit from the Bible in the story of the Fall, but it makes me wonder if it was a mango. Even the name implies that, doesn't it?"

The boys looked puzzled. Both had attended church with their families, but most of what the minister said went straight over their heads.

The soldier explained. "Mango as in 'Man Go,' as in leave." He chuckled again. "In other words, when God cast Adam and Eve out of the Garden of Eden. I'm well-versed in the Bible, but I'm not sure I believe what I was told."

The boys had both heard that story. They gave smiles that showed they only partially understood what he meant.

Foveaux shook his head. "I'll explain later, but you two should at least know your Bible stories."

George frowned and said, "I do, to a point, sir. But what do they have to do with fruit?"

Foveaux smiled. "As I said, I'm sure the captain will explain when he has time. For now, we are heading off on an adventure, and you will see sights that most boys in England would give their eye-teeth to view." He explained the political instability of the area, then said, "Do not wander without armed escorts. Bill Felton and his friends can accompany you, but you must always stay together. As tempting as the women are, this is not the place to play fast and loose with the desires of the flesh. If you succumb to their wiles, you will pick up more than information."

He had been watching the foreshore as he spoke. He had seen a small group of ill-clad women on the shore. He now turned to the boys and saw them both open-mouthed with astonishment. "Lads, those women willing to offer their services are probably well-used by sailors from all the ships. The girls who hang around the dockhands are, more often than not, diseased and filthy. Keep your trousers buttoned, and do not slake your lusts with loose women such as these. Keep yourself clear of the temptations of your nether regions until you find a woman who will give you her heart, love and trust."

Two red-faced boys listened glibly. Only last night, Bill, Ben, and George had gathered in George's cabin and discussed the possibility of experimenting with the easy women of the dockland. Grant, one of the sailors, had told them about the exquisite pleasures to be had in such a place as this. The three young men had never had a chance to enjoy such delights as the girls in each of their towns were far too well known to them to violate without the threat of marriage to that girl. At sixteen, eighteen and nineteen, the boys wanted to experience everything they could. Women were on that list. With the warning now given, the boys grudgingly accepted an alternate activity. None wished to contract the French disease, known as the clap.

With a sigh of frustration, George said, "Oh, sir, we'll come and force a smile on our faces."

Foveaux laughed out loud. "It will be worth waiting for. Trust me about this."

Ben frowned. "Are you married, sir?" There was no sign of a wife.

The soldier shook his head and gave an embarrassed grin. "I'll give you thirty minutes to get ready. You will need hats and shoes; please also bring water or another beverage to drink. I would suggest nothing with alcohol in it. It will go to your head in the heat."

A hired carriage and a large flatbed wagon were awaiting them.

Bill and a few younger soldiers were to follow the carriage on the wagon. The journey inland was mainly intended to keep the younger members of Foveaux's team safe and to source fresh food for the ship. Although they could have purchased it at the market, this trip was a way to keep the youth engaged and healthy. William was to keep Mopps on board with him.

Rio had only just been returned to Brazilian ownership, so many farms had fallen into disrepair. When Foveaux inquired, he discovered that those inland were still producing good crops. Others, nearer to town, were now abandoned. While Captain Jackson dealt with the official side of things, his regiment had orders to assist with restocking supplies from whatever was available.

The boys had seen dark-skinned people before, as some of the servants in England were from Africa, but the squalor in which these poor people lived silenced the chatter from inside the coach. When the Portuguese had left the town, their slaves and staff had been abandoned. Poverty was rife, and hunger and squalor followed hard on their heels.

Neither lad had ever faced the hunger and poverty they were now witnessing. Skeletal children ran after the carriage until their strength gave out and they collapsed.

George brushed away a tear as one child screamed, "Have mercy!"

Even the Lieutenant Colonel was quiet. The country had looked nothing like this on his last visit. He expected it would be the beautiful tropical countryside it had been on his previous stay. "Boys, I'm here to buy fruit. If we can find a ripe bunch, we'll leave it for them when we return."

Two nodding heads were his only reply.

Within two hours, the wagon was full of green banana bunches and crates of assorted tropical and citrus fruits, from the giant yellow pomelos to small green limes. Case upon case was piled on the wagon. The citrus fruit took priority over the tropical delights. Even the carriage had its share of fruit. There were three cases of papaya, all packed in dried banana leaves. These were for immediate consumption. However, they also arranged to send the wagon back tomorrow to collect more fruit and green coconuts. They gave the children a bunch of ripening bananas and a basket of eggs as they passed.

While living in Sydney, on his earlier posting, the Lieutenant Colonel had often come across whalers and amongst these men were some islanders. They had taught him to marinate raw fish in lime juice and serve it in a cream coconut sauce. When first offered some of this dish, he refused to eat any until he saw his officers devouring it. He took a small amount and discovered it was better than fresh-boiled lobster. It was so delicious that his father, who had been a French chef in the Earl of Upper Ossory's household at Ampthill Park in Bedfordshire before becoming his steward, would have been proud to have served it. Since then, he had eaten his fish like this when he could. When living on Norfolk Island, fish was on the menu regularly. However, coconuts were difficult to obtain, so he arranged for some germinated nuts to be planted in the settlement. Unfortunately, only one tree grew, but it was near the front of his house, so he claimed the nuts.

The younger boys resisted the provocative offers of the women who appeared on the docks at dusk, but some older sailors fell victim to their wiles and accepted all the wanton girls had to offer. The rutting couples rarely moved out of sight, and the boys found it hard not to watch. With a hitched-up skirt and a flap unbuttoned, the act was cheap and degrading.

After watching what was happening, George moved to the other side of the ship. His body was in turmoil. He was torn between unaccustomed desires and gross disgust. He was unaware that he was rocking back and forth as he leaned against the gunnels.

The Lieutenant Colonel came to his side. "Remember, I told you they were cheap and dirty. Those crewmen from the other ships will probably need to be treated for the clap soon. The streetwalkers here have little choice but to ply their trade where they can. They have no other means of supporting themselves or, in some cases, even their families. Life in poverty is not pleasant or easy in a place like this."

Ben came and joined them. He, too, could no longer stomach the degrading scene occurring in various places along the dockland. Crewmen from various other vessels were queuing for the girls. He had missed the earlier conversation and said, "How can the girls degrade themselves in such a way? I had no idea they would be so blatant in plying their trade." He joined George, looking out over the bay in the opposite direction.

Foveaux said, "I told you they were bad news. They are only beaten by the Irish whores that I had to cope with on Norfolk Island. They breed like rabbits, and when I left, there were over two hundred illegitimate brats that we were supposed to feed, clothe, and educate. That was about one-third of the population. Flogging was the only way to control their evil ways. The more you give, the more effective the discipline is." He grunted with disgust at the memory.

This comment was the first he had made about the punishment of flogging, but George's friend Bill had already mentioned that Foveaux was known to give punishments of over two hundred lashes regularly. The boys had not believed him... until now. Bill told them that men deliberately committed crimes so they could be sent back to Sydney for punishment rather than be dealt with by Flogger Foveaux.

Dusk closed in quickly, and the wanton activities on the dock were no longer visible. The grunting sounds of rutting couples were soon out of earshot as the boys descended into their cabins. Thankfully, they had opened their portholes before leaving on their trip, as it had been extremely hot. Their cabins had caught the full morning sun. The open converted gunport allowed most of the heat to escape.

George watched as Foveaux walked past their small cabins and moved towards his large suite on the far side of the corridor. George grabbed Ben's arms and pulled him into his room. Knowing his voice would carry through the open porthole, he whispered. "Ben, Foveaux may have been right about the street girls, but don't cross him. Bill told me that his men in Norfolk Island call him a sadist. There is even a story about him ordering a naked woman to be flogged. Foveaux ordered a man to inflict the punishment, and he refused."

Ben was stunned. He said, "Cor George. Foveaux seemed so nice."

George nodded. "He is, as long as you're not Irish or free with one's manhood. You know what we were listening to tonight. He hates the streetwalkers and punishes them by flogging them. More so if they are Irish women. According to Bill, two hundred lashes are not uncommon for Foveaux to order."

Ben sank onto George's bed. "Oh golly gosh, George, we're going to have to watch ourselves. I wonder if Bill knew what he was getting into." Mopps licked his hand as he gazed at his friend.

They kept talking and soon heard booted footsteps outside the door. They stopped talking until they passed.

George nodded. "And we're going to knuckle down and do our leatherwork. He watches but leaves us alone."

The footsteps returned, and this time, they stopped at the door. A knock was followed by the door swinging open without invitation. The captain stood there, glanced down the corridor, stepped inside, and closed the door behind him. "I've come to warn you both that sound travels over water. Thankfully, his cabin is on the other side of the ship. But you are right. Take care, stay out of trouble, and you will have none. Savvy?"

The boys had learned what this word meant. "Do you understand?"

They responded with a nod.

Captain Jackson said, "Good. Now come and try this coconut fish Foveaux has been raving about. Mopps, you too. Dinner is ready."

The three departed the stuffy cabin with the dog hard on their heels and went to the mess room for their evening meal.

The boys were seated on the extended bench and placed on either side of the captain. Usually, they sat beside Bill, but he was next to Foveaux. With what they had heard about him, they decided to stay clear of that soldier if possible and be very polite to him when required.

A bowl of soft, white cubes was placed in front of the captain on the table. Foveaux had already piled his plate from another bowl and encouraged everyone to "Hoe in, chaps. You'll love it."

After hearing about the taste, the boys each took a spoonful. Neither had tried lobster, so they had no point of reference to compare it to. They tentatively put one cube into their mouths and tasted the white creamy juice. Not knowing what to expect, they were surprised at the tart but creamy sauce. The fish cube was firm but not chewy, and it was delicious. Before the bowl was passed along the table, they each took a heaped serving-sized scoop of the treat.

The captain waited until the boys tasted it before trying it himself. He, too, then took a large serving of the dish. "Foveaux, when you told me about this, I doubted you. But it seems you are correct. It's not bad, even if I say so myself. Similar texture to lobster, but still good."

An exotic dessert of fresh fruit followed the meal. Mangoes, papaya, pineapples, passionfruit, and other local fruit were served on a large platter. These were also devoured quickly by everyone.

The upshot of this meal was an order to purchase several cases of limes, lemons, and numerous crates of green coconuts, along with a vast array of local tropical fruits. They discovered that pineapples also transport well.

The stay in Rio de Janeiro lasted ten days before they set off again. After another few days in the bay, the ship set sail again. The weather was fine, and the breeze was blowing at a steady rate of knots.

~

Foveaux ensured that his soldiers were drilled regularly to maintain their skills. Uniforms had been stowed, and the soldiers were as relaxed as they could be.

With little to do on board, the boys set up their temporary saddlery again. There were many hands to assist in setting up their class on the poop deck.

Mopps was always on guard nearby.

The way Ben had packed the partially assembled saddles meant that each one had been stored in a calico bag. This contained the wooden tree, leather, twine, thonging, a roll of leather for the stirrup straps and a smaller bag of the required metalwork, such as buckles and stirrups.

The tools for assembly were kept in his room, as these were his livelihood. If they were to go missing, he would be unable to work. His pride and joy were his small anvil, along with packets of rivets, hammers, carving and sewing tools. He permitted no one but George to handle them, and even then, that was only in the privacy of their cabins.

George produced many of his grandfather's old tools, and it was these that the others used. He was now thankful that Miles insisted that he take most of the small things. He had only left a few large items behind, like the big anvil. In these bundles was what Ben called a pricking iron or stitching chisel. It was a bit bent, but Ben quickly straightened the wonky teeth.

The onboard sailmaker had purchased an extensive collection of needles and twine in Rio.

George's pierced leather off-cuts gave each man something to work on to occupy their time. Mastering the double-sided sewing skill was challenging, but with the additional tools now available, those interested could attempt to acquire the skill.

The sailmaker also brought out some of the old sails, and one was so severely torn that the group turned it into an awning for the workers to sit under while working through the summer heat.

Chapter 4   Towards the New World
April 1808

*T*he ship's arrival in Cape Town saw both boys dressed and ready to go ashore for another adventure. Rather than don their Sunday best, they dressed down. The wide-brim hats they had purchased in Rio were now part of their daily attire. It was the end of March, and the weather was still quite hot.

After months at sea, Ben was cleaning up when he opened the second bottom drawer in George's travelling case. He had intended to pull out the lowest drawer to stow the tools, but grabbed the wrong handle as he was not paying attention. An odd-shaped box sat alone in the drawer. "Hey, George, what's that?"

George had not dared to bring out his fiddle in public, but Ben was now a firm friend. "It's my grandpa's fiddle." He did not explain; he just answered his question.

Ben was not one to hold back, and he asked, "Can you play it?"

George nodded. He had practised for hours after work each evening since he was a child, but he'd not dared to touch it while on board. He played at the village dances and weddings, but few knew of the talent he had not revealed. Bill thought he could only play a few dances and not much else.

Ben asked, "Can you play me something? My Grandad used to play his fiddle, but his instrument broke, so I never got to learn. He played something that he called 'my song'. It was the Hallelujah Chorus. Can you play it?"

George smiled. It had been months since he had pulled it out and practised. He had not wanted to be teased about his skill. He quietly closed the cabin door and then took out the instrument bag. The warm red timber of the violin glowed in the dim porthole light of the cabin. George almost caressed it as he picked it up. Moments later, the small room was filled with sounds of Johann Bach's *Violin Concerto in A minor*, then *Canon in D* by Pachelbel, followed by Handel's *Hallelujah Chorus* from *The Messiah*.

Ben's jaw dropped open. He had expected a few cheap and nasty dancing tunes, but for George to be a classical violinist astounded him. "I do like the last one, George. That's the one my grandad called 'my song'. He could play, but not as well as you."

His friend played a few more short pieces before hearing approaching footsteps. The instrument was hastily stowed, and Ben was sworn to secrecy. The case was lovingly placed back in its drawer, and George closed it carefully. His hand caressed the closed cover.

Ben finally recovered from his astonishment and asked, "Why didn't you tell me? How come you can play like that?"

George shrugged. "I'm a tanner, not a musician. Bill knows I can play, but not about the classical stuff."

Ben chuckled. "Well, I bet he'll know now. If our voices carry, then the music sure will." As he spoke, he shivered as the music penetrated the depths of his being.

Bill stuck his head in the door. "Was that you?" His eyes sought out George, who was once again sitting innocently on his bed.

George nodded, then gave a mischievous grin. "Shh! Keep it quiet, Bill."

Bill swore. "I won't lie; you're blooming brilliant, George. I used to hear a violin in the village, but no one ever knew where it came from. I suppose that was you, too?"

George nodded. "If it was at night, then it was probably me. Rob hated me playing indoors, so I would go into the shed and fiddle away."

Bill almost choked. "That's not fiddling; you're a blooming maestro!"

A cold draught blew down the corridor and in through the open door. All three shivered. George closed the drawer that held his valuable instrument lest the cold affect it. "Pipe down, Bill. I don't want everyone to know."

Bill lifted a hand in farewell. "I'll do my best, but they will guess soon enough."

The cold was penetrating, and both boys had dug out some soft pelts to put on their beds. Being so far south, there were icicles on the rigging each morning, and the larger ice shafts were dangerous when they broke off and fell. The music became a phantom, as no one claimed to know anything about it. The three boys kept quiet, but silent smiles were shared between them.

Over the months on board, every now and then, the haunting sounds of the violin floated through the ship. George never had to acknowledge it was him playing, because no one ever asked. The others remained silent.

The day before landing in Cape Town, Captain Jackson showed George a knife and sheath he had purchased on his last visit to Cape Town. The tanner confessed that he had never seen anything like it. The leather used was unlike anything George had ever seen before. The captain chuckled. "I don't think there would be too many hippopotami in London, lad. And that is what I was told it was made from."

That one comment inspired George to pump him for as much

information as possible about the extraordinary leather. He was itching to have a look at what else was available. With his new skills, he wanted to experiment with various hides. Captain Jackson could not escort them, but he did ask the harbourmaster to supply a guide for them. Bill and two of his soldier friends accompanied them while the captain and William kept Mopps with them.

After visiting various shops, the guide asked George if he wished to see how the locals tanned hides. After he nodded his head, they were taken out of the town to a wide area where many mounds covered the field. They were greeted with a wave and beckoned to look at what the group of digging men were doing.

George expected the usual vats of stinking, partially decomposing hides soaking in salt; however, there was little, if any, smell.

The fresh skins and raw hides were buried and left to partially rot underground. The visitors watched as the hides were removed from their earthen holes and laid out to scrape clean.

George was intrigued. He discovered that not only were oxen and sheep hides being tanned, but also those of hippopotamuses, rhinoceroses, zebras, elephants, crocodilians, antelopes, ostriches, lizards, snakes, and various other animals. He watched as some workers scraped the remaining fat off the skins, while others worked on the hair. A short distance away, he noticed someone was pounding roots and animal fat into a pulp. They smeared it onto the hide and rubbed it in, just as they used to with the dog poop. The added benefit of doing this was the lack of smell; his process stank. After much questioning about the ingredients, he was determined to try this new tanning method when he set up his equipment.

He plied the guide with numerous questions, which were duly translated in both directions. George took copious notes on the various processes and asked if they had any tanned hides for sale.

On hearing that question, the lead worker, who George thought spoke little English, grinned and dropped what he was doing. "You come! You come now. I show. You look, you buy good skins."

After consulting his companions, George was keen to take advantage of this opportunity. He knew he could fit in many more crates, as Captain Jackson had permitted him to buy what he pleased.

George and Ben followed the big African as he walked into the scrub. Bill and his armed friend were close behind and walked beside the guide.

By the time they arrived back at the ship, George and Ben's pockets were a bit lighter. On their way back to the ship, they visited two other places. George bought some leather-working accessories and rolls of leather sewing thread. He had seen an old Zulu shield made from a thick, crudely tanned hide. The slashes cut into it were unusual, but the leather was so thick that he could not bend it. They purchased all the tanned hides the first man had prepared and hoped they would arrive on board tonight. Another place had more, which George purchased as a job lot. This shipment included over one hundred pelts, from snake skins to an enormous elephant hide. All were soft, supple, and ready to use.

Ben was only interested in leathers he could use for saddles, so he kept to the traditional brown leathers, but George didn't care. He had enough money, and the five pounds in coins covered the cost of the hides and transport to the ship, leaving him with some money over. He gave the guide and manager a generous tip before bowing his thanks.

Captain Jackson and Lieutenant Governor Foveaux were on deck as the boisterous and excited group returned.

Bill reported to his commanding officer on arrival.

The captain questioned him. "Did they purchase anything? George asked if he could, and I approved."

Bill flicked his gaze from one man to the other and back to the captain. "Um, well, yes, you could say that, sir. Ben purchased about a dozen tanned hides for his saddles; however, George purchased the rest." He dropped his eyes to the deck, embarrassed at what he had to reveal to the captain.

Foveaux recognised that mannerism was one of being ashamed. "Felton, when you say 'the rest', how many are we talking about? Ten, twenty?"

Bill shook his head, but his eyes remained on his boots. He dared not admit that an entire flatbed wagonload was about to arrive.

The silence was punctuated by the crunch of wheels on the gravel road. The captain saw what had just arrived on the dock. "Cor blimey! Did he have to purchase the entire animal herd?"

Bill moved so he could see the flatbed wagon. The pelts were now crated up and ready for loading into the hold. He gave a wicked grin. "They are so worth it, though, sirs. I had no idea you could tan so many sorts of animal skins. The bulk of these skins are hippopotamuses, rhinoceroses, zebras, elephants, crocodiles, alligators, ostriches, and snakes. But, sir, you really must see the first zebra skin. They kept the fur on it, and it's incredible. If we had been here next week, there would have been about three more crates of monkey, lion, and something called a warthog, included. They only had one lion skin, and George claimed that." Bill watched as the cart pulled up and the driver hopped down. He waved to him, and the African tentatively pointed to the narrow gangplank and shook his head.

The captain saw the man's fear and said to the soldier next to him, "Foveaux, can you get your men to unload the wagon and bring the crates aboard? I don't think the driver wants to come on the ship. Knowing that many have been stolen as slaves, I can understand why."

Foveaux swore under his breath. "If I must!" Then he turned to order some of his men to help.

George appeared and almost bounced down the flimsy boards. The gangplank bounced as he jumped off the end. He checked that all his purchases were included, and after he had unloaded the crates from the wagon, George gave the driver a generous tip.

Ben's few hides were marked separately and stowed with his luggage.

Within an hour, the new crates were off the dock and on the deck, awaiting storage in the cargo hold.

Some crew members had witnessed the arrival, and knowing they would benefit from additional lessons and potentially more free items, they all pitched in to help secure the cargo.

Soon, the new leatherwork was safely stowed and tied down.

As George had not packed these, he didn't know what was in them, but one had an easily recognisable skin, as there were irregular black and white stripes poking out. He placed that crate on top and pried off one of the boards to pull out the zebra hide. He had never seen such an unusual pattern and was determined to keep this one whole. He hoped there would be more of these included in the consignments, as they had promised. He had never tanned a hide, keeping the hair on, and his questions today gave him ideas on how to do this. With the black and white pelt over his arm, George decided to take it to dinner to show everyone before keeping it on his bunk in the cabin. It was surprisingly soft. Bill had already been raving over it, and everyone clustered around him to feel the somewhat prickly hair on the tanned hide. The tanned leather side was surprisingly soft and supple, despite its wiry texture. It would also be warm when the weather cooled down.

The African tanner had told him that sometimes they used these pelts to make shields, as the thickness of the hide made a thick, firm leather. He didn't care; this one was his, and he intended to keep it. He couldn't wait to unpack the remainder of the crates, but if they were treated as well as this one, he would be in seventh heaven. He intended to return to ask why the hair stayed firmly attached. He had already filled pages in his journal.

Restocking the ship at Cape Town took a week, and they were soon on their way again. Mopps was taken on regular walks onshore, and she was even permitted to have a long run around the dockland in the mornings.

~

On leaving the safe harbour, the *Lady Madeline Sinclair* headed directly east. Most other captains took the shorter route, much further to the south, but the seas over winter could be treacherous. They were terrible at the best of times, but with no hurry to arrive, he took the safer northern route. Even now, the ship was occasionally rocked to the scuppers by the giant waves.

Working outdoors was abandoned, and more often than not, the boys would sit on George's berth and work in silence. They flipped over the zebra skin, and it made an excellent work area, providing a reasonably firm surface on which to work. Mopps was content to stay with them in the cabin.

While Ben worked on the central part of the saddle, lining and cladding the saddle tree, George prepared the straps, flaps, and smaller leather sections. His stitching was so good that he could double-sew the buckles on rather than rivet them. He had learned to use the V-shaped edger that took off the sharp sides of the cut leather. He discovered it was called a skiving cutter beveler. To chamfer the ends, a broader version was used that reduced the leather's thickness by half. Then, a decorative edge creaser was used to make a line along the edge of the leather. This needed to be heated, so George often took his work along to the galley and did this in the relative safety of the mess room. The wet weather had set in, and a storm was brewing. The barometer was dropping quickly.

Over the hurried meal of stew and tea, Captain Jackson had said, "We're heading into a bit of rough weather, chaps, so batten down the hatches. Stow everything away, and you must sit tight for a while. Tie up Mopps."

If this was not rough, then what was to come?

Ben's eyes grew large. "Cor, Captain, will it get worse than this?"

Mopps' grass was moved into the galley and tied to the leg of a table.

The captain added, "Yes, lads, much worse. When I said, 'stow your gear,' I meant to ensure that everything movable is securely strapped down. George, tie down your large travelling case, and I suggest you close it up and strap it to your bed. Ben, if your small anvil goes flying, one of you will get hurt or even killed. Store it in a safe location and take a few days off from work. Stay in your cabins unless you really must move around. Above all, do not use the head. The water will flow in and flood the compartment. Confine yourself to using the chamberpots until it calms down. There will be a lidded barrel in the mess to empty it into. Needless to say, keep the porthole closed." He was then gone. A few minutes later, he returned and said, "George, keep Mopps indoors. If she goes overboard, we won't be able to turn around."

~

The blow lasted four horrific days. The two boys stayed in George's cabin so they could at least be deathly scared in the dark together.

Mopps snuggled between their legs. She hardly moved off the bed.

It was too rough to do more than hold on for grim death. Their portholes, usually well above the waterline, were completely covered for most of those one hundred hours of hell on high water. Being a modified gunport, it leaked like a sieve. The only food available was the hard-tack biscuits, but no one wanted anything else anyway. Their water had run out, and neither had wished to refill from the barrels in the mess room just down the corridor. They drank cider and stout that George had forgotten he had stowed under his bunk.

Mopps loved her treat of stout, and it made her sleep. Neither beverage sat well on their stomachs, but it slaked their thirst. The only time they left the cabin was when one of the crew came around to empty the chamberpots into the barrel. Even that was done quickly and carefully.

After four days of terror, wondering if the ship would make it over the next vessel-eating wave, they woke to find the wind had dropped. By midafternoon, the seas were quieter, and the stars were out by nightfall.

At dawn on the fifth day, the seas had returned to the usual rolling movement they had become accustomed to. The boys emerged somewhat green around the gills but ravenous. The cook relit the fire that had been out for the past four days and had a cauldron of porridge cooking over it. It was consumed quickly by everyone, but that was merely a stopgap while he cooked something nourishing for luncheon. He was about to break open a barrel of pickled pork when a cry came from above. They had a fish on the troll line. Word soon spread of excitement on deck.

Mopps was still on a lead rope and all but dragged the boys out of the cabin and up on the deck to see what was happening. After relieving herself on the grass pad, she sat watching with her tail never still.

Cook joined everyone and watched a life-and-death fight of whatever had taken the trolling line. Some thought it might be a shark, but hopefully, it was a fish. Bets were soon being taken.

After the trauma of the storm, the excitement of an enormous fish was enough to blow away the cobwebs. Somehow, in the middle of the storm, a troll line had been washed overboard from the top poop deck, where it had been stowed for safety. It was three levels higher than the sea and had snagged an enormous tuna. The thick line was thankfully tied to the base of the mizzenmast, and it was only when the rope was seen moving sideways that anyone realised they had a fish on it. With one hundred and eighty on board, this giant tuna would feed them for many meals. None had ever seen a fish this large.

Captain Jackson realised that the only way they would get the leviathan on board was to use the anchor capstan. It took over an hour, but finally, the exhausted fish lay on the deck. It had lost its fight and was soon despatched. The ten-foot-long Bluefin tuna must have weighed at least a thousand pounds. Even with so many on board, they could not eat that much fresh fish in one day, so they set about preparing some to be preserved for later use. After letting it bleed, long machetes were used to cut into the fish and fillet it. Cook sent for an empty barrel and salt. One filet would be skinned and pickled for later consumption; the rest would be prepared for eating. Foveaux told the cook he could dice the fish and leave it in the citrus juice overnight. This would still leave enough fresh meat for two meals and the skeleton for a fish soup the following day.

With so much fish available, the tuna head would be used as bait in a day or so. If they could catch another one, they would salt, dry or smoke some of it. The sea was still too rough to set up a smoking area on the deck.

Mopps ran around in circles with delight at being outdoors again. She was given many off-cuts. The boys were also on watch for more tuna. The troll rope was now permanently hung over the back of the vessel, as it worked much better there than off the side where it had usually been used. It only took days for the seas to quieten completely, and with the calmer weather, the boys resumed their work outside.

In the following days, two more tunas were caught, and while smaller than the first one, having a stock of preserved and dried fish was beneficial.

Foveaux asked for a half-tail fillet from one of the fish and a small empty keg. He added various ingredients to the barrel and mixed them well before adding the fish segments. He made a slurry of cooled, boiled water, salt, molasses, a few crushed garlic bulbs, some sherry that he had produced, and some pungent black fish sauce that he had purchased in Cape Town. After tasting it, he added the raw fish. Once the keg was full, he added a bit more salt and sealed the barrel. Once done, he said, "This will last for a few weeks, but I wouldn't leave it much longer." He loved fish, and his father had told him about preserving excess fish this way, but it needed to be eaten reasonably quickly. It sat for ten days before it was cracked open.

A seagull landing high in the rigging was the first sign that land was close. Ben felt something drop onto his shoulder and discovered a blob of white, foul-smelling bird droppings on his shirt. When he looked up, he saw the grey and white gull sitting atop the main mast. "Hey George, look, a bird."

George was not the only one to look up. Grant scurried up the rigging and into the crow's nest near where the bird had sat. With all the noise on the deck, it had already taken to wing and gone. The "Land Ho" call came from above only a few minutes later.

By the time the ship sighted land in May, all the preserved tuna had been eaten. Even the barrel load of pickled fish that Foveaux had made was gone. He had been correct; it was delicious, much tastier than the salted fish the cook had preserved. A few smaller fish had been caught and eaten immediately, but they were minute compared to the first giant Bluefin tuna.

Captain Jackson had his sextant out and took bearings to determine their location. The crew soon scurried around, readying the ship to change direction. They quickly tacked to the south. He said, "With land in sight, Sydney should only be about eight weeks away."

Days passed in expectation of seeing more land. When they finally did, it was off to the side. Towering cliffs were seen in the distance and vanished as the ship turned further south to skirt the bottom of Van Diemen's Land. Whales appeared occasionally, but birds were now plentiful. It was far too cold to sit outdoors working, so once again, they remained in George's cabin and worked to finish the saddle before landing in Sydney. The open door was all the light they had.

Chapter 5 Unstable Landing
Mid 1808

By early July, they were sailing northwards up the coast of New South Wales. The boys had finished the saddle they were working on and decided to pack away the rest of the kits. They concentrated on the girth straps and making long rolls of rein strapping. Sewing on the buckles was enough work to keep them occupied.

Mopps could sniff the difference in the air and often stood at the bow with her nose towards the land. She released a howl of delight. The land itself was not always within sight, but when it was, the grey-green vegetation exuded a strange, almost pungent scent.

Birds were now regular visitors to the rigging and were no longer only gulls. At one point, two large black and white pelicans investigated the ship, but they were shooed off after depositing large white dollops of foul, fish-smelling excrement on the deck. William had a slingshot and was a crack shot at aiming for the large feathered fish-eaters. The ship had to tack and wear up the coast because the wind was a headwind. The average ten-day trip turned into three weeks as the winds were also light.

By the end of July, the end was nigh. Sydney Heads were now in sight, and the boys were advised to watch as the vessel approached the land. Rather than stand on the poop deck, they were next to Captain Jackson at the helm.

Ben could see the land mass in front of them and exclaimed, "Cor, skipper, we're going to hit that headland, aren't we?"

The captain laughed. "No, watch! I love sailing into this harbour. I consider this one of the best and safest in the entire world, and trust me, I have sailed into many. Lieutenant Cook, as Captain Cook was in 1770, didn't know what he was missing when he didn't investigate this harbour properly. Governors Arthur Phillip and John Hunter discovered the vastness of this incredible bay. I think it must also be one of the largest in the world. I would go as far as to say that this is the best anchorage that I have had the pleasure of sailing into. The weather is sublime, with only the occasional storm. It doesn't snow, but the summer can be quite hot, though not as bad as the tropics."

The ship was now heading directly west. Captain Jackson and the crew were in their best uniforms. All the military personnel were in full military uniform, and they had done a practice drill that morning. The crew was up in the rigging, ready to furl the sails when ordered. Foveaux had done a few dry runs of their positions for when they entered Sydney Cove. He wanted his regiment to be resplendent. With a whistle and hand signal from the captain, half the sails were furled, and the ship's speed dropped in consequence.

On the 28th of July 1808, the ship headed for its destination. As the land approached, the single line of the cliff was varying shades of green. The middle section was slightly lower, and as the vessel approached the land, the opening into the harbour became visible. In front of them was what appeared to be a single, substantial, and continuous cliff; however, it was three separate headlands. The three promontories were easily seen once in through the towering heads, and the middle head had bays on either side. Captain Jackson gave another whistle, and more sails were furled. He spun the wheel with a practised hand, and the ship turned slightly to the south. It was now headed toward a cluster of anchored vessels deeper into the extensive bay.

Foveaux came to the captain's side. "Something is not right, John. The flag on the headland has not been raised. By now, there should have been a pilot boat come and meet us from Watson's Bay."

With a flick of his hand, Captain Jackson motioned for the boys to head up to the poop deck. They did, but overheard his reply to the soldier. "I was wondering that myself. I wonder if Bligh has pushed the Corps too far?"

Foveaux grunted disapproval. "That would not surprise me at all. I was on the verge of speaking out against him over his treatment of Captain Short on our first trip here two years ago, but I refrained from doing so. He already has two mutinies under his belt. The first was the infamous *HMS Bounty* incident, and then there was the mutiny at Nore, when he was captain of the *HMS Director.*" He gave another disgruntled sniff. "If push comes to shove, I must take control of the situation unless Paterson is back from Van Diemen's Land."

Captain John Jackson nodded. The captain knew of the tension Bligh had already elicited and had little doubt about his ability to cause tension. He knew him well, as he had captained the vessel that brought him here only two years earlier. Captain Short had ordered a cannon to be fired over the bow of his ship; thankfully, he had seen the change of order from their sister ship and corrected his direction in time to avoid this. Bligh had been livid that he had overridden his orders. John knew that his fellow captain was a good shot. He was not going to risk losing his ship.

After they dropped anchor in Sydney Cove, a much-delayed pilot finally met the *Lady Madeline Sinclair*. Things ashore certainly did not look right, as soldiers seemed to be everywhere, especially around Government House. This was unusual, as they usually would be on duty supervising convicts in their various patrols; for large groups of slovenly dressed, red-coated men to be lolling around the dockhand was undoubtedly not the norm.

Captain Jackson last sailed into this port one week shy of two years ago. He knew the process of how an arriving vessel was supposed to proceed. This was not it. He brought Governor-elect Bligh and his daughter, Mary Putland, who would act as the first lady instead of her mother. Bligh had been sent to relieve Phillip Gidley King and assumed the colony's leadership. Commander Joseph Short and Mary's husband, John Putland, had been on the *Porpoise*. Short and Bligh fought over who commanded the small fleet of five ships. The *Elizabeth*, *Justina*, *Alexander*, *Porpoise*, and *Sinclair* carried supplies, convicts, and the new governor to relieve the ailing Governor King. When the pilot's longboat drew aside, he climbed on board and reported the unusual state of the situation ashore.

The astonishment at what they heard made their jaws drop.

Captain Jackson knew the pilot, Gareth Molyneux, well, and they had spent many happy hours together on his last stay in port. He reported that a coup had occurred six months earlier, and the governor was under house arrest.

Mopps had not seen new people for months and could not be restrained. She scooted down the steps from the upper deck and rolled on her back for a tummy rub. The pilot laughed. "What on earth is that shaggy mongrel? It looks like a giant mop without a handle."

The captain chuckled. "Oh, she has a handle. It wags nonstop."

The men around him shrugged. One said, "No idea of her breed, but she's friendly enough."

As the boys heard the question, George's voice carried to the questioner. "I'm guessing she has some sheepdog in her, but her parentage is somewhat ambiguous."

The pilot's portly belly shook as a rumble of laughter emanated from his lips. "She's a mongrel mop." Mopps licked his hand as he bent to pat her. "Cor, laddie, I needed that belly laugh." He bent down and brushed the fur out of the dog's eyes. He loved dogs and said, "Oh, you're a good girl." He turned back to the captain and explained, "John, things here have been on tenterhooks, as one might say, for nigh on six months. The governor has been under house arrest since January 26th. The military has taken over the town. I do my job and keep my head down, but it's not wise to take sides if you get my drift." He eyed Foveaux's uniform. "You, sir, may not have the choice but to take command."

Foveaux and Jackson looked at each other in astonishment. Each was about to reply when the pilot continued. "Sir, I have little time before the military comes aboard, so I will tell you Bligh has also dismissed D'Arcy Wentworth and Thomas Jamison. The Rum Corps is running everything, and it started soon after you left." The portly pilot blew out his cheeks in utter frustration. With his voice lowered as the second longboat drew close, he said softly, "Rum is still the tipple of choice and officially the main currency. It was the attempt to halt this that brought the governor undone. Well, that and land grants. An incident with Macarthur brought it all to a head." He glanced over his shoulder to see how close the boat was before continuing. "As you know, Bligh drew a line at land allocations, and that got enough members of the Rum Corps on the wrong side, but when he stopped them lining their pockets, that was like waving a red flag to a bull. Major George Johnston has taken control, but you outrank him. Take care, good sirs, and be careful of which side you choose. London will need to have the final say about all this."

The captain swallowed nervously, knowing he carried one thousand gallons of grog in his cargo. The second longboat had now tied alongside and contained some red-coated soldiers from the 102nd Regiment. A black hat and red coat appeared at the top of the rope ladder. The uniform showed that the man held the rank of major.

Both knew him well. Major George Johnston stood before them and saluted. He looked at the Lieutenant Governor and said, "Major Johnston at your command, sir. As an officer of senior rank, I bow to your seniority and relinquish command of the colony to you. Lieutenant Governor Paterson has taken ultimate authority; however, he is still in Van Diemen's Land at Port Dalrymple."

Foveaux was stunned. He had arrived to take command of Norfolk Island and shut it down. Now, he needed to handle the colony following Bligh's third mutiny. He discovered he was tongue-tied. Rather than answer, he cleared his throat, frowned and nodded acceptance. This situation had been wholly thrust upon him, and as much as he disliked Bligh, he had the authority of the Admiralty. He was supposed to return to Norfolk Island, but now he must deal with this fiasco. He wondered if he should reinstate the governor.

Up on the poop deck, the two boys listened to every word spoken. They had not expected to arrive after a military coup had taken place. They had no idea what this meant for their life ahead, but they would take the pilot's words to heart and choose their side carefully. Hopefully, they would not be forced into a situation where this would be necessary. Fence sitting looked to be a good option. Fleeing from the main settlement seemed preferable, but how?

~

In the following days, the boys were advised to remain on board until the situation was resolved. The captain sought them out and said, "You lads are lucky. The new commander likes you and has recommended that you bypass Sydney and head to Parramatta. I'll see what I can find out for you. All the whispers you have heard about the military coup are accurate. Keep well away." Captain Jackson kept them informed about the situation on shore.

Lieutenant Governor Foveaux had taken command of the situation, and surprisingly, he sided with the Corps rather than Governor Bligh. The governor was still under arrest, but Foveaux was now acting leader.

Captain Jackson remained tight-lipped about this decision. With the disembarkation of the military passengers, he told the boys they still had free range of the ship. The two boys looked at each other with a touch of fear etched on their faces. They had no accommodation on shore and had no idea what to do. They had somehow expected there would be a place or someone they could talk to about starting a new business, but there was nothing.

A week after dropping anchor, following a cursory knock on the door, the captain entered the larger cabin, and as he had done before, he entered without invitation and closed the door behind him. He said softly, "Boys, I do not think you should stay in Sydney Cove at all. You can return for a good look around once things have quietened down. I have made enquiries and found that Parramatta is located to the west of the main settlement and requires both a tanner and a saddler who possess good knowledge and are willing to teach. If you are willing to work together for a while, you will each be given a grant of land and assistance to set up your businesses there. Foveaux has agreed to support you if you are happy with his arrangement. He has assumed command, and although he has sacked John Macarthur, he has sided with the rebels. He suggested that Macarthur and Johnston leave for England sooner rather than later." He paused and watched the boys as they consulted each other. He continued, "We can head out that way tomorrow, and you can look around the town. There is a place you can store your cargo and move it when you build your homes."

Ben was thrilled. "You will come with us, sir?"

Since most passengers had vacated the ship, the *Sinclair* had moved further offshore. As it was mid-winter, the porthole was closed, and no one was around to overhear their conversations.

The captain nodded. "I will, as I wish to see the area myself."

George was open-mouthed. "You mean he will just give us some ground? For our very own, without paying anything for it?"

Ben was equally shocked. "You mean Foveaux wants us to really work together?"

The captain chuckled. "Yes, you may not like the fellow, but you both kept your mouths shut and didn't rile him when you discovered his enjoyment of inflicting harsh punishments. I know he's known as a sadist on Norfolk Island. When he left for his health's sake, I believe the islanders cheered as his ship departed. He knows you are both skilled at what you do and intends to see that you are kept out of the way of the troubles here. Plus, Sydney Cove is not the place to set up a stinky business like a tannery, but Parramatta has land a-plenty out of the town, and I think it may grow faster than Sydney."

George questioned him again. "You truly mean we will be given land for free that we will own outright? I'm not even of age; will that make any difference?"

The captain shook his head. "No, Foveaux knows you have the skills required to teach your craft. I wondered why he wanted to sit in on those initial lessons you ran. Now I know why. Not that he knew he would be in control." He made as though to leave and then turned back to George. "It was you, wasn't it, the violinist? You were the only one missing each time I heard it." George nodded, somewhat embarrassed.

The captain asked, "Where did you ever learn to play like that? I've never heard better, you know, and I catch whatever concerts I can when I'm ashore. Well done, lad. Keep it up."

George flushed scarlet and grinned. "I learned from my mother, sir." He muttered "Thank you" as the captain departed.

~

Within a week, the boys had found lodging in a small room on the outskirts of Parramatta with a family named Rosedale. Foveaux had processed a two-acre land grant for George between Parramatta and Rosedale's farm. Ben wanted to take time to look around the area. The family owned a farm closer to their new block of ground than the town. Although they were currently caring for a convict's baby, the family seemed to consist mainly of girls. Even better, this family had a bevy of beautiful daughters, some of whom were their age. Margaret, Patience, Victoria, Katherine, Charlotte, Emily and Rebecca were delighted to have two attractive young men move into their guest room. Two were engaged, but the other five vied for the boys' attention. Emily and Rebecca were too young, and as Margaret and Patience were planning their weddings, that left three eligible girls and two boys.

The room they were allocated had been used by Governor Hunter while the official house in Parramatta was being built.

Although the family used this room for guests, it only had one double bed, so the boys had to share it.

Captain Jackson was familiar with the farm, as nearly ten years earlier, Governor Hunter had brought this family to the colony to teach farming. He had visited them on his last trip, carrying letters from John Hunter. Linus and Agnes Rosedale arrived in 1789 with fourteen of their sixteen children. Their eldest daughter, Helena, had been sent out as a convict and married one of the governor's personal guards. She was a brilliant gardener and mentioned that her father had taught her all she knew. Governor Hunter needed such skilled farming families, so he sponsored the Rosedales to emigrate. They did and then taught others to farm the compacted, virgin soil. They arrived at the same time as three other families who had come to farm in the colony. Linus Rosedale and his family set to work tilling the virgin land, and with the aid of only his family, they soon had the land productive. Admittedly, the governor had pre-cleared many acres and built them a substantial house. Governor Hunter befriended the family and used the farm as his own retreat. He often came and oversaw their work, encouraging the education of many convicts and ex-military men who wished to learn how to farm. The family were currently caring for a convict's child. She was born with a deformed hand, and had she been sent to the orphanage as she should have been, it was likely she would have died. Mary Jensen was a little over a year old when the boys arrived, and as cute as a child could be. Her father visited after church on Sundays, but as he was a felon, he was unable to remain for long. They discovered the child's mother was dying of syphilis, hence the child's deformity.

Margaret was a year older than Ben and was engaged to one of the security guards at Government House, who was primarily based in Parramatta.

Patience was engaged to Algernon Darnley, one of the soldiers based at the Redoubt in Parramatta. When the girls married the next month, they planned to remain at home as Parramatta had no married soldiers' quarters. Even though engaged, Patience was the same age as Ben and had shown interest in him from the moment they met. Victoria was a year younger and also tried to catch his eye. At nearly eighteen, Katherine was a year older than George, but she had caught Ben's eye as soon as they met. She was as vivacious as Ben was quiet. She had a riot of curly, fair reddish-coloured hair that kept escaping from her mob cap. Her infectious grin was slightly lopsided, but it added character to her. She had a somewhat unusual gait as she had broken her ankle years earlier, and it had never healed properly. Charlotte was the next youngest girl and was nearly sixteen years old.

George found he was tongue-tied when she was around, but he was often found gazing at her. Her huge blue eyes were rimmed with dark lashes, which was unusual as her hair was light with a strawberry and cream hue. He had never seen hair this colour before. Their eyes locked when they were introduced and only broke their gaze when Charlotte's mother, Agnes, tapped her daughter on the shoulder. George soon discovered that Charlotte's only drawback was that she was overly chatty. However, this may have been due to her nervousness. He certainly was jittery when she was nearby.

Rather than the extensive family spread into rooms, the six youngest women had three sets of double bunks in their large room and shared a wardrobe and clothing. They were content to share everything, but when the boys moved in, Patience and Victoria soon vied with their younger sisters for the handsome lads' attention.

Agnes chastised Patience, saying, "You are engaged, dear; leave the lads alone." The girl huffed and walked away from her mother.

After only three weeks, Linus Rosedale realised that he needed to move the boys out sooner rather than later. Rather than cause a rift in his family, Linus called a meeting of the men in the family. His twin sons, Gerry and Jem, his sons-in-law, Crispin, Jonas, and Arnold, and the two newcomers were called to a gathering to discuss building a house for Ben and George. Linus used this meeting to address the growing issue. "Boys, I know this is not of your making, but for the first time in my life, I have my children at odds with each other. Therefore, we are teaming up with a convict crew and building you a house as soon as possible."

Ben and George hated being the centre of attention. George spoke up first. "Sir, we had no intention of causing trouble. We will leave immediately and camp out on our block."

Crispin Milroy replied. "George, this is not your fault. You have done nothing to attract their attention, but you have. You are male, single, and breathing. Those three things all but sealed your fate."

Linus chuckled. "I have ten daughters; trust me, I know what I'm talking about. Crispin married our eldest, Jonas and Arnold had a double wedding with the next two. The remaining girls should know better than to cause a rift, but that's females for you. Margaret and Patience will be married next month, so it's not as if either is available, and Vicky, Kath, Charlotte, and Emily should know better. Emily and Rebecca should not be interested in boys yet, but that is what happens when you have so many children." He sighed. "Ahh, the joys of having ten delightfully attractive daughters! We lost our eldest and youngest girls."

Ben, now twenty, had already spoken to Linus about courting Katherine and was told he could, but not until the following year, when he turned twenty-one. However, they had to make their business profitable before they could marry. Now seventeen, George had four more years to wait until he reached the age of maturity, and he was not happy about that. Charlotte had undoubtedly taken his eye, but he knew he needed to establish himself before he could think about a relationship.

One of the benefits of living on the Rosedale farm was that they kept well out of the politics that were going on in the colony.

Ben discovered that Jonas had ties to Admiralty House in London, as his uncle worked at the Home Office. They found that he also held a title. This came about when a letter from England was handed to Ben to deliver. It was addressed to "The Honourable Jonas Thistlethwaite," written in fancy calligraphy. He had walked into town to collect a cart he and George had ordered. They had purchased it damaged and needed to replace a wheel before re-upholstering the seats.

George had heard of a pony for sale and had accompanied him to purchase it so that they would have transport for their new business. They had never planned to work together, but after Foveaux's message, they had little choice. Ben had not decided where he wanted to live, so he delayed choosing his land grant.

As both were young, working together would be good. George had learnt different tanning techniques in Africa; he was prepared to try various methods. Replacing the dog poop was the first thing George wished to experiment with.

Chapter 6   A Growing Family

September came all too fast.

Margaret and Patience married, and the boys were invited to the wedding.

Mopps was happy staying with the Rosedale dogs. However, it was time to move, and she would not leave. George soon found the reason why. She had befriended one of Linus's working dogs and was expecting puppies.

During the months with the family, they saw their new house reach completion. It was harvest time on the farms, and the boys promised to assist in payment for their new abode by helping with the harvest.

If they thought they knew what hard work was before, harvest time brought new meaning to the word. Hired labourers worked side by side with the household members, the boys and some of the local tribe. Only Agnes was exempt from the chore, but she had to feed everyone. All this grain was for use within the family cluster. None was to be sold as they refused to support the rum production.

Once one farm was finished, the next was started. Crispin and Arnold each had forty-acre farms further west at Toongabbie. Jonas had two blocks of forty and fifty acres, and the twins had fifty-acre farms each. Thankfully, not all of it was under crop. Some were used for stock feed, and these fields were strip-grazed. The twins mostly had mixed stock, so the grain stalks were kept as chaff and added to silage pits for feed over the lean years.

What surprised the boys was that they worked shoulder to shoulder with the Aboriginal people who lived at the back of Linus's farm. These lithe and near-naked people hardly took a breather. They could scythe a crop faster than the boys. They only asked for food as payment.

Linus also supplied them with clothing, blankets, and medical help.

On meeting one of the elders, he introduced himself in English. He executed a perfect bow and said, "Hello, I am Bennelong. These are my people. Boss Linus calls me Ben."

Ben Parker grinned. "I'm Ben as well, but I'm Benjamin."

At night, the boys were so tired that they slept on the shed floor of whatever farm they were working on. A fire was lit in a stone ringed pit, and the chill was taken off the air by the many sweaty bodies sleeping around it. Everyone rose at dawn, and within an hour, everyone was back in the fields.

Mopps was growing fatter by the day, and it didn't take long to realise she was expecting lots of pups. Although one of Linus' mongrel dogs had shown great interest in her, no one realised they had mated.

On the final day of the harvest, Mopps decided it was a good day to give birth. She had been left at Rosedale's Farm, as she now found walking hard. Agnes and the younger girls kept an eye on her. George had just arrived to collect her when she delivered her first pup. Nine more followed, and each of the tiny pups was alive. No wonder she was so big.

They had stopped taking her to the twins' farms as she kept rounding up the sheep. Even though she walked at a slow pace, the flock was often cornered, and eventually, George was required to leave her at the farm so they could complete the work. The entire birthing process took hours, so George did not go to work that day.

Agnes brought George food and tea as he sat with his beloved companion. Other family members came and went, but George barely acknowledged them. His concern was for his beloved dog.

By the time the tenth puppy was born, it was dark. Agnes and Charlotte came and assisted in cleaning up the birthing area, helping George show the puppies where to feed. The black and white border collie cross mongrel father hovered around his family and nuzzled Mopps. Some pups were his colouring, but the majority had patches with grey spots on their predominantly white coats, although each had a large dark patch across their shoulders, as Mopps had. The pups certainly had the shape of an Old English sheepdog but were oddly marked. The dog looked at her master lovingly, her tongue lolling to one side in a lopsided grin. It was as though she said, "Look what I made."

Linus eventually came to inspect the new arrivals. He stroked the head of his ill-bred mongrel and addressed it. "Well, Fergus, my boy, you have some explaining to do. Ten pups! I hope we can find homes for them all when the time comes." He brought a lamp with him and carefully checked each pup one by one. "Six males and four females, that's a good split. If they are as good working dogs as Fergus, we shall be able to get a good price for them."

Thankfully, Mopps had a nipple for each pup. They sat cooing over the newborns and helped them find a teat through Mopps' thick fur. Margaret bought a tea tray for them as they watched to ensure the pups could latch on properly. Mopps happily licked each baby clean and settled to rest with her new family. Fergus lay beside the bed with the other dogs on their blankets further down the verandah.

The following day, he was exhausted after a day of harvesting, so George stayed in the visitors' room that night. He was asleep, still fully clad. He had removed his boots but then collapsed onto the bed, planning to undress later. When he woke at dawn, he realised someone had come in and covered him with a blanket. His first thought was for his dog. The chill September morning made him keep the blanket around his shoulders while he checked Mopps. He crept out of his room and out the front door to find Fergus curled up with Mopps. He had dragged his blanket to his family, and they were snuggled up under it in the basket. He realised Mopps was better off here for a few weeks than at their house. There were more than enough people here to look after her. He slid down next to her head and stroked her lovingly. Her big brown eyes sought his approval, which he willingly gave. He caressed her head and said, "I'll miss you while you are here, my girl, but they will look after you. I'll ask Ben if he wants one of your pups. I will keep the one most like you, but Linus can have the rest."

George did not hear the door open, but Charlotte slid down to the other side of the basket. "How are they all?" She eased up Fergus's blanket and peeked under it. All the pups were asleep.

George grinned at her. He had seen her in work clothes but not in her night attire and dressing gown; with the sleep still in her eyes and her long, light-strawberry blonde hair out and hanging down to her waist, she looked ravishing. She had not brushed it yet, and he had not realised it was so long and wavy. He wanted to run his fingers through it, and... he halted his thoughts. Yes, he certainly did wish to do all those things and more, but they were too young to court. "You're up early. Couldn't you sleep, Charlie?"

Charlotte gave him a shy smile. "I heard you get up and wanted to spend time alone with you. I put a blanket over you last night; I hope you don't mind, but don't tell anyone." She put her finger to her lips.

George realised that meant she had come into his room. "I won't, but you should not have been in there, Charlie. You know how I feel, but we're too young. I should not have said anything, but your sisters were... well..." he couldn't finish. How could he say, "getting catty" without being nasty?

She chuckled. "I waited until they were all asleep. I was going to say good night, but you were out cold and fully dressed."

George realised the pups were waking and pulled back the blanket a bit to watch them feed. Mopps moved a little and gave the pups easy access to her milk. Her teats were now full, and the pups were beginning to suckle.

George reached out to move one of the smallest puppies onto the teat at the same time that Charlotte did. Their hands met, and so did their eyes. George moved the pup and then reached for her hand. He caressed it with his thumb, then said, "Charlie, you must be careful. As much as I appreciate you covering me, I do not want you to compromise yourself. We have time on our side."

Charlotte nodded and said, "I know, George, but..."

George shook his head. "No 'buts' Charlie! I'm not going anywhere. Mopps has given me a reason to call in frequently over the following weeks, but please be careful."

Charlotte's face showed her abject misery. "I'm sixteen now, George, and I can legally marry with Papa's permission."

He took a deep breath and slowly exhaled. "I know, but I can't until I'm twenty-one, and your Papa won't even consider me unless I am established. I could seek his permission, but I won't. I have no income and no idea how long it will take to establish myself in business. Ben is in the same boat. I know he wants to marry Kath, but he can't until we have set up our business and got it going. Once they are married, you are welcome to visit our house, but only after that.

Charlotte pleaded, "But if we were to marry, then I could help you. Papa let Phoebe and Arnold marry that young."

George shook his head. "He had a paid job, I don't. I want to have something to offer you, Charlie. An empty house and a few pounds in a safe spot are insufficient. What if we have a child? They cost money, which I don't have. Give me a few years to set myself up, and then we can discuss this with your papa. Ben is three years older than I am. He is in a much better situation than we are, and he still isn't planning on getting married for at least a year. Just be patient, my dear."

As he spoke, the door opened, and Linus exited. With a tilt of his head, Charlotte fled indoors. She was aware she should not be outside in her night attire, but she couldn't risk dressing for fear of waking her sisters.

Linus took her place beside the basket. "I heard what you said, lad. I didn't realise you were that serious about her."

George looked almost guilty, not that he'd done anything wrong. "I am, sir, but we are too young. I told her that, but…"

This time, it was Linus who halted his sentence. "But nothing, lad, you did the right thing. Though I have a suggestion, and this is for my sanity more than your situation. It will also give you two a bit more freedom. If I agree to an understanding that when you are old enough, you will marry, the other girls will hopefully leave you alone. Charlie has been moping around the place until you appear."

George opened his mouth to reply, but Linus held up his hand. "I also heard her creep into your room last night. If you had encouraged her, I would not have made this offer, but I knew you were out cold, as I had looked in on you only a short while before her. I know she brought you a blanket, as you are still wrapped in the one her mother made for her." George's acute embarrassment made him chuckle. Linus asked, "Do you need time to consider my offer?"

George shook off the blanket and said, "You really mean that, sir? I'd love it. But I'm only seventeen myself. I won't reach my majority for four years, and she will want us to wed before that."

Linus smiled, "She's immature and needs to grow up. We shall endeavour to nurture her over those years and encourage her to learn more than just how to cook and sew, to run a household. Let us say we will use a long engagement, like a dangled carrot, to encourage her to continue her education. Until now, she has been somewhat lacking in motivation when learning household skills. Mind you, we have enough hands in our house to hardly notice what everyone does or doesn't do."

George was delighted. He realised she was a very pretty face, but if she was to be a tanner's wife, she had to learn to cope with smells and filth. An understanding would give them time to get to know each other and see if they were suited before they committed to an engagement. He was overwhelmed but managed to say, "Sir, I thank you from the bottom of my heart. I had never even thought of mentioning my feelings for some years. But this will give me something to strive towards. She will certainly need to hone her skills in stain removal. She may even wish to learn some leather decoration. That would certainly be useful."

Linus reached out his hand to the lad. "Shake on it, my boy. But don't expect her to be too happy about this. However, it will hopefully mean that peace will return to our home. Trust the good Lord that He will lead you both. I expect you to treat her like a lady and no sneaking off for illicit liaisons at all."

George was horrified. "Oh, no, sir. I would not dare lay a hand on her in such a way. You have my word about that."

Linus chuckled. "Good, but it's a pity you don't have a few friends to foist two more girls onto." He sighed. "For the moment, I only need to hunt for a husband for Vicky."

George swallowed. He thought of Bill. Would he be interested? He was more of an acquaintance than a friend, but he was trustworthy. He would invite him out to meet the family, and over time, they would get to know some of Bill's soldier friends. For the moment, he smiled and said, "I have only one friend, and that's Ben. But I know one of the new soldiers from home. Bill is also of good character." He swallowed nervously, then said, "Sir, there was another thing I wished to talk to you about."

Linus's brow lifted.

George paused, trying to gather his words. "It's your faith. I could feel something different about the whole family the week we moved in here, but I couldn't put my finger on it. When we went to church with you last week, we were still getting to know the area. But discussions after the meal with Jonas and the baby's father, Obadiah, got me thinking. I didn't get much out of the long-winded sermons, but then, in the wagon on the way home, you summed up what Reverend Marsden said in a few sentences. However, it was over our luncheons that things started falling into place, but there is much I still don't understand. I hoped you would be open to explaining things to me. Obadiah said he and Jonas talk often, and that's why his child will move there soon."

Linus's smile took George's breath away. It was like a mantle of tranquillity had descended on his prospective father-in-law. "Ahh! Yes, lad. I would be delighted, my boy; however, the house is stirring, and the day has begun. You can look forward to many lively conversations in the years ahead. Ben has already voiced a similar interest. Cris, Arnie and Jonas are all firm believers, as are Margaret and Patience's beaus. Some dinner-time conversations become very interesting. These started when my friend John Hunter used to stay with us. Obadiah is just learning and has some way to go. Jonas has taken him under his wing and will care for the man's child until his time is up. With you lads here, the baby will move to Jonas and Mary's house. Obadiah is working nearby and will see her more often."

George's eyes nearly popped. "Do you mean the governor? I knew he stayed here, but did not realise he was a personal friend." He wasn't so worried about the baby leaving as she cried quite a lot.

Linus nodded. "He is indeed. He also taught me to read and write during his various visits. John Hunter studied Latin and Divinity at Edinburgh University before the call of the sea won. However, his faith never faltered, and our friendship grew from that. I miss him greatly. Cris still writes to keep him informed about what we are doing and what's happening in the colony. Foveaux's ship brought more letters from him. Your captain delivered them. John warned London about the Corps more than eight years ago, and they didn't believe him or Jonas's uncle. Admiralty will regret they ignored them now."

Chapter 7   The New Business
Spring 1808

By early October, the first locally obtained skins were ready to process. Linus's Aboriginal friends had speared and skinned a wallaby without burning off the fur, as they usually did. They brought the boys the hide, then gave Agnes the tail. It had a spear hole in the hide; therefore, it would only be used for small things, like thonging. The skin had been salted and left for a month. Other pelts had been added since then, but the first one was nearly ready for processing.

In the intervening month, huge coopered tubs were purchased and set up at the back of their new shed. This building had a rock base and a brick top. The floor was also brick, so rats could not dig through it. They had added massive barn doors so one entire side could be opened. It had a loft where the crates of pelts were to be stored. The back also had a door and two timber shuttered windows. This created an excellent cross breeze. The crates of hides and equipment were due to arrive any day from the Government Stores warehouse in Sydney.

One of the first things they needed was scudding posts. Sourcing the correct size was not a problem, as Linus had trees of the correct diameter ready for felling. A four-foot log was needed, and it then needed to be split in half lengthwise.

As weekends were spent with the family on one or the other farms, the first weekend in October, they felled a tree perfect for scudding posts. The top had been hit by lightning and split down the centre to the roots. As it fell, it broke apart perfectly. Two four-foot sections were cut and loaded onto the boys' cart; the rest would be used for firewood.

George had already made the two frames for legs, and on the following Monday, the scudding logs were put to use.

This was the first time Ben had made the leather he would later use for saddle making. The pair decided that if they could each learn the other's trade, they could eventually start their own businesses.

Ben had already been to the Hawkesbury River and found an area he liked. He liked to be near water, and the high riverfront block he had seen looked good. There was an elevated area for his house and workshop, and the river frontage he would use for his livestock.

Ben applied for a land grant near the new town of Penrith, and Foveaux had said he would look into seeing if this land was available for him.

George was happy with this arrangement and was content to put his money into the tubs and equipment to set up his tannery. When the time came, George promised he would go and help Ben set up his business.

Although the first tannery was up and working, their house still needed furnishing. They had grass-stuffed mattresses and minimal furniture. Their kitchen contained an open fireplace and a few pots and pans. It was certainly not suitable for either of the girls to live in. A single roof over their heads was not enough.

With the first skin tanned, the boys were now ready to put the business into full swing.

George spoke to the butcher and arranged to get what hides he had. He collected the first load, and they were salted in a covered vat. The salt came from boiling seawater on the foreshore of Sydney Cove. John Boston was the salt maker and supplied them with the coloured, contaminated dregs from the tubs, once the potter, Colin Osborne, had had enough. George treated a few roo skins; the first one was ready to process.

With access to numerous kangaroo and wallaby skins, George thought he would apply what he learned in Africa in a modified way. Rather than using the dog poop to treat the hides, he used a puree of vegetable matter mixed with animal fat. The mix of what the African man told him was essentially unprocessed dog poop, and it smelled a lot better. After George rinsed the salt from the first skin, he spread the pelt over the log and, with his curved blade, he removed the fat and then the fur.

This kangaroo skin was much thinner than a cowhide but seemed strong and flexible. It was similar to tanning a rabbit's or hare's skin. Those were the only ones he had cured with fur. He thought back to an experiment he did with a rabbit pelt when he was fifteen. However, he must have overdone something, as the fur came out in clumps a week after tanning. Sadly, with that experiment, Rob ended up plucking the rest of the rabbit skins he had done at home and making them into a purse lining.

With further experimentation, he discovered that the thin skins only needed to be soaked overnight in salt, then drained and rinsed. The roo skins he left for only twelve hours. This cut the waiting time down dramatically, but it meant that they often had to scud many hides in a day.

With an eighteen-hour salting, George rinsed it and placed the odd-shaped pelt over the *scudding* log. He set to work de-fleshing and trimming the skin. He checked it and saw that the skin had survived unscathed. Next was the new treatment for batting. He had purchased some damaged vegetables from Linus that had started fermenting after being cut when harvesting. He mixed the raw puree with some unclarified lard from the Rooty Hill Government Farm near Crispin's property.

The mixture smelled quite reasonable. He wondered what it would taste like if he cooked it; moreover, it seemed to work as well as the poop, if not better. It certainly did not smell nearly as much as the foul-smelling dog excrement, and was easier to use. He didn't gag as he smeared the goo on the skin.

George pounded the rawhide and worked the congealed lump into the new skin. Even his hands liked working with this substance. He was even tempted to taste it. His hand was nearly at his mouth when he realised what he was about to do. That made him gag.

George was astounded by how supple the skin was, and he wished he could show his father and discuss other options for the tanning treatment. He thought back to all the excrement he collected and realised he should write to Miles at home and let him know.

The next stage in tanning was a long soak in a tanning solution. Again, he had a new process to try. He learned about the use of acacia tree bark in Africa and discovered that a black wattle tree in the colony had similar tanning properties. As this was only a test hide, George left the hide in the tanning solution for two days rather than a week. It was thinner, so it may not need to stay in the solution for as long as a thick cowhide.

~

The first skin was nearly finished at the end of the first week. The hide came out of the final solution late on Friday afternoon. George pegged it out to dry by mounting it on a stretching frame. He should know by next week if the new tanning process would work.

While he waited for each process to work its magic on the skins, he had built a series of drying frames. He had spools of thick twine that he purchased in Africa, and he used them to sew the tanned skin into the frame. He knew he would need to rub and stretch the drying skin a few times over the next few days, but if it worked, this leather would be amazingly versatile, and he could make saddles, whips, and even belts.

The boys were keen to test it for strength, but could already see many potential uses. It was so thin that they would not need to slice it in half.

Waiting was frustrating, but Ben and George could hardly wait to check the skin on Monday morning.

They had rubbed it twice yesterday, in the morning before church and on returning from Rosedale's farm.

Ben could tell the quality of this skin was going to be amazing.

The leather was supple but incredibly strong. The tannin from the black wattle had given the roo leather a lovely red hue, and there was a natural gloss to the hide.

Spring arrived with heavy rains. This meant crops would germinate and animals would reproduce.

As the family meandered around the grassy area outside the church, more people arrived. John Macarthur and his wife, Elizabeth, stepped out of their carriage. She glanced at her husband to ensure he was not looking. Then, she waved hello to Agnes. Her guarded smile spoke volumes. Crispin and Elizabeth had been experimenting with cross-breeding sheep, but John had not yet discovered this. She had lent him a purebred Merino ram.

Once the Macarthur's entered the church to take their seats at the front, Agnes turned to Linus and whispered, "I so feel for her, dear. I do wish there was something I could do, but I dare not even approach her when that man is nearby."

Linus agreed. "Love, she knows you want to be her friend and that alone is valuable. Take every opportunity you can to let her know you're there for her if she needs you. Be there for her as she needs friends. He'll be returning to London soon, so she will be alone. She will need friends then."

The following morning, Ben undid the final length of twine on the stretching frame. Rather than being stiff, the soft skin all but collapsed into a heap. "Cor, George, I've never seen leather this soft." He picked up the entire skin and held it to his face. "Can you make me more of this? This will make the most incredible saddles. Not only that, imagine whips and riding crops. They will be so supple, they will fly off the shelves. You have a winner with this roo pelt." The new tanning process required some adjustments, but it ultimately worked.

George had wondered how best to use some of his African hides. "Ben, you know those patterned hides I bought in Cape Town? I thought about using some of those for the tongue end of the riding crops. Can you imagine how they will look? The red leather with a black and white zebra skin popper tip. The rough bits of zebra skin can be used. Did you know they included more than just the one striped skin? There must be a dozen or more."

Ben swung around and looked at him. "George, why did I never think about making a selection of riding whips? I have only ever made shaped crops, but do you know there are at least six sorts?"

George's nose screwed up. "I was thinking more of the plaited whip handles. There's no reason why we could not invent our own. I have seen a long cracking whip, and I want to try making one of those and a riding crop with a sword stick in it. I know carriages need longer whips, but what other sorts exist?"

Ben said, "The ones I know are ones called joking bats, dressage, trotting, touchier, stick drop lash and lunging whips, but there may well be more. Some are long, and some are short. We can always experiment, and I'm sure someone will buy them. We can make them to order. I've also heard of hidden sword sticks in crops. We'll need to talk to the blacksmith for that."

George said, "You forgot hunting whips and all the flexible ones. I might play around and see if I can figure out something unique we can put our names on."

On the first Sunday morning in November, the Rosedale wagon stopped by the boys' house and collected them. The other families arrived in various vehicles and gathered at St. John's Church in Parramatta.

The large family group squashed into two rows halfway down the aisle. Obadiah had relieved Jonas of his child and sat at the back with the convicts. There were many small children now, and Crispin and Helena had nine of them; the youngest, Jeremy, had been born in February, only days after the Rum Rebellion. At nine months old, the little boy was adorable. He had his father's dark hair and eyes. He took to George at first sight. Every Sunday, the little boy would reach out for him, put his thumb in his mouth, and then settle down to sleep.

George had never had much to do with children, but Charlotte adored them. She usually carried the baby into church and took it upon herself to keep him quiet. Helena had her hands full with the other eight imps.

As the family knew the young couple now had an understanding, they could sit together. Ben and Kath were usually squeezed in next to them. Neither couple minded being so cramped, as it meant they were touching each other throughout the service. Admittedly, this often made George take his mind off the sermon, but Charlotte and he frequently held hands under the guise of caring for the child.

Sunday luncheon discussions usually made up for what he missed in church. These meals were now often more picnic-like than sit-down dinners. They were generally held at Linus and Agnes's house, but if the weather were fine, they would travel to Toongabbie and one of the four family homes.

Crispin and Helena Milroy, Linus's eldest daughter, employed some of the younger convict girls, and they were training them to be housekeepers, maids and nannies. To assist in the training, the family often descended on them *en masse*. These days, each household brought their own food, but it was put out to share.

~

As the weather warmed, the ladies went to the waterhole behind Linus's house. The tribe had gone to Kissing Point, so the swimming hole was private. This time gave the men time to talk, and talk they did.

In the weeks leading up to summer, the two boys sat and listened as Linus explained his faith. They were intrigued that the women were encouraged to join the discussions and, more often than not, contributed regularly to the lively conversation.

One question that had fixed itself in George's mind was about the Fall. Foveaux's comment about the mangoes inspired this. He had wanted to ask someone, but he knew by Ben's blank look that he did not know either. As they sat in the Spring sunshine, Linus was relaxing next to him. George knew it was time to ask his question. "Sir, can you explain what happened in the Fall in the Bible and what it has to do with fruit?" George swallowed nervously, expecting to be ridiculed. He wasn't.

Linus smiled. "I've been wondering where you would start with your questions, but the very beginning is as good a place as any, and the Fall is right at the beginning. I will start by saying I am an uneducated man. I learned to read and write well after I turned fifty. As I told you, John Hunter taught me and then gave me a Bible. Before that, I had to wait until Sundays before the words were read to me, but that was never enough. I found my mind was like a dry cloth, eager to absorb more but with no opportunity to do so, until I met John." Linus smiled, thinking back to those happy days with John and the strong friendship they had. He inhaled and looked at Ben, then released a deep breath. "Now, I shall tell you the summary of the entire bible in five lines. This is how you can both remember and understand what Christianity is about. John told me, so it is easy to recall."

The young man beside him gazed expectantly.

Linus was about to start when Ben moved closer. "Sir, may I listen in too?"

Linus nodded. "The outline is three words and two questions, well, one question, in two parts. The words are *'God, Man, God,'* and the question is, *'What if you do?* And *What if you don't?'* Just that, and it covers everything."

The frowns on the boys' faces mimicked his when he first heard this. John explained it to him.

"The first words in the bible are 'In the beginning God…' Well, that's because God made everything. Our minds are finite, which means fixed. We see everything in terms of black and white, but God sees it far more deeply. Anyway, we don't need to get into trying to understand His mind, only His love for us. Okay, God created everything we see, hear, or feel, but He also created us in His own image. He also made us perfect. That surprises many, but it's true. He made the world perfect, but then sin came into being. One of His angels, Lucifer, rebelled against Him and thought he could do as much as God. God cast him out of heaven."

Both boys had their full attention on the older man.

Linus said, "Now, this next bit, George, answers your question. Lucifer, who we also know as Satan or the Devil, knew how to tempt the two perfect beings God had made. We call them Adam and Eve."

He saw the boys' heads nodding in agreement. Linus continued. "In the centre of the garden were two trees. One was the Tree of Life, and the other was the Tree of Knowledge. God gave Adam one rule when he made this beautiful garden. That rule was not to eat from the Tree of Knowledge, or he would die. That's it! One rule. They could do anything else they wanted to: eat, sleep… absolutely everything."

The boys gasped.

Half under his breath, Ben said, "Oh, now that would be nice."

Linus chuckled. "I know! Anyway, the couple loved living in the garden, and God regularly came to speak to them. Though naked, they were not afraid, and as God said, it was good. Then, one day, and this is the fruit connection, George. Lucifer, now in the form of a snake, saw Eve near the Tree of

Knowledge. It lied to her, saying that the fruit would not kill her, but it tasted delicious. Eve succumbed and took a bite. Her eyes were opened to her nakedness, and she realised the fruit was indeed delicious and that she wasn't dead. She shared the fruit with Adam. That decision is called 'the Fall'. It was the fall from God's perfect will. However, that one action had enduring consequences. That night, when God visited, He found they were covered in leaves. Their nakedness had never worried them before, but now, for the first time, they were ashamed and hid from Him. God knew what they had done, and they were cast out of the beautiful garden we call Eden."

Linus heard both boys gasp.

As they did so, Crispin, Arnold, Jonas, and the twins Gerry and Jem moved closer to listen.

Crispin said, "This never grows old, sir. I could listen to it a thousand times and still learn more."

Gerry smiled, "Go on, Papa, get to the good bit."

Linus gave a single nod and continued. "So that explains the first words of my quote. 'God Made,' and the second being, we disobeyed, so the words, 'Man rejected.' So now the third word is God again. The sin of rejection and separation from God was just one of the things that occurred. You see, the world became unbalanced as sin has many far-reaching consequences. That we are all sitting here today in a penal colony proves that. But that sin did not just affect humanity; it also brought earthquakes, thunder, lightning, and unknown calamities, as well as sickness. The land was also no longer as productive. Adam now had to work tilling the earth to produce food, whereas previously, he ate what God grew."

Linus paused, gazed over the beautiful farmland before him, and said, "But God loves us. He does not want us to be separated from Him, so He gave us a way back to Him. Do either of you know how that would be?"

George frowned and shook his head.

Ben said tentatively, "Jesus? Is that how He fits in?"

Linus nodded. He looked at his sons and son-in-laws and smiled. He knew each had come to him with discussions like this. He nodded and said, "Boys, before we came here, Cris was a lamplighter in London, and Jonas is an earl's son. I was an illiterate farmer, but before God, we are all equal. There is no sin that is too big or too bad that God won't forgive. If you truly repent and ask, he will listen. That is where the second 'God' part of the statement fits in. He loves us and wants us to love Him too. So, yes, this is where Jesus comes in. Jesus is God's son, but He is also God Himself. Jesus is also the doorway back to God's side."

Linus sighed, "Sometimes, we are told that we only have to believe and we will be saved, but that is not true. Believing is only the first step. Even Satan believes in Jesus, so consider that. No, what we have to do is believe and then act. By that, I mean we must put Jesus' teaching into practice. Many call themselves Christians, but that is only a name. We are called to care for the sick and wounded, putting Christ's love to work. It's what our family have tried to do here. I see God's hand in what happened to our Helena and her being sent as a convict. It's also why we have been caring for Obadiah's daughter."

He cleared his throat before continuing. "Here, we have a good life… no, a great life, and with what I now know about God, we have taught others. As my friend, John Hunter, taught me, so I now teach you. And that is where we get to the two questions. 'What if you do?' and 'What if you don't?' Well, as I said, they are really only the two options to one question. Do you follow Jesus and His teachings so that we can one day walk with God? Or do you reject everything and do as you please? There is no third option. You may have fun while alive here, but then what? I believe in Eternal Life after I die. I want to be with God at that time. I want what Adam and Eve rejected and then tried to reclaim. So I choose 'Yes.' We must repent of our sins and accept the gift God is offering us, then try to live as though Jesus walked beside us every step of our lives."

Crispin nodded.

Jonas chuckled. "I had much to give up. I was born with a silver spoon in my mouth, so to speak. I liken myself to the rich young ruler. But money means nothing compared to the peace I have now. I can truly say I am happy. My father still begs me to come home, but I realise home is now here. Mary and I have a big house, but if it burned down, I wouldn't care a fig as long as the family and our rescued convict girls and Obadiah's child are safe. However, we use that home for God's purposes. Boys, take it from me, money is nice, but it is more of a burden than a blessing. Linus and I had some interesting discussions on the way out here. He had no idea I had a title at the time. Lad, his faith was in action even then, and I saw in him what I was missing in my empty life. I embarked on this journey for different reasons, and I won't go into that now, but once I had decided to put into action what I had learned in church, my life finally fell into place. Don't get me wrong. God never promised us happiness, but He did promise us joy."

George glanced at Ben, frowning.

Jonas saw the puzzled frowns on their faces and explained. "Mary and I lost two babies before we had our son. I know our little ones are now with God in Heaven. Without my faith, I would have lost hope. Cris and Helena lost their first, and sir, you lost a child after the twins, as well as your last little girl, Samantha."

Linus nodded.

Jonas continued, "Those children were never able to sin, and I firmly believe they are in Heaven in grown perfection. Oh, don't get me wrong, we hurt; it still does. But you cannot get through the bad times without faith firmly anchored in God. You have both lost your families, but somehow, you have ended up together here. We are now here for you both, and I know that any of us will be able to answer any of your questions."

George had been thinking while he spoke. "I have never really done anything much wrong, like theft, murder, or the like, but I still don't feel, well, clean, I suppose. I'm guessing that the sin makes me feel like that?"

Ben nodded, but he was confused. "Me too, George. We have always been honest; we don't cheat, lie, steal, or womanise. What do we have to repent for?"

Linus released a rumble that sounded like laughter. "I love you two. You are but innocent babes."

George flushed with embarrassment.

Linus smiled at the young men. "Sin is not always in action, but in thought or word, too. Have you ever wished to do something you knew to be wrong?" His eyes moved from one to the other.

George glanced at Ben and thought about the girls in Rio. He nodded, too ashamed to confess what those thoughts were. They had both come so close to succumbing.

Ben also shrugged in acknowledgment, followed by a nod. He also thought of the lusty feelings he had not only for the girls in Rio but also for Kath. Only yesterday, they had kissed behind the shed, and he found his hands wandering over her luscious but thin body. Goodness knows what would have happened if they had not heard the back door bang closed.

Linus said, "Although actions speak louder than words, the thoughts and words are also to be acknowledged and confessed. Have you never lusted over a lady or more money?" He hit the nail on the head as they both gasped.

Both boys nodded, finally understanding.

George asked, "So, how do we do this repentance bit? Do I have to flay myself or what?"

Cris chuckled.

Arnold, who had been quiet until now, said, "No, George, all you have to do is have a conversation with God. You don't need big words or even set prayers; you need to be serious. You must say sorry for all your thoughts, words and deeds… and mean it. If you go straight out and do the same thing again, then it shows you are not serious. We will all need to stand before God and be judged. From the king to the newest babe, no one will escape."

Jem now chipped in. "George, if you are an alcoholic and want to lay off the stuff, would you hang around a public bar?"

George gasped. "Cripes no, Jem."

Gerry added, "Well, if you find yourself tempted somehow, ensure you avoid whatever that temptation is. Drink, women, gambling, cheating and the like. Here in this place, it's hard to make an honest living. But I have found that even selling grain at an elevated price was a temptation. I knew it would be distilled, so I refused to sell. I was so angry at the chaps that I said no to them when they approached me. I could have doubled what I eventually got, but it's not worth it."

Jem put his hand on his brother's arm.

Gerry smiled, took a deep breath and finished his story. "When they destroyed the rest of my crop, I felt like hitting back. Instead, I did only what I could think of: I no longer grow grain. As you can see, I still get upset. I now only have stock. Colleen is too precious to me to risk our lives together, so I removed the temptation that also brought danger to my family. Jem had a similar experience. It's why we now only grow vegetables, stock feed, or grain for the family's use."

Crispin gasped. "I had no idea that was why you both went out of cropping."

The twins nodded.

Jem said, "You didn't need to know, Cris. But Erin suggested it before we married. Some years ago, our two girls had just been approached to join the Irish uprising and fight the English shortly after Governor John left. Colleen and Erin had not been assigned to the Rosedale Farm for long. As Irish convicts, they were enticed to rebel. They thankfully told us, and we sent word to Parramatta. Troops were ready and waiting when the first breakout occurred. Had they kept silent, we all could have been burned while we slept."

Gerry added, "Like you two, we had to wait until they were old enough to marry our girls. Living in close quarters with a girl you fancy is much harder than seeing her occasionally. Temptations present themselves all too often. Eventually, Jem and I decided to move to our farm rather than stay here. We planted a grain crop that first year, and that was what happened. John Hunter told us to be careful, but admittedly, we didn't listen. We thought we knew better and tried to beat the Rum Corps at their own game. It backfired. So yeah, I know about repentance."

Jem nodded in agreement.

George's attitude to life changed after that conversation. If God truly were in control of his life, then who was he to fight against it? He had more questions, but he was sure that there would be more conversations.

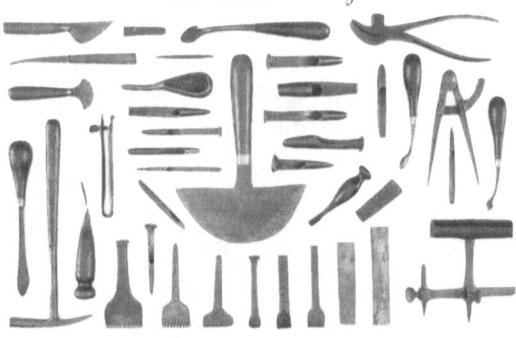

Chapter 8   *Work Begins in Earnest*

*T*he extended Rosedale families continued to attend St John's church in Parramatta. They heard that Foveaux had called Lieutenant Governor Paterson from Van Diemen's Land.

Paterson finally arrived and took control of the settlement after their first Christmas in the colony, but he did little to change what Foveaux had established since his arrival. Paterson did extract a promise from Governor Bligh that he was to return to England. He went.

All were pleased that Bligh had left Sydney. That was until word had filtered back that he had only gone as far as Van Diemen's Land.

At church for Easter in 1809, Paterson was visiting Parramatta. Paterson wondered how Lieutenant Governor David Collins would cope with the arrival of Bligh in the Derwent River settlement and anxiously awaited word of the outcome.

Linus overheard precisely what occurred. Lieutenant Governor Collins refused permission for Bligh to disembark and would not permit his vessel to remain at a mooring in the river. Bligh's vessel, the *HMS Porpoise*, was anchored in the mouth of the Derwent River, where he intended to remain.

After Paterson arrived, Foveaux had intended to return to Norfolk Island to assume command there, but Paterson had suggested that he stay to assist him in the colony. Things were still unsettled.

George and Ben did not realise Foveaux accompanied Paterson to the church service. They were discussing the ousting of the leader of the coup, now referred to as the Rum Rebellion, and they were surprised when their travelling companion came up behind them and placed a hand on each shoulder.

The boys jumped.

Foveaux released a belly laugh. "You really should not eavesdrop, gentlemen. It is not polite."

Both young men flushed scarlet.

George said, "I was hoping to hear where you were, sir. I thought you must have returned to Norfolk Island as planned."

Foveaux shook his head. "Paterson has ordered that I remain here until London sends a replacement leader. I believe Major-General Miles Nightingall's name has been mentioned as the possible new governor. I dare say we won't know until our new commander arrives. I'm expecting that it will not be for months."

George was about to ask about the man he mentioned when Foveaux continued.

His lips pursed. "Enough talk about politics. I get enough of that every day. Tell me about your businesses. George, I believe you have been experimenting with the vegetable tanning you saw in Africa. Does it work?"

George was happy to discuss leatherwork. He proceeded to wax lyrical about the kangaroo leather he had made. It was thin, strong and supple. He grinned and nodded. "Too right it does, sir." He enthused about the hides.

Not to be overlooked, Ben said, "Sir, I used some of this new leather for my saddles and discovered it is an excellent medium to work with." He spoke highly about the quality of George's pelts and how easy it was to work with. "Sir, I am astounded by the superior strength of the kangaroo leather. As a saddler, I need thin skins for some of the more intricate areas. Usually, I must split the bovine hides into one-eighth of their thickness. However, the roo hides are so thin, I use them as is. The leather is incredibly strong. I tried to do this with calf or lamb's skins, but they ripped."

Foveaux was intrigued. "It's that good?"

Both boys nodded.

George admitted he made riding crops from it with exotic poppers. "Sir, my brother, Rob, could not walk, but he could use his hands and made an astounding range of items our mother sold at the markets. Rob used to make riding crops from the offcuts of leather, and as he taught me to plait the casings, I tried making a whip out of this new leather. Oh, sir, the roo skin is superb to work with. I can cut it into fine thonging, and it has the most incredible stretch while still retaining its strength. It's like weaving silk ribbons. I had always wished to make a cracking whip, but I had never been able to achieve the thinness of the leather. With roo skins, it's easy. The vegetable tanning is also much less smelly, and I now use black wattle bark to tan and colour the hides. The result is a shiny, almost deep red leather that is soft to the touch and stronger than any I've worked with in London. Another plus is that the thinness of the hide means that they take about a quarter of the time to tan."

As he spoke, Charlotte and Katherine Rosedale walked to his side.

George introduced them.

Foveaux cocked an eyebrow as each attractive young lady hooked their hands through the elbow of the two young men.

Ben had been permitted to propose to Katherine, but they had no plans to marry for nearly a year or more. He informed Foveaux that they were recently engaged.

A look of almost jealousy flashed across Foveaux's face before he congratulated the happy couple. He addressed Katherine. "Well, my dear, I congratulate you heartily. Ben, have you thought about where you will live? As I know, you are currently in George's dwelling. I gather you are still keen to move westwards? I thought you had chosen somewhere. Did you change your mind?"

Ben nodded. "Yes, sir, Penrith is a new area that is growing quickly. I like the land at Castlereagh, and I was hoping to speak to you about finalising it sometime."

Foveaux's eyebrows shot up. "You did, but has that grant not been completed yet? I thought that had been done. I shall see Macarthur about it now. Hold your horses for a bit, lad." He turned and walked away.

The two young couples stood awaiting the soldier.

When he returned to their side, he was no longer alone.

Neither boy had met the infamous John Macarthur, but they knew all about him from Gerry, Jem, and Cris. All three said that he was the motivating force behind the coup. Macarthur had been tried and acquitted locally, and it was the arrest of his six companions that was the final straw. They knew him to be someone to be kept at arm's length.

The four young people bowed or curtsied when the new Colonial Secretary arrived in their midst.

Foveaux was not happy. His voice held animosity. "Macarthur, I put a request through months ago for a land grant for Benjamin Parker. Why is this not yet finalised?"

The younger soldier shifted his weight from one foot to the other. Macarthur shrugged rudely. "I didn't know who he was, sir. Atkins was given the paperwork, but I didn't push him to finalise it."

Foveaux had intended to embarrass the soldier beside him, but the man was as slippery as an eel. Atkins was known to enjoy a tipple.

John Macarthur gave Foveaux a look that froze him. John had no qualms about ignoring an outright order issued by this man. He was aware that Paterson was in command, not Foveaux. He would process this grant when he had time and not before.

Rather than rile the egotistical man any more, Foveaux merely asked politely, "Captain, if it could be completed with all possible speed, I would be appreciative." He knew that that comment alone could imply that a favour was owed. He should have rephrased his words, but they had been said. He added, "This man is a saddler; you know how short of skilled craftsmen we are. His skill is required, and he must have a base to work from."

Macarthur didn't miss the innuendo of a possible favour that would remain outstanding. He smiled knowingly. "I'll get on to it tomorrow, sir. I'll also send a crew to clear the land. I presume you want a house, a stable, and a workshop. I'll sort that out, as well, as I have been tardy in filling out the grant paperwork. I have convict crews in need of work and no jobs." He had no intention of complying, but he would inform Atkins and hope that the man would remember to complete the land grant paperwork at some point.

Ben wasn't sure about having convicts clearing his land, but it meant he could have somewhere for them to live when they married. He felt Kath's fingers gently squeeze his arm and saw a subtle nod.

Ben reluctantly acquiesced. He bowed. "Thank you, good sirs. We accept with pleasure."

Both soldiers gave a nod.

Foveaux turned his attention back to George. "I must come and see this amazing leather you have been working on. I might commission a saddle if it is as good as you say. Have you found someone to make the trees for you, or do you make them yourself?"

With the conversation safely turned back to their crafts, Ben and George were content to chatter away for some time.

Macarthur was thankfully called away, and he had the decency to bow before departing. However, he did not return Foveaux's salute.

Foveaux waited until the Macarthur carriage left before growling. "That man infuriates me. You would think he would be grateful that I sided with him when I arrived, but he's a thorn in my flesh as much as he was with Bligh. Paterson and Macarthur have already come to blows, well, pistol blows, as they had a duel eight years ago. Macarthur shot him and had to return to England to stand trial. He was gone for four years. There is bad blood between anyone who stands between what that man wants and his goal. So be warned. Stay clear of him."

Ben and Kath were unsure of what to say.

Thankfully, Linus and Agnes approached, and the conversation returned to leatherwork.

George had not had a chance to reveal a small sample of the roo leather in his pocket. He now did so. The reddish-coloured sample was extracted and lay in his hand. "Sir, I did not expect you to be here, but others are interested, and I brought a sample with me. This is what it looks like. The finished leather is strong and supple. Ben will be able to craft the most incredible saddles with this. I believe that the ladies' side saddles may benefit the most, as they require smooth and lightweight designs. I will freely admit I have never seen leather this fine." He watched as the soldier examined the swatch of leather. "Sir, sourcing pelts will be our biggest challenge. I know that the Redoubts process meat. I wondered if the skins are discarded or if we could have them?"

Foveaux nodded. "I'll sort that." He took the sample from the young man's hand and fingered the soft swatch. "This is kangaroo leather? Really?"

George's mouth twitched. "To tell the truth, it's wallaby skin, sir, but I have some big red kangaroo pelts in salting. Over the next few weeks, I will experiment with various African techniques and treatment times. Overall, I have a product that no tannery in England could surpass. Personally, I believe the saddles Ben will make from this will outshine any saddles made in England. The cedar here for the bases is both light and strong."

Paterson overheard the comment and all but elbowed into the

conversation. He saw the swatch that Foveaux held and reached out to feel it without asking for permission.

Linus had seen the full hide but had given little thought to its uses. He looked at his future son-in-law in awe.

George watched the acting governor pull, stretch and rub the leather.

Paterson said, "Boys, can you make me a new saddle with this? If suitable, I'd like to replace some worn ones for government use. If it works out, as I presume it will, I may issue a temporary Government Warrant for their replacement."

The four young folk gasped in unison. Their business would thrive if they had a steady stream of customers, such as a government contract. A warrant meant that Ben and Kath could marry sooner rather than later. With a large order possible, the boys knew they needed to hunt around for help.

~

Ben made the new saddle for Paterson and took it to Government House in Parramatta, where the officer was residing.

The two officers visited the tannery a week after it was delivered.

Both soldiers were suitably impressed, and they pulled and stretched various samples of tanned leather. Local cedar trees made the saddles both light and robust.

Business picked up after Lieutenant Governor Paterson issued a complete resupply order for saddles, and the word quickly spread about the quality of workmanship by the lads. Though there were few horses in the colony, they all needed new tack, including harnesses, bridles, and saddlebags.

~

By May, Ben realised he needed to make a concerted effort to source more hands to work with him. He wanted to focus more on the leatherwork than on making the bases.

Hopefully, they could find an orphan lad who wanted to learn how to make the tree bases for the saddles and other carpentry work. George wanted more workers for the leather.

At the end of the month, the Sydney Gazette carried an article with an assortment of carpentry tools for sale.

Macarthur did not make good on his promise of building on Ben's block as he left for London in October, so Ben poured his funds into building the house himself. As Ben's meagre funds were almost exhausted after prepaying for the foundations of his house, George purchased all the tools required for a new branch of their business. While collecting the tools, they intended to visit the boy's orphanage in Sydney to seek assistance.

Both lads were astounded to discover that there was no such thing as a boys' orphanage anywhere in the colony. There was a girls' one, but young orphan boys were assigned, like felons, to live with Ticket of Leave convict families. The orphan boys had a rough life and were often treated as slaves by most of the families. Many wanted to leave but had nowhere to go.

A lad named Quinn had been living with a convict family until he grew too old to do so. For some months, he had been living on the street with a group of younger boys. He voiced an interest in the job. He was ready to travel back with them. He had few possessions.

Their sparsely furnished house had a third occupant. They were now in great need of more furniture.

~

A month later, George saw an advertisement for a house full of furniture for sale, which included a few pigs and other assorted items. The whimsical wording of the advertisement captured George's attention, and he wondered what 'other items' might possibly be included. Without telling the other two boys, he made a trip to Parramatta and informed the agent that he would purchase the lot sight unseen. The inclusion of two wagons and two horses with the consignment would be beneficial for the budding business.

The items George didn't want could be given to the extended Rosedale families, as there were enough family members to use what was unwanted. Even the pigs could be gifted to the wider family.

The addition of a nanny goat meant they could have milk, and this odd collection of items prompted him to bid eight pounds on the auction lot. His offer was the winning bid, but the agent only paid £3.3s for the entire enormous consignment.

George paid the agent his commission and arranged for the furniture to be delivered on Wednesday.

The pigs were crated and taken to Linus. He had wanted some to root out the field after cropping. George decided to keep the two goats and chickens, which were not mentioned in the advertisement.

~

Mid-afternoon, in the middle of June, their work was interrupted by the arrival of six wagonloads of furniture and other extraneous paraphernalia. Work in the shed was abandoned for the day, and they assisted the six drivers in unpacking the vehicles.

George's eyes widened when he saw the items that had arrived. He had no idea that a small boat was included. It was on a wagon and filled with boxes of household items, such as bedding. The boat was a rowboat with a fold-down mast. It also had a red sail attached to a boom. Once the small vessel was emptied of its contents, all nine men struggled to lift the small clinker boat off the wagon. It was dragged to the front garden and left there. The boat now sat in the front yard, glaringly out of place since they were atop a hill, just west of Parramatta. George had no idea what to do with it.

Ben grinned. "Hey, George, did you see that one of the boxes was full of fishing tackle? I'm guessing you don't fish?"

George shook his head. He didn't have the time or patience for fishing. "If you want it, it's yours. When I bought their entire consignment, I knew there would be stuff I didn't want, but feel free to take all the fishing gear. I would only on-sell it for a pittance to get rid of it."

Ben chuckled. "I'll take you fishing one day and see if I can persuade you to change your mind. It's why I wish to be near the river."

"You'll have to twist my arm, but I'll go because it's you asking." George hoped to find someone who actually enjoyed fishing. He thought it a waste of time.

The second wagon contained two large double beds with feather mattresses, a sideboard, a dining table and chairs, and an entire crate of kitchenware. The third and fourth wagons had three wardrobes, settees, and some armchairs that were packed high. It also contained an assortment of crates they would unpack later. These were placed in one of the spare rooms.

Four of the wagons left when unloaded, but they now had to find a place for their new vehicles and steeds.

The remainder of the day was spent finding places for the numerous pieces of furniture. When Linus had arranged for the house to be built, George expected it to have a room each for them and maybe an eat-in kitchen. The six-bedroom house was enormous, and half of the rooms lacked anything. They sat shut and unused. They never had visitors overnight and, therefore, did not require furniture. Amongst the deliveries were some mattresses without frames. These were only horsehair, but they were better than Quinn had ever had before. He had never slept on a feather mattress and thought he was in seventh heaven to be surrounded by such luxury. He felt somewhat guilty that he now had a home, but flopped back onto the soft mattress and chuckled with sheer delight.

The consignment also included oil lamps, as well as a large drum of whale oil. Previously, they had only homemade rushlights, which didn't last long. The lamps meant they would be able to work into the evening indoors. The three oil lamps were filled, two placed in the sitting room and one in the kitchen.

The house was starting to feel lived-in. Once the beds were set up and in place, the three boys went to make their beds using the sheets that came with the purchase.

Quinn stood looking at the flat linen lengths. He had no idea how to use them. "George, can you show me how to make a bed? I have no idea where everything goes. I've never had a bed before, let alone sheets."

The two older boys felt guilty. They had never experienced such poverty and were still accustomed to cooking to make ends meet. Quinn had rarely had enough food, let alone regular meals, clothes or his own room.

Agnes taught them how to make porridge, stew and bread, so they lived on that. Occasionally, a few family members would bring a box of damaged, unsellable vegetables for the boys, or they would make a stew and leave it for them to eat.

When they visited the Rosedale's farm, which was often, they were sent home with a loaf or two of bread and the leftovers.

Thirteen-year-old Quinn was in seventh heaven. For the first time, he had stability in his life. The two older boys were like brothers that he'd never had before. He threw himself into learning everything he could about timber and the skills needed to make the saddle-trees.

Ben was patient with him and explained the properties of the special joints, including their grain and strength.

Quinn learned to make the four main components of the tree. The various sections were the horn, swell, cantle and two sidebars; all were made individually and then assembled. Quinn was learning about the different types of wood and experimenting with them. He found that the gum tree timber was hardwood and much more challenging to work with. The black pine had a lovely aroma, but his favourite was the spotted cedar tree.

Linus had his family cut a cedar tree some years earlier. It lay where it landed. Linus' sons used the large tree for building and repairs for their house.

Ben was given numerous cedar offcuts to work on. As all the individual sections of the saddle tree were relatively small, the large crate of cedar offcuts could be utilised for his work.

Ben showed Quinn how to craft the numerous parts of the saddle tree from the chunks of timber in the crate. The thicker branches were firm enough for pommel skeletons; the curved sides cut from the planks were the right thickness to make the cantle and sides. Quinn rarely had a thick enough section to create a swell, but Ben taught him how to laminate a few thin chunks of wood together and then shape them for the front section. He loved making the dovetail joints to ensure the sections didn't separate. Each time he finished another item, they would hear a cheer from his workbench. Meanwhile, George was busy making the leather for the saddles while Ben converted all the bits into a completed item.

At night, the three boys could now work on some small saleable items by lamplight.

George was making a cracking whip. He had wanted to try the new roo-leather as thonging. The first hide he had tanned had been an experiment, and he now cut it into thin strips with a special knife and plaited long lengths to make a whip. The wooden handle he was using was a whittled length of gum. It was eighteen inches long and would have a snapping popper. This was only an experiment, so he didn't want to waste too much leather. He had a roll of rawhide cord that he had brought from home, which they used for the whip bodies. George cut a four-foot length of this and glued it into a small hole in the handle. With four rolls of roo thonging, he wove the outer casing. The whip so far was light and supple, but would it crack? When he reached the end of the rawhide centre, he had lots of thonging left, so he kept weaving. By the time he had used the lengths of leather, the whip was eight feet long. He still had to make a cracker for the end. He chuckled as he snipped off some hair from one of their horses' tails. His father would have been furious if he had done this at home. He chuckled at the guilty thought.

He finished his whip and watched the other two boys working away in the lamplight. A wave of nostalgia washed over him at the thought of his father, and the dim light and working bodies reminded him of the evenings he spent at home with his family. Since Quinn had arrived, he had not brought out his violin. He packed up his things and quietly went to his room. His instrument transported him back to his happy home. His large travelling case was still in pride of place, but it now held his work clothes, excess tools and finished small items for sale.

The violin was still in the second bottom drawer. He eased the draw open and extracted his beloved instrument. He needed no music, so the leather satchel remained in the drawer. He tuned and tightened the strings, then rubbed the bow with rosin. He left the case on his bed and snuck out the back door. As the boys were busy in the sitting room, he exited through the kitchen and went out to the shed in the backyard.

The moon had just risen, and the stars were out. Mopps heard his exit and came to sit at his feet as she did at home. It was a perfect evening.

He settled himself on a large log, then stretched his neck backwards, and then side to side. It cracked delightfully, and he already felt the stresses and uncertainty of his new life leaving his body. He tucked his instrument under his chin and raised his bow. He wondered what to play first when he glanced up at the moon. With a smile, Beethoven's first notes of *Moonlight Sonata* soon floated across the land.

The haunting cry of the exquisite music silenced the crickets, cicadas, and birds. Music like this had never been heard in this land.

George played on. He had not realised how much he had missed his violin. Tune after tune followed, and it wasn't until he began to feel cold that he thought he had better head to bed. The last long note seemed to echo through the valley as he played it. He drew the tune to a close, rose and walked to the back door.

Quinn sat on the doorstep and greeted him. "I've never heard a violin before, George. Ben said that is what it was called. You made it, and me cry, and I haven't done that for years. At my old place, we were told, 'Big boys don't cry,' and I hadn't until tonight. It was beautiful."

George sat down beside the young lad. "Thank you, Quinn, but the family you lived with got that saying wrong. My papa used to add a bit to that saying. He said, 'Big boys don't cry, real men do.' Never be afraid to show your emotions. Life is too short not to laugh, cry or love. There is nothing shameful in any of them. You know how I feel about Charlotte. I tell her of those feelings, and she tells me as well. I'm an orphan too, but my folks and brother died of disease. I miss them like crazy and wish I had told them how much I appreciated them. They knew, but I didn't say it enough to them. Mama, especially, I took for granted. So never hold back telling people how you feel." He tousled the boy's brown hair and said, "Now, bed for us all. If you like the music, I'll play it more often. How about that? I may even teach you one day."

Quinn's eyes bulged with delight. "Really, truly, you would let me touch it?"

George chuckled. They stood, and he slung his arm around the lad's shoulders. "Yes, one day I will, but for now, it's bedtime for us all."

Quinn opened the door for them and stepped aside.

When George entered, he was encased in a bear hug from the younger boy. "Thanks for taking me in, George. For the first time ever, I'm happy and safe." He released him and turned to lead the way to their rooms.

Ben had long since retired. He had hardly been able to keep his eyes open over dinner. After George left, he had managed to cut a few tongues for some riding whips before heading to his room to bed. These were for some specialty riding crops, and the tongues were made from the trimmed African hides George had purchased.

One skin now lay in front of the fireplace in the sitting room. It was obviously a male lion's skin, as the fluffy mane was still there. The headless, tawny hide was Mopps' favourite place to sit. One of the puppies, which Charlotte named Muffin, was now eight months old. She had returned home with Mopps after the other puppies had found homes. Mopps nuzzled her pup, and the pair snuggled up on their giant cat skin in front of the open fire.

George crept into bed. It was hard to believe they had been in the colony for over a year. He had recently turned eighteen, and only Charlie wished him a happy birthday.

With the government contract to replace the saddles, they had done little about any other sales. Now empty of the heavy tools, other than the single roll of excess of his grandfather's unwanted tools, the bottom drawer in George's travelling case was nearly full of completed nick-nacks, purses, whips, crops, and small leather items they had made to sell but had never gotten around to.

One day…

George sighed, closed his eyes and slept.

Chapter 9   The Macquaries
Christmas 1809

George's second Christmas in the colony was spent at Rosedale's Farm. Every household had to bring something, and their house was not exempt. Kath and Charlotte had come over to raid their larder to see what they could make. There were very few options; it was custard or boiled eggs and goat's milk. Ultimately, they made both as they needed to use up the eggs. None of the boys could cook well, so the girls made a giant custard and brought a basket of hard-boiled eggs. Their hens were laying well, and the goat was producing a lot of milk, having just given birth to another kid.

As the weather was extremely hot, the custard was made the day before and brought to the farm to set. It was then placed in the cool cellar under the house.

~

On Christmas morning, the Rosedales' farm wagon paused while the three boys hopped onto their smaller cart. As the family passed, the jovial group travelled to church, singing Christmas carols.

They had just turned onto the main street when Quinn hopped off the back of their small cart and headed down a side street. "Gotta go, George. It's them."

George had seen a young boy poke his head around a building and whistle. Quinn's head had jerked up, and moments later, he was gone. As the apprentice fled, George called, "Quinn, we'll meet you at the church."

Quinn raised a hand in acknowledgement. He didn't pause in his flight. He knew some of his friends had no family to live with, as they had been booted out of their homes due to their age. However, he had no idea where they had gone. With rooms spare at the house, the two older boys had suggested that Quinn see if he could find the other orphans and offer them a forever home. They had room for more helpers if they wanted to learn. Quinn had not seen or heard from his friends for months. That was until today.

Linus saw him scurrying away from the cart and asked George, "What is wrong. Is he not joining us?"

George thought he had better explain his offer. "Sir, I think Quinn has just found some of his orphan friends. I have offered to train them, but we may have to miss Christmas luncheon if he finds them today."

Linus nodded but said, "Rubbish, George, there is more food than we can eat, and they will need feeding. I say the more the merrier. I think Bennelong and some of the tribe will also be coming. We never know how many we will be feeding. If they are good workers and willing to learn, then I think we can all find a place for one or two of them. Tell Quinn to bring who he wants; however, I suggest you all go for a swim to clean up before lunch."

The various family wagons and the boys' cart arrived at church with everyone still singing. George hopped off and flicked the reins of their steed to the hitching rail. Charlotte did the same for their wagon. Even though it was early, other families were already waiting, and they were greeted warmly. Jonas passed little Mary Jensen to her waiting convict father, then went to join the extended family in church.

Bill was in uniform as he was guarding some of the convicts. He greeted George with a smile, then shyly waved to Victoria. Linus had asked to meet Bill soon after George's mention of him. The handsome soldier immediately captured Victoria's attention. He and his two fellow soldiers, Harry and Algernon, were to join the family for the Christmas meal after they had gone off duty. Bill was delighted and thanked George.

George gasped when he saw the subtle wave. Bill's face showed he was as smitten with Victoria as she was with him. He grinned.

As the family meandered around the grassy area outside the church, more people arrived. Agnes was about to say something when she saw movement out of the corner of her eye. "Linus, look!"

Linus turned to see Quinn with three bedraggled boys behind him. He glanced around and saw George close by. "Look smart, son, Quinn is back."

George looked up and saw the small group approaching. He turned to Charlotte and said, "Stay here, Charlie." He was gone before she could object. He greeted Quinn with open arms and welcomed his friends with a friendly smile. He then asked to be introduced. They stank, but he would not let them know he had noticed. The three boys were even skinnier than Quinn had been when he arrived.

Quinn grinned. "See, Pete, I told you they would welcome you. George, this is Pete, Eric and Wendell. We grew up together on the streets. You said you wanted some help, and they said they'd like to learn even if it's for a roof over their head and regular food. I told them it's dirty, hard work, but worth learning." Three dirty-faced boys nodded.

George was thrilled. Having seen Quinn when he arrived, he knew that three more boys would be easily absorbed into the household. With such a large house, they could share a room or have one each. From now on, they would have a voice in what happened in their lives. "I did, Quinn, and they can have a safe forever home with us if they are willing to work and learn."

Three thin, filthy faces of the urchins grinned. "We can come, mister?

Really? Quinn wasn't kiddin'? He says you don't flog him, neither."

George beckoned to Ben, who was waiting to be called. "I'm not kidding, and there will be no floggings. I'm George, and this is Ben; he lives with us and is a saddler. I'm a tanner and make leather. It's dirty, smelly work, but you'll get a room, food, and clothes in return for your labour. You will also learn a skill and earn some money when you are good enough. Then, you can start your own business if you wish. Will you come? We'll teach you how to do bookkeeping as well."

Three heads nodded again. This offer was beyond their wildest dreams. These poor mites had been abused since they could remember. Quinn was assuring his friends that they would be safe. He was thrilled.

George said, "Fine! Now, because you have not had a chance to clean up before church this week, we'll sit at the back with the convicts. Part of the deal for new clothes is a weekly bath on Saturday nights. I wash daily, especially in the summer, due to my dirty work. You can if you want to as well. That's the deal after today, okay? Quite honestly, you all stink." He chuckled as he spoke.

The boys knew they smelled, but the only food they could get was from the pig troughs at the various houses. Bathing was not an option as they had seen a shark in the river. Again, the three grinning boys' heads nodded.

Until the coup, they were required to attend church each Sunday with their Ticket of Leave families, as holding such a pass was a condition of their Tickets. Foveaux changed that when he arrived. He made the services in Sydney at six o'clock instead of seven, and few now attended. All the boys had been required to have a lye bath on Saturdays. It was more of a dip, but it stung, and they hated it. However, if it meant food and lodging in exchange for work, they would take it.

Wendell said, "Church is okay, mister, but I know I could do wiv' a bath."

George sent Ben to sit with the family while he stayed with the four boys. "We'll go in last and leave first." Pointing to the wagon, he said, "That's our cart next to the big wagon. So if we get separated after church, go and sit on it, and I'll meet you there."

Again, the three heads bobbed assent. Quinn could not wipe the grin from his lips. He was almost dancing with happiness.

The bell pealed a Christmas welcome, and the last stragglers fed into the building. The five boys followed the latecomers and sat near the doorway.

Even the convicts who sat at the back turned to see where the smell was emanating from. George was sure that one or more of the boys had fouled their trousers. The stench was stomach-turning.

The Christmas service was joyous. Surprisingly, the boys sang well and joined in loudly.

George was surprised that they hardly missed a response or verse.

The lengthy sermon was over by nine o'clock, and as soon as the Blessing was given, the boys raced out of the church. Rather than run away, they ran directly to the wagons and patted all the horses tied along the hitching rail.

George watched as the boys plucked some of the clumps of long grass and hand-fed the various beasts tied up in the shady lane.

The boys obviously loved animals. With a smile, George stood and waited for his new family to leave the church.

Charlotte was the first to arrive. She made a beeline for him. "Georgie, are they coming?"

George nodded. He expected her to release some form of delight. He wasn't wrong.

She squealed with joy. "Did I tell you Quinn told me all about them? They have lived all their life as orphans, and when they turn twelve or thirteen, they all get thrown out of the convict houses."

George's face showed his sadness at their story. He nodded again and said softly, "Would you like to meet them? They need a long bath, so we will stop at my place and wash them before lunch. They need feeding as Quinn did, so I hope there is lots of food."

She giggled. "Far too much as usual. Mama is expecting an army, I think." She hooked her hand onto his arm possessively, and they walked sedately to the boys.

Rather than vanish at their approach, the three new lads gathered to meet the lovely lady drawing near. At seventeen, Charlotte was only four years older than they were.

Quinn had told them about the Rosedales and Kath and Charlotte, who was called Charlie, so they waited to meet the first of their new family.

After the greetings, the assortment of family vehicles loaded up and returned to the main farm. As all were heading to Rosedales, some family members shuffled onto other vehicles.

Linus said, "George, if you have spare clothes, grab them as we pass, and the boys can swim in the waterhole at the back of our place. In fact, please bring your own swimming clothes as well. As they are children, Bennelong will get his wife, Boorong, to take them to the tea tree swamp to de-louse them. Bennelong's family are back here for the week and doing a corroboree for us tonight." He wasn't going to mention that there was now a white girl living with the tribe. She was Obadiah's friend.

George grinned and nodded. "Will do, sir."

Linus continued, "Six of you won't fit into your cart, so Ben, Quinn, come on the wagon with us, and we'll drop you off later tonight." He paused, then said, "Better still, we'll pause at your house and load Mopps and Muffin on the wagon and tie Daisy on the back. She will need milking tonight anyway. You can all stay for the night."

When they reached the boys' house, the ladies stayed on the wagon while the boys scattered inside to gather the required items and animals. Ben unharnessed their horse and led her into the back paddock.

The new boys were each handed a rope lead with a pet attached. Daisy and the two dogs all ended up on the big wagon, much to the delight of everyone. The goat was supposed to walk, but the nanny goat hopped on the back before anyone could argue.

Ben, Quinn and George returned laden with night attire, bedding, clean clothes for the boys, and an armload of towels. The linen was piled onto the wagon, and the girls made room for the seven lads. The younger Rosedale boys, Nick and Tris, travelled with Crispin and Helena.

By the time the slowest wagon reached the farm, the other family members had the food prepared and were setting out the Christmas luncheon feast.

The pantries at each house had been raided, and the food was plentiful. It was currently under a series of covers on the verandah.

Agnes said, "We have half an hour until we eat. Any boys who wish to swim, go now. Bring any of the children from the tribe back if you wish. There is plenty of food available. Now scoot!" Her hands waved to shoo them all away.

George carried an armload of clean clothing and a few towels.

On arrival at the waterhole, Linus introduced Bennelong and some of the younger tribe members to the three new boys. The tribal children soon led the four new boys to the best place to swim. They needed to wash before heading to the de-lousing swamp.

The three boys all dived in fully clad, then stripping off in the water, they swam naked, emerging from the cool water. They donned clean clothing. Their old clothes would need a proper wash later, but for the moment, they were dumped unceremoniously on a rock.

After they were clean, Boorong and two older women took the four lads to another special waterhole. This tea tree swamp was a brown, still body of water. It didn't look inviting, but the four boys did as they were told and crept into the brown water.

Boorong said, "You need to go under and wash your hair. This special water. Brown water will kill the itch." She pointed to her hair.

The four lads did as they were told. They stayed underwater for as long as they could hold their breaths. Resurfacing only to submerge again.

After ten minutes, Boorong beckoned them out of the pool.

Bennelong had a small boy in his arms and introduced them to his son, Dicky.

The child's grin showed he was content to be in his father's arms.

By the time they returned thirty minutes later, the boys were clean.

None of Bennelong's tribe accepted the invitation for luncheon as they were all coming for dinner and a dance.

On their return, more tables had been added, so that the food tables now covered one side of the verandah. As they appeared, the protective covers were removed.

Four pairs of eyes boggled, and their jaws dropped in astonishment.

This was the first time Quinn and the boys had ever had a family

Christmas, and they were somewhat overwhelmed by the astounding abundance of food.

Agnes called the three new boys over and introduced herself properly. She said, "I'm Mrs Rosedale. Boys, you will be like Quinn and not be used to so much food in your stomachs. Eat slowly and start with small portions at a time. There is plenty to go around, and you won't miss out. There is so much food that you will need to take a hamper with you. I suggest you start with something plain, like bread with a bit of butter. If that stays down, then nibble at anything you wish. I know Quinn knew how to use a plate and fork. Therefore, I presume you were taught manners at your homes? Well, the same rules apply here. No greed, understand? You can graze all day, every day. You will all be given a lot of food to take home, as we don't have room to keep it."

The four heads nodded. All were grinning. Their mouths were salivating. Wendell reached out to take something, but Quinn grabbed his hand. He whispered, "Wait!"

Agnes said, "After we give thanks to God, then we will all eat, but it will be orderly. The older ones feed the younger ones, and so on. You are to go first, but only take some bread. You will know if you feel sick when it's your turn again. You can come back and take more all afternoon."

Linus gave thanks to the Lord for the feast, and the family lined up behind the hungry boys.

When lunch was finally over, everyone had eaten so much that they almost rolled off the verandah and moved into the shade under the trees. The new orphan boys had done as Agnes had instructed and grazed all afternoon.

Late in the afternoon, all the males and older children went to the waterhole for a swim, while the ladies prepared more food for the evening corroboree.

While the men and children were away, Bennelong appeared with his tribe and prepared the fireplace and surrounding area for their corroboree and another feast.

After scything the grass, Agnes and the women of the tribe spread the coals to cook the food.

When the fire had died down a little, a collection of clay balls was placed around the fire's edge in the coals. These balls were whole, feathered ducks encased in clay. Twenty of these clay balls were being cooked tonight.

The swimmers returned refreshed and clean. The new boys had scrubbed their old clothes in the waterhole, and they were hanging over the verandah railing.

The afternoon sun soon faded into twilight. However, it was still hot.

Food was again brought out. It was all consumed; the clay-coated roast ducks were quickly opened, and the aroma wafted over the hungry hoard.

Again, everyone ate until they were full, and there were still leftovers.

Knowing the tribe, rather than the lads, would claim any of the leftovers, Agnes packed food for the boys' house, and they would take it home when they left in the morning. The tribe knew they could take whatever they wished, and all the children raced to collect any leftover cakes and sweet foods.

Bennelong called everyone to attention and had them sit along the verandah and on the grass around the fire, then he vanished.

Out of the darkness, an eerie roar whirred with alternating speed, tempo and loudness. Eric whimpered at the noise.

Quinn chuckled but didn't tease him. Having never heard such a frightening sound, the four boys huddled together, unaware of what would occur.

Bennelong, Bidgee Bidgee, Bungaree and some older men slowly emerged from the gloom, twirling something around as they walked.

The sound ceased, and they took their places around the fire.

George leaned across and softly said to the boys, "That noise was made by a contraption called a bull-roarer. I'll get them to show you later."

The four heads nodded, their eyes fixed on what was happening around them. The four imps' eyes were large with anticipation.

For the following hour, dancers performed and changed places after each performance. Each dance represented an animal, a hunt or a story, which Bennelong explained to the watchers. The performances were so realistic that an explanation was hardly needed. The body painting of each person represented the character they portrayed. Some had feathers stuck into the clay daub. The dances were accompanied by women playing tapping sticks and men on the haunting didgeridoos.

Bennelong described his Dreamtime stories of their creator being. He said, "When the rainbow is seen in the sky, it is said that the creator serpent is moving from one waterhole to another."

Linus took over and explained. "The tribe, along with many others, also believes in a divine being. This tribe says it's why some waterholes never dry when drought hits." Because he was sitting near the boys, he didn't need to raise his voice to make his explanations. "Lads, I'm intrigued that after many conversations with an assortment of people who have travelled to many places, most primitive groups seem to have a Creation Story. They each seem to have a deity responsible for bringing things into being. In Christianity, we believe in the Creator, and that is God. Jesus is His son and a pathway back to Him."

Bennelong grinned. His missing front tooth was obvious, as the rest of his smile showed his white teeth with a gap. "You good *yellomundie*, boss Linus. You tell really good stories like me."

Linus chuckled. "I learn a new word with every conversation, Bennelong. So *yellomundie* is a teller of Dreamtime stories, eh?"

Bennelong nodded. "You *biyanga* to all these people. That means 'father,' boss Linus. You good man and kind to my people. Remember what I tell you before? I learn in London when I meet the big king man, George the Third, 'The enemy of my enemy is my friend'. I like that, as I know you do not like the bad men who hurt us fellas. You give us a safe place and help with food. Just like Mister Squires, where we live down bye'm'bye, that way." He pointed towards Kissing Point, where the tribe spent most of their time. "You big father to us people, too. You *dadyibalung*! That means good, boss Linus!" He caught sight of the white girl on the far side of the fire and said, "She Em-*buyi*. A ghost girl. Boorong look after her for O'buddy."

Linus gave a nod of his head in thanks. He knew Obadiah had a friend called Emily who came from England, only to discover he was already married. Being alone, she befriended Boorong and went to live with the tribe.

Bennelong smiled and hooked his fingers together as though linked. "We work well together, good. I like it here, no bad booze. Hard to stop drinking." He shook his head and looked sad.

Linus laid a hand on his friend's arm. "You are my friend, Ben."

The interchange was watched and overheard by the four boys.

With heads together in discussion, the boys were excitedly talking about their new family and their unusual friends. They had been told all Aborigines were bad and would harm them if they came near them. They realised that what they had been told about the native people of this country was untrue. The indigenous boys had taken them to a safe place to swim, and after they stripped off, they joined them in the water. The boys, with skin as white as snow and black as ebony, played together, and they realised that they were all friends.

Being unable to swim, the four new boys stayed in the shallow water. However, at one stage, Eric ventured out a little too far, and one of the older boys in the tribe came to his aid and dragged him back into the shallower water. A bond was forged.

Most of the tribe spoke a few words of English, but they said their names so fast that they did not know any of them.

Eric grinned. Life with this family was going to be both good and exciting. He had not laughed as much in his entire life as he did today.

~

The following day, the boys arrived at George's house. They had returned late in the afternoon and stored the leftover food first. Quinn showed the new boys the ropes. The boys spent hours puzzling out who was to sleep where. They investigated everything.

They sat around the table and ate leftovers for their evening meal. While the new boys were shown how to wash the dishes, George vanished.

Another haunting sound made them freeze.

Quinn put his finger to his lips and explained that it was George playing his music. He made them follow him to the back doorstep to listen.

The lads crept out and sat on the back steps, listening to the exquisite sound of the violin as it wafted on the evening air. Ben was already there as he had seen George leave with his instrument tucked under his arm.

The hot summer night carried the music on the breeze. Again, the crickets and cicadas fell silent as the violin's melodies filled the air.

As the house sat on a ridge, the sound carried down the valley on both sides and drifted over the evening breeze. No one knew how far the sound would travel, but the four boys and Ben listened spellbound. Wendell swiped away an errant tear. He had never heard anything so beautiful.

For nearly an hour, they remained still. They were captivated by the beauty of the music and events of the last two days. When the music stopped, Ben silently ushered them indoors. "George doesn't know that the sound carries so far. He gets lost in the music. I adore listening to him, so say nothing, or he might not play any more."

~

The week after Christmas, the settlement buzzed excitedly as a ship carrying the new governor arrived in the harbour. At church, a contingent of new soldiers from the 73rd regiment surrounded an unfamiliar couple. They were dressed in red coats outside St John's in Parramatta. The new viceregal couple's appearance at church was unexpected.

Linus pulled into the usual parking area, and Nick hopped down and tied the reins to the hitching rail. Lieutenant Governor Foveaux saw the family's arrival and called to Linus. "Rosedale!" He beckoned Linus over to introduce them.

Linus turned to the wagonload of people and said, "Everyone, stay here for a bit; I'll go and see what's going on."

Knowing that his word was law, no one moved. However, their eyes followed his path across the grass. As they waited, the other family vehicles drew up beside them.

Crispin noticed the new people. Like Linus, Crispin, Arnold, and Jonas were called to meet the strangers.

The men all bowed as they were introduced. The thin man was dressed in an unusual uniform. He returned their greetings with a crooked smile. The woman looked nice, and they saw her exchange a friendly word with Elizabeth Macarthur before she walked into church alone.

John Macarthur was on his way to England, so Elizabeth could converse with whom she wished. The ladies touched hands, which they didn't immediately drop as they parted. The action inferred a friendship of some standing.

After a few minutes, Linus beckoned to the large family group. He was now holding a thick letter in his hand and had a big smile.

The large group moved towards the newcomer in an orderly fashion.

A Scottish lilt carried over the air. This was not Major General Miles Nightingall; everyone knew he was English. Who was this man?

Linus did the honours and introduced Agnes, then waved his hand over the remainder of the family. "Sir, there are far too many of us to introduce individually just yet, but be assured that I vouch for them all." His grin showed that he was not afraid of whoever this new man was. "Everyone, this is Major General Lachlan and Mrs Elizabeth Macquarie, and they are our new governor and first lady. He comes bearing letters from my friend, John Hunter, and wishes to visit our home to share more about what John is doing. John has filled our new governor in about who you all are, except your household,

George."

Standing beside the new governor, a tall soldier was quite wary of the large group. The governor turned to him and said, "Duffy, can you arrange a visit to…" Lachlan turned to Linus and asked, "Where do you live?"

Linus smiled and replied, "Rosedale Farm, sir. It's along the Windsor Road, then a bit to the east. The extended family lives in half a dozen houses, some of which are located at Toongabbie, near the government pig farm. I may need some notice if you wish to meet with the younger men unless you know when you can come."

The security guard, Captain Mark Duffy, said, "Tuesday is free, sir."

Lachlan gave a nod to the guard and said to Linus, "I think that would be good later, but for the moment, until I sort things out in Sydney, I may just meet with you and Milroy on Tuesday. Mrs Macquarie and her companion will accompany me if that is permissible, so mayhap Mrs Milroy could come too?"

Agnes and Helena both gave a bobbed curtsy of acknowledgement.

The Macquaries were escorted into the church and took their seats in the front row. A bevy of officials juggled themselves to better their positions.

Linus watched their antics, and Agnes saw him roll his eyes in frustration. She subtly dug him in the ribs, and they took their place in their usual pew about halfway down the church.

Reverend Samuel Marsden started the service with an official welcome to the new vice-regal couple. Linus gave a soft chuckle as he saw Lachlan Macquarie's shoulders slump. The body language he had just witnessed suggested that this man disliked the limelight. If he were a friend or even an acquaintance of the ex-governor, John Hunter, he would be worth getting to know. For once, Linus focused on the man in the front row rather than the normally wordy sermon. He was tempted to pull out and read John Hunter's lengthy letter, but that would set a bad example for his family. He knew his son-in-law, Crispin, had a lengthy epistle as well, and as he caught his eye further along the pew, he tapped his pocket with a smile.

Cris nodded, then grinned. Crispin had been the personal bodyguard for Governor John Hunter, who had befriended him and become a father figure to the younger man. After Cris married Helena, she worked in the gardens at Government House. Governor John was a godfather to their first child, Jasper. When the governor saw Helena's gardening ability, he sponsored the Rosedale family to come to New South Wales and teach farming with the promise of a land grant. They had arrived in 1798. John taught Linus to read and write. This activity drew the two men close. When John returned to England two years later, the three men kept in contact.

Linus still struggled with the written word, so Crispin usually wrote the letters as Linus dictated. Linus always added a paragraph or two in his own hand. The letters informed John of what was occurring in the colony far better than any official despatch. John had foretold the coup years earlier, but London had refused to believe things were as bad as he painted. He had been proven correct. John was aware of the coup before London was, thanks to

Linus. Lachlan Macquarie happened to visit John soon after receiving his detailed missive. John suggested Lachlan head to London as he had an invitation to the palace to meet the prince. He was there when Miles Nightingall refused the governorship. Lachlan jumped at the chance to step into his shoes. Now he was here, and he had a big job to do.

With the service over, the group mingled outside. Luncheon was on at the Rosedale Farm, and the wagons and carriages were readying to head off when the new governor's very tall bodyguard made for Crispin's side. "Hello, sir, I believe you once held my position for Governor John Hunter?"

Crispin nodded. "I did, sir. Crispin Milroy at your service." He gave a polite bow.

The tall man grinned. "I'm Mark Duffy, and if you don't mind, I would like to catch up when we come out. I want my new wife to meet your family, as she is unfamiliar with anyone here. We married on the voyage out, but that's another story completely. I could use a friend who knows the work and the clicks of who's who and who we can trust."

Crispin was a little surprised. He saw that the man held the rank of captain. "Of course, Captain Duffy." A microfrown crossed his brow.

Mark saw and said, "My stepson, Cathy's lad, arrived as a convict and... and..."

Crispin understood. "...and as my wife was a convict, you would like an off-the-record chat?"

Mark nodded, replying with a lowered voice, "Amongst other things, yes, if possible; and please, call me Mark."

Crispin's chuckle was comforting. "That's fine, Mark. I'm Crispin, but most now call me Cris. You will find being a convict causes no problems here, unless you are talking to the reverend. He will not even give the time of day to my lady wife. Others are not so narrow-minded."

Mark gasped. "Seriously? The reverend is biased against convicts?"

Crispin glanced to where the rotund reverend was standing. "Absolutely! I'm not sure he understands the word 'emancipated', but others are far more generous. So be warned. He will talk to you, but expect him to ignore her unless the governor is at her side. Even then, it will be a nod, but he is unlikely to converse at all. His nickname here is the 'Flogging Parson' as he seems to think the whip is a curative for all evils. I'm not sure he doles out more floggings than any other magistrate, but none of the others are clergymen, and he should be more compassionate. Two magistrates, Simeon Lord and Andrew Thompson, are emancipated convicts, and he refuses to sit at the bench with either of them. I've seen Marsden order a man flogged to an inch of his life. Foveaux has the reputation of being a sadist in much the same way when on Norfolk, so keep him at arm's length as well."

Mark turned to where the minister stood in deep discussion with the new governor. Marsden was bowing in a very overawed way. He wondered how long that would last. He was glad he now had that titbit of information, knowing that was not what Lachlan Macquarie would like. Lachlan caught his eye with a plea for rescue. Mark said, "I must away, Cris, but I look forward to our visit. I shall pass on the information. Until Tuesday, then!" He clicked his heels, bowed and returned to his post beside the Macquaries. He beckoned his wife, Cathy, to his side. Her presence made the minister depart after a cursory nod. Lachlan frowned. Mark said, "I'll explain on the way home, sir." He caught Crispin's eye and smiled.

Everyone once again enjoyed the Sunday luncheon at the big farm. The four new boys soon realised one way they could repay the family's kindness. Firewood was always in demand, and as they walked to and from the waterhole, they collected kindling and small branches for the household fires. This job also cleared the track of the debris and fallen trees.

In the week just passed, the three new lads had found that having a single room each was strange and asked if they could share. Mattresses were juggled, and they now had two boys in each room. The rooms were large enough for all four to share, but George wanted them to get used to living in a real house rather than sharing everything as they would in a dormitory.

~

On Tuesday, a small black unmarked carriage made its way out along Windsor Road. The rutted track was not in good condition, and the occupants were bumped and jostled as the vehicle moved. Lachlan muttered as he held tight to the wrist straps. "One of the first things I will order is for crews to patch the roads. The road from Sydney Cove is even worse than this." As the other passengers had already commented on the appalling track, he spoke to himself.

The first lady turned to the soldier and said, "Captain, are you sure it was all right for us to come with you?"

Mark gave her a reassuring smile. "Yes, ma'am, the Milroys and Rosedales are keen to make your acquaintance."

Chapter 10 We Are Sailing

*T*he New Year brought forth a suggestion from Ben. His land grant had finally been approved, and he was eager to see the land he had chosen. He also had another suggestion. The boat was still sitting in the front yard of George's house. It now had grass growing all around it as they were not used to using the scythe to cut the lawn and were scared they would hole the dinghy. A picnic was planned. It was too hot to do much work, and the six boys decided to take a day or two off. The weather was fine, and the four younger boys had never had a holiday. For that matter, neither had the two older boys. When the outing was mentioned, some of the younger Rosedales and other family members expressed a desire to accompany them. The older Rosedale boys and their wives were also due to join them for a few days, but they were unable to travel with them. The presence of the married couples would ensure that their younger sisters were suitably chaperoned.

The boys at the tannery decided to have a short week and shut on Thursday, January 4th, then stay two nights on Ben's new land and return on Saturday evening. That would give them an entire day on the river.

It took most of Thursday morning for the wagons to traverse the distance from Parramatta to the Hawkesbury River at Penrith.

They parked the big wagon on the block near a small creek, and before they unharnessed the horses, they all went to the river and hauled the boat off the back of the smaller wagon. They unloaded the two oars, mast, sail and boom before heading to the campsite. They left the vessel sitting on the river rocks, but away from the ford, before setting up camp. They had brought scythes to cut the grass where they intended to camp. However, they discovered that someone had recently had a campfire there, and the grass had recently been burned to clear the area. The wagons were soon emptied, and their camp was set up.

Ben and George were eager to try out their boat and left the others to gather wood and prepare for a two-night holiday. Ben led the way towards the river.

George had not been out this way before and did not realise the river was not a wide-flowing one, as at home. This river had areas of gravel blocking the flow of water. Peach Tree Creek was the side boundary of Ben's land, and launching their boat here meant they could only go upriver and not sail down to Windsor as he hoped. When Ben first viewed this land, the river level was much higher, but it had hardly rained since they arrived.

The group of boys dragged the clinker boat over the river rocks that were used as a ford for the prison farm, and then to the water's edge.

George was not keen on leaving dry land again. "Ben, are you sure it won't leak? I've had enough water under my feet to last a lifetime. I can't swim." The river water was icy cold.

Ben chuckled. "I've got no idea, George. But we won't know if we don't try." He set about preparing the vessel by erecting the orange mast through the hole in the seat. "So far, no water has leaked in."

The sail was an old red sheet of canvas permanently stuck to the mast and laced to the boom at the bottom. The ropes looked old and worn, but they had given them a pull, and they seemed firm enough. They pulled off their boots and threw them onto the shore before dragging the dinghy the final few feet to the water's edge.

Ben said, "Hold it here for a bit, George, while I check things over. You know, leaks and stuff. I've already checked the bung is in."

The small wooden craft was now floating, and there did not seem to be any water coming in. "So far, so good," said Ben with a smile.

George was still unsure about leaving *Terra Firma* and heading onto the river. "Do you really need me? I can stay here and watch."

Ben's laugh echoed up the river. "Don't tell me the brave tanner is afraid of a dip in the river?"

George shrugged. "Paddling on the edge of Bennelong's waterhole is not the same as heading into the middle of a river. You know I can't swim properly. What's more, the water is darned cold."

The boat was now ready; Ben made George get in and sit in front of the mast. He pushed off from the shore as some others came to see them off. George's heart was in his mouth.

Ben chuckled. "Just do not stand up."

The group watched them sail away, then returned to the campsite to set up for the evening. The four young boys, the four youngest Rosedale girls, plus Harry and Algernon, set up the camp while George and Ben played on the river. Bill was on duty, so Victoria didn't come. With a group of twelve, plus the two dogs, they intended to have a good time. The girls were to sleep on the wagons, while the boys and men slept around the campfire on the ground.

Mopps and her pup had been clipped for the summer and looked like different animals. They were sleek and had a lot more energy without all the mattered fur. Mopps sat on the river's edge, barking as the boat caught a puff of wind and headed around the corner and out of sight. Mopps was nearly frantic at seeing George vanish and took off across the river gravel and up the far side of the river embankment. The diminishing sound of her barking was heard as she chased the boat as it sailed away.

After an hour, Quinn returned to the crossing. He was so jealous of his friends leaving him behind that he was in no mood for company. He had donned his tattered trousers that now only reached halfway up his calves and intended to have a paddle. The river's edge was overhung with she-oaks. It was cool in the shade, and although the water was cold, it looked inviting. Having regularly swum at the waterhole on the Rosedale Farm, water no longer frightened him. He had nearly drowned once, but that was because he had walked out into the water and discovered the large rock he had been walking on had a drop-off. He was in over his head so silently that if the tribe's boys had not been watching him, he would have drowned. The bottom here was smooth river rocks. The heat at the campsite was oppressive, and he expected the rest of the group to join him at any moment.

Before they arrived, he stripped off his shirt and plunged into the cool water. He stretched himself out to fully submerge, leaving only his face out so he could breathe. As he did so, his hands were on the gravel riverbed. His fingers explored the rocks, and he discovered a few that were uniformly shaped. Grasping them, he sat up in the shallow water and looked at what he held. The two rock shapes were almost identical, but these were not natural river rocks. They had been shaped and even had a groove in the same place to tie onto a handle. He sat chest-deep in the water, gazing at his finds. Were these grey rocks axe heads? He wondered if this was the area Bennelong had told Crispin about at Christmas. He overheard their conversation about places along the river where the various tribes met to make stone implements. He tossed these two on the shore and hunted around for more. If these were man-made, they may have been some of the discards Bennelong had spoken about. The water was too murky to see, but he found six more by feeling around.

Approaching voices disturbed his hunt, and he knew he needed to dress as he could hear the girls were coming. He now had eight of these stone axeheads, and his foot touched another, larger one as he stood. This was about eight inches in diameter. The others were two by four inches and about an inch thick, but tapered to one end, just as this one did. Most had a big chip. He picked the big one up, uttered a swear word, and then said, "Cor" as he saw how large this one was.

Eric appeared first and saw that he had something in his hands. "What you got there, Quinn?"

Quinn waded out of the water and showed them his finds. "Look behind you; I have a pile of those axe heads Bennelong told Crispin about on Christmas Day. I think these are the discards as they all have a big chip out of them." He emerged dripping and held out his hand to his friend.

Eric took the large rock as Quinn hastily donned his shirt. For the first time in ages, he felt cool, clean and relaxed. He was beginning to enjoy the work with the two older boys, as he now had his three friends living with them. It was almost as though they were a family. Admittedly, it was an all-male one, but belonging somewhere was nice. Mrs Rosedale and their daughters were kind and supplied the feminine presence in his life. Yes, he was happy. He had never known his mother.

The rest of the group, including the pup, joined them. They found more chipped stone axeheads as they paddled in the cool river water. After they had all had a dip, the girls moved a little further up the gravelly riverbed and found a protected waterhole to swim in.

Nick, Tris, and their wives, Rachel and Rebekah, also known as Bek, arrived and later unloaded their wagon. They joined the noisy group in the water so their children could cool off. Both had one-year-old babies, and they were flushed and hot. The boys unharnessed their horses, hobbled them and left them to graze so they could join the others at the river.

As the young folk frolicked, the sun moved across the sky with hardly a second thought about the two lads in the boat. It was not until Muffin started whining that they wondered what had happened to their friends. After trying to get someone's attention, she took off over the ford and disappeared.

With their notice drawn to watch the dog, they realised what had caused her to vanish. Further up the river, they heard another dog barking frantically.

It was Nick who frowned. "Is that Mopps barking? She sounds distressed."

Quinn didn't need to hear any more than that. He took off after the dog and followed the two-wheel track that led to the prison farm.

He was hardly out of sight when Nick and Tris followed. The three younger boys were told to stay with the girls.

Quinn saw Muffin running along the top of the high embankment. He could hear that she was barking, and she was distressed.

The river at this point was a long, straight section, and he could see a long way upriver. The boat was not visible. In the distance, he saw Muffin's light-coloured coat. She stopped and stood at the top of the riverbank. As he drew closer, he could hear both dogs barking in unison, but still, there was no sign of the boat. He mused, "Where could they be?"

Nick and Tris had caught up to him by the time he reached the dogs. Now he could see the boat from the top of the high river bank. At least he could see what he thought was the boat. In the middle of the river, a puddle of red cloth and the blurry outline of their dinghy were visible, but it was underwater. He could not see either of his friends.

Quinn began to panic, and his heart was already pounding from his run after the dog. As he tried to peer over the bush embankment, he called, "George, Ben, where are you?"

Muffin heard him and began to whimper, then vanished.

He called again. "Ben, George, are you there?" He caught movement further along the river and saw Mopps through the bush. The scrubby river bank showed signs of the recent floods that had passed through some months earlier. There was debris right along the flood line.

Muffin reappeared and was still sniffing around the top of the high bank when Mopps appeared. She ran to her pup, then to Quinn. After a welcome sniff, she returned to where she had appeared.

Nick, Tris and Quinn followed her, and they saw a goat track that led to the water. Mopps scurried back down the narrow path, barking encouragement as she did. The three boys were hard on her heels. As they reached the waterside, they saw Ben trying desperately to hold George's unconscious body out of the water. Ben struggled to stay afloat and was going underwater with the added weight. As he surfaced, he said, "Can't hold him any more."

Nick and Tris grabbed George's shirt, then his arms, and dragged him up the last yard of the river's edge. Quinn held on to Ben's hand and kept him above the water. Once George was safe, the two young farmers took Ben's hands and dragged him out of the frigid river water.

As he lay face down on the grassy verge, he vomited up some water he had swallowed. Quinn sat with him as Nick tended to George.

Ben hauled himself up and said, "Is he alive? The boom hit him, and then the boat capsized in a gust of wind. He was knocked overboard, and I knew he couldn't swim, so I dived in after him. The boat tipped when I tried to get him back in."

Nick nodded. "He's alive. Ben, you saved his life. How long have you been there?" Ben vomited again. He felt terrible. He was so keen to get on the water he'd not even thought of any possible danger. "It must have been more than an hour. The sun was on the water, but it's nearly set now."

Mopps was licking George's face and whining. Muffin had returned to the top of the riverbank and was barking at something.

Quinn had just asked how they would get George up the riverbank when a shout from above was heard.

"Hey, who's down there? Come up, or we'll shoot."

Tris replied, "We're farmers; we need help. We have an unconscious friend here and…"

Quinn moved to see the speaker. A glimpse of a red coat caught his eye. He whispered, "They are soldiers!"

Nick grinned and thanked the good Lord. "Sirs, do you, by any chance, know how we can get him up there?"

One of the men up top said, "Give me ten. I'll return in a jiffy with some help."

The remaining soldier said, "Are you the chaps I saw in the rickety sail tub?"

Ben mournfully acknowledged that he was the skipper of the stricken vessel.

George was rousing but still far from being able to help himself. Nick said, "Ben, can you and Quinn take Mopps up, as that will give us more room down here." The narrow section of grass did not leave room for much manoeuvring

Ben nodded. His energy was fading fast as the cold set in. Nick and Tris stripped off their warm coats and wrapped them around the wet men.

Quinn saw and said, "You go first, and I'll push from behind. I don't think Mopps will leave George." He was right; she refused to go.

The two younger lads made their way to the narrow track. Ben all but crawled up the path and was nearly exhausted by the time the soldier hauled him up the steepest part. He collapsed onto the grass, panting, and then vomited again.

Muffin came to his side and licked him. Ben rolled onto his back, and she burrowed into his arms. Her body soon started warming him.

The climb had taken longer than they realised, and by the time Ben regained his breath, the second soldier had returned with a rope, a blanket, four more men, and a stretcher.

The long rope was folded in half, and a soldier took the loop end down the path. With the help of beefy men, George's extraction took little time. The rope was looped under his arms, and as the three below supported him, the ones above gently dragged him up the cliff.

Mopps was hard on their heels, and she appeared over the top as they carefully laid George down. She went to his side and again licked his face and whimpered. She rested her head across his neck.

"Loving beasties, aren't they?" The man who spoke was the major from the prison farm. "Okay, chaps, we'll need to get him to the sawbones at the gaol, but I think he's going to be fine." He tried to pull Mopps away, but she snarled at him. Rather than becoming angry, he presented the back of his hand to sniff. "Come on, poochy, we need to get your master some help."

Ben called her, and she reluctantly went to his side.

With both dogs under control, the soldiers gently rolled George onto the stretcher and covered him with a blanket.

Ben was jealous of that warm covering. He snuggled into Nick's coat but still shivered; his future brothers-in-law pulled him to his feet. The group slowly made their way back along the track. Nick slung his arm around Ben to ensure he didn't collapse.

What had seemed like seconds when running after the dog now took forever. The trail of rescuers, two dogs and a mournful sailor meandered their way towards the prison farm buildings. He glanced back at his sunken boat. He could see the sail under the water in the dim light, and the vessel's outline was still visible, as was a splurge of red.

Back at the river campsite, the remainder of the group had left the crossing and returned to stoke the fire for dinner.

Charlotte was fretting. "They should have returned by now. Where are they? Why have they not come back?"

Kath was equally as worried but remained silent.

Emily and Rebekah set about preparing the camp for their evening meal. They had brought a small chunk of pickled pork and a box of fresh vegetables. They prepared a stew for everyone and set up camp for the night.

Charlotte's eyes kept flicking towards the track to the river. Finally, at dusk, she heard voices coming from the path. Ignoring decorum, she dropped what she was doing and flew towards the ford with her skirts hitched up. Kath was hard on her heels.

As the two girls reached the top of the track to the river, the boys' heads appeared. Kath ran into Ben's arms, but George was not with them.

Charlotte's scream pierced the twilight stillness. She saw Ben looking bedraggled, but there was no sign of George. "Ben, where's…"

Nick grasped his sister's arms to silence her questions. "Charlie, he's okay. George is staying overnight in the gaol hospital. He was knocked out, but Ben saved his life. He'll have a hell of a headache, but he's fine."

Charlotte's gaze lifted to her brother's face. "Sure?"

Tris came to her side and hugged her. He nodded and replied, "He had woken by the time we left. His speech was clear, and he was aware of our presence. He kept apologising to Ben, so I presume he knew standing up in a small sailboat was a stupid thing to do."

Charlotte reached out her hand to Ben to thank him.

He nodded, but he was exhausted and just wanted to sleep. He was chilled through, and even though the soldiers eventually gave him a blanket, he continued to shiver. Kath and Quinn escorted him towards the fire.

Charlotte stayed with her brothers.

Nick tightly tucked her under his arm, saying, "Offer your thanks to God that George is safe, sis. If the dogs had not been with us, they both would have drowned. Ben couldn't hold him any longer; they had just gone under when we arrived. You owe that man big time, Charlie, so do not go off half-cocked and blast him for taking the boat out."

Charlotte nodded. Nick knew her too well. She had been ready to tear into Ben for making George go with him, but realised he wasn't looking too good himself. She watched him walk away wearily as they followed them to the campsite. Their holiday had nearly turned into a tragedy.

~

The following morning, the campsite occupants were up and eating porridge for breakfast. They paused as they heard voices approaching.

Ben had slept well and was feeling much better. He stood as he recognised the major's voice from the gaol.

George waved as he topped the riverbank and was thankfully prepared for Charlotte's enthusiastic welcome. Her bowl was dumped and tipped over, and she ran to close the distance between them. His arms were open and welcoming.

"Georgie," was all she could muster to say. Her body was pressed close to his as she wept against his shoulder.

He wished to kiss her, but they were not yet engaged. He rested his cheek on her hair and said, "I'm okay, Charlie, thanks to Ben. He saved my life, and it was all my fault. I stood up in the boat when he told me not to."

After her warm welcome, he introduced the two soldiers who had escorted him. The billy was boiling on the campfire, so they all sat down to share a mug of sweet black tea and discuss the previous day's happenings.

After finishing the strong brew, the soldiers returned to duty. It would be another hot day, and there was a sniff of smoke in the air, but it was not from their campfire. Their parting shot to the group was, "If a bushfire starts, go and sit in the river. You might be safe here as this has already been back-burned, but the river would be your best bet if it gets out of control. There are no sharks up this far."

Ben returned the blanket, and he and Nick thanked them again as they departed to cross the ford. After the boat was lost, the group stayed on the riverbank.

By noon, the heat was almost overwhelming, so they decided to take a dip. The girls walked back to their cloistered waterhole, and the boys stripped down to their drawers and sat in the cool water.

The day passed with much laughter, but Charlotte was fussing over George, which was beginning to frustrate him. He wanted to lie down for a rest, but she kept chattering. His head still ached, but he didn't want to acknowledge it and sound weak. Everyone treated Ben like royalty, which he deserved. Rather than feel guilty, he realised how valuable these people were to him. Ben apologised to George for making him go with him, but the incident had broken down any remaining barriers between the group, and they bonded in friendship.

At dusk, two of the younger boys went to the river to get water. They returned with the buckets of water, but they called everyone down to the water's edge. They had found something.

The boat had drifted down the river. Although submerged, the vessel was firmly wedged in the shallow rocks near the ford.

With boots discarded, the boys dragged the vessel into the shallows and bailed it out.

Charlotte kept fussing over George. "Georgie, you really shouldn't be lifting anything after spending a day in the hospital."

He growled. "I'm fine, Charlie. I can't let them do everything." She wanted to cling to his arm, but he shook her off. He said, "I have to go." For once, she was getting on his nerves. He turned to the boat and saw that it looked to be undamaged.

Ben and George passed dubious glances at the boat and then at each other. A chuckle was followed by a full-blown belly laugh from them both. Both knew they had been goofing around when the incident occurred, but it could have ended so differently. He said, "Thanks, Ben. Sorry!" George had tried to stand in the rocking boat when a gust of wind hit. He said, "It seems that I can't even sink a damned boat properly. I have a new name for it. 'Boomerang' seems apt, as it keeps coming back. I suppose we had better keep the thing, but I absolutely refuse ever to set foot in a boat again! Is that understood? It's now yours. Totally and absolutely! Are you sure you want it?"

Ben grinned with delight. "You bet! I suggest we leave it here on my block. There is nowhere we can use it in Parramatta anyway."

George grinned. "Done! Just never ask me on the water again!"

It had been dragged half out of the river and then turned on its side to drain it. The now-empty dinghy was clear of the ford, and the last of the water was tipped out. The oars were gone, and the sail was torn, but the mast and boom seemed intact, but were dislodged. They carefully untied them and laid them in the hull of the boat. Ben untied the torn sail and said he would need to make a replacement or have this repaired.

With all hands helping, the small vessel was dragged up the hill and unceremoniously dumped onto the grass. The mast and boom were placed on the ground, and the hull was flipped over to cover them. The craft would remain there until Ben decided what to do with it.

~

The following morning, the camp was packed, and the wagons loaded and readied to leave. Charlotte had been stirring up the dogs, causing them to bark nonstop. Her giggling was the last straw.

George had asked her to leave them alone, but she kept playing with them instead of assisting with the pack-up. She didn't listen, but she did hover beside him. He would reach for something to pack away, and she would grab it and stow it on the big wagon. The two dogs were at her heels, and she continued teasing them.

Eventually, George snapped, "Sheesh, Charlie, leave the darned dogs alone, will you?" Rather than wait for her to reply, he stormed off. He didn't want to admit it, but he wasn't feeling so good. His head ached, and his chest felt heavy. He thought he was coming down with something. He had vomited up a lot of river water when he roused.

Mopps and Muffin were still getting in everyone's way and not obeying anyone. Ben eventually tied them onto the seat of his wagon. They had decided to pack all the belongings onto it as it had an edge around the tray, but George's smaller wagon didn't.

With the campfire out, the last of the water was used to douse the hot coals and rocks, to ensure the campsite was safe.

The wagons were about to load up. Tris, Nick and the first two wagon loads set off. The three youngest boys went with them.

Ben called out to George and heard a grunt in reply from near the river. He went to find him.

George was sitting under an overhang along the edge of the river.

Ben went to his side and said, "What's up?"

George couldn't face his friend. He was angry and felt sick. He had spewed into the river soon after he left the campsite and was close to doing it again.

Ben didn't push him.

They sat in silence until George turned to his friend. "It's Charlie! She's on my back, niggle, niggle, niggle. She's driving me crazy and won't stop fussing over me or the dogs."

Ben was stunned. He knew George adored her. "It's only because she cares."

George nodded. "I know, but I don't want to admit she's right. I don't feel one hundred per cent. I just spewed and can't cope with anyone fussing right now. I just want peace and to go to sleep. The accident took more out of me than I thought. My head is pounding something bad, but I can't take any more of her giggling. Normally, it goes in one ear and out the other, but today…" He groaned. "Well, I need some peace and quiet, and I can't get that with her on the wagon. Her immature behaviour shows how young she is, and I'm not sure I can put up with that for the rest of my life. What do I do? I wish she would shut up sometimes."

Ben placed a caring hand on his friend's shoulder. "Do you want me to take her home with us? I'll tell her you need some time alone."

They heard a rustle in the grass above them, and Charlotte said, "Don't bother answering, George. I'm going with Kath and Ben."

George said, "Damn! She must have heard me." He was going to stand, but Ben put his hand on his shoulder.

Ben said, "Stay here for a bit and tag along in your wagon in a few minutes. Are you okay to drive home?"

George nodded. He could stop and spew without worrying who saw him. He hoped he was well enough, but he was teary and emotional. He dared not admit that he also felt hot. He managed to utter, "Thanks, Ben."

His friend looked back at him as he returned to camp. "See you at home tonight, George. I'll take the dogs and your stuff." He raised his hand and was gone.

George could hear them pack the remaining things, and then the big wagon moved off. He remained where he was until the dogs' barks faded, indicating they were well away from the campsite. He stood to follow them, but not too closely or quickly.

Chapter 11 Missing
January 1810

By the time George emerged from the river's edge, all was quiet up on the flat. Ben had put his horse in its shafts but tied it to a tree so it could graze on the long grass.

George had nothing to pack. His bag and violin were on Ben's wagon.

Other than the boat, the campsite was clear. Someone had tied a water flagon under his seat; otherwise, his wagon was empty. He untied the reins of his steed, climbed up on the flatbed wagon seat, and flicked the reins. He would not hurry home, as he planned for his horse to walk the twenty-six miles rather than take it at a trot. He would give Charlotte a week before seeking her out and making up. He knew he would have to apologise, but he was so sick of her fussing. He wasn't feeling up to coping with her juvenile antics at the moment.

For an hour, he needed to concentrate as he negotiated the rough roadway to Penrith. Once the town was behind him, the horse only needed to follow the well-worn track. He loosened the reins and let the horse walk at her own pace. He didn't care how long it took to get home.

The sun's heat beat down on him, making the road ahead shimmer like water. He was glad he had his hat on. He could see a dust cloud well ahead and presumed it would be Ben's wagon. Another plume to the south was more worrying. It looked to be a campfire. He figured that they would also only walk on the return trip. He had no intention of trying to catch up.

For the next hour, he happily plodded along. He spewed twice more but had not even dismounted to do so. He was so tired. He wished he could sleep. The summer heat made the road dusty, and he knew that dust would be kicked up as each wagon travelled along the dry road.

Mid-morning, the dust cloud ahead of him stopped. George realised the wagon ahead had probably paused for the dogs or girls to have a comfort stop. He pulled over, not wanting to get too close. He didn't feel like being near anyone.

He waited.

After relieving himself and vomiting again, he saw the dust cloud reappear, and he set off again. He was feeling decidedly not himself. Even his thoughts made him angry. The sun beat down on him relentlessly. It was hot, so darned hot.

Perspiration was trickling down his back, and his clothing was sticky. He took frequent swigs from the water flagon but knew it had to last all day. He wished he had a corned beef and egg sandwich. He was so hungry. He loved the way Charlie made them for him. He realised she had noticed everything he liked and usually had them ready for him. He felt so guilty about his harsh words to her, but she really did annoy him sometimes. His head still pounded from the thump of the boom. He had a big, egg-shaped lump where it had hit.

The miles rolled by as he enjoyed the quiet of the bushland around him. He spotted an occasional flight of wallabies or a kangaroo standing tall in the long grass near the road. Twelve nearly grown emu chicks followed a father emu, and George trailed them along the road for a few hundred yards. They had lost their stripes, so they weren't quite that young. He had no intention of hurrying them along. He had to slow his wagon even more as they ambled along the road, but he was glad to watch the waddling birds. Eventually, they headed into the bush. He hadn't had much chance to interact with the wildlife, and seeing one of these giant birds up so close was incredible. He watched them run off into the scrub as soon as they reached an open area. He wondered what spooked them, but saw nothing.

George had lost sight of the dust cloud. He had forgotten to keep his eye on it. He stood and looked around him. He couldn't see it. He was approaching a sweeping bend as the road climbed a small hill. Maybe he would see them from there.

The horse could smell water and picked up its pace a little. George knew there was a hollowed log near the waterhole down the road a bit. With nothing to eat on board, George took a long drink from the water bottle before re-corking it and stowing it under the seat.

As the wagon neared the crest, the horse's ears flicked.

George noticed her tense and said, "What's up, girl?"

He had hardly finished speaking when he heard a branch crack.

Three scruffy men appeared out of the bush just before the top of the rise. They were armed, and George had nothing with which to defend himself. He didn't have the energy to argue when they told him to put his arms up. He dropped the reins and put his foot on them lest his horse take off and he get shot.

He could tell from their appearance that they were probably escaped convicts who had turned to bushranging. One of the men came and took hold of the bridle. "Get orf! We want the wagon!"

George wasn't going to argue. He could buy another wagon, but he only had one life. He dismounted and stepped away from the other two men, backing away.

"The mare's thirsty," was all George said.

One of the other men said, "She's ours now, mate, so leave her to us."

George turned to watch the two men climb onto his wagon.

The third man said, "Step away now, laddie, and you won't get hurt."

No sooner had he finished speaking than George's world went black.

The man who had been holding the bridle sideswiped him with the butt of his musket. George collapsed in a heap in the middle of the road.

No sooner did he crumple than one of the men on the seat said, "What the damn hell did ya do that for, you stupid clod?"

The clod shrugged. "Well, now he can't follow us, can he?" Rather than leave George in the middle of the road, he dragged him by his foot and rolled him into the gutter against the embankment.

With George now off the road, the man hopped onto the seat of the wagon, and they took off slowly. Instead of turning the vehicle on the narrow section of the road, they knew the water hole was at the bottom of the hill. Other wagons that had passed were packed with young folk, and the last wagon had three people on it, so they let that go. They would water the horse and then head back west. They had no fixed plan for where to go, but they were sure they could eventually reach China if they headed westward. They'd heard rumours of great wealth and riches in China and planned to travel overland to get there.

An hour passed before they returned. George had not moved. Rather than check if he was all right, they figured he was dead.

One man said, "We'd better scarper, lads. If he's dead, then we are too." The lead man flicked the reins, and the horse merrily tripped along the dusty road.

Having had a long drink and a rest, she was happy to pick up speed a bit, especially as it was downhill.

~

Miles away from George, Ben saw the dust cloud follow them for most of the morning. He noted that it stopped when they did, and he smiled. He admitted that Charlotte had overdone the fussing that morning. He was amazed how George had stood it for as long as he did.

Since they left camp, she had said nothing. She wouldn't even sit on the seat with Kath. He wasn't sure if she was sulking or worrying. Either way, it was nice not to have her incessant chatter. Kath often complained that her little sister was like a bubbling brook. Mostly, it was innocuous gibberish, but occasionally, she would unleash her tongue on someone.

At their lunch stop, Ben searched the skyline for George's dust cloud. Nothing. He was sure he would have caught up with them by now, as he had nothing to eat. They had caught up with the other two vehicles. The three wagons stopped for lunch near Rooty Hill.

Ben had seen Charlotte leave a bottle of water under the seat of George's wagon, but there was no food.

After an hour, they continued their journey eastward, hoping George would catch up with them.

Ben paused at the top of a hill just west of Parramatta and looked westward. They could see out to the Blue Mountains from here, and he should have seen George's dust cloud. Nothing! He stood on the seat, and his eyes scanned the horizon. He saw a slight puff of dust to the far south near a plume of someone's fire, but nothing on the westward road.

Charlotte realised what he was doing. "Can you see him?"

Ben shook his head. He had not told her that George didn't feel too good. "He's probably just stopped for a sleep under a tree somewhere."

Charlotte blanched. "I should have stayed and travelled with him." A tear escaped. "I know I fuss, but I was worried about him." The pair on the front didn't know that she had wept for most of the trip. She knew she was a chatterbox; her siblings always told her to shush, but she had not realised that it annoyed George so much. She was determined to grow up.

Kath reached out and gently squeezed her sister's shoulder. Ben had quietly told her what George had said, and she encouraged Charlotte to travel with them and the dogs. Kath now added, "He'll be fine, Charlie." She hoped and prayed he would be.

Ben eventually sat down and said, "I'd better get you two home. I dare say he'll come in late. He won't come to your place tonight, so don't expect to see him." Ben sat and gee'd up their horse.

Within half an hour, Ben was pulling into the front yard of the Rosedale house. The four boys were there and would return with him to their home. The girls hauled off their bags and waved to the departing vehicle. They would meet at church tomorrow morning.

~

Out on the western road, George lay in the gutter. He had not stirred since he was hit. Ants were now crawling over him, and the sun had burnt the back of his neck as the thieves had taken his hat. It had been hours since he had had a drink.

A late messenger from Emu lock-up had been sent to Parramatta to inform them that there was a wisp of smoke in the south. If a bushfire started, they may need to send troops to help fight it if it spreads.

The rider had periodically galloped and trotted, thinking he should arrive in a little over an hour. The stallion he was on was a magnificent beast with the stamina of a steed twice his size. He knew he was more than halfway and would soon reach the waterhole. As he topped the rise that overlooked the creek, his eyes were drawn to a white lump on the side of the road. He realised it was a man in the gutter. He pulled up and dismounted. Presuming he would be dead or drunk, he was stunned to hear a soft groan as he rolled him over. The poor sod was covered in ants and had bites all over his face. He was also hot to the touch, and he could feel that the man was burning up. After brushing off the ants, he pulled out his water bottle and held it to the man's lips. No response! He poured some over the man's face to cool him. This seemed to rouse him.

George stirred and grabbed the water bottle. He drank thirstily and collapsed back into his rescuer's arms. "Thanks!"

The soldier said, "Can you answer some questions?"

George dared not nod. His head hurt like hell. He croaked a "Yes. I was held up, and three men took my wagon. One hit me." He felt ill and pulled out of the soldier's arms, twisted and vomited where he had previously lain.

The soldier swore. He wondered what to do. "Do you think you can stand? I'm on a time constraint and need to reach town tonight." The sick man was in no state to answer anything. He was fighting even to stay awake.

George rolled over and crawled to the horse. "You'll have to help me up." He managed to stand and was hanging onto the stirrup.

Thankfully, the soldier was strong and manoeuvred George onto the saddle. After retying the water bottle onto the saddle bag, he hauled himself behind George. The saddle was one without a prominent pommel, so they managed, even though it was uncomfortable. The burly soldier put his arms around George, and it was just as well he did, as George passed out as they reached town.

Rather than go directly to the captain's cottage, the soldier knew he had to get this man to the hospital. He had not been fully coherent since he had managed to get up on the horse. He kept saying, 'Charlie,' so they presumed it was his name. On arrival at the hospital, he called for assistance.

In moments of his call, a bevy of orderlies and a doctor had eased the swollen, mumbling man from the horse. With the scant information provided, the soldier departed to fulfil his duty. Once done, he would return and give the rest of the information, such as he had.

The horse was exhausted. Carrying two men for ten miles was stretching the stamina of the amazing animal. To do half of it at a trot or canter was incredible. The stallion could hardly raise his head.

Realising the state of his mount, the soldier hopped off and led the beast to the stables. After leaving him there, he went to find Captain Phillip Margate. With the suspected fire reported, he returned to the hospital to see the patient. He wondered how 'Charlie' was going. How bad were his injuries? Would he even pull through?

On arrival at the hospital, the doctor reported the man was now entirely unresponsive and was not calling out any more. He drank a pitcher of water and then collapsed. "I checked his eyes but couldn't see if the pupils even moved in this light. I will have to wait until daylight to provide you with a more detailed report. If you had not brought him in, he would be dead by morning."

The soldier wiped his brow. "He's that bad, doc?"

The doctor nodded. "Yes, he is. It may well be touch-and-go if he survives the night. He's strong, but I can tell you that he has two head injuries, and one looks a little older than the other."

The soldier sighed. "I do hope he pulls through. Did he tell you his name? He kept calling out Charlie, so that may be it."

The doctor shook his head. "Sorry! By the time he arrived, he could not answer any questions."

With a nod, the soldier said, "Thanks, sir; I shall call in again tomorrow and see if he made it through the night." He glanced at the patient. "Oh, doc, a fire is starting near the river to the south. It's why I'm here." He gave the doctor a bow and departed.

~

By eight o'clock, it was dark outside. George had still not appeared, and Ben was now apprehensive, knowing they had to get up for church the following day. After unpacking the luggage, they retired for the night. Ben carefully put George's violin case in the second bottom drawer and dumped his bag on his bed. He, too, had swallowed a lot of water, but he had vomited most of it up pretty well straight away. Rather than cook a meal, the boys cut slices of bread and slathered them with honey before heading to their rooms.

Ben woke in the pre-dawn light and rose to see if George had come in while he was asleep. He padded to his room and slowly opened the door. His bag was still sitting in the middle of his bed. George had not returned. Now Ben was distraught. He knew he had to tell Charlotte and the rest of the family. Thankfully, they would meet in town at church.

Ben roused the four boys, and they set about preparing for the day. All were hungry, and Eric checked the chicken coop, finding fifteen eggs. They had been sent home from the Rosedales with two loaves of bread, so they quickly fried ten eggs and had two each on toast. Now fed, they dressed for church. At half past six, the family wagon passed their door and stopped to collect the boys.

When only five emerged, Charlotte let out a cry. "Where's George?"

Ben hopped up beside her and said, "I don't know, Charlie, he didn't come home?" Kath pulled her into her arms. Her eyes met Ben's over her weeping sister's head. She turned and saw that both her parents were watching them. She mouthed "Help" to them.

Linus said, "We'll report him missing after church. Then, instead of a picnic today, we shall go hunting for him."

Ben was relieved. He said, "Thanks, sir."

When they arrived, Reverend Samuel Marsden greeted them and then turned his back on Crispin and Helena. Although she was now free, his attitude to emancipists still rankled. Helena had served her time years ago, but the minister still shunned her.

The greater Rosedale group was about to go inside when the governor's carriage arrived. They stood back and watched as they alighted.

After being welcomed by Marsden, Lachlan Macquarie paused and spoke to Linus. "You look worried, Rosedale. Is something up?"

Linus nodded, acknowledging the honour of the conversation. "Somewhat, sir. George Ellis is missing, and we were coming to report this after church."

Macquarie frowned. Captain Mark Duffy was summoned to his side with the flick of a finger. "Duffy, can you get some details about the lad?"

The vice-regal couple proceeded into the church, leaving his head of security with Linus. Mark pulled out a notepad from his pocket.

Linus motioned for the family to take their seats as he and Ben told the captain what they knew. Mark looked puzzled. "Did something occur that might have made him hide?"

Both older men looked at Ben. He swallowed nervously. "Well, sir, first, we had an incident with the boat. George was hit by the boom and knocked overboard, but it wasn't that, sirs. When he returned from the prison hospital at Emu Ford, Charlotte was fussing to the point of making him storm away after nearly biting her head off." He looked apologetically at Linus, who nodded his understanding. "Well, I followed him, and as we sat talking on the river's edge, he mentioned that he wasn't coping with her fluster and fussing. Plus, she was teasing the dogs. We had no idea she was above us and overheard. She flung a reply at us and stormed back to camp. He said a few other things."

Linus didn't look angry. "She does tend to do that, Ben. But did he chase after her?"

Ben shook his head. "No, sir. He was not well. Our wagon left when I returned to the campsite. Charlie left some water on his wagon, but as we left the boat there, his wagon was empty. Even his bag and fiddle were on my wagon. Sirs, he has nothing with him but his hat and some water."

Mark Duffy said, "Nothing at all? So he has not fled?"

Ben shook his head. "No, sir, he's missing, not run away. He would not go without his violin. I saw the dust from his wagon until just before Rooty Hill. We had paused for a comfort stop not long before that, and I saw his dust stop. So I know he followed us. I know George, and he would have left her to cool down, but he would have come home. It's not like him to vanish."

Linus agreed.

Mark jotted notes as Ben spoke. "I'll get on to this after the service, but we'd better take our seats."

For Ben and Charlotte, the service and sermon seemed to go on forever. Both wished to leave and hunt for George.

~

Over at the military hospital, George had not roused. His eyes would open but were glazed, and he had not spoken. This may have been because his lips were so swollen. The ant bites had affected his face and hands, leaving him almost unrecognisable. The orderly could sit him up, and he would drink, but he remained all but unresponsive. When the orderly said, "Come on, Charlie, you need to drink." George's eyes followed the man, but he was expressionless. After each drink, George would collapse back on his bunk and sleep. T h e orderly placed a cold, damp compress over his face to ease the bites, but the blisters on his neck from sunburn caused more discomfort. George soon threw off the compresses in an effort to turn over.

~

With the service now over, the governor made a beeline for Linus. "Mark told me that it's not like George to vanish, so I shall order a posse to search for him."

Elizabeth Macquarie, Kath, and Agnes were comforting Charlotte, who was weeping. Yet, she turned to Helena and whispered. "It's all my fault. I made him leave." Helena enfolded her sister into her arms. No one knew what to say or do, so Helena escorted Charlotte to the waiting vehicles.

A large group of soldiers, including the soldier who had found George, left at dawn. They headed west from Parramatta to attend to reports of the possible bushfire south of Penrith. Within an hour of the service finishing, various other search parties were organised. Small groups of soldiers were dispatched and headed along multiple possible routes to look for George. Hopefully, by dusk, some word of George would have been heard. The family had no option but to return home.

No one associated the unknown man at the hospital, 'Charlie,' with the missing George Ellis. 'Charlie' lay in his bunk, thrashing in agony. His lungs laboured as he breathed, and his face and neck were burning in pain. The inflammation of the bites was now secondary to his breathing difficulty. The new orderly, Greg, sat by his bed and bathed his head. His patient's hacking cough almost hurt his ears. 'Charlie' had trouble breathing again, so the orderly rolled him onto his side. Almost instantly, his breathing eased. He remembered his mother patting his back firmly when he had a chesty cough. He rolled the man onto his stomach and patted his back with cupped hands. The patient coughed and spewed up some vile-smelling, slimy fluid. His breathing eased, and his patient fell asleep peacefully. Rather than sit at his desk, he moved his paperwork to the table next to the sick man. At one stage, 'Charlie' choked on something, and Greg patted him hard on his back again to assist him in dislodging it.

'Charlie' coughed and disgorged a plug of mucus. With it gone, his breathing eased for a while. He was still burning up.

By noon, the swelling from the bites had subsided slightly. Throughout the day, the various groups of soldiers returned and reported to Captain Duffy, having discovered nothing. There had been no sighting of either George or his wagon. He seemingly had vanished. However, the fire had spread into the bush and was heading northeast of where it started.

Chapter 12 Smoke

*F*or two days, 'Charlie's' hold on life was touch-and-go. His fever raged, and his hacking cough dislodged a lot more mucus. Although he was hot and perspiring, he was shivering.

Greg covered him with blankets but also sponged his forehead. He and two other orderlies attended to his needs. The doctor visited regularly and was astounded that the patient was still alive. Greg was off duty when 'Charlie' was brought in, but took over his care. The blisters on his neck filled with yellow pus, and they had become flyblown. No one had picked it up. Greg discovered maggots on his pillow and knew he needed to act quickly. Something similar had happened to him when he had been burned. He poured neat rum onto the raw wounds and expected a cry of pain. Nothing! 'Charlie' seemed to be getting worse. He managed to sit him up and get him to drink, but the towel between his legs was hardly damp. He knew he had to get more fluids into him.

With most other patients discharged, Greg focused on fighting for 'Charlie's' survival. He took up his place beside the hospital bed. He rested on the unmade bed beside his patient. Greg forced the man to sit up and drink every hour. Sometimes, it would take twenty minutes to get him to take a glass of water, and at other times, he would devour a jug full in minutes. Greg didn't care as long as his patient took the fluid. Occasionally, 'Charlie' would murmur, saying, "Sorry, Charlie, I didn't mean it." His words made Greg wonder if his name was indeed Charlie. Soon after he spoke, he choked again. He had discovered that when 'Charlie' choked, a firm pat on the back would ease his patient's laboured breathing, and often, he would cough up another lump of foul-smelling green mucus. Greg rolled his patient on his side and gave him some cupped pummelling every hour or so. Each time 'Charlie's' breathing eased. He was still sweating profusely, but the shivering stopped. Greg also kept up the cool compresses on his face. There was no ice, just a bucket of cool well water, and some flannel cloths.

After some hours of pummelling and cool compresses, 'Charlie' was breathing normally for the first time since he had been brought in. Greg was pleased when the doctor checked him that night to hear that his fever had broken. 'Charlie' slept on. However, it was now peaceful. The maggots had been killed, the swelling from the bites had eased, and the sunburn blisters had reduced. His face looked almost normal. An occasional coughing fit would rack his body, but he would fall back to sleep quickly.

Greg made him drink deeply after each coughing spasm.

While the doctor was at the hospital, word came that Mrs Ovens, the Macquarie's cook, had been burned. The doctor left to attend to her at Government House rather than get her to attend the military tent hospital.

Cathy Duffy was at the cook's side when the doctor arrived. "Thank you for coming, doctor. She was in too much pain to move."

The doctor brushed his nose nervously as he was wont to do. "It is of no matter, Mrs Duffy, as there is only one patient at the moment. We don't quite know who he is, and he's been in a bad way since he was brought in from Emu. The orderly has been at his side for the past three days. I'm unsure how the man survived, but his fever broke earlier today. I think the poor chap will live."

Mark came in while the doctor was speaking. "Excuse me, doctor, but did you say you have an unidentified man in the hospital?"

The doctor nodded while he washed his hands before treating the cook's burnt arm. He walked to his new patient and said, "I did, Captain. One of the soldiers found him unresponsive by the side of the Parramatta Road late on Saturday afternoon. He brought him to us. I didn't think he would make it through the night, but he's a fighter. He kept calling out 'Charlie', so we presume that is his name. Perchance, do you know anyone missing by that name?"

Mark gasped. He replied, "No, but a man named George Ellis is missing, and he had a misunderstanding with someone he called Charlie shortly before he vanished."

"Do you mean the young tanner?" The doctor was now drying his hands. "Ahh, well, that could explain his strange ramblings. The size of the lad made me wonder if he was a smithy. His words didn't make sense to me, but that explains a great deal. I doubt you would recognise him as his face is severely swollen from multiple ant bites. His lungs are also affected. He's coughing something bad."

Mark nodded. "That makes sense. He nearly drowned on Friday. So, he's still at the hospital? May I go and see if it is our missing lad?"

The doctor was now checking the burn on Mrs Ovens's arm. "Yes, yes, by all means, go. I shall be glad to know if you can give my patient a name." He waved Mark away.

Mark blew a kiss to his wife over the heads of the other two people, then, with a wave, approached the governor and asked for permission to leave and go to the hospital. He had met George a few times, and he was sure he would be able to identify him. He knocked on the governor's office door. T h e call from inside said, "Enter!"

Mark did. "Sir, I may have a lead on George Ellis. There's an unknown patient at the hospital. If you're not planning on going out, may I check if it's him? Apparently, he's in a bad way."

Lachlan looked up when Mark entered. Usually, his security guard would wait to speak until he was given permission. "Go, Mark, and report back to me as soon as you know. Linus's girl is beside herself, not to mention the boys he lives with. I do hope it's him."

Mark realised he'd broken protocol and now stood to attention. "Sorry, sir."

Lachlan gave a single choked laugh, "Oh, for goodness' sake, relax, Mark. You're supposed to be off duty, anyway. Henry Antill is here. Yes, go and return as fast as you can. I freely admit I'm worried about the lad. Check the state of the fire if you can while you are out."

Mark saluted, turned on his heel, and soon paced down the hill towards the tent hospital at the bottom of the compound. He entered through the wobbly hospital door at the front of the insubstantial structure. This building was little better than an oversized wattle-and-daub cabin, but it was known as the hospital tent. It provided little shelter and was not only rat-infested, but patients often got flyblown. The earthen floor was impossible to keep clean, and the pallet beds wobbled severely. As the doctor said, there was only one patient.

Greg looked up and saw who had entered. "Hello, Mark. Did the doctor send you?"

Mark nodded. He came to the bedside and looked at the unresponsive man. "Cor! That is George Ellis, all right. What happened to him? He looks like he's going to explode!"

Greg shrugged. "The lumps are from ant bites, but he's got two head wounds, one on either side. He also has sunstroke, and when the blisters ruptured, they got flyblown. I doused the maggots with overproof rum."

Mark's face screwed up in disgust. "Is he going to make it?" He liked the burn-scarred orderly.

Greg nodded. "I think he's through the worst. He rouses now and then, but he doesn't respond to the name Charlie. Having said that, if his name is George, then that would explain it."

Mark gave a strangled chuckle. "Greg, George's girl is named Charlotte and gets called 'Charlie'."

Greg nodded in understanding but replied, "Ahh!" The two men sat chatting for some time. Mark heard the details of his patient's arrival and what the soldier from Emu Prison Farm had told him. There was very little information, and no mention was made of George's wagon or horse. Mark knew he should send a messenger to the governor, but there was no one to send.

George stirred occasionally and had a coughing fit. Greg rolled him on his side and gave him a pummelling on his back. Once again, George spat up a plug of mucus. A paroxysm of coughing followed, and Greg tended to his patient. More muck was coughed up, followed by a long drink. Greg changed his towels and settled him down again. As he did so this time, George woke and looked around him. His eyes focused on the thatched roof above him, then he looked around and took in his surroundings. "Where am I?"

Greg was emptying the vomit basin, and Mark came to George's side. "You're in the hospital at Parramatta, George. Do you remember what happened?"

George's eyes focused on the tall, red-coated soldier next to him. "Who are you, and why am I here?"

Mark had met him a few times in the week before the accident. They spent time together after church and participated in many discussions. He was surprised George didn't remember him. "I'm Mark Duffy. I head Governor Macquarie's security." He saw George frown. "Do you remember meeting Governor Macquarie?"

George was about to shake his head, but his hand went to it. He said huskily, "Ouch! No. Who's he?"

Greg returned and overheard the comment. He took over the questioning. "Do you remember your name?"

George shook his head slightly. "Oooh, I should not move my head. What happened to me? I ache all over. You called me George, so I presume it's that."

Greg met Mark's gaze over the bed. His eyes dropped again to his patient. Greg asked again, "Do you know your full name?"

George was struggling to sit up. Having found his voice, he was full of questions. "No! What the blazes is going on? Why am I here? Who are you two, and what is this place? Where's Papa, Rob and…" The struggle to sit made him dizzy. He collapsed back onto his pillows.

Greg left to see if the doctor had returned.

George's unfinished question made Mark gasp. He remembered George telling him he was an orphan. Greg returned to the bed and gave him another drink. Footsteps sounded behind Mark, and he turned to see the doctor enter. Mark released a long sigh of relief. He said, "He's awake, Doctor."

The doctor came to George's side and looked down at his patient. "Well, you look a hell of a lot better, young man. Can you tell me what happened?"

George had no idea. "I don't even know who I am, let alone tell you anything about how I got here." The effort of talking exhausted him. He looked around for something to drink and spied Greg holding another glass of fluid. With Greg's assistance, he downed two more glasses of water and then collapsed back on his pillows.

Mark pulled the doctor away while he drank. "Doctor, what's wrong with him? Why doesn't he remember anything? Not even that his family is dead."

The doctor rubbed his nose again and said, "I remember reading about a case. I think it was called amnesia. It's a form of memory loss caused by a head injury. In most cases, the patient recovered fully in several days, if not weeks. He may never recall certain things, such as the exact details of what happened to him. Time will tell, and you can't hurry him. For now, he's alive, and we must focus on getting him home. So, he is this missing George Ellis, eh?"

Mark nodded. "I must report to the governor. We've had a posse looking for him." Without returning to George, he left to return home. He knew he had to send word to the family that he had been found and was alive, but far from well. After leaving the hospital, Mark went to the barracks next door and sent a messenger to Ben and the Rosedale farms. He then walked up the hill from the military redoubt towards Government House. As he did so, he saw the growing plume of smoke as he topped the hill. The fire had fanned into a full-blown bushfire, and the wisp had grown dramatically since yesterday. He knew at least one problem was solved, but with the westerly winds behind it, the fire could burn towards the town. In the dry weather, everything could burn. He hurried indoors to report his findings.

Cathy greeted him with a kiss. "Who is he, Mark?"

Mark slung his arm around his wife. "It's George, love, but he doesn't remember who he is. How's Mrs Ovens?"

"She's fine. I sent her to lie down. Jenny and I will prepare dinner tonight." They chatted quietly as they walked towards the governor's sitting room. Cathy informed him that the vice-regal couple were waiting for his return. Mark gave her another quick kiss. She told him last night that she was carrying their first child. They had only married in September on the voyage out. He was still getting used to having a lovely wife, let alone her two older children, Josh and Jenny. Both lived with them at Government House. Josh, who had arrived as a convict, became the governor's apprentice groom. M a r k knocked, and they waited until they heard the call to enter.

Lachlan was standing at the window that overlooked the front gardens. He turned and asked, "Was it George?" Elizabeth patted the seat next to her for Cathy.

Mark nodded. "It was, sir. He roused while I was there and asked where he was. Sir, he's lost his memory. He didn't even remember his name. I hardly recognised him as he is covered in welts from ant bites; therefore, his face is swollen, and he's also severely sunburnt." There was no way he was going to mention the maggots in the blisters in front of the women.

Lachlan paced the room. "Did you send a messenger to the family?"

Mark walked to his side. "I did, sir, and also to the boys. They are going to have their hands full caring for the lad. It could be a long recuperation."

Lachlan nodded. He turned to look at his guard-cum-friend. "You're pensive, Mark. What's up?"

Mark turned his back on the ladies and lowered his voice. "Sir, I think the bushfire is heading our way. The plume of black smoke out west has grown, and we have not heard back from the men we sent out to assist. It's been three days now, and we should prepare for the worst. I don't wish to worry the women, but we could be in for a bad time."

Lachlan uttered a quiet "Darn!" He glanced over at the ladies. "Can you send one of the front door guards down to the barracks and mobilise the troops? I won't leave the town unprotected, so I will not send more soldiers west. This place is so different from Scotland, and I have yet to acclimate to the weather. India and Egypt are hot, but not like this." He took a deep breath and turned to look back out his window. "Mark, this climate is sapping. If George was left out in the sun for any time, I'm surprised he survived."

Mark frowned. "He nearly didn't, sir. The doctor also said that his lungs are affected. If what we heard from Ben was true, then George nearly drowned. I dare say that was what caused the problem with his lungs."

Lachlan nodded. "Mark, duck out and send the message to the regiment to prepare for fire. I'll get the rest of the story when you return."

~

Linus Rosedale was sitting in his rocking chair in the cool shade of the verandah. From this site, he could see the plume of smoke in the far distance. Thanks to a warning weeks earlier from his indigenous friends from the tribe, the family slashed and burned all the stubble near the house. The homestead sat in the middle of a blackened paddock as Bennelong insisted they back-burn everything around the home. All the stock feed was covered with canvas, and the hay had been raked up and wrapped with a sheet of old sail, then covered with a layer of dirt. Along the verandah, full buckets of water sat with rags in them to beat out any embers that landed nearby. The boys doused the thatching and shingles on the house and shed. There was little more they could do. Linus was drinking a mug of tea and frowned as he watched the plume grow. The sound of a galloping horse drew his attention. This drew him to his feet. "Agnes, Charlie, come quick!"

The sound of running feet followed his call. As the rider drew closer, they realised it was Algernon Darnley, Patience's husband. She came and stood with them.

Algernon reined in and jumped off his horse. "He's alive! He's sick as a dog, but he's alive." He flicked the reins around the railing, grabbed Patience, and swung her around. With his arm around his wife's shoulders, he said, "I don't have all the details, but he's in the hospital. He doesn't even remember his name, so he's pretty crook."

Charlotte asked nervously, "Can we go and see him?"

Algernon shrugged. "I don't see why not, but don't be surprised if he doesn't know you. Ben's already on his way in, so I'd leave it until tomorrow if I were you. He might have regained some memory by then. In the meantime, the fire is approaching, and we must prepare to fight it. Captain Duffy told me to say you can head into town if you feel unsafe."

After a glance at Agnes, who had arrived on the verandah, Linus said, "We'll stay, thanks, lad. We're ready if a fire comes. The tribe told us to head to the waterhole if it got any closer. There are caves to shelter in, and they have shown us where they are."

With little more to do, Algernon took the opportunity of a bit of unexpected time off. He had not seen his wife for two days. Once his message had been delivered, Linus waved the pair away. Patricia was tugging at his arm, and he hoped she would take him to their room. Algernon had barely closed the door when she started unbuttoning his jacket. After she hung it on the valet stand, she paused and said, "Algy…" Words failed her. She took his hand and placed it on her stomach.

His eyes flew open, and he said, "You're late, or you're sure?"

She blushed and admitted, "Both. I nearly told you on Sunday, but with George missing, it could wait. I was late for my monthly flow, so I wasn't sure. It still has not come. I will need to wait another few months before I tell everyone, but I wanted to let you know."

The couple had been married for over twelve months, and each month, she would be in tears as her monthly flow came. She hid her distress from her husband, but he knew. He had been surprised she had not conceived as the more buxom Margaret had. She already had a babe in her arms. Algernon was delighted. He swung her around and was about to disrobe her when he paused. "Can we still… you know?" he asked somewhat shyly, glancing at their bed. Her nod saw the rest of their raiment quickly divested. He knew he needed to return to duty as soon as he could.

~

All the while, George slept on. He had relapsed and fallen back into a delirious slumber. With the fire approaching, the doctor, one other orderly, and Greg planned to sleep at the hospital, in case they were needed. Greg had been a patient here for many months the year before. He'd been severely burned in a fire and could no longer serve as a soldier. Greg moved his things onto the pallet bed beside George and intended to nurse him through the night. The building often smelled of smoke, but the odour was not too heavy.

Mid-morning, the hospital door opened, and a shadowy figure filled the doorway. His silhouette showed he was tall, but Greg could not see his features. The man drew near, and Greg noticed he was young. "Can I help you, sir? Are you injured?"

The young man shook his head. "No, I have come to see George." Ben walked to his friend's side and took his hand. While addressing the orderly, but looking at George, he said, "Cor, look at his face!" A moment later, he added, "He's so hot. Come on, George, you have to fight like hell."

George groaned for the first time in a while. Greg moved closer and said, "If you are his friend, I shall tell you what I know. He's got two head injuries, ant bites, sunstroke, and his lungs are putrid. Do you know how he received any of these injuries?"

Ben finally looked at the man. His scarred face indicated that he was clearly very familiar with hospitals. The orderly's forehead was burned and severely scarred, but his smile remained untouched. Ben nodded and said, "My name is Ben Parker, and George and I run a small tannery and leatherwork business on Windsor Road." He recapped their activities from last Friday, detailing how George had sustained one of the head injuries. Without taking his eyes off his friend, he confessed, "He had a bit of a tiff with his girl, and instead of travelling with us, he decided to follow later. I saw his dust until about halfway here; then, the hills obstructed the roadway from view. He never arrived home that night."

Greg said, "So you are none the wiser either?"

Ben shook his head. "Was his horse and wagon at hand?"

Greg shrugged. "Apparently not, as a soldier found him face down on the side of the road. If he only had one head wound before, then I gather he has been attacked. It must have been stolen by the people who attacked him. He told the soldier who found him that three men stopped him, but he no longer remembers."

Ben pulled up the chair nearby and sat beside his friend. He knew he couldn't stay past noon as he had to return to the boys to help with fire protection, but he needed to see George for himself. Ben's presence meant that Greg could have a break. "Can you stay for a bit? He needs to drink as much as he can when he rouses. I'm beat, so if you don't mind, I'll have a nap while you are here. He had a bad night last night, but call me if you need me." Ben didn't take his eyes off George's swollen face. He nodded assent.

Outside, the gusts of wind stirred the leaves. The wind was picking up, and Ben realised this would fan the flames. At the barracks, the troops rallied and prepared for the approaching bushfire. Barrels were filled with water and distributed throughout the small town. Convict teams were recalled from road and building duties to slash long grass and cut back overhanging vegetation wherever possible. Birds screeched overhead and were seen flying eastward. Snakes, wallabies, and other animals headed to cleared areas or the water. A colony of flying fruit bats took off and left the town.

Ben returned home after an hour beside his friend. George's condition changed little, but his breathing was undoubtedly easier. When he left Greg, he said, "I'll try to return tomorrow, but that depends on the fires." With a final glance at his friend, he said, "Thanks, Greg, for your care of my friend. I won't ask when he can come home, as there is no way we could look after him. We are six single lads sharing a house and running a business. We make do as best we can, but he would die if I attempted to move him."

Greg nodded. "I'll take good care of him, Ben. I know what fire and sickness are like." He brushed his hand across his forehead. "I got this from my first attempt at fighting fires. I spent months in the hospital healing, so I know what pain is. Take care, and I'll see you when I see you."

When Ben finally turned to leave the hospital, he gave a final glance at his friend. He said again, "Thanks, Greg, for your care." Ben arrived home at noon. The wind was carrying burnt blades of grass and small leaves, and it was picking up strength. It was so thick that it was nearly dark by mid-afternoon. The gloom showed that the blowing leaves were not black and dead but live embers. Each one was a small incendiary device ready to start another blaze. Every ember carried the potential for total disaster. The darkened sky looked alive with fireworks. By six o'clock, the heaviness of the oppressive smoke made everyone aware of the danger they were in.

The convict crews, overseen by the soldiers, acted quickly. As fast as an ember landed and caught fire, an observant watcher extinguished it. All the felons were kept on duty, and after a quick meal, soldiers, convicts, and free fighters fought side by side to save the town. The blessing of the descending darkness meant they could see where each ember landed. Although exhausted from having spent a day on road gangs or crushing rocks, the convicts fought on. Mark sent half the men away at midnight and told them to sleep as they would take over at dawn. A fresh team battled each small spot fire.

Throughout the night, George slept on. The hospital staff tended to a few walk-in patients with burns or other injuries. One was brought in with a broken arm; a few came with cuts that the doctor needed to stitch up. A falling branch knocked one out, and it had dislocated his shoulder. He was treated while out cold.

Sunrise saw a line of blackened, exhausted men relieved of duty, and they went to their various abodes to grab what food and sleep they could. They downed fluid enough to drink the sea dry, then collapsed, exhausted, onto their beds. Although the wind dropped overnight, the heat blasted down like an inferno. Birds were found dead at the base of trees; heat-affected, thirsty possums were scattered amongst them. No one went to their aid, though the children placed buckets of water at the bases of trees. The day wore on, with more spot fires starting here and there, but the raging inferno had not eventuated. The town was safe... for now.

By Wednesday morning, nobody had the energy left to fight. Some paddocks of stubble were left to burn, and trees that caught alight were no longer cut down. Linus stood on his verandah, watching the approaching wall of smoke. Agnes came to his side and slid under his arm. He looked down at his beloved wife and said, "We could lose everything if this gets any closer, but we started with nothing and will leave the same way. We can lose the house and farm, but as long as the family is safe, that is all I ask."

Agnes saw the worry written on his face. "Can we pray for that, then?"

While enfolded in each other's arms, they prayed for the safety of all their extended family and friends, including George, and that God would intervene and save the town and their farms. Linus's voice was never quiet at the best of times. His children knew he could roar better than a lion if required. He was a man of God who truly believed the Lord listened to their prayers. Crispin called him a prayer warrior. This morning, he prayed from his heart. His beseeching words to the Lord carried to those inside.

The front door opened, and one by one, they were joined by those indoors. Rebecca, at thirteen, was the last to arrive. She had heard her father's earnest prayers from the kitchen at the back of the house. As she joined them, an enormous explosion carried across the air. The air was thick with black smoke, and they could not see where the noise came from. Had the ammunition store caught fire at the Redoubt? For a moment, Linus fell silent.

Once again, his words beseeching God to keep them safe flowed like liquid gold from his tongue. Another explosion was heard, and this time, it made everyone jump. From the corner of his eye, Linus saw movement on the verandah. Without releasing Agnes, he said, "Hello, Bennelong. Is everyone safe?"

Bennelong nodded. "Yes, boss Linus; all good! A big storm is coming. Safer here. Cooler soon. You feel. Flood now." No sooner than the last of his tribe stood on the deck than the first drop of rain hit. It had not been an explosion but thunder and lightning. Bennelong walked to his friends. "Bad storm, hit now, Linus. We shelter here from the rain. Many trees fall, caves not safe. Flash floods come quickly. Stand back near the wall."

The Rosedale family saw a growing pile of animal skins, *coolamon* bowls, and baskets carefully placed on the verandah. Each of the bowl-like containers was filled to the brim with food. The loose-weave baskets contained what appeared to be freshly killed ducks.

Boorong, Bennelong's wife, said, "Agnes, we brought tucker for everyone." Having lived in Sydney with Reverend Johnston for nearly two years, Boorong spoke English well. Back then, she was known as Abaroo. Bennelong spoke well, but his time with his people had made him lazy. He journeyed around the world to England and returned with Governor John Hunter in 1795. The tribe adopted the Rosedales and became friends through John. They lived at Kissing Point on James Squire's property for most of the year, but they still had their place at the waterhole just off the Windsor Road.

Linus had left a large section of his land grant uncleared so the tribe could have a sanctuary. The tribe members were never any trouble. They were more often a blessing. They were always welcome in each other's homes.

Drop by drop, the rain grew heavier as the thunderclaps neared. Lightning strikes could still start more fires, and they expected some to do so, but hopefully, the gathering storm would quench the flames. All were relieved that the noises they heard were one almighty storm.

Linus glanced at Agnes and grinned. "He heard, again!"

Agnes nodded and moved to snuggle under her husband's arm.

Chapter 13 Aftermath

*T*he fire had spawned the storm, which exploded over the area from the foothills of the Blue Mountains to Parramatta. From the safety of the verandah, the family and tribe had watched as the fast-moving tornadoes of fire were quenched by a drenching from the Almighty hand above. An occasional black plume was seen from the direction of Parramatta. They realised some of the buildings were burning. They prayed the boys would have survived, but it was far too dangerous to venture out and check on them.

For four hours, the elements raged above them like a battle of good and evil. By the time the sun set on the second day, the worst was over. Rather than cook the ducks encased in clay as usual, everyone set about plucking the birds, and Agnes gutted and quartered them and slid them into the oven. The smell of roasted duck wafted through the house and out to the waiting, hungry horde.

As they had potatoes and vegetables a-plenty, the ovens were packed to the brim, and the cooktop had pots of other vegetables waiting for the ducks to roast. Soon after Governor Hunter returned to England, he purchased a large cast-iron stove for Agnes and shipped it out for them. This behemoth of a stove had two full-size ovens and an immense cooktop that made catering easy for a family of fourteen children, along with all their spouses, children and friends, not to mention the unexpected arrival of Bennelong's clan. However, the tribe never arrived empty-handed. This time, it was ducks, but often it was a wallaby or sometimes fish or possums.

With the meal eaten, the household settled down for the night. They needed to catch up on some missed sleep. The weather was still hot, and the danger was not over, but at least they had an evening of temporary relief. Some of the tribal men took turns on watch.

No further news arrived about George, so Charlotte didn't sleep well. She had extracted a promise from her father that he would take her in to see George the following day. They also had to check on Ben and the boys. Knowing she was to see George, she rested as best she could. At least he was alive.

Dawn brought more nerves for Charlotte. She would finally see George and hopefully manage to sort things out with him. She was up and dressed before anyone else and had most of her sisters' chores done before they were even out of bed. Although she was keen to go, she knew her father would not leave until the work at the farm was finished.

With a breakfast of cracked barley porridge prepared for the hoards, Charlotte went to harness their horse. She would only put him in the cart's traces once the household had eaten.

An hour after rising, Charlotte, Linus, and Kath set off for town. They planned to stop in and collect Ben if he wished to come. Otherwise, they would leave Kath at the tannery.

The trip was slow by necessity. They collected Ben and heard the saga of their close call. The grass around the house had been cut short, but they planned to keep it for dry fodder. The boys had neglected to remove the piles far enough away. The four younger lads decided to stay at the house and continue with the work, keeping watch. One fodder heap had nearly caught alight, and they could have lost the shed and stable. The boys managed to douse the smouldering ember before it set fire to everything.

The journey to town took them through areas blackened by the fires. Logs still smouldered, and they had to dodge fallen branches from the burnt trees. More than once, Ben had to hop off and pull branches from the roadway. The ground was scorched, with only a few patches of green or the occasional unburned tree or pocket of green scrub visible. The normally hour-long trip seemed never-ending.

When they arrived in town, they picked up speed a little. The wide road was empty, and they saw an occasional burned area or thatched wattle-and-daub cottage shell that had not survived the inferno. Parramatta had fought back as best it could, and only the storm had saved it.

Their path took them past the church, where they saw numerous bodies asleep on the grass. They presumed that these people had been the occupants of the burnt cottages or firefighters. They didn't stop but headed to the military Redoubt and hospital on the lower grounds of Government House.

Linus was quite surprised that the rickety twenty-two-year-old Redoubt had survived the storm. The hospital was in little better condition, but somehow it, too, had made it through the firestorm and the downpour. Linus shooed the three young ones into the structure while he saw to the horse.

Charlotte entered, clutching Kath's hand. Ben strode to his friend's side and was greeted by two smiling faces. Only it was Mark Duffy's and Greg's, not George's.

George was still asleep, but his face had almost returned to its normal state. It still was covered in red welts, but the swelling had all but gone.

Charlotte came to the bedside, and Ben stood aside to let her see her beloved. Her gasp of horror made Greg wince. That was not what he wished to hear. If George were to regain his memory, he would need support. This pretty girl was supposed to love him. "Miss, are you Charlie?"

The pretty head nodded.

"Come and take this seat." Greg moved aside to let her sit.

Linus joined his daughters and Ben at the bedside. Directing his question to Mark, he asked, "Has he woken this morning, Captain?"

Mark stepped away from the bed slightly and shook his head. "I've just arrived, sir, but Greg said he's had a good night. I was hoping to see if his memory was any clearer this morning." He glanced at the patient and noted he was stirring. "I will tell you we think we know how the fire started. Ben, this will answer your question about the whereabouts of his wagon. His wagon, along with the horse and three bodies, was found on the road to Macarthur's new five-thousand-acre grant at Cowpastures. The wagon was his as his name was on the burned-out vehicle, but the horse, which was still in the shafts, was dead, as were the three bodies sheltering under the wagon. We presume that these men attacked him and left him for dead. We may never know, but it appears that their campfire ignited the grass, which was the source of the fire. They must have been on the run for some time, as they had an established camp out there." Mark blew out his cheeks in frustration. "We don't even know who they were, but they were probably escaped convicts. Reports have been circulating among the convicts of false rumours that China is located on the other side of the mountains. The sooner we find a way across those hills, the better."

Ben groaned. "George loved that horse. Thankfully, I had taken his possessions back on our wagon, so he didn't lose anything valuable other than the vehicle and his steed." He turned to look at his prostrated friend. As he did so, George stirred. Dropping Kath's arm, Ben went to his side. "George, can you hear me?"

A groan emanated from the bed; then, his eyes fluttered open. A croaky "Yes" was the reply. "Thirsty!"

Charlotte was closest to the jug and poured him a full glass of water. Ben had seen how Greg raised him to drink, and he did the same. Charlotte handed him the glass and stood back. She was determined not to fuss over him. She had not said a word and hoped George would say something nice to her. He didn't. He barely noticed her. He gave a nod of appreciation but remained silent.

As Ben held his friend close to drink, he whispered, "Charlie is here to see you."

George's eyes flicked around the bed. He croaked, "Where?"

Ben winced, as did Charlotte. "Beside you, George. Charlie is Charlotte."

George turned towards the girls.

Hope was written on her face. Would he recognise her?

George's eyes rested on her and then flicked to Kath behind her. He smiled but didn't recognise either of the ladies. He gave a half smile and turned back to Ben. He whispered to the man holding him, "Which one?"

Ben met Charlotte's devastated gaze. He said softly, "She's the one closest to you, dear friend. The one behind is her sister Kath, who is my fiancée."

George turned back to the pretty girl beside him. With a frown etched on his brow, he gazed at her. Eventually, he said, "Pleased to meet you, Miss Charlotte. Thank you for coming." He watched her reaction. It looked like pain, but why was that? He didn't remember her and didn't know if he should.

Linus drew his daughters away as Greg reappeared. He could see the distress on Charlotte's face. He said, "Let us leave George to recover for a bit, my dears, while we step outside." He could tell that Charlotte was about to dissolve into tears, and George didn't need to see that. He and Kath hurriedly escorted Charlotte outside before that occurred. As he left, he heard the three remaining men talking to George. With a short sigh of frustration, he opened the door to tend to his daughter.

Mark sat on the foot of George's bed. "Hey, laddie, Charlie's your girl, you know."

Ben and Greg now had George sitting up in bed.

George showed both shock and horror. "No! Is she? I don't even remember her. She's pretty enough, but isn't she a bit young? She only looks fifteen or so." George looked at the red-coated soldier on his bed. He vaguely remembered seeing him earlier, but couldn't remember his name. As he had rallied, he was given some thin broth to drink and sipped it from a mug. Greg had brought him some earlier, and he devoured it. After some minutes, he said, "I don't even remember who you all are. Do I know you as well?"

Ben closed his eyes, drew a deep breath, and released it slowly. Deciding to fill in a bit of their background, Ben said, "George, we share a house with four orphan boys. You are a tanner, and I'm a saddler."

George was listening intently. He said, "I am? Tell me more."

Ben pulled up another chair and recapped their history and the activities of the weekend that had just passed.

Greg and Mark anxiously watched the patient's face to see if any inkling of his memory was returning. His interest in Ben's story showed that it was all news to him.

George flopped back on his pillows at the end of the lengthy story. "So my family is dead, and I'm on the other side of the world? I didn't think this looked like Doctor Jamieson's clinic."

Ben shook his head. "You've been in the hospital since Saturday night, and it's now Thursday, I think." He saw Mark nod.

George let out a "Cor! Really? I don't remember much except my face hurting and the smell of burning." He paused. "I still smell smoke. Did something catch fire?"

Mark nodded again. "It was a bushfire, George. The town was saved when the good Lord sent a huge deluge last night." George's light brown eyes burned into his as he spoke. "Do you remember anything about your attack, George?"

George's head shook very carefully. He turned to Ben and asked, "Is she really my girl? What did you say your name was?"

"It's Ben, and yes, she is, at least..." He paused and wondered if he should say anything about the overheard conversation.

George picked up on his hesitation. "At least, what, Ben?"

Ben glanced at the two men near the bed. Both nodded. "Until she overheard you say that her endless fussing annoyed you no end, and you wondered if you could cope with that for the rest of your life. She threw some words at you and stormed off. I took her home on our wagon."

George groaned. "Ooh! I remember that! You leaving, that is. But what happened before that?" He put his hand to his head. It hurt.

Ben rehashed the boat incident and pointed to the injury on the right side of his head.

The incidents of that day returned as a hazy picture. The more Ben spoke, the clearer the memories became. That became obvious when George said with horror, "Where's my fiddle? Is it safe?"

Ben choked a laugh as the magnificent violin was no ordinary fiddle. Ben nodded. "It's at home in its safe place, as are your dogs." He was well aware of the instrument's value and what his mongrel pups meant to George.

George relaxed. "Thank you."

The doctor came in and shooed the visitors away. "I need to check him over. If he's well enough, you can collect him tomorrow. But I'd leave him here another day or so, at least. You say there is no one to care for him at home?" Ben shook his head. The doctor frowned. "Fine, then he stays here! Thankfully, we're not overworked, so he will remain until his bed is needed."

Before Ben and Mark left, they heard George ask, "Doctor, why can I remember some things and not others? People are a blank to me, as is my name, but I remember my music and my dogs. I also remember saying some mean things, which is unlike me, but I can't remember who I said it to or even what or why. I am surprised that I know I'm not usually mean."

Ben heard part of the doctor's reply. "It's the head injuries, laddie. I've known stronger men than you to be knocked out and wake up with no idea of who they are. One later regained his memory after hitting his head again."

George frowned and then replied. "Twice is enough. My head hurts enough as it is. I don't particularly want to be thwacked again."

The doctor made him lean forward, and he checked the burns on the back of his neck. He said, "You also had sunstroke, and when the blisters ruptured, they got flyblown. However, the maggots seemed to have cleaned up the wound nicely. That is a blessing, as I've seen burns like this go septic. The ant bites on your face have also eased, so you look more like yourself."

George groaned as the doctor poked and prodded him. Maggots, flies and ants, plus two head wounds, near drowning, an attack and sunburn; no wonder he felt terrible.

Greg followed the visitors outside as the doctor tended to his patient. They were standing next to the wagon and talking to Mark. He walked to them and said, "I'd give it a couple of days before the girls visit again, but Ben, you seemed to get through to him. Do you think you could return tomorrow for a while? The more you talk to him about the past, the better."

Ben said he would, and the group soon took their leave. The girls didn't return indoors to say their farewells.

George was pleased the strange girls didn't come back. He still didn't remember them, but then, he didn't remember anyone, including himself. Various conversations and situations flashed into his mind, but the actual people involved remained hidden. The effort of conversing had worn him out, and by the time the doctor had checked his injuries, George had succumbed to deep slumber again.

Charlotte remained silent on her journey home.

Kath tried to lighten the mood, but her conversation efforts fell flat. After they dropped Ben at his house, the three Rosedales remained quiet.

~

The family did not return to town again until Sunday's church service. By then, the tribe had vanished as quietly and quickly as they had arrived.

Charlotte returned home as almost an empty shell. She wept while doing her chores, and her effervescent nature had left her.

Agnes tried to do what she could, but Charlotte gave her mother a vacant look and walked away. Her daughter would walk off in the middle of a conversation, and she barely touched her food. As thin as she was, she shed what curves she had. It was as though she were in a deep state of mourning. Agnes was confused because George was still alive.

Thankfully, the storm not only quenched the fires, but the weather also remained overcast, with intermittent showers of rain. Their journey to church on Sunday to gather together and praise God for the thunderstorm was enough cause for celebration, but when they stopped to collect the boys, Ben let them know that George would be returning home with them.

At church, Crispin and Helena saw the state of Charlotte. She was a mess. Gone was the clean and neat girl. Her tear-stained face was swollen and puffy. Before they entered, Helena took her aside and said, "Charlie, is he dead?" she asked, knowing that he wasn't.

Her young sister replied, "No, but he may as well be. He doesn't remember me."

Helena giggled, which Charlotte had not expected. Her eldest sister said, "You have a unique opportunity, sister dear. Not many get to fall in love with the same man twice. George may not remember you, but you still love him. Is he worth fighting for?"

Charlotte nodded.

Helena continued, "Then fight for him. Be the woman he needs you to be. Stand by him for better or for worse. It's what marriage is all about. I was sleeping in a doorway when I met Crispin. I thought life couldn't get any worse for me, but then I was attacked, arrested, convicted, and then sent here. Crispin sold everything and followed me. He did it because he loved me. If you love George, he will need you more now than ever. Do things for all the boys, not just for George. Do things because they need to be done, not because you expect anything in return. But above all, try not to fuss over him. Men, on the whole, hate that. Having said that, do not ignore him. Go the extra mile, but know he probably won't even notice."

Charlotte nodded. She knew her sister's story and that she had served her time as a convict. "I'll try, but I don't know how to, Nella."

Using her pet name showed Helena that she had touched a soft spot in her little sister. "You won't be alone, but don't try to do everything at once. Be in the shadows rather than in his face. He fell in love with you once; he'll do it again. Just give him a chance." She tucked her arm around her sister's shoulders, and they entered the church. "Your strawberries and cream hair and big blue eyes captured him once; I'm sure they will again. Don't push him."

Charlotte nodded as she walked. Her heart was a little lighter.

After the service, Linus, Ben, and Quinn went to collect George from the hospital. Everyone else waited impatiently under the trees at the church. The heat was building again, and the nerves were showing on Charlotte's face.

George had healed to the point where he looked normal. The welts were entirely gone, and although his sunburn was still peeling, it was progressing well towards healing. He felt nervous in case he became overwhelmed by a large group of strangers.

Agnes had warned everyone not to overcrowd him with well-wishes upon his arrival. They waited for most of the congregation to leave before allowing the children to run around on the church lawn. They were not permitted to make much noise or kick a ball, but the exuberance of so many children needed an outlet. Even the stern reverend suggested that they be allowed to play on the grass now that the rain had cleared.

As the wagon returned, a select group stood waiting to greet them. Charlotte was one of them. Agnes listened to her daughter breathe deeply and release. She did this three times before lifting her head slightly. "Mama, Nella told me this is the 'worse' before the 'better'. Now, I have to make him love me again."

Agnes smiled when she heard her daughter say to herself, "I can do this! I *can* do this." Charlotte stood and waited in the shade. She wanted to run to him, but he didn't need that. She had to do what was best for him, not her. What did he need?

The wagon pulled up next to the other three family vehicles. Each had baskets of food spread out and ready to be consumed.

The following hour, George greeted everyone as if they were strangers. He coped well but was keen to head home.

Quinn and Ben stayed near George and introduced him to the other three boys who lived with them. George shrank closer to Ben. Their faces rang no bells. Ben waved the boys away.

Quinn, Pete, Eric, and Wendell hovered nearby but didn't crowd him.

Charlotte handed him an empty plate, showed him where the food was set out, and left him to help himself after pointing to the corned beef slices and boiled eggs.

George murmured, "Thank you," and followed her to the food wagon.

She knew his favourite foods but left him to help himself. She stood back and let him make the decisions. Typically, she would have filled his plate, as Kath did for Ben, and then handed it to him while he was busy talking.

She already had her meal, so she wandered away and sat alone rather than ask him to sit with her.

The family group sat in silence, eating for a while.

Minutes later, he joined her, as did the five boys. George said, "Ben said I was rude about you. I'm sorry."

Charlotte was stunned. Not knowing exactly what to say, she admitted, "I deserved it. I fuss far too much. But may I ask, do you remember anything about that weekend?"

George shook his head. "I get flashes, a boat, the dogs barking, foul-tasting water." He shook his head to clear his memory, but it didn't work. "So, no, not really." He tucked into the meal.

Charlotte watched as he peeled two hard-boiled eggs, squashed them onto the bread, and covered them with a slice of corned beef. She had made him these open sandwiches many times over several months that they had been unofficially courting. It was one of the little quirks she adored about him. He sank his teeth into the open sandwich and chewed, emitting a groan of delight. Halfway through his meal, he froze. He grasped his head and groaned again, but this time with pain. As he had finished his mouthful, he said, "There were three of them." The food had triggered his memory. He had been thinking of this exact meal when he was stopped.

Charlotte asked, "Three of whom, George?"

He started panic-breathing, stressed. He was reliving the attack. Placing the plate beside him, he bent over and put his head in his hands. "They wanted the wagon. I gave it to them, and then one hit me." He fell to his knees. He moaned again, muttering "…three escaped convicts."

The moan he made sent Quinn to get Ben and Linus. They were not far away, but he said, "Come quick. He has remembered the attack."

~

Over the next two weeks, much of George's memory returned. He still had gaps, and one memory that did return was of his beloved instrument. He dared not touch it, fearful he had forgotten how to play.

A fortnight after his release from the hospital, he returned from the usual post-church picnic and sat in his room, gazing at the travelling chest that remained in pride of place in his bedroom. It was a link to home. After a while, he took out his violin. Instead of playing it, he tested the strings to see if they were still in tune. He was surprised that he knew what to do.

That evening, he sat outside in the twilight for over an hour and caressed his instrument without putting the bow to the strings. Fear ate at him. He tested the bow and gave the end a few turns to tighten the hairs.

Ben knew where he was and why. George had fled the boys' chatter to find solace under the stars. Eventually, the three younger lads took themselves off to bed. Quinn came and joined Ben on the back step.

The crickets and cicadas fell silent as the first haunting sound of the violin bow was drawn across the strings. Then, for the following hour, the most beautiful music emanated from the tanner's shed. *Romance No. 2 in F Major* by Beethoven was followed by *Chaconne* by J.S. Bach. Other tunes followed, but Ben had no idea what they were. It just sounded heavenly. The complexity of these pieces made Ben think that George was testing himself to see if he could still play. He had only heard one or two of these compositions before, but knew George's repertoire was far broader than he realised. His friend had lost none of his skills. Ben was awed that George could play these complex compositions from memory. The previous pieces he had played had been slow and melancholy. The two boys sat enthralled by the beautiful music.

The final slide of the bow at the end of the piece he had just played signalled for Ben to send Quinn to bed. He needed to have a chat with George, and he didn't want ears around. Knowing that George would need to enter via the back door, he stayed put on the back step. With the music silenced, an occasional chirp of a cricket broke the stillness of the evening. Eventually, the crunch of a twig signalled that George was approaching through the gloom.

Rather than move, Ben said, "Take a seat, my friend. We need to talk."

George did. The moon had just poked its head above the trees, and a dim light was spreading. He still cradled his beloved instrument, and Ben thought it was a good place to start.

He was about to say something when George said, "I thought I had forgotten how to play, Ben. I was too scared to touch it, and I realised that leaving it unplayed would not help me find out if I had forgotten my skill."

Ben chuckled. "Trust me, you haven't. I've never heard you play better. I don't even remember you playing one of those complex pieces before."

The silence hung like a noose between them. Ben knew he had to discuss Charlotte. She was hurting and needed to know where she stood with George. "Dear friend, we need to talk about Charlie."

George knew that but groaned. "I know, but Ben, I don't know what to do about her. Don't get me wrong, I like her, but how do I say I'm sorry for words I don't even remember saying?"

Ben jolted. "You still don't fully remember what happened?"

George shook his head and then realised Ben couldn't see him. "No, not really; I remember sitting on the riverbank and talking to you. I remember being mean, but not exactly what I said or even about who it was." He groaned, "Ahh! Why can't I remember? Why does my head feel like it's full of fluff? I have no recollection of Charlie at all. She is a complete blank."

Ben gently placed a hand on his friend's shoulder. "You've come a long way in three weeks. Please, don't push it. I'm sure it will come back to you in time. However, you must think about what you will do about Charlie."

George knew that. "I like her, I really do. I remember someone who used to be so chatty; I presume it was her. Now, she hardly says anything."

Ben swallowed nervously. "I think that's because she took your angry words to heart. Your words were hurtful, but my friend, it was how you said them. You told me, and I shall quote you, 'that she fussed far too much and never shut up,' so I think it's why she was so hurt. That, and the addition of you not being sure if you could live with that for the rest of your life."

Ben knew the conversation needed to be repeated so his friend could understand the hurt she was feeling. He told George precisely what he had said and what Charlotte had overheard. When he had mentioned it before, he had not told his friend how hurtful his words had been. George had almost spat out the comments with venom.

George remembered someone teasing children and dogs. The girl relished teasing the boys and her younger sisters. He was stunned to hear that it was Charlotte. He remembered a girl who was always the life and soul of the group, but often her antics went too far. George usually didn't mind, but she needed to grow up. Thinking back to the scraps of memory of the immature girl and his desire for a wife, he could not put the two together. If he were courting the naughty girl, he wasn't sure he could live with a wife who constantly annoyed everyone. Had he made an error in encouraging her? Emily and Rebecca were much quieter.

George thought about Charlotte now. He had seen her a few times over the past two weeks. The giggling girl was gone, and the teasing was absent. Even the dogs were now ignored by her. He knew it was time to have a long discussion with her. Could he fall in love with her again?

When he was in the hospital, he let his facial hair grow because shaving it hurt too much. His beard itched, but his moustache had filled out well, which surprised him. He decided to shave off the beard but leave the top lip for now, as there were a few scabs under it.

Chapter 14 The Way Forward

*T*he opportunity for a deep and meaningful conversation occurred only a few days after the boy's discussion on the back step.

George dressed in his best outfit and borrowed Ben's best hat. He felt he looked silly, but he knew he had to resolve the situation with Charlotte, so his feelings were irrelevant.

That week, he purchased a new horse and buggy and drove it to Rosedale's farm.

Linus greeted him with a smile, took the reins and flicked them over the hitching rail. "Are you staying for a meal?"

George smiled. "I'm not sure, sir. It depends on how a certain conversation goes."

Linus said, "I was wondering if that was why you had come. Have all the memories returned?"

George shook his head. "No, sir, at least not about her. But Ben has told me enough to know I must apologise to her."

Linus had his arm around the lad's shoulder. "I think you may find it works both ways, George. She's done a lot of thinking over these weeks, and she's changed. I'm not sure it's all for the better, but neither is it for the worse. She needed to grow up, and I think she has finally done so. I'm sure you can work it all out if you are willing."

George sighed. "I am willing, sir, but I feel we will need to get to know each other all over again."

Linus nodded. "That won't be a bad thing. This could be the means by which you both grow up. I have not been willing to permit her to marry, as she has not yet demonstrated the necessary maturity. Give it time, and thankfully, time is on your side, laddie. Neither of you is in a hurry. Get to know each other again and grow up together. Remember, she's only seventeen."

The men walked up onto the front steps of the verandah and were about to enter when they saw Charlotte disappear out the back door.

She had heard George's voice and felt she could not face the rejection she was sure would follow.

Linus sighed in frustration. He muttered, "Women!"

Agnes greeted George with the caring love she had always shown. After having given birth to fifteen children, George and the boys were drawn into the extended family. "Welcome, George. She just left."

George nodded. He knew that already. He remembered that these two people had almost replaced his parents, whom he missed dearly. He remembered his parents and brother before he had returned from the hospital, and saw the travelling chest. His breath caught in his throat when he saw that. Memories of their loss washed over him.

Crispin took him under his wing as a little brother, and George had spent the previous day in deep conversation with him. Cris had doled out the same advice his wife, Helena, had given Charlotte. "George, if this was the 'worse' in your relationship, then you are lucky. Most married members of the extended family have lost at least one child, as we have. Trust me, a small disagreement can strengthen, not break, a relationship. Talk to her, George. Open yourself to her and reveal your innermost thoughts, feelings, and wishes. It may hurt, but it will be worth it in the long run. Bottling up things only leaves grey areas. In your situation, she needs to understand exactly what you are thinking. Get your brain straight before you talk to her. Know your own emotions. Work out what you need. She is walking a tightrope and is sure you will call off the relationship."

George spent the evening after their meeting in deep thought and prayer. He realised that he wanted Charlotte, even if she did chatter. He had come to sort things out. George knew that some of the newer family members were orphans like them. Nick and Tris's wives, Rachel and Bek, had been Irish convicts, and both had lost babies before they met the boys. Their abuse on the ship had been horrific. The girls arrived battered and beaten. They both were recovering from difficult births, where the babies both died. The boys had been part of their healing as the girls learnt to trust again. In the years the girls had been on the farm, those four young people grew close and eventually married.

Agnes greeted George with a motherly hug. She pulled back from the embrace and said, "You've been through a rough time, love, but we're here for you. And that remains, even if things don't work out between you and Charlie. If you wish to see her, she's fled to her favourite log."

George hugged Agnes back. He needed that comfort. She reminded him so much of his mother, and her sage advice was always apt. He was stunned that he had remembered his parents and even his brother, Rob. Their faces flooded his memory, but he recalled little about Charlotte.

Fighting his unsteady emotions, he said, "Thanks, Mrs R., I'll go and find her."

Mrs Rosedale said to call her Agnes, but he could not bring himself to be so familiar with either of them. He and Ben shortened it to Mrs R.

With the tip of his hat and a nod of thanks to them both, he went to find his quarry. The door banged quietly behind him. He knew he was about to have one of the most critical conversations of his life, and he was as nervous as heck. He wandered down through the blackened back paddock and towards the stand of trees that escaped the ravages of fire. Sure enough, she was sitting on her log with her back to him. He gingerly approached and, when standing behind her, intentionally stepped on a twig. "Hi, Charlie! May I sit down?"

She gave a wan smile, followed by a nod, then moved to the end of the log.

George seated himself. "Charlie, I first wish to say I'm sorry for all the hurt I have caused you. I was wrong to say anything, and I'm not usually mean like that. I beg your forgiveness." He expected her to lash out at him as she usually did verbally. He remembered that much. He was stunned to see her remain sitting meekly and giving a nod. He heard her breath hitch. "Charlie, look at me, please."

She shook her head.

He saw a tear fall. "Charlie, love, don't be sad. I'm sorry I hurt you. Can't you bring yourself to forgive me? I want you so bad that it hurts."

This time, she gasped and looked up at him. Her red-rimmed eyes were pools of blue sadness. "You still want me? I thought you had come to tell me to leave you alone. I know I talk too much and tease everyone and the animals, but it's because I'm nervous." Her hand flew to her mouth. She was doing it again. George chuckled. It was not the reaction she expected.

He said, "It seems we must get to know what we each want. We are both young enough to change, and I want to grow old with you. Maybe a little less fussing, but I love your chatter. Charlie, I will be of age in less than two years. I know we have an understanding now, but I would like to officially court you rather than just the family knowing about us."

Her freckle-spotted, porcelain-like face broke into a beautiful grin. "You mean it? I haven't chased you away?"

George reached out for her hand. "No, dear, but we both need to grow up. We are still young, and we have much growing to do. But, sweet Charlie, I want to do that, growing with you beside me." His eyes dropped to where his thumb was caressing the back of her hand. A tear fell onto it, and he looked up to meet her gaze. "Charlie, can we go back and ask your Papa for permission now?"

She needed the truth. "Do you really want me? Or are you just being nice?"

He answered honestly. "I want you, Charlie, but I don't remember what we had. So, we'll need to start from scratch if that's okay." He was delighted that her head was nodding in agreement. "Charlie, I still don't remember much about that entire weekend. Don't hold that against me, please."

She smiled. "I won't. I nearly lost you; that's why I was fussing. I want to change. I want to grow old and wrinkly with you as well. I don't want to lose you again."

He released a long sigh of contentment. He continued with a chuckle. "I want to kiss you so much, but I won't until we have your papa's blessing."

A giggle followed the gasp she gave. "I've never been kissed, Georgie."

He sighed with delight. "Good, because I've never kissed anyone before either. At least, I don't think I have. We'll learn about that together, as well."

Rather than hook her hand through George's arm, she slid her hand down to hold his. They dawdled back to the house, stopping often to chat.

Permission was granted. Linus was thrilled that another child was settled, as he knew his life was drawing to a close. Agnes and his older children knew, but they kept his ill health from their younger daughters and the boys' household. Linus had fallen ill some years earlier, and his chest never fully recovered. He coughed a lot and now only pottered around his home garden. He knew he was living on borrowed time.

~

1811 to 1812

The following year, in August, the family banded together after the sudden loss of Linus Rosedale from a lung complaint. He had been unwell for most of the year.

Macarthur left the colony soon after making his promise to build Ben's house, so the extended family built his buildings and workshop on the outskirts of Penrith. Ben was not yet ready to move. He didn't wish to go into tanning hides in an area with no market for them. He knew that his newly acquired knowledge would enable him to work effectively with the leather. His focus was on saddlery. However, moving away meant that he would be completely alone. The outcome was that he and George entered into an official partnership.

Kath saw some leather carving in a shop in town and asked Ben to visit Richard Hunt in Parramatta so she could learn how to do it. Richard's family were about to leave the area and return to Sydney with his wife, Lydia and family. Although Richard would ply his trade in Sydney, he was closing the saddlery in Parramatta. The timing was perfect for the boys. Richard willingly taught both Kath and Charlotte the technique of his decorative craft. George discovered some of the required carving and embossing tools amongst his grandfather's old things that Miles had refused to accept. He had never known what they were for.

With the skills Ben taught George and Charlotte, they tanned their own leather and focused on making sidesaddles. Like Kath, Charlotte discovered the joys of decorating the kangaroo leather with inked designs and stamping or embossing them. However, amongst George's grandfather's tools, she also found some small implements that she used to slice the tanned hides into even, eighth-of-an-inch-wide strips or smaller. She took great delight in making this thonging so that when it was too wet to work outdoors, they would plait-weave the various styles of whips now sold in their small shop. These were exceptionally popular, as all other whips and crops were imported. Eight-ply plaited leather belts were also popular.

At the beginning of 1812, Governor Macquarie decided to hold a concert. This was to be a celebration of the change in the colony. New buildings were under construction, and there had been an amazing transformation of the colony since his arrival to quell the insurrection of the Rum Rebellion.

Gone were the bark hovels, the squalid conditions and the filthy streets in Sydney. Fires and age had dealt with many of them, but others were cleared to make room for permanent dwellings. Gone was the stench of the dirty water and streams. Wells were sunk, and community buildings were constructed. New buildings were cropping up everywhere, and the colony was growing fast. New barracks were built for the troops and convicts, and plans were underway for various new buildings, some of which were in different stages of construction throughout the area. New farmland was being cleared, and efforts were underway to eventually find a way across the Blue Mountains. Therefore, there was much to celebrate, and many wished to attend the concert. The only problem was that there was no suitable venue for such a performance in Parramatta.

The governor decided that the front lawn of the official residence was the only venue that would accommodate everyone, and the elevated hillock would serve as an amphitheatre. The concert was designed to reveal the hidden talents of those in the community.

Unbeknownst to everyone, Mark Duffy had discovered George's skill. When George mentioned the fiddle to Ben in the hospital, Mark realised there was a slight possibility that George was the mystery virtuoso. He knew the sounds came from that direction. When he asked about it, George's following silence confirmed his supposition.

Later questioning of Ben revealed that George was, indeed, the mysterious violinist. Many mentioned hearing hauntingly beautiful music in the stillness of a summer evening. If the breeze blew from the north on a summer evening, they could even hear it at Government House. Mark broached the subject by saying, "George, can you play for us? I know you can, as why would you have a fiddle with you otherwise?"

George nodded, but his mind was distracted. He wondered how much his friend knew, and he hoped not much. Charlotte had matured into a wonderful helpmate in the year since the attack. George knew it was time for him to propose. He received permission to propose to her shortly before her father died. Linus had called George in to see him while he was bedridden. He gave his blessing on their union when George was ready.

Agnes knew, and George was waiting for the opportunity.

Charlotte was now nineteen, and he was nearly twenty-one. The concert would be a perfect opportunity, but he was unsure whether to do it privately or in full view of everyone. He would think about whether the time was right. He eventually replied. "Yes, Mark, I will do it, but can I be put on last and play the finale?"

Mark grinned. "I'm doing the programme so I can manage that. Any idea what you will play?"

George nodded. "Um, yes; as it is on Sunday night, I thought of a hymn duet with Charlotte. What about 'When I survey the wondrous cross'? Charlotte will sing it as I play."

Mark was delighted. "I shall add it as 'hymn finale' and leave it ambiguous. How about that? There are a few other appropriate items to satisfy Reverend Marsden. He objected to holding the concert on the Sabbath, but he said he would approve if some hymns and the like were added."

As the evening concert drew closer, Charlotte and George practised secretly at the boys' house. The occupants were aware of George's skill, but Kath was sworn to secrecy. While Kath was at their home, they chaperoned each other, but the girls were not allowed to stay overnight.

For weeks, they rehearsed until they felt they were ready. Charlotte had a beautiful voice, and she sang her heart out. Her face glowed with happiness. However, she needed to know the words by heart as there would be no lights for the performance.

Agnes had suggested to George that Charlotte would cope well with a public proposal, so his mind was made up to do it that evening.

The concert started after a noon picnic. Everyone brought their food and drinks and sat on the grassy slope to eat and share their feasts. At three o'clock, the governor opened the concert. The Reverend Marsden said a prayer, and then the first entertainer took the stage.

As performers moved from their positions, one by one, they entertained the masses. Participants ranged from playing a gum leaf to an amateur opera singer. Singers, flautists, and poets recited their compositions. There were ballads of the bush and Irish convicts singing some songs from home. A bagpiper made many an eye glisten and heartbeat faster with his excellent rendition of a collection of songs from Scotland.

The governor and his wife had their eyes glistening with memories of their beloved Scottish soft, misty rains. The loudest cheer for the piper's skill came from the small portico where the Governor and Mrs Macquarie sat. He called for an encore, which the piper was delighted to do. 'Scotland the Brave' echoed over the town, followed by the 'Skye Boat Song.'

As the evening approached, the performances were getting somewhat risqué and almost groan-worthy. The reverend had been called away. In his absence, the convicts and soldiers swallowed their fear of flogging and offered some impromptu performances.

Eventually, Mark gave George and Charlotte the nod to take their places. Their hymn was the last item on the program. The concert lasted four hours, and the crowd was preparing to pack up and head home for dinner.

When George moved to his place, the sun had reached the horizon. There was sufficient light to see, but summer darkness would quickly envelop the stage area. Twilight in this land passed quickly.

As she walked on stage, George heard her say, "I can do this!" Charlotte took centre stage with George standing off to the side. She stood meekly until the first notes of the beloved hymn silenced the multitude. Rather than acknowledging the crowd, she dropped her head and waited. Her voice began somewhat nervously. She sang

When I survey the wondrous cross…

Her voice was shaky.

One man from the gathered convicts yelled for her to sing louder. He was booed to be quiet.

George saw her lift her head in defiance of the jeers, but did as he requested.

On which the Prince of Glory died,
My richest gain I count, but loss,
And pour contempt on all my pride.

The depth of her contralto voice floated over the audience as she continued with the first verse. The hymn was sung with love.

George stepped closer at the end of the first verse.

Forbid it, Lord, that I should boast,
Save in the death of Christ my God:
All the vain things that charm me most,
I sacrifice them to His blood.

By the third verse, George could hear an occasional sniff from those near him. The audience once again settled on the grassy slope. All thoughts of leaving were forgotten. Isaac Watts's words hit home. There were no more jeers.

Mark was not watching Charlotte, but George. Even for a reasonably simple hymn, George's fingers caressed the strings, and the vibrato of the notes added depth to the music that astounded him. He even double-stopped some of the notes. His incredible skill added depth and meaning to the spiritual music. He made it sound like there were two instruments.

During the Macquaries' visits to the tannery and the Rosedales, they discovered the depth of faith in the vice-regal couple. George's choice of a hymn was not hard. However, tonight, he decided not only to propose to Charlotte in front of everyone but also to serenade her with a romantic violin solo beforehand. Tonight, his secret would be revealed. The town would find out who the mystery violinist was.

Charlotte sang her heart out for the last three verses. As she sang, she didn't just stand in front of everyone, but acted out the words. Tears glistened on her cheeks as she sang the well-loved lyrics of the beautiful hymn. Others joined in softly. A magical murmur of voices joined her.

See from His head, His hands, His feet,
Sorrow and love flow mingled down!
Did e'er such love and sorrow meet,

Or thorns compose so rich a crown?

His dying crimson, like a robe,
Spreads o'er His body on the tree;
Then I am dead to all the globe,
And all the globe is dead to me.

Were the whole realm of nature mine,
That were a present far too small;
Love so amazing, so divine,
Demands my soul, my life, my all.

Sobs were heard from those close enough to see her actions.

As she sang the last line, George walked behind her and dropped to one knee. He had her ring on his little finger, ready to offer it to her. He was sure she would say "Yes," as long as she was not too embarrassed.

Charlotte was aware that he had drawn close, but did not know why the audience was gasping until she turned and saw George's stance.

The grin on his face made her giggle. He had not put his instrument down, but now held the bow in the same hand as his fiddle. He offered the ring to her with his free hand.

George's words were for her ears only, but everyone could see what he asked her. "Will you marry me, Charlie? I need you to make harmony with me as we fit together like a violin and bow."

With her hands clasped at her chin in delight, she nodded her reply. "Yes, of course, I will, you wonderful man."

He took her outstretched hand and kissed it, then slid on the ring, and she placed her palm on his cheek and caressed it with her thumb.

Although George wanted to draw her into his arms for a big kiss, he couldn't. Even in this convict-stained town, he must do as society demanded.

However, the crowd erupted in a huge cheer.

But George wasn't done...

He didn't leave the stage, but stood and took a position next to Charlotte. He tucked his violin under his chin.

Tonight, everyone would know how he felt about her. He would play for her in front of everyone. His anonymity would be shattered.

As he had finished the hymn, rather than the stage area being enshrouded in darkness, Mark and a team of soldiers lit oil lamps around them, and the soft glow of the lamps made the evening almost magical. Mark knew that this man was no ordinary fiddler. He hoped tonight that he would share his talent.

The audience waited breathlessly. They realised George was not finished.

The first piece that George played was an original composition that brought tears to the eyes of everyone there. He had written this piece and poured his heart into it, especially for Charlotte. It started slowly and held a melancholy tone, but then moved to a joyous melody of love.

She listened in rapt awe. As he played each movement, the story of their love was clear to anyone who listened.

The light was fading fast, and as the moon rose above their heads, his violin sang as the crowd wept. A rapturous round of applause rolled across the listeners as he lifted his bow to play again.

Knowing that this next piece was Ben's favourite music, George struck up the notes of the *Hallelujah Chorus* from Handel's Messiah.

He heard Ben's loud cheer. "Yeah, you're playing my song!"

This was followed by a rendition of *Romance No. 2 in F Major* by Beethoven, then *Air on the G String* by Bach, and *Divertimenti Carnevaleschi, No. 1,* by Paganini. This piece was written for an instrument made by the same maker as George's. George followed that with another Beethoven piece, the beloved *Moonlight Sonata,* to bring the evening to a close. The moon had fully risen, so the timing was perfect. More than half an hour had passed since he proposed. Many were familiar with this music and were moved to tears.

Mark had undoubtedly kept the best for last.

George was no fiddler but a concert violinist. As he pulled his bow across the strings for the final notes, the hillside erupted in rapturous applause, and many rose and gave him a standing ovation.

George felt like singing, not for the adulation, but because Charlotte was his. He had had a wonderful evening. He was ready to leave the stage and kiss Charlotte. However, the evening was not over.

From up on the top of the hill, the Scottish voice of the governor called for an encore. He yelled, "Do not think you shall escape that easily, George Ellis! We want more, laddie! Encore!"

The masses took up the call.

"Encore!" "Encore!" "Encore!"

George bowed. "I will play a new piece written for an instrument by the same maker as this. *Caprices* by Paganini is a complex fingering work I do to exercise." He drew a deep breath and settled the rosy instrument under his chin. The complex double and triple stopping, as well as left-hand pizzicato and spiccato bowing, left the uneducated audience astounded. Those who lived close to him had heard this on a still evening as he warmed up.

Mark had attended many concerts in London as a child, but he had never heard anyone as skilled as George Ellis. His jaw dropped open as he watched the speed with which George's fingers moved.

The crowd stood and applauded, still calling for more.

With another bow to the crowd, George tucked his red fiddle to his neck again, and with his head lifted, he thanked God. He then dropped his chin and played an abbreviated version of Vivaldi's *Four Seasons.* His rendition lasted only twelve minutes, rather than the forty-two minutes required for the complete piece. George could have heard a pin drop during his performance if he had listened, but his eyes remained fixed on Charlotte. His music was for her. He was unaware of the hundreds of people listening, spellbound, to his love of music and the strawberry-blond girl who had promised to be his wife.

Once more, the crickets and cicadas were silenced. Babies were lulled to sleep, and many a handkerchief was used to mop away tears.

Mark's jaw had dropped as George played the first of the classical pieces. He was stunned by the unassuming virtuoso who performed so magnificently. He had never heard a better performance. Having spent his childhood in Covent Garden, London, he had attended many concerts. None held a candle to this man. Mark's eyes were fixed on George, but George's gaze never wavered from Charlotte's glowing face. He played for her and only for her. Charlotte was serenaded with the most beautiful music the colony had ever heard. The deep timbre of the Guarneri violin made the hearts of the most brutal criminals melt. The haunting notes of the superbly played instrument floated across the evening air and echoed through the town. Even those locked in cells at the gaol sat back and listened.

As the final notes drifted away on the evening breeze, the magical performance held the audience spellbound for some moments. George ushered Charlotte from the stage and disappeared into the darkness before anyone realised they had gone. As George passed Mark, he shoved his violin and the bow at him. "Mark, hold this for me, will you?"

"Sure, I'll take it inside to keep it safe." Mark knew that as Master of Ceremonies, he still needed to close the evening, but he planned to prolong his final speech as much as possible. He was aware that the young man, in particular, would be overwhelmed once the night drew to a close. He allowed them time to leave. Mark returned to the stage, holding the valuable instrument. To give the happy couple more time, he spoke at length about the well-known, mysterious melodies carried on the breeze during many summer evenings. He raised the precious instrument high for the crowd before him.

Someone in the audience called out. "Do you mean to say that that music we've heard some nights is the young tanner?"

Mark gave a bow of acknowledgement. "That it is, my good friend, and played on this very instrument. This fiddle was his grandfather's, and he learned to play as a boy. As his secret is now out, I dare say we will hear more of the tanner's songs in future concerts. His friend, Ben, the saddler, has already claimed the *Hallelujah Chorus,* as you heard. However, I beg you to remember that George puts as much love into his leatherwork as he does into his music. Consider this when you appreciate the sheen of your new saddle or the weave of your new whip. Ben Parker is soon heading out to Emu Ford along the river, but will remain in partnership with George. Our land will produce saddles of the best quality from the unique hides of the kangaroo. One day, it may even seat a monarch."

Governor Macquarie heard the audience gasp, but he was now watching a dramatic performance that the audience was unaware was occurring. Sitting in such an elevated position, the governor and his party watched as the young couple fled around the side of the hill. The moonlight lit their path. Lachlan's gaze followed the movements of the young violinist as he dropped to one knee again and asked her to marry him in private. She no longer had the pressure to reply. Lachlan chuckled as he saw Charlotte all but throw herself at the tanner. They stood in a shaft of moonlight. He hoped that Reverend Marsden was not watching them, but he knew the joys of young love all too well. He had lost his beloved first wife, Jane, to illness, but then found love again with his cousin, Elizabeth Campbell.

Lachlan leaned over and nudged his wife. "Look, down there, Elspeth." He lifted his chin and pointed with his nose, as he didn't wish to draw attention to them. They watched as George pulled Charlotte into his arms and then kissed her. Few others knew where they went, as their eyes were still on Mark. Lachlan leaned across to his wife and said, "We missed out on the young love, Elspeth, but I do hope you know my affection for you is equally as strong."

Elizabeth squeezed his hand and softly said, "Mine too, Lachy. Later…" He grinned, knowing how their night would end.

Cathy Duffy stood behind the couple, her two older children, Josh and Jenny, on either side of her, and her seven-month-old baby, Gideon, whom she held in her arms. She was already carrying their second child but had not told anyone but Mark. Her eyes followed the direction of the young folk in front of her. She watched the couple remain in a tight embrace. Her eyes turned back to her husband on the stage.

Both Mark and Cathy grew up near Covent Garden in London. When she was a child and later a newlywed teenager, she would sit and listen to the arias and cantatas performed in the Covent Garden concert hall. Mark confessed that he did the same. Tonight's performance returned her to those happy times with her first husband, James, the father of Josh and Jenny. Memories of her beloved James rarely surfaced as life with Mark was safe and secure. After James was murdered and then Josh was arrested a few months later, she thought her life was over. She had used the money Josh had stolen to follow his convict ship. On the boat here, she met a red-coated soldier as she boarded. They married three months later in Cape Town.

Mark left the stage, so Cathy watched the young couple who were so obviously in love. Their life was just about to change. She sighed with happiness at how her life had turned out. From absolute poverty and a life of hell, she now had a home, hearth, and a secure future. Tomorrow, they were to move to establish the new toll gate in Parramatta. Mark was a Godly man who willingly accepted her two older children. She caught movement off to the side and saw Mark walking up the edge of the crowd. He was trying to reach her before the seething mass of humanity started surging towards the exit gate of the official residence. She knew she had to get everyone indoors quickly. This was Mark's final official duty before they were to leave this life and take over running the new tollgate in Pitt Row. They would have their first home together. Josh was to remain at Government House as the head groom. He would be trained to take over the tollgate in the years to come, but he had years to grow and learn. First, he needed to serve his term as a convict. In the meantime, he formed a close bond of friendship with the governor. Josh found the father figure that he needed in this regal gentleman. Hopefully, one day, Mark would fill that role, but sixteen was an awkward age at any time. For Josh, his world turned upside down far too quickly. She felt her heart skip a beat as Mark drew near with the violin in hand. Their son wiggled as Mark arrived at her side.

He bent and kissed them both quickly. He said, "What an incredible finale! I think the town will remember this for many years to come." He lifted the instrument case and said, "I shall stow this carefully before the crush occurs. I have no doubt we shall soon be inundated." He had seen where George had placed the case when he arrived and placed the instrument in it.

Lachlan said, "Put it on my desk, Mark. It will be safe there."

"I will, thank you, sir." Mark vanished inside, and Cathy and the group followed. George entrusting his violin to Mark showed two things. First, he trusted Mark, and second, he loved Charlotte more than this instrument.

As they moved indoors, the discussion turned to the instrument. Elizabeth Macquarie was well aware of the value of these violins. She said a Guarneri violin was more valuable than a Stradivarius instrument.

Mark did not understand the value, except that the music it made turned his heart to mush. He slid his arm around Cathy's shoulder and dropped a kiss on her lips.

After the night's performance, Lachlan knew George could have made his fortune in the world's concert halls. Instead, he worked as a lowly tanner with a saddler on the outskirts of Parramatta. Lachlan would ensure this lad had a fine future.

Chapter 15 Family Stick Together

*K*ath and Ben married a few months after the concert. Kath's eldest brother, Gerry, walked her down the aisle.

Everyone dearly missed Linus. Rather than leave the boys' house and start out on their own, the young couple decided to remain until Ben thought the Penrith area was large enough to require a full-time saddler.

Life at the boys' house settled into a new routine. Kath's presence meant the four younger lads had to use the manners Ben and George had taught them. Meals were at the table, and they had to use the cutlery properly.

~

At the end of summer, about fourteen months after the concert, George and Charlotte finally married. Charlotte said that now that she had grown up, she didn't want to be called Charlie anymore.

The governor and Mrs. Macquarie had attended their wedding, as did the Duffy family. The wedding feast was held at Rosedale's farm, and the elderly Bennelong, Boorong, and the rest of the tribe were invited.

By the time of their wedding, Kath and Ben had been married for over a year. Each month that passed, Kath's monthly flow brought more tears. Charlotte conceived reasonably quickly, but she lost the baby six months after their wedding. She had never liked spiders, and when bringing in the washing one afternoon, a huge one crawled up her arm, around her neck and sat on her other arm. The creature was so large that its legs overlapped as it circled her upper arm. Her bloodcurdling scream brought George, Quinn, and Eric at a run.

George flicked off the offending beast, and the two boys despatched it. Charlotte collapsed, and George carried her to bed. She was four months along, and the baby should have been safe, but the shock of seeing the spider caused her to miscarry that night.

When her bleeding started, panic set in, and Agnes was fetched. There was nothing anyone could do, and Charlotte lost the baby.

Agnes stayed with them for two weeks. Her mother explained to the household that Charlotte would experience much moodiness and weeping after such a loss.

George wondered if they were being punished for something.

Crispin took him aside and explained that that was not how God works. "George, Linus spoke to you about the creation story and what happened in the Garden of Eden. I shall tell you what Reverend Richard Johnston told me when we lost our little one. He said that sin entered the world at the time of the Fall. That's when Satan tempted Adam and Eve, and they succumbed to his lies. It is not through any fault of our own that bad things happen, but rather, they are a consequence of what happened so long ago. Because of the Fall, sin dwells in the world, and bad things like this happen. Trust that God will receive the glory; I believe you will hold healthy children in your arms, just as we have, but it will be in His time. I have said the same thing to Ben and Kath."

George hurt. He had been sorry for Ben before, but now he understood the depth of his sorrow.

Having Agnes at hand had been a Godsend for the household as Charlotte curled up into a ball and wept a lot.

Kath hid as much as she could because she had not even conceived.

Lachlan brought Elizabeth to visit the grieving couple. They, too, had lost numerous children to miscarriage and knew the pain of such a devastating loss. Their first child, a girl named Jane, died when she was only a few months old. They had some stillbirths and were still childless. Charlotte and Elizabeth wept together and discussed the grief of such a loss.

Months later, Kath and Charlotte had still not conceived.

~

After eighteen months of marriage, Kath finally missed a flow. Her entire manner changed, and although coping with the household chores, she glowed. However, her confinement was extremely difficult. The morning sickness set in early and remained throughout the entire confinement. Agnes and Helena attended the birth, but Ben and Kath's perfect son was stillborn.

The loss of their baby boy hit all of them hard. The young couple found living in a house full of young boys was difficult. Their home on the river awaited them. Ben knew they should move, but here they had support.

Charlotte and George discussed the names of their children before they married. Their first son would be Albert, after George's father, and if they were blessed with a second son, he would be Robert, after George's brother. However, they discovered that the blessing of children didn't always happen easily.

By the end of 1814, Kath and Charlotte found solace in each other's company. Elizabeth Macquarie finally gave birth to a living child, but Charlotte did not conceive again that year ...or the next.

All three women had experienced deep grief from the loss of babies.

Neither Rosedale girl had a child to cradle, and both felt the emptiness of their arms and hearts.

~

For another year, the sisters continued to grieve.

Elizabeth Macquarie was a regular visitor. She usually came alone, but sometimes, she brought a friend. Today, she was accompanied by new friends. The lady, Katy White, was a convict, but her husband was not. Today, Perry White escorted the ladies because he wanted to meet George and watch him work. The three ladies remained indoors for tea while Perry went to watch George and Quinn work.

Lachlan had sent advance notice to the Ellis's about their new friends, and the message carried a warning. Perry White was severely burned, and half his face was melted and grievously distorted. He was even more horrifically scarred than Greg at the hospital. It was as well that the governor forewarned them, as the man's arrival caused the household to gasp.

Perry walked to the backyard to watch Quinn and George work. "Mr. Ellis, I hope you do not object to an audience. I am intrigued by how leather is made."

George had been scudding a hide, and thankfully, was not too dirty. He held out his hand to the visitor. "Mr. White, you are welcome. However, I do ask that you call me George."

The visitor nodded. "Thank you, George. Then, please call me Perry." He looked around for a perch and noticed a slab bench off to the side. "May I sit here and watch?"

George grinned. "You certainly can, sir; sorry, Perry." George returned to his work and explained the tanning process. "What I'm doing now is working both sides of the skin. However, before I do this, the first treatment is salting, and then I need to remove the fat from the underside of the pelt. How long I leave it salting depends on whether I wish the hair or fur to stay on. I have found that a day is long enough with the roo skins. Their fur is much softer than a bristly cowhide, so it comes off easily." His spiel about the tanning process was occasionally interrupted by an intelligent question or six from Perry.

Perry really did wish to know about the work. He plied George about his skills. After a while, he asked, "George, where does dog poop come into the process? You have not mentioned it, but I have heard at home that it is integral to making leather flexible."

George replied with a chuckle. "I was a pure collector for my father when I was a lad. That's what you call dog poop collecting. We certainly used the foul commodity until I was on my way out in 1808. We stopped off in Cape Town to resupply. Ben and I were taken on a tour of a local tannery. They used a different process, and it's a lot less smelly."

As he was talking, he beckoned Perry to follow him. He walked to a small keg off to the side. A loose-fitting lid was removed, and a gooey substance nearly filled the container. "This is a mixture of vegetable slurry from damaged crops from the various family farms, mixed with clarified animal fat. In essence, it is unprocessed dog poop. It works brilliantly and doesn't stink nearly as much. I used to retch whenever I had to do that tanning stage. I now buy the suet fat from the butcher and clarify it. As both the soap and candle-making industries continue to grow, I'm finding that I need to order my supplies well in advance. I make up a big tub of this mixture and ensure that I order more suet when I get halfway down my bucket. This is the end product."

Perry gave George his lovely lopsided grin. "So, no doggie poop anymore."

"Nope," said George gleefully. "And I hope I never need to use the wretched stuff again." He looked up and saw his wife approaching. He said, "I think Charlotte would throw me out if I came in smelling like I used to."

Charlotte brought out a tray of mugs filled with hot, sweet tea and slices of cake and left George to bring in the tray when it was empty.

Quinn was parched and joined them as they sat on the bench. The other three lads took their beverages back to their work areas.

Perry and the boys devoured their delicious treat.

This visit from Perry was the first of many such sessions.

~

On subsequent trips, Perry pumped Quinn for his story. He had seen other street urchins in town, and he knew they were having a tough time. He wondered how he could help them. Lachlan was in the process of building a girls' orphanage in Parramatta, and after his conversation with Quinn, he suggested that Lachlan use the old girls' home in Sydney as a boys' orphanage and school.

Over the following months, Perry and Katy often arrived unannounced and helped where they could. Perry would come dressed in work clothes and help with whatever the boys were doing.

Charlotte adored Katy, and the two had become fast friends. Kath held her at arm's length but often sat and listened.

Katy had also lost her first child, and this was one of the reasons she was here. She mentioned to Charlotte that she believed their dead children would be in Heaven, and they would be awaiting them there.

Charlotte needed to hear that. "Oh, Katy, do you really believe that?" Tears of loss trailed down Charlotte's cheeks.

Katy moved to sit beside her new friend. "I do, dear girl. I believe that wholeheartedly. Those little ones are pure and innocent of the evils of this world. I am sure our Lord has them safe in His care already. I said the same thing to Elizabeth Macquarie."

Charlotte wept for a while before a smile eventually appeared on her lips. "I think I can cope with that, Katy, but I so wish to have a child for George." She looked up shyly and added, "For me, too, of course. I do so crave a baby, and so does Kath." Kath nodded. She had surreptitiously wiped away a tear or two. Was her son really alive in heaven?

It was eighteen months before Charlotte and Kath conceived again. However, midyear, Charlotte fell as she hung the washing and hit her head on a flagstone, knocking herself out. Kath was visiting Agnes, so Charlotte had been alone. Ben, George and Quinn had been at the markets with the boys. When George found her on his return, she had been on the ground for hours.

She ran a fever for a week and delivered their stillborn child prematurely. Charlotte refused to rise from her bed. Having Kath nearby in the last stages of her confinement made things awkward for everyone.

A month later, Kath delivered another stillborn baby.

This little girl was also perfect, and Kath had felt her moving until the day she was born. The baby arrived with the cord wrapped tightly around her neck. The two girls consoled each other. Ben was pleased they had not yet moved. To say the family was shattered was an understatement.

They all needed a break. As soon as Kath was well enough, they packed for a holiday at the empty river house.

George left Quinn in charge of the business to spend a week with Kath and Ben at the empty house near Penrith. They took bedding as it was still unfurnished. They planned to build some shelving and storage in Ben's workshop. George packed his fiddle and hoped to sit with Ben on the riverbank, playing for him.

As the business picked up, George played his violin less often. They missed the closeness of the music they all loved. Ben needed more leather for his saddles, and George struggled to keep up with the demand. More helpers were needed. The summer evenings melted into autumn, and as the evenings cooled, they sat on the wide verandah. George played for them all. The two couples were hurting, and the melancholy music eased their pain.

After ten days of refreshment, they returned home to try again.

Agnes was always available for the girls, and she was kept busy with the arrival of numerous other children. All the young couples were having babies. Nick and Rachel, Tris and Bek, Margaret and Harry, Patience and Algernon, and Vicky and Bill Felton produced numerous children. Grandmother Agnes was kept occupied, but all knew of her loneliness. Emily was recently married, so she expected more children to arrive soon.

Many of Agnes's daughters lived nearby, but Kath and Charlotte withdrew from the family when the households gathered. They struggled with their losses and turned to each other in their grief.

~

In 1818, Charlotte conceived their third child. This time, George asked the governor to assign a convict maid to them to assist Charlotte and serve as a companion. He did not want her unattended, even for a moment.

The seventeen-year-old girl who arrived was a convict who had been vilely abused and was very timid. Her name was Willow with no last name. Charlotte adored her. The girls worked together on all the household chores. Charlotte's laugh once again sounded through the house, and she set to work on decorating some of the leather.

Charlotte taught her new companion to cook. She refused to call her a maid and treated her as a friend. Willow would prepare food for them all. She loved the safety of the kitchen, and having come from the slums in the Rookeries in London, where Mark and Cathy Duffy had grown up, the food she now had access to was a delight. Cathy Duffy came to meet the girl from home shortly before they moved to their new shop near Camden. Their backgrounds were disturbingly similar.

Charlotte discovered that after Willow's adoptive mother died, her adoptive stepfather violated her from when she was six until she turned twelve. Then he sold poor Willow to a madam. He got rid of her, having found another young girl for himself. The madam who bought Willow pimped her out to various gentlemen of society who liked their girls very young.

It took more questions before Charlotte discovered the origin of her name. Willow wiped a tear away with her knuckle. She shook her head and replied. "I was an unwanted baby, and I was found under a willow tree on the banks of the Thames River. No one knew who I was, but I suppose my mother wanted me alive as she could have thrown me in the river." Willow told how happy she had been with the couple who found her, but added, "Sadly, my adoptive father died when I was five, and my adoptive mother remarried a few months later. Less than a year later, she was dead, as well." She sniffed. "I'm sure he killed her as he had tried to get to me earlier, and she stopped him."

Charlotte enfolded her into her arms. "You are safe here, sweet girl."

Willow lifted her tear-stained face to Charlotte. "Can I tell you the rest because I want you to know? It's why I'm here." Charlotte nodded. Willow continued her saga. "Well, one man, I found out he was a baron; he liked things rough and hurt me real bad. He wanted me again the next week, but I was still sick from his last visit. He forced himself into my bed. He used me then, as he got off me, I fought back. I pushed him away with both feet, and he fell and hit his head. Mrs Simmons couldn't wake him and had to call a doctor. Because I had hit a peer of the realm and knocked him out, I was arrested." She sniffed and wiped her hand under her nose.

"As sick as I was, the doctor got the Bow Street Runners onto me, and I was taken to Newgate, sentenced, and transported. Life there wasn't good, but not much worse than what I had left. At least I was locked up with women. A lady called Elizabeth Fry had the gaolers leave us alone. These matrons are now looking after the women. But the men gaolers still used to take their fill. I was ever so pleased to see the back of that place. The gaol here seemed like heaven on earth in comparison. I was only there for a week before I got sent here. I was right fearful when I found I was coming to a house full of men."

Charlotte enfolded the poor lass into the biggest hug she had ever had. Tears flowed, but they were tears of happiness. Willow had found a refuge and safety with the Ellis's and settled into her forever home.

~

After losing her first two confinements, Charlotte finally managed to carry a baby to term. Albert George Ellis was born in mid-May 1819.

For the first time, Kath was jealous, and she didn't want to have anything to do with Charlotte. Tension in the house could be cut with a knife. Bertie's constant crying didn't make life any easier.

When Ben heard the news of the live arrival, he half-heartedly congratulated George. For George to have a son was wonderful, but he had no children at all. He and Kath had lost two full-term babies. Even though their house was ready and had been for ages, it had only been used occasionally for holidays. Ben had not moved earlier as Penrith and the surrounding areas were not big enough to support a full-time saddler. However, with the crossing of the Blue Mountains, the growth and development of the foothills had now made the move viable. Their new house beckoned them, and they planned to set up a new branch of the business. A new inn was being constructed across the river.

George tried to delay the move, but Ben was adamant. He had delayed long enough. Ben knew that he had to get Kath away.

Ben, Kath, Pete and Wendell finally moved into their home and set up the new branch of the business.

The two younger boys, Pete and Wendell, went to help Ben set up the workshop, but they planned to remain with the Parkers. They had become skilled in saddlery and loved the work, but this was only the first step towards their future. Ben and George had trained the boys to start their own saddlery, including keeping the books balanced, and this was the beginning. They had dreams of crossing the mountains and starting their businesses. This was something they had never thought possible until George took them in.

Quinn, Ben, and George had built the lads a small cottage behind the saddlers' workshop. They only slept there as they ate their meals with Kath and Ben in the main house. The hut had a small hob stove, but it was for warmth. It usually had a kettle of water boiling for the never-ending tea everyone in the colony consumed.

The boat now had its own boathouse and a slip for easy access to the river. The three young men often took it out on the waterway, and it had never tipped over again. Ben realised that only George standing up and unbalancing it was the problem.

The house and business were located on the banks of the Nepean River, near the junction with the Hawkesbury River at Castlereagh. It was a pleasant walk to Penrith. The two rivers were the same body of water, with a shallow section separating them, except during times of flood. Decades earlier, both rivers had been named without realising they were the same body of water. One flowed east-west and the other north-south, hence the confusion.

To recover from the loss of their last child, Kath put her skills to good use and decorated the saddles that Ben made.

Ben purchased his tanned leather from George as part of their business arrangement. His top-quality saddles were a high-priced commodity, and he and the boys found that their English saddles were in high demand.

However, George's skills surpassed Ben's in terms of side saddles, something Ben didn't mind at all. They were fiddly and didn't have as much need for them that far west.

Quinn made their side saddle trees out of the beautiful red cedar, while Pete and Wendell made Ben's from more sturdy gum or black pine timber. Ben would not swap timbers, as he considered the gum to be more durable. The cedar was strong and exceptionally light. Therefore, so as not to tread on each other's businesses, George focused on the ladies' saddles and leather whips while Ben made the military and stock saddles.

Ben used traditional bovine leather for his saddles, while George preferred the roo-hides and even made a couple of ridiculously small racing saddles and traditional English saddles.

Ben laughed at him; however, all varieties sold quickly.

George's whips were popular. He perfected the crops and the poppers on the end in various stunning African hides, adding something to the style that no one else had supplied. He also made carriage and stock whips that gave an earsplitting crack when expertly flicked.

Charlotte loved using her small strap-cutting tool to cut the tanned hides. She expertly shredded the damaged leather and wound the long lengths into balls. From these, George wove the whips.

Kangaroo skin was perfect for these lightweight items, and the red-tanned hides were so strong and flexible that they coped with a lot of stress and movement as the saddle was ridden. Because these hides did not need to be thinned, their strength was far superior to that of cowhide.

~

By the time baby Albert arrived, Quinn and Willow were courting.

Shortly after Charlotte's fall and the loss of their second child, Eric moved south near the Duffys' new store to start his own leather tannery.

Life was changing, and Kath refused to come to see the family, no matter what the celebration. The Parkers shunned all visitors.

Quinn stayed close to his adopted brother, which is how he saw George. He was saddened that his group of friends had separated. As all could read and write, mail was delivered quickly. He extracted promises for at least a monthly update from each of them. George was unsure if Quinn intended to leave with Eric, but when Willow arrived, all thoughts of his departure fled. Quinn was besotted.

With the baby's arrival, Charlotte's bubbly attitude to life returned. Her laughter was a delight to George's ears. It was he who started calling their son Bertie.

In the years since the identity-revealing concert, other performances had followed. George was often asked to play at a concert or some official function and frequently did the finale, followed by the now-usual encores. Trips to Sydney were made occasionally when an important function was held. The Ellis's were happy. Business was good, Bertie was healthy, and the young couple were as in love as ever.

Ben and Kath, however, grew further away from everyone. The arrival of Bertie had built an almost insurmountable wall between them.

Ben had not issued any invitations for visits. George and Charlotte dared not visit uninvited. Quinn made the deliveries and brought orders.

~

In early 1820, Governor Macquarie called in to see George. He wanted a birthday gift for his wife, and a new side saddle was what he had decided upon.

By now, Mark and Cathy Duffy had moved to Camden to set up a government store, and Cathy's older children, Josh and Jenny, took over the tollgate with their spouses. A retired soldier from the governor's regiment ran the northern one between George's house and town. Today, a new young soldier accompanied the governor. This new man was a friend of Perry's, and because of that, Lachlan trusted him. Well, that, and a lengthy letter of introduction from Vice Admiral John Hunter, which Lachlan had shared with few. The letter mentioned that this young man was the Vice Admiral's distant cousin. Lachlan needed men he could trust, and this lad was one of them.

The new guard was a towering blond giant over six feet tall. The young man was obviously a toff, as his mannerisms were not what you would expect to find amongst the rabble in a soldiers' mess. This fair-haired young man had charisma. Although young, George could see why he had chosen Major Ned Grace as his security guard.

Lachlan and Major Ned entered the house and perused the front room, which Charlotte had converted into a shop. Over the years, they had built shelving and display cabinets, but the most unusual thing was the polished log on a frame under the window. On this were six of the most exquisite side saddles that Ned had ever seen. However, they were displayed on some of the African hides George purchased in Cape Town. The striped zebra skin was always a topic of conversation. This had long since been removed from the floor of George's room. The tanned lion skin still sat on the floor in their sitting room.

Muffin still had her place there, but Mopps had died three years ago. Her granddaughter, Molly, now lay in her place amongst the fluffy mane of the lion. Crispin's ageing English Springer Spaniel cross was her father.

The shelves around the room displayed an eclectic assortment of other handmade leather goods, from sword-stick riding crops to full-size bullwhips with horsetail crackers on the end. There were carriage whips and riding stocks. Ned's eyes were everywhere. He fingered the carriage whips expertly. George smiled as Ned handled it like an expert.

Charlotte and Willow also made suede reticules with tassels and edges with painted designs. These spawned the idea of coin purses with drawstring ties. Plaited belts were made from one long piece and woven without cutting the thonging. The tongue was the end of the wide strap. These were popular among men because they could be adjusted to fit their girths. The buckle's prong fitted through the plaited thonging.

Quinn made knife sheaths, and the blacksmith, Thomas Tindale, made a selection of knives for them, as well as the required buckles for the saddles.

Charlotte's brothers taught her to whittle, and she made handles for the blades from horn or wood. Every item for sale was a masterpiece. All the pieces in the room could be handled to feel the quality of the leatherwork or the craftsman's skill.

Ned lifted his gaze and grinned. "Mr Ellis, I've never seen quality like this. The governor and Perry said they are made of local hides. Are those sweet bounding creatures the source of this red leather?"

George picked up a riding crop with a cheetah skin popper. "The red leather certainly is, Major Grace, but the poppers are from some hides I purchased in Africa. I did not realise the man I bought them from included some of the most incredible furry pelts. The lion on the floor next door, the zebra, and this cheetah are some of the more distinctive. However, these crops would be nothing without the decorative poppers on the end."

Ned felt one was especially heavy.

George put his hand out. "May I?" Ned passed it over. George flicked up a leather latch and extracted a lethal sword-stick from the riding crop sheath.

Lachlan, who had been silent until now, muttered something in Gaelic. Ned chuckled. Lachlan apologised. "How do you know what I said, Grace? It was Gaelic."

Ned grinned. "My mother is a Scot, sir."

Lachlan laughed. "I'll need to watch my language around you then." He turned to George and said, "You could kill someone with that."

George nodded. "That's the whole idea, sir. I only have one, and I would be thrilled if you would accept it as a gift. You will never be unarmed again. With so many felons and bushrangers, you can't be too careful."

Lachlan was delighted. "I would be honoured." He accepted the gift with a reverent bow.

Chapter 16 New Friends

*M*arket day in Parramatta was always enjoyable. Over the years, the Ellis's had met many people, but through the Macquaries and the Whites, three new families entered their circle of friends. They initially met at church, where the governor introduced them to each other. The first to arrive were the Millers. Bill and Molly had been hand-picked to run a new upper-class inn on Church Street in Parramatta. There was another inn nearby, but Joseph Hawley ran the Bird in the Hand Inn down the street, and it catered to the rougher clientele. The young convict, Obadiah Jensen, whom George had met through the Rosedales, now worked there with his wife and child.

The young Miller and Ellis couples grew close, as Molly and Charlotte often discussed the problem of trying to have a baby. Both women were woefully thin.

Perry and Katy White also had some new staff. Charlotte sat at the rear of the church with George during services, as she had a teething baby. This was a convict area, but from here, she could easily stand at the back of the building and rock the baby when required. The Whites' new convict servants sat with the Ellis's. Charles Lockley and Sal McCarthy were assigned to them on arrival. After an attack on the way to clean Major Ned's cottage, Charles proposed to Sal to protect her. However, it was obvious to everyone that they were smitten with each other. It was no surprise that Major Ned fast-tracked their union. The Lockleys married only six weeks after they were assigned. The somewhat buxom Sal conceived immediately. The stick-thin Molly Miller smiled through her sadness, but Charlotte knew the pain of empty arms. Bertie was her pride and joy, but she had lost two other babies. Kath still had none.

Through the governor and the Millers at the Rear Admiral Duncan Inn, they met Jennifer Kellow. She was an unmarried Cornish convict who arrived expecting a child. However, she came bearing a letter of introduction from a duke. Jennifer was later followed by her fiancé, Billy Williams, and his parents, Bryn and Delen. They arrived on the day she gave birth to her son, Christopher, to be known as Kit. Billy married Jennifer the following month.

These four believers were welcomed into the ever-widening group of friends.

A baron had violated Jennifer while she was delivering her gourmet cheeses and then accused her of defrauding him. Much to the shock of her new friends, Jennifer had conceived after that single incident. Charlotte wondered if it was the same man who abused Willow, as the descriptions were similar. Jennifer worked hard. She was busy converting the pitifully small new dairy behind Government House in Parramatta into a cheese-making hub. Charlotte adored cheese, so when Jennifer asked them to join her tasting group, she jumped at the chance.

~

Late 1821

Katy and Perry White were delighted with how all their friends had settled. However, they shocked them all by announcing they were going home to England. Perry, Katy, and their household were returning home with the Macquaries. George and Charlotte were saddened that these two families were leaving, as they had become good friends. The two men were part of an eclectic group that would meet and have a Bible study around Perry's large dining room table. George found that it was through this group that his faith grew.

Lachlan confessed to this group that he had resigned but had to face an inquiry in London due to John Bigge's report. Everyone knew Bigge and disliked him. He had come to investigate the colony on behalf of the government in London. Rather than do a thorough job, he only interviewed friends of John Macarthur. None of Lachlan Macquarie's supporters were approached, so the report was heavily biased against Lachlan.

Many letters preceded his return, as they were aware of the reason for his resignation. If the replacement governor arrived in time, their departure was set for early in the New Year. Lachlan refused to leave the colony without a leader after what had occurred when Governor Phillip departed in 1792. George would miss their friendship. He could not come every week, but he managed as often as possible, usually when it was raining or too hot to work in the shed. Near the end of the year, Sal and Charles Lockley welcomed a son, Charlie.

Before Billy Williams' arrival, Molly, Katy White, Charlotte, Helena, and Agnes surrounded the Cornish girl. Throughout the year, the three little boys — Bertie, Charlie, and Kit — adored the Sunday picnics that followed church. Molly and Bill often joined them, but she became increasingly quiet.

Agnes and Sal took the unhealthily thin Molly aside and explained that she had been so malnourished during the voyage that she needed to gain weight before her body returned to normal. Jennifer offered to supply extra cream, cheese, and milk for her. Molly agreed. They had tried to talk to Kath, but she would not listen. She ate like a sparrow, only picking at her food.

Perry told George of the Lockleys' new placement. "George, our friends, Charles and Sal, will not be far away. They have been asked to run a new inn near the river wharf. Charles will oversee the Government Stores for

Parramatta. Sal and Molly will take over looking after our waifs, strays and abused women." Perry chuckled. Few knew they had leased a cottage for abused wives. He added, "Charles is somewhat overwhelmed with gratitude but knows not whom to thank." Perry knew Charles suspected Major Ned Grace had something to do with his placement, but he dared not ask. Perry was about to leave when he turned back to George and said, "Oh, for a belated wedding gift, I gave my big table to Charles. You will be able to continue your studies around it. Ned is adapting the new building so the table and sideboard fit."

George was thrilled. His grin revealed his delight. Perry smiled as he thought about his unusual friends. The men in their group included two convicts, a cheesemaker or two, a tanner, a tutor, the governor, any of the extended Rosedale men, and himself. Only Ned and the governor knew he had a title. Being an earl in a convict colony would have made life impossible, so they kept it under wraps. Here, he lived under the name of plain Mr. Perry White. Lord Jonas Thistlethwaite also maintained a low profile, but Perry knew Jonas's family from London. He was the youngest son of a peer. They both kept quiet about their backgrounds, as Lord Jonas and Lord Peregrin would have been targets of hate if word spread. Ned also held a title, but he was not even using his real name. He shook off his Lord Edward moniker.

The three men cherished the informality of life and the anonymity it provided. Now, Perry had to leave and return to the society he despised. However, since his time in New South Wales, he had plans to shake things up a little in London when they returned home. Katy's friendship with Mrs. Elizabeth Fry would help achieve that. He smiled at the thought. He knew his father, the duke, would welcome involvement in the work and use his title to lend assistance.

Perry's mind drifted back to Ned and Charles. Their friendship was quite unusual. The two men bore a striking resemblance to each other. They were nearly the same age, both had white-blond hair, blue eyes, and deep dimples on both cheeks. They could easily be mistaken for brothers. Knowing Ned's family well, including his three brothers, Perry knew Charles wasn't one of them, but who was he? Ned had no cousins. Perry had asked Ned, but he said he knew of no connection.

Nevertheless, neither man spoke openly about their resemblance. Ned informed Perry that they had not known each other in England and had only met before departing from London on the same ship: Charles, a felon, and Ned, a guard.

When the subject came up in conversation with his friends, Charles replied to Bill and George, "Grace and Lockley are names I have never heard linked before. I do know the Duke of Gracemere lives near our home in Kent, but I have never laid eyes on him. My father, John, may have met him at some time, but I have not." If Ned and Perry were near, their eyes would meet. Ned wondered if he would ever discover the answer to the puzzle. None of his friends inquired further. Other than Perry, no one dared to ask Ned if there was a connection.

Bill Miller and Charles had arrived as convicts in 1819 along with Jack Turner, who was now assigned to the Duffys at their new store. Charles and Jack met on the same ship as Major Ned. Ned was caught staring at Charles more than once. Billy Williams and George had come as free settlers, but neither was prepared to seek clarification from the young major about his connection with either Charles or Perry.

~

The official household left Parramatta the week of the governor's birthday, and they had a celebratory meal before departure. Jennifer made a unique smoked ricotta cheese for the event. Mrs Ovens and Betty Eccles served it with a berry *coulis*, dollops of clotted cream, and a crispy toasted oat and treacle biscuit topping. It was delicious. In 1822, the time of the governor's departure arrived. He was loved by many, and the multitude didn't want him to go. The departure date was only days after Lachlan's sixtieth birthday, and they had celebrated with a final meal at Perry's house in Parramatta before it was handed over to the new owner. Ned was remaining in the colony but travelled to Sydney with the governor, his wife, their eight-year-old son, Lachie, and the White household to say farewell on the ship.

The departure of the Whites left a massive void in Ned's life. He had known Perry since he was in short coats at school when Perry had been a senior. Due to various delays, the ship finally departed on February 12, 1822. Ned's heart almost broke. He was left halfway around the world and totally alone. Twenty-one-year-olds did not weep, especially if they were majors in the British army, but Ned wished to. He walked to the headland overlooking the expansive harbour and watched the ship carry his friend and mentor away. A tear slid down his cheek, and he brushed it away angrily. Governor Brisbane seemed able. He was keen to get his teeth into the work, but Ned knew things would change. He was no longer part of a personal security detail, as he was now responsible for supervising female convicts, among other duties.

~

Shortly before Easter, Charlotte suspected she was expecting again. She remained silent, having had numerous false alarms in the past. Over Easter, at Agnes's family gathering, Kath told Charlotte she was also expecting. With news of new babies on the way, each couple promised to write to share their news.

As before, Kath and Ben's third child died the day it was born. The tiny baby was emaciated and so small that even if he had breathed, he would not have survived. They named him William, but he could not be buried in consecrated grounds at Penrith as he had not been baptised. Ben took his son's tiny body and buried it on the top of a hill in the growing town of Emu. It was just across the river from their home, and they could see the rise from their verandah. With no children to nurture, Kath refused to leave home for any reason.

With the house more like a mausoleum, the boys, Pete and Wendell, purchased everything they needed to start a new business and moved to the new settlement of Bathurst.

Ben kept working, but no longer contacted George unless it was to place an order for leather. The house by the river fell silent. The laughter had gone, and although Ben and Kath still adored each other, any conversation was rare. Work became their all-consuming passion.

When the Rosedale family gathered *en masse*, Agnes would insist that the Parkers attend, and Kath would occupy herself in the kitchen or take a long walk. She shunned any contact with her fertile sisters and often returned home tear-stained. Ben didn't know what to do. He was so in love with his beautiful wife, but having a child did not seem to be God's plan for them. He didn't want one for himself. He wanted one for Kath. He even contemplated adopting one, but even that had not worked. He found a new friend in Emu. His name was Jack Turner. He was the man who had arrived some years earlier with Charles Lockley and Jack's wife, Martha. She took Kath aside and gave Kath a good talking-to about her weight. Ben and Kath visited the Turners for a Sunday brunch to say some prayers. Emu Ford had no church, and the Turners couldn't leave the inn unattended to go to Penrith. This suited both families. The Murphy family joined them. After seeing Maureen Murphy and Martha with their heads together, Martha drew Kath aside.

Kath was woefully thin as she would still only nibble at her food, and it was this that Martha addressed. "Kath, Kath, Kath! You say you wish for a child, but you are doing everything you can to lose weight. You are stick-thin already, and if you lose any more weight, you will be a walking skeleton. If you don't eat right, your body will fight you."

This comment brought Kath up with a start. "What does food have to do with babies?"

Martha led her into the kitchen, sat her at the table, and then explained the basics of a woman's fertility. "I learned this in Africa when sailing with my parents." She described the woman's menstrual cycle and the role of body fat in conception and the development of a healthy child. "Your cycle must be regular before anything can occur, and your body needs a little meat on you for that to occur. You have no weight for the growing child to feed from, so it will starve."

By the time the Parkers left, Kath had a reason to smile. She had now lost three full-term babies, and goodness knew how many she had lost early on. She lost count of the months she had missed a flow, only to have a really heavy one the following month. Was each one a lost child? Kath returned home, intending to gain weight in order to have a baby. She was now determined to eat correctly. As she left Martha's house, she looked down at her gown, stretched it over her stomach and noted that her hip bones were easily visible. Her hands were skeletal. She gave a humph of frustration. Most of her other sisters were curvy. She had never had the voluptuous bumps her elder sisters did. Patience and Charlotte were the only sisters as thin.

~

By August, Charlotte could not hide the bump under her gown. They had not advertised her condition, as Molly still had empty arms, just as Kath did. Sal Lockley could not help but notice her expanding waistline as they sat in church. Sal leaned over and whispered, "I'm expecting again, as well." She was due in the spring. Her sons were eleven months apart. Eddie, their second son, was born on the sixteenth of October, 1821, which was Major Ned's twenty-second birthday. He was named Eddie after Major Edward Grace. Sal had gone into labour in the middle of Ned's birthday luncheon. The Williams, Millers, and Ellis families were missing from the celebration. The Williamses had to tend the dairy, and the Millers had Molly's mother, stepfather, and their daughter staying. The Ellis's had gone to the Rosedales farm for a family luncheon to introduce their newborn to everyone. Much to the delight of George and Charlotte, Robert Linus Ellis had arrived at the end of September.

~

In November 1822, Charles and Sal Lockley's third child, Elizabeth, to be called Liza, was born thirteen months after Eddie.

Molly Miller was excited as she had just realised she was finally expecting a child. She blurted out her news to Jennifer when she and Billy delivered the latest cheese samples to take to the luncheon. "It's happened. We're having a baby." Molly was almost dancing a jig of delight. Finally, her once curvaceous figure was filling out again after her near-starvation convict voyage. Jennifer laughed as she, too, danced with joy when she found she was carrying Billy's first child. She confided that she was also expecting a child. The ladies worked out that they were due at about the same time.

Bill Miller permitted George to install a small display cabinet in the front room of his inn that stocked small, saleable items. The items included knife sheaths but no blades, riding crops, and an assortment of whips. Charlotte was making coin purses and fob tags to add to the display. These items were constantly breaking and needed frequent replacement.

George had received another shipment of tanned African hides, and all the small off-cuts she cut into the fob button ends, whip poppers, and crop tips. The zebra skin crops were especially popular.

Governor Thomas Brisbane heard about George's prowess with the violin and asked to visit and listen to him play one day. Ned Grace often accompanied Sir Thomas when he came. Although he was no longer the governor's security guard, he was trusted. The governor's new man, Captain Guy Manning, was on his second tour of duty to New South Wales, or Australia, as it was now called. Ned and Guy were good friends.

George and Billy Williams drew close. They were happy to spend time with the extended group. Sir Thomas was cordially invited to join the bible study, but politely declined. Guy came when he could, but this was not often. The smaller gathering met around the big table in Charles's dining room. Guy's young wife was a convict he had married on the journey over. Martha Manning was expecting their first child.

~

Quinn had no idea what his last name was, so he took Ellis as his family name. He did this officially so that when Willow and Quinn got married, he would have a surname to put in the register. George was delighted as he now had a family again. Within weeks of the wedding, the now slightly buxom Willow announced that she was expecting a baby. For the first time in her life, she had access to good food and delighted in every mouthful and then some.

Howard Marlow, the man running the new boys' orphanage in Sydney, had other older boys he needed to place. Rather than booting them out at ten years old, he converted the attic and kept them for as long as possible.

Out on the Nepean River, Kath and Ben had lost more babies to miscarriage, but they told no one but Jack's wife, Martha Turner.

By the time Robbie was six months old, Charlotte could hardly pull herself around with exhaustion. Chasing after a toddler and caring for a baby was exhausting. One afternoon, Charlotte went to visit her mother with George, leaving Bertie with Willow. Upon her return, the house appeared to have been hit by a storm. Charlotte was not often in tears, but it got to her today. She lay on her bed and wept. Their two little boys were always on the go, and the house was often in disarray. Adding to the chaos of two families sharing one home, they had numerous cats, dogs, and other animals that Bertie regularly brought inside. Half an hour later, the reason for her moodiness hit home. As she was feeding Robbie, he accidentally hit her breasts. She noticed they were exceptionally tender. She wondered if she was expecting again. She had not had a monthly flow since Robbie was born, but she had only had one after Bertie before she fell with Robbie. She dared not even mention her suppositions to her beloved George. She knew he would fuss and give the secret away. However, a few weeks later, when she was sure, Charlotte told George they would have three children under three. They were both reeling with the news.

~

Amelia Agnes Ellis, known as Milly, was born at the end of 1822. She had a mass of red hair, bluish-coloured eyes and her mother's infectious giggle. By the time Milly was crawling at four months old, her eyes had turned green. Her two big brothers idolised her. Muffin had taken to sitting at the foot of her basket and defending it as though her life depended on it.

Life in the Ellis household settled into a routine.

In Parramatta, Molly Miller and Jennifer had their babies on the same day in March; both girls had sons, four months younger than Milly Ellis.

The tannery grew so much that Quinn and George employed four more boys from the orphanage in Sydney. They asked Ned to arrange a team to construct a second dwelling on their farm as a dormitory for their workers.

George had plenty of money to buy the materials, but he lacked the skill to build a dwelling. He assisted with Ben's house, but that had been to hammer a nail here and there or follow an order from one of the Rosedale boys. Ned took over the plans for a dormitory for more orphans. With a smile, he enlarged the design. If George had room, then more boys could be housed.

George was delighted. He liked Howard when he went to Sydney to discuss their plan. The new dwelling would have eight small rooms; the boys could choose if they wished to share or have a room each. Each lad would be paid a fair wage and taught the skills needed to set up their own businesses, should they wish. They would also learn how to manage the bookwork necessary for a business to be successful.

The log dormitory house was completed in eight weeks. Ned and George furnished it with horsehair mattresses and timber bed frames. These beds were chunky and could be turned into bunks with the addition of two-inch dowels drilled into the head and foot frames. Instead of timber slat bases, Quinn used some damaged, semi-tanned cowhides that came with the African consignment. They were cut into two-inch strips and woven into a sprung base. This gave the mattresses some give and made them far more comfortable.

George grinned. Rather than choosing the boys himself, Quinn volunteered to go and talk to the lads in the orphanage. He knew the ropes, having grown up alone. Six young lads returned with him. Each was carrying their worldly possessions in a small swag. These boys were clean, well-fed, and happy. George's heart went out to them. Amazingly, all were literate. The current lads moved into the new dormitory with the new residents, allowing two new convict girls to move into the old rooms to assist with the cooking and cleaning. The boys' dorm room was warm, dry and comfortable.

Ned was thrilled as he had more than a dozen young Irish girls to place. Agnes took one as a companion, and the Milroys and Thistlethwaits each took two. Three were heading out to a dairy near the Macarthur's farm.

Business was growing. George and Quinn still made sidesaddles and numerous other small items, but the tannery was the money spinner. The quality of George's kangaroo and wallaby hides was top-notch. He was getting orders from far and wide and found it hard to keep up. Expansion was the next step. However, that took money and time. He had the former but not the latter. He needed even more help.

Chapter 17 The Instrument of Joy

$\mathcal{F}$our years after Milly's birth, her sister, Isabella Charlotte, joined the family. Belle was as quiet as the boys were noisy. Bertie was seven, Robbie was nearly five, and Milly was four. Charlotte was delighted but exhausted.

The house was packed to the rafters as Quinn and Willow's growing tribe outnumbered theirs. All the children shared two rooms, with all the boys in one room and the girls in the other. The youngest babies slept in cane baskets with their parents.

One night, when all the children were quiet, the four adults sat in the sitting room, having packed away their weaving early. The four adults barely had time to scratch. They were all so consumed by work and family.

George was stunned when Charlotte said one evening, "You never play for me anymore."

George had not touched his beloved violin for more than a month. "How about now? But let's go outside as the children are all asleep."

Charlotte nodded. The evening was warm, and she would not even need a shawl.

Quinn and Willow loved these evenings. They would follow them out the back door and wait on the kitchen step.

Charlotte sat on the bench in the tanning shed, and George played for her. She was waiting with her hands clasped to her chest. Her eyes were fixed on her husband, and her love and adoration of him radiated from her face. Her quiver was full with four healthy children, her husband was loving, and their business was going strong.

George picked up his instrument, and soon, the melody of the *Moonlight Sonata* was floating across the evening air. It was followed by song after song that carried unvoiced words of love for his wife.

Unbeknownst to them, Bertie had been woken by the beautiful sounds. He stole out of bed and joined Quinn and Willow. His parents didn't know he was awake until, at the end of one song, they heard his voice ask Quinn, "Is Papa playing to the angels?"

The moon had fully risen, and the couple on the back step could easily see George as he serenaded his beloved.

Quinn chuckled and replied, "Yes. Bertie, I think he is. Well, one angel at least; that is your mama."

Willow tucked the young boy under his arm. "It's beautiful music, isn't it?" She felt the boy's head nodding.

After the end of another melody, Bertie whispered, "Do you think he would teach me?"

Quinn answered. "I think he would. He told me he was about your age when he started to learn. I always meant to learn, but never made the time."

Before he could stop him, Bertie flew to his mother's side.

Charlotte caught her son and pulled him up beside her. "Shh, son, and listen."

Bertie did, and he loved what he heard. The strings of his heart wanted to play the music. He had expected chastisement for being out of bed, but he received love and acceptance instead. He sat listening to the beautiful music.

At the end of that piece, George noticed his son. "Bertie, do you know I was a bit older than you when I first saw this fiddle? My mother taught me how to play later that year."

Bertie adored his father, and the music had just kicked him up a notch in his hero worship of him. "Am I too young, then? Do I have to wait another year?"

Rather than answer him directly, George chuckled and turned to his wife. "Do you think you could cope with a small boy learning to do something that will become an obsession?"

Charlotte giggled. "I think it is more likely that we will need a second fiddle, as there is no way you will not wish to accompany him when he plays better than you."

George crouched before his son. "I think that means, yes. Would you like to start right now?"

Bertie's head nearly nodded off.

George did something he never dreamed he would ever be able to do. He passed his beloved violin to his son and showed him how to hold the bow. His heart was bursting with pride.

The child had a long reach for his age, and George folded his fingers around the neck of the instrument and bowed a note.

George said, "You know how gently you must be with a chicken; you must care for your instrument the same way. Gentle and loving, then it will love you back. It will take a lot of practice, but it's worth it."

After a few slides of the bow, George asked, "How about we try a tune?"

"Yes, please, Papa, but I won't be able to play real music, will I?" Bertie asked excitedly.

George smiled. "That depends on what you call real music. The tune we shall first play is 'Twinkle, Twinkle Little Star'. It was written by two sisters, Ann and Jane Taylor, when I was a lad. Are you ready?"

Bertie grinned. "Yes, Papa. Can you show me how you make it shake with love?"

George chuckled. "Of course. To create a pulsating change in pitch, the finger moves sideways on the string. This is called vibrato. This rhythmic movement is used to add expression, warmth, and life to the tone"

Bertie nodded and moved to stand between his father's legs.

George felt excitement growing within him. This is how his mother taught him to play. He said, "For the first time, I shall push your fingers on the strings but try to remember where they go, and then you can have a play yourself."

Bertie bowed like a natural and only had to be shown twice before playing the nursery rhyme himself.

The boy was delighted. "But, make it shake, Papa."

While Bertie moved the bow, George showed him how to make the note reverberate by the quick movement of his fingers.

Bertie sighed with delight. "It makes my heart happy, Papa."

Charlotte brought the evening back to earth with a crash. She drew her son close and said, "Papa will play one more song for us all and then bed for you, my boy."

Once more, the soft notes of love floated over the evening air. At the tune's end, George ruffled his son's hair and said, "Bedtime, son!"

Later that month, George managed to buy Bertie his own fiddle. It had belonged to an Irishman who had recently died. None of his family could play, and they needed the money. George paid them more than it was worth, but he knew that £2 was a fortune for them. It needed a new bridge, as the original one was flatter. With no access to maple, George thought he'd try to make a bridge from the seasoned cedar he had in the shed. The bow that came with the instrument needed to be restrung. George knew his horse would need to lose some of its tail for the bow to be of use. For the moment, Bertie would need to use George's spare bow.

As soon as the instrument was refurbished, Bertie demanded a lesson.

With the apprentices now keeping up with the orders, George set aside an hour every morning for Bertie's lesson.

The child practised whenever he could. Like his father and great-grandfather before him, music was in his blood. At one stage, they needed to confiscate the instrument so the family could get some sleep.

George was right when he warned Charlotte of the overwhelming passion. Bertie discovered an obsession with the beautiful, haunting music.

Within a short time, a duet of magical notes floated across the night sky. Many residents would take their evening tea outside, hoping the haunting tunes would fill their evenings.

~

1827

By the time Bertie was eight, his playing was so skilled that he could accompany his father for duets at wedding breakfasts. He had heard of a new piece that was perfect for a solo violin and written by Franz Schubert.

Bertie found the score in a new book his father had purchased. Someone must have slipped it in by accident. Bertie didn't mind at all and wanted to copy it before returning it to the shop. However, when he took it back to the bookshop, no one had reported it missing. The storekeeper told him he could keep the score. Bertie waited until his family was busy, and then he played the new music quietly. He gasped for it was divine.

For the next wedding, Bertie played *Ave Maria* in church. This was a German adaptation of Sir Walter Scott's poem *"The Lady of the Lake."* In German, it was called *Ellens Gesang III,* and this was the new music by Franz Schubert that Bertie had heard mentioned.

After a year, George upgraded his son's fiddle to a much better and beautiful mellow instrument. It had been damaged in transit but was not beyond repair. George and Bertie set to work to reattach the sprung back.

Bertie's fingers were able to work in the small places of the back. As the instrument was currently unplayable, George dismantled it and scraped off all the glue. George had never dismantled his violin, so he let Bertie try his hand at repairing it. With a new cedar bridge, the sound of the repaired violin was mellow. Bertie loved it and could make it cry; this is what he called the moving music. His playing was good, very good.

George knew that his children needed a formal education to succeed. Part of that education was the responsibility of completing a job. The three older children did chores around the property. They were only permitted to play with the animals if they completed their list of jobs and did some reading lessons.

Willow joined them because she wanted to learn how to read.

For the two older boys, this meant an hour of reading and writing with Charlotte as their teacher; however, her education was limited. With only a charity school in town, when Bertie was eleven, George arranged for the boys to be educated with their cousins at Toongabbie.

Bertie was thrilled but only agreed to go if he could keep practising his instrument.

Robbie shrugged. He knew he had to learn to read, but he'd rather make things to sell. He had no interest in music of any sort but loved the clink of the coins when he sold something.

Their Uncle Jonas and Aunt Mary had hired a tutor for their children, and Bertie and Robbie would stay with them from Monday to Thursday and ride home for the long weekend. The poor tutor coped with a vast range of family children from ages six to eighteen.

~

Ben ordered six more tanned hides by mail, but Quinn was too busy to deliver them. After nearly sixteen years of marriage, Ben and Kath had not attended any family gathering for almost eighteen months. Although Kath had managed to put on some weight, she remained withdrawn and moody. The last time Charlotte saw her sister over a year ago, Kath spat the words, "Just stay away from me. You have everything you want, as you have four children, and I still have empty arms." She turned and walked away.

Charlotte was worried. Her sister's words hurt. She said, "George, can we deliver Ben's hides ourselves? If we take an overnight bag, we can spend time with them. Belle is weaned, and Willow can care for her for one night. If we're not welcome, we'll stay at Turner's Inn and return tomorrow."

George's arms slid around her waist. It was no longer as trim as it had once been, but then again, neither was his, and he had not borne four children and lost two more. "I do like the way you think, my dear. How about I take my fiddle?"

Her coy nod made him smile. She asked, "Can we go now? Like right now? I feel we are needed."

After more than a decade and a half of marriage, Charlotte only had to smile a certain way, and he was putty in her very capable hands. Knowing they had no time for a quick romp as he had hoped, he shook his head to make himself concentrate. He was aware that she had had premonitions like this before. It was only after a conversation with one of Kath's friends on their last visit that Charlotte started acting on them. He wasn't sure who that was. He knew they should go as soon as possible if she said to leave today.

With Quinn and Willow left to run things and care for their young daughters, George and Charlotte went to visit the Parkers unannounced.

Taking the children was not an option, as their four imps had become a wedge between the sisters. The boys were at their aunt's place for another two days. Quinn and Willow would take care of things at the tannery.

The carriage was loaded with hides and pelts for Ben. The trip was an excuse to deliver the leather he had ordered. They expected to be shown the door. However, as promised, George packed his instrument.

Charlotte also added some home preserves and ginger cookies for Kath. She knew they were her favourites.

Their arrival that afternoon was not as they expected. The piercing screams emanating from the house were eerily familiar. The sounds were as though a woman was travailing in birth pains. Ben was nowhere in sight, and there was no hammering noise from the workshop.

Charlotte hopped out while George looped the reins onto the hitching rail. She followed the moans into the master bedroom. A woman was kneeling in front of the bed. A birth was undoubtedly in progress, and Kath was screaming in agony.

Charlotte did not even know Kath was expecting a baby. She realised the midwife was Martha Turner when the woman on the floor said, "Oh, thank goodness! I need some help." She nodded to the other side of the bed.

Charlotte saw a pair of men's feet sticking out from beyond the end of the bed. Ben had obviously passed out. Charlotte giggled. "What do you need me to do, Martha?"

Martha said, "We're going to sit her up and get her to deliver squatting. She's too tired to push. Have you done it this way before, Charlotte?" Martha's reputation was well known to all the family, but few had met her. She spent her first sixteen years on her father's ship, travelling with her parents as they circumnavigated the globe for his business.

Charlotte knew her well, but she hitched a breath. "No, but I've seen it done and had four babies myself."

Kath was moaning in agony but unaware of her sister's presence.

Martha settled her friend into position when the contraction finished. Kath was hardly aware of being moved. She was exhausted and barely *compos mentis*. Ben was useless, and George was not welcome.

Charlotte had been through this four times and had been at hand for her mother when Willow gave birth, as well as Kath's first two deliveries.

After sixteen years of marriage, Mary Kathleen Parker arrived clenched fist first and screaming enough to wake the dead. It was even enough to stir her father from his impromptu nap. Ben groaned from his safe position on the floor but didn't move.

Once the afterbirth had been dealt with, George came in and lifted Kath into bed, then nudged Ben with his foot. "Hey, Dad, wake up and meet your daughter."

Ben's eyes opened, and he caught sight of his friend. "Why are you here?" He sounded dazed but grumpy.

George reached down to grab his hand and pull him up. "Charlotte said we were needed, so we came. We made it in time to help Martha deliver your beautiful daughter." George swallowed. He knew just how much this would mean to his friend. "Ben, you're a father, and she's beautiful and healthy."

Ben scrambled to his feet. He ignored his child and went to his wife's side. "My darling beloved wife, I told you I was no good with blood or pain. How are you?"

Kath giggled like a silly schoolgirl. "I hurt, but I'm surprisingly well, and so is our baby." She reached out for her husband, and he enfolded her in his arms.

He had not even looked at his daughter. His concern had been for Kath. He blinked. "She's alive?"

Kath nodded. "She is, and she's a fighter. Look." She beckoned Charlotte to her side while she still held the baby. Kath took the baby from her sister, and as she did so, she squeezed her sister's hand in a wordless gesture of thanks. Her tears of happiness welled and slowly overflowed.

Now swaddled, Mary lay in her mother's arms. She was not red and wrinkled like other babies, but her skin was as soft and smooth as a pink magnolia. It was creamy and unblemished.

Ben had his arm slung around his wife; he could hardly see his daughter as tears blurred his vision. A sob escaped him. After sixteen years of marriage and four full-term, stillborn children and numerous miscarriages, they had a healthy, breathing baby. He choked back a sob.

George walked to his friend's side, put a comforting hand on his shoulder, and gave a squeeze of compassion.

Charlotte stroked her sister's cheek and then giggled. "Now you will discover what the lack of sleep is like. You will also find that she will twist you around her little finger in a way you have never believed possible."

Martha cleaned up the birthing area and stood watching the two couples. She asked, "Are you staying for the night? If so, I shall head home to my family." She stretched, and Charlotte saw that she was about six months gone with child.

Charlotte gasped. "Oh, Martha, I didn't realise you were having another one. When are you due?"

Martha grinned. She glanced at Kath and, lowering her voice, said, "This one is number five. We already have two boys and two girls. If this is a girl, I may call her Catherine, but spelled with a C, not a K. After Cathy Duffy and your dear sister."

Charlotte and Martha moved a little away. They chatted as the new family bonded.

Charlotte smiled. "I have four, and my companion, Willow and her husband, Quinn, have six as they had twins. So, our house is in permanent mayhem. Add four adults, two maids and ten orphan boys to that. Meal times are crazy."

Martha was stunned. "How do you cope?"

With another glance towards Kath, Charlotte admitted, "I didn't, Martha. Thanks to you, I asked Major Ned to find two young girls who needed a safe place. I had them assigned to me, and they break the back of the work. Willow and I can handle the rest."

Martha gasped. "Oh, what a pretty name, but it's unusual."

Charlotte explained, "She was apparently abandoned under a willow tree and then found by a nice couple who were both dead by the time she was six. Things got worse from there, and she's ended up here."

Martha grimaced. "Oh, the poor dear! So, even mentioning her name is almost rubbing in her past. We may have to make up a special nickname for her."

George walked to their side. "You were spot on, Charlotte!" He turned to Martha and said, "Have you ever heard of someone who just knows when to be somewhere at a given time?"

Martha chuckled, looked at Charlotte, winked, and walked away, shaking her head. She had to head home.

George said, "Did I say something wrong?"

Charlotte replied, "No, silly, she's the one who told me to use my intuition. She has the same gift."

George looked embarrassed. "Oh!"

Charlotte had a thought. "Darling man, is the carriage still outside?"

He nodded. Charlotte asked, "Can you take Martha home? She's six months gone with child and has four little ones and Jack waiting for her."

With an arm slung around his wife's shoulder, they followed Martha's path out the front door. "Sure, sweetie! I wasn't sure what was happening. But I'll message your mama from Martha's Inn. She should be able to come and stay with Kath for a while. I'll also need to let Quinn and Willow know we will be delayed. The messages can go on the afternoon mail coach. We'll stay until your mama arrives."

Chapter 18 A Tanner's Life
Years later

$\mathcal{B}$y 1834, Governors Brisbane and Darling had come and gone, and Richard Bourke now held the reins of the colony.

Bertie was fifteen, and he played as well as his father. They swapped fiddles occasionally, as George's instrument had a more mellow tone. Bertie could make it hum in a way even George couldn't.

Robbie and the girls showed no interest in the music. Robbie was still more interested in selling the products, taking over the shop, and hawking their wares at markets. He had a knack for persuading people to buy something they didn't need.

With the family growing, the house could no longer accommodate everyone. The girls, who were twelve and eight, no longer shared a room with the other children; they moved into a guest room.

Quinn and Willow's brood had outgrown their rooms.

After long and tearful discussions with George, Quinn finally moved his family to start his branch of the business. He wouldn't go far, but he needed to establish a branch for his children to inherit. Four of the trained orphan boys left with him. He refused flatly to go out on his own. He would still make the saddle trees for Bertie, but would set up an exclusive kangaroo tannery as the demand for this fine leather increased. George focused on cow hides and fluffy sheep skins. He planned to export most of his tanned hides. The prices of these rose as the animals became harder to source. With more beef available, kangaroos and wallabies were now rarely on the menu.

Ben and Kath now had two beautiful, fit and healthy daughters. Violet Agnes, now four, arrived a shade over two years after Mary. If that was all the children they had, then they were content. Kath had come out of her shell and threw herself into the family life again.

With Ben and George's friendship once more on a firm footing, visits to the river were frequent. Now, middle-aged, the men were sitting on the verandah, drinking their hot mugs of tea.

Ben said, "I need to apologise, George. My jealousy of you and your family nearly overshadowed our long-standing friendship. I know I've said it before, but I really am sorry."

George placed a caring hand on his friend's arm. "Ben, we both went through a lot before we met. We both tossed in everything we knew to come here. God brought us together back then. We only had each other to rely on, but God had already given us the Rosedales as our new family here. If we had fallen for the same sister, things might have become very awkward, but we didn't. We four fell in love. Charlotte and I nearly didn't make it. After my accident, which I still don't remember all the details of, Charlotte and I... well, let me say it wasn't smooth sailing. We both changed after that incident. We were not the same young, idealistic couple we had been before. She had lost her spark, but I didn't remember much about anything for a long time. I had to learn to be me again. Then Linus died, and it threw us completely. Back then, I existed on flashes of my past, and it took months to regain most of my background."

Ben looked horrified. "No kidding, George? I thought you remembered everything at that first church picnic after you left the hospital."

George shook his head. "No, but that was the beginning of it. It took months. I remember my attackers; at least, I recall there were three of them. The hospital already knew that, as I said something when the soldier found me. To this day, I can't recall their faces or the soldier who helped me. I winged most situations and threw myself into work. If I made myself busy or looked interested, I could fool everyone. My greatest fear was whether I could still play my violin. I was worried about it to the point of making myself ill. I was vague and standoffish when I was in a group, as I felt overwhelmed. People seemed to leave me alone. I listened a lot, but Ben, I also did a lot of thinking."

Ben bit back a gasp.

George paused, remembering those years. "I had no direction. When I left home, I think I was running away from death. Of course, that didn't work. I had nothing, and I hurt. I think you were much the same. But we never spoke of our feelings back then." He saw Ben shake his head. "Well, we've been here for over twenty years and have both faced death squarely on. We found the love of a good woman and a faithful family. Praise God, we still do, and now we sit here as two nearly forty-something-year-old men who have full and enriched lives."

Ben relaxed in his wicker chair. A soft chuckle emanated from him.

George fell silent as his eyes roamed the vast expanse of the riverbank in front of him. "Ben, I am happy. I have a deep-seated sense of contentment within me. Linus's many discussions about his faith firmed mine. I realise that everything I ever wanted has been achieved. We have a fabulous partnership. All the boys still contact us if they need help, and our children are fit and strong. Do you know how many orphans have been through our 'tanning school,' as Quinn used to call it?"

Ben tried counting. "Twenty-three? Or did I miss a few?"

George gave a deep-throated laugh. "More than a few! There have been fifty-six. Fifty-six young men who would have otherwise lived on the streets now have their businesses or continue to work for us. All can read and write, and all have a strong faith. Our first four boys also have apprentices, so the work has spread. Pete and Wendell were right. Across the ranges was the right move for them. One of their lads has set up a wagon with mobile leather repairs. He travels from property to property doing small repairs using Wendell's tannery and saddlery as a base. If a saddle needs major work, he leaves a temporary one in place and sends the original back for an overhaul. I was thinking of having a few saddles available to do the same. What do you think? Good idea?"

This time, it was Ben's turn to laugh. "Who do you think suggested the idea, George? I've always had an old saddle or two for such use. I buy them from the paper and then refurbish them. Then, I make them as ugly as I can, so that they won't get stolen. Even the new repairs I distress and rough up, so they look beaten up." He reclined and relaxed. "I admit, I thought you wanted to dissolve the partnership."

George gasped. "Oh gosh, Ben, no way!"

The two continued drinking their now-cooled black, sweet tea.

Ben released a long, contented sigh. "I'm happy too, George. I'm glad we married sisters, as you are the only family I claim to have. I know many others are in the extended Rosedale family, but we're more like real brothers. Plus, we have known each other longer."

George rarely teared up, but he found that he could not reply. The lump in his throat made it impossible to swallow. He looked away, upstream, so Ben wouldn't see him wipe a tear from his eye. Since Quinn left, he'd grown close to Ben again.

Ben saw his friend's action and mopped his own eyes. He elbowed his friend lovingly and said. "Golly, George, so much for being tough blokes, aren't we?" He sniffed. "Is this what fatherhood does to a chap?"

George gurgled a laugh. "I think it must. I was thinking about my family at home. Our first three little ones are named after my father, brother and mother. Milly is the only full redhead amongst them all. Belle is a strawberry blonde like her mother. As you know, our boys are nondescript, brown like me. We are totally boring, with nothing special about any of us."

Ben nearly choked as he finished the remnants of his mug of now-cold tea. "Are you kidding? George, you should have been a concert virtuoso, not a tanner. You are brilliant, and Bertie will be as good, if not better than you."

George shrugged and replied, "Possibly, but it's not about that. It's all about the lifestyle and using the gifts for the right reasons. I would have hated to be togged up every night and play to packed concert halls around the world. When I need to play in Sydney for a fundraiser, I do so because I know the charity money is for God's purpose. I never wanted the fame. I only wanted the music. Bertie and I play in church for weddings and other events that we enjoy. I admit that when I played for that first concert, it never occurred to me that I was anything special. That night, I played for my Charlotte and only for her."

They spoke about the astounding impact the concert had on their business. Almost overnight, Mark's spiel transformed it from a small, practically unknown backyard business into a money-making factory.

They fell silent for a while before Ben said, "Did I tell you I have a new apprentice, and he's not an orphan?"

George was surprised, as the last two boys had left, and Ben mentioned he didn't want to take on more orphans.

Ben smiled. "It's Martha and Jack Turner's second son. Alex wants to be a saddler. He's thirteen and is a brilliant worker. He said inn-keeping is not for him. His big brother, Marcus, will inherit the family inn, so Alex knew he needed a skill."

A cocked brow was followed by, "Any good?"

Ben gave a nod. "He has great potential." Ben had plans for Alex, including the day when he would hopefully marry one of his daughters and take over the business. Mary was only seven, but she already idolised Alex. He would do everything he could to encourage that relationship. Ben swallowed, thinking about losing his daughter to marriage. "Cheer me up, dear friend. Play my song, please."

George had brought his fiddle with him but, so far, had not put bow to string. He leaned down and took his cherished instrument from its velvet-lined case.

As twilight fell, the birds on the river landed for the night. Dinner was an hour away, and the two friends settled back to enjoy the evening.

George took a deep breath and lifted his bow. The notes of the *Hallelujah Chorus* floated up and down the river.

All was right with the world for these two not-so-young men.

Inside, the sisters caught each other's glance and smiled. Hearing this particular song was a delight. Both girls knew that their men were happy.

Chapter 19 Life's Twists and Turns
Early 1840s

*L*ife in Parramatta had changed dramatically over the thirty-three years since George and Ben arrived. George was scudding hides, and doing this job gave him time to think. His mind wandered.

A conversation from early that morning made George reflect on his years in the colony while he worked scudding. The town would soon be abuzz with a new project and the change in his family. Most of the residents in town were now emancipated convicts.

Two years ago, it was announced that no new felons would arrive. Soon, the colony would be filled with free settlers or emancipated felons.

George reminisced about his family. Soon after the announcement that was transforming the colony, Bertie married Charles and Sal's daughter, Liza Lockley, in November 1841. A month later, her second brother, Eddie, married Martha and Jack Turner's daughter, Jenna.

The three families were friends, and the intermarriages drew them closer.

George did not realise that Charles Lockley and Jack Turner had arrived together as convicts, as no one had ever spoken about their pasts. He was surprised Ben had known all along. Having reported an attempted mutiny on the way out to Major Ned Grace, they were given early Tickets of Leave and then lost contact.

It turned out that Jack and Martha had both been assigned to Duffy's new store in the Camden area. Though they had met in England, they arrived six months apart at the behest of William Wilberforce, who was familiar with their backgrounds. Ned knew where they were, but he kept silent about Jack, as he eventually discovered Jack's background from Lachlan before he departed. Ned obviously knew far more than he would say.

George didn't ask. He smiled when he thought of those early days living under Governor Macquarie's leadership. George and Ben's ship arrived shortly after the Rum Corps rioted and ousted Governor Bligh. They had been sent to the Rosedales farm for their safety. This was a blessing as it was here they met their future wives.

When John Macarthur and the ring leaders left for England, a collective sigh of relief circled the colony. Macarthur was gone for nine peaceful years.

In 1809, things changed dramatically. Lachlan and Elizabeth Macquarie arrived, and the colony was quickly brought under control. The dour Scotsman had put his big broom to work and sorted out the military while Macarthur was absent. Many were shipped to India. Tariffs were placed on the importation of alcohol, toll roads were built, and new buildings popped up everywhere. Macquarie expanded the farming land across the mountain range, and the production of grain crops there removed the monopoly and price gouging by the Rum Corps. However, introducing local currency by purchasing the Spanish coins and re-minting them changed the balance of power. Lachlan was unconventional, but his methods worked. He turned a penal colony into a decent town.

George's mind wandered as he worked. He and Bertie played for Eddie and Jenna's wedding party, where Milly met Jenna's eldest brother, Marc Turner. Marc became putty in Milly's very capable hands. Another romance budded and blossomed. They were now engaged.

George knew this lad well. His younger brother, Alex, had already spoken to Ben about courting Mary when she was old enough.

Ben and Kath had willingly agreed on one condition. Alex was to one day take over the business. Ben was over the moon. This union was to be a love match. Mary idolised Alex, and it was reciprocated fully.

Jenna and Eddie's wedding also brought about another union. Fourteen-year-old Wills Lockley met Jenna's little sister, Cathy. They were moon-eyed over each other, as was Charlie Lockley over Grace Miller.

George laughed. The four families would have more connections than he could count. There was a rumour of a triple wedding later that year, but Charles Lockley had not confirmed that yet.

George smiled, but he felt his life was passing far too quickly. Charlotte never carried another child to term. They kept their losses close, knowing they had four happy, healthy children. They had given each lost baby a name, and they were sure that one day, they would meet them in heaven. He smiled again at that thought. There were six he knew about after Milly, but he had a feeling Charlotte had not mentioned some early miscarriages.

Bill and Molly Miller's four children would be related by marriage to the Lockleys, the Turners and the Ellises. Tim Miller was a lawyer who married Liza's sister, Anna. She was Charles Lockley's second daughter.

Sam Miller had spoken to George about courting Belle, but at fifteen, George considered she was far too young to marry. They were in no hurry as they would need to live at the inn, but Sam wished to stake his claim.

George wasn't too keen on permitting his daughter to live at an inn for some years yet, but he gave his permission for them to court.

Bill Miller's youngest girl, Ellen, was Belle's best friend. They were often seen together, and Belle frequently stayed overnight in her room. George knew Ellen Miller was keen on the youngest of the six Lockley children, but as yet, Luke had said nothing to her. Her eyes followed him everywhere.

One of the church ladies, Mrs Meadows, tutored many girls in grooming, deportment, and household skills. He chuckled to himself when he thought about this beautiful woman. When Ned Grace retired and moved two doors down from a stunning widow, George wondered if Ned was finally showing some interest in the lovely lady. He was right.

Numerous other girls had come under Ned's care, but Ned was a gentleman and never put himself or them in a situation that could compromise them. However, since retiring two years ago, Ned had become very secretive.

They discovered why when, out of the blue, at age 42, Ned had married the beautiful widow. Because Ned had helped hundreds of young women over the years, no one gave it a second thought when he was seen with this woman. No one realised that she would become his wife. Ned secretly married Christina Meadows on Christmas Day. Nothing was exceptional about that, except when they married, both signed their names with titles. Mrs Meadows was, in reality, the daughter of an earl and, therefore, Lady Christina.

George turned over the skin he was scudding. Ned's marriage was not the biggest surprise. When a soldier from Ned's old regiment married a few weeks later, he read the wedding register and realised that Ned had signed as the Duke of Gracemere. George smiled, remembering the congregation's astonished looks.

Doctor Gerald Winslow-Smythe, Ned's childhood friend, had come looking for him. The three had just left for England. George chuckled that he was on first-name terms with a duke. He shook his head in disbelief, thinking back to the other revelations. Perry White was an earl, and the Sydney builder Sam Garney was also an earl. That title was inherited upon his brother's death. All of them had since returned to England.

George knew that Ned and some of his military friends had safe houses scattered throughout the area. Over the years George had lived in the convict town, he knew that Ned and his team had saved many of the younger, uncorrupted convict girls. His friends worked subtly, and consequently, no one realised Ned had secretly been placing many of the younger or abused women in safe houses. Ned had perfected his skill of not letting his left hand know what his right hand was up to. He was seen everywhere, often accompanied by women. No one realised he had been caring for and later courting the beautiful widow on the sly for over two years.

Bertie did most of the heavy work at the business now. George changed hides and kept scudding. Scudding hurt his back, but it was easier to stay in one position than move and cope with the pain. He stretched before starting the new hide. His scudding pole was now more elevated than it had been, which certainly helped his back. All the families were growing up around them, and keeping track of who was who was becoming problematic. Many individuals shared the same selection of names, and most had nicknames. Charles and Charlie Lockley came to mind. Bertie had named his son Albert, but he was called Albie. Although unrelated, Ned and Eddie were both Edward. At fifty-two, George was still fit and healthy.

Bertie and Quinn's youngest lads worked with him, and a string of new boys from Howard's large orphanage, now situated at Cabramatta, had recently arrived. These boys were beginning their training. George, Ben and Howard had a system where six boys could be trained together. Once they had skills, they would finish their apprenticeships with one of the other boys who had started their own businesses. This way, all the boys would have a secure future.

Robbie was the frontman of the business and sold their products in the markets. He preferred working in the shop at the house; however, it wasn't very busy. George knew he needed to do something about that, but wasn't sure what. He would leave that in God's hands. He had learned to put his trust in the good Lord years ago. He and Charlotte prayed each night before they blew out their lamp.

As George kept scudding the hide on his post, he smiled. He missed Ned and Perry. Ned and Christina left in March this year, shortly after she told Charlotte that she was expecting a child. Ned was stunned when he learned he would be a father at long last. George knew that feeling. He remembered when Bertie was placed in his arms. Tears of delight dribbled down his cheeks. He had been much the same when Liza and Bertie had their son, Albie, the same day Eddie and Jenna had twins.

Charles, Bill, and he had met Ned and discussed fatherhood with him. Eddie and Jenna had gone to see them off in Sydney and returned in shock.

It was suspected that both Christina and Jenna were carrying twins. Well, Jenna certainly had been. He wondered if Ned and Christina had also had two children. Had they even survived? Ned promised to stay in contact with everyone.

George was sure Ned would meet up with his other friends in England and help the less fortunate in some way. Ned could not stop helping people. It was in his nature. Perry and Katy were heavily involved with Elizabeth Fry's work with the female convicts before they were transported. He looked forward to the next mail delivery.

Chapter 20 A Fortunate Future
Early 1843

*G*eorge and Bertie were scudding hides when two of the Lockley men

paid a visit. However, his friends were not in their usual work clothing, but were garbed in their Sunday best, if not better. Their clothing looked like new outfits.

Charles Lockley arrived in his small gig with Eddie. Charles spent a few minutes inside with his daughter before coming to find George in the tannery.

George greeted his friend. He presumed that Charles had heard from Ned and wondered how their friend coped with being the Duke of Gracemere.

Addressing his friend, Charles asked, "George, is Robbie around? We want to talk to the three of you inside, please." Charles turned and walked back inside. His walking stick tapped as he walked away.

Robbie was rinsing some salted hides at the back of the shed as the skins George and Bertie were working on were nearly ready for the next stage.

George replied, "Sure, Charles. Is something wrong?" As he spoke, with a wave of his hand, he sent Bertie to get Robbie. George wiped his hands and called one of the younger boys to finish the scudding. Hurrying after his friend, he asked, "Charles, you are worrying me. What's up?"

Charles grinned from near the back step. "Nothing! Come inside." He didn't wait but turned and limped inside. His broken leg from a decade ago had never healed properly.

Charles was waiting impatiently for his friend to join him.

While they waited for Robbie, Charles gave some information that made George chuckle. Christina had delivered twins, a boy and a girl. Ned had an heir.

George wondered how Ned was coping with screaming babies. Being a duke meant he probably had hordes of staff at his beck and call. Presumably, the ducal estate was large.

Charles acknowledged that it was immense. Although he had never been there, he knew the area well. It could be seen from a distance.

Eddie waited for the two younger men. Bertie was his brother-in-law, and they became fathers on the same day. As the three babies were now nearly a month old, the men compared notes about fatherhood whenever they could.

Robbie arrived at their side and was greeted with a nod.

Eddie asked his brother-in-law, "Is Albie sleeping any better yet?"

Bertie was in the middle of a yawn.

Eddie chuckled. "I'm guessing not."

Bertie shook his head. "No, and I'm beginning to wonder what the desire to have babies is all about. Liza is exhausted, and we share the night duties. The little chap has certainly got good lungs." Bertie groaned.

Eddie chuckled. "Try having two! Neddie is a terror, but Tina is the opposite. She wakes for a feed and then is asleep in a flash. Neddie is the night owl. He kicks off his blankets and then screams the cottage down." He gave a frustrated sigh. "I know what you mean, Bert, but Jenna takes it in her stride."

Robbie grunted with disinterest and walked through the kitchen, following his two friends, and into the sitting room. His parents and Charles were waiting for them.

Charles met his son's smiling eyes and grinned. "Take a seat, please, gentlemen."

Charlotte left to get them some tea.

Once everyone was settled, Charles waved his hand to his son. "The floor is yours, Eddie." He relaxed and settled into the padded cane chair.

George's brow furrowed. What had occurred?

The news that Charles brought stunned him. They had a proposition for the family.

Eddie felt like standing, but didn't. His gaze flicked around the room before settling on Robbie. "For a belated wedding gift, Duke Ned sent me £1000. My wage as a junior in the blacksmith forge is £15 per year. However, as a junior shareholder of the smithy business, I also get a percentage of the sales."

George caught his eye.

Eddie grinned at his friend's surprise. "As you know, Major Ned always had a soft spot for me. Since I was born on his birthday. However, I played a crucial role in his ability to marry Christina. Bertie, when we married, the major had little money to give us a wedding gift, so he sent some money to Dar for us. Bert, you and Liza will also get some, as will each of my siblings, but that is by the by. Dar will tell you about that later. I have come to say that I will build a mixed emporium with some of my money. At first, Jenna and I planned a proper shop at the forge, but with this money available, I have decided to make it a one-stop shop for all farm equipment, saddlery, tools and the like."

George gasped. He hoped he knew where this conversation was

heading, but kept quiet. Charlotte entered carrying the tea tray. He moved a small table so she could place the tray down.

Bertie's eyes were fixed on his brother-in-law.

Robbie was reclining in an armchair, cleaning his fingernails. He was bored stiff; he hated tanning. He wasn't listening. He hated these family meetings. A dark-haired, pretty face made him smile. He sighed with resignation. Maryanne's father had already warned him away from her.

Charles watched the younger man intently. He knew what his son was about to say and didn't wish to miss Robbie's reaction.

No one spoke as Charlotte passed around the mugs of tea.

Each man received them with a nod of thanks.

Charlotte then sat next to her husband.

Eddie sipped his hot, sweet brew and continued. "Mr Ellis, Bertie, Robbie, we want you to sell your goods from the emporium. We would add ten per cent to your current price, which we would take as our commission, and you would receive the original sale price. There are no additional costs involved for you. You can still sell from here if you wish."

Charlotte grabbed George's hand and gave it a squeeze and a micro nod.

George had already decided to hunt around for a shopfront but had said nothing to anyone but Charlotte. He was planning to ask Robbie to run it. He didn't let on about his mounting excitement at this prospect. "Go on, Ed. I'm sure there is more."

Eddie grinned as he nodded. He noticed Robbie's distraction and turned his attention to his childhood best friend.

At twenty-one, Robbie had never found his niche. He looked positively bored. However, he was a brilliant salesman. He knew how everything worked and could fix nearly anything. He and Eddie were the same age and had been friends since before they could walk. Bertie and Charlie were as close.

Eddie continued to watch Robbie as he spoke. "Well, it's good to have a shop here at the tannery, but everyone must pay the toll to reach your store, so not many come out this far just to browse. As we will sell other people's things, we need someone trustworthy to run it." He paused. "Robbie?"

George saw Eddie's gaze rest on his younger son. He gasped but remained quiet.

Eddie didn't say anything. He waited for Robbie to look up from his hands.

Eventually, Robbie realised everyone had fallen silent. Why had the conversation ceased? He realised all eyes were on him. Rob squirmed uncomfortably and said, "What? Why are you all looking at me?"

"Did you hear what I said, Rob?" Eddie asked.

Robbie flushed. He shook his head. "Sorry, I wasn't listening. I was woolgathering!"

Eddie said, "Did you hear any of it? I want to open an emporium, and I was wondering if you would run it for us."

Robbie sat up quickly. Maryanne was forgotten for the moment. "Me? You want me to run it? Why?"

Eddie laughed. "Yes, Rob, we want you and your exceptional sales skills. We all know you hate the work here at the tannery, except for the sales. We know that your heart is in the markets and selling stuff. You could sell ice to an Eskimo, a blanket to a hot Indian and sand to an Arab. Maryanne Connor, our new cook's daughter, said she would like to work in a shop there. But she wants to run a tea shop and sell the fresh produce her father grows. She is the girl who worked with Christina Meadows before she married Major Ned. Sorry, I mean the duke."

Robbie knew exactly who this girl was. He had taken every opportunity possible to seek her out and chat with her. He had just been daydreaming about her. Sadly, he only ever saw her at church. He said, "Really? We'd be working together?" That alone would be worth it. He would no longer have to make the dirty leather, but he could have a small workshop at the emporium and continue to craft his saddlebags and other small items, as well as do repairs for people. Yes, he would love that.

George thought it amusing that his son, Robbie, was so much like his namesake uncle. Moving into the emporium would mean they would regain their big front room. Of course, he would agree.

Robbie realised everyone was waiting for his reply. He grinned. "Too right, I'll do it. I'd be thrilled, but could I have a workbench? I could also do some small repairs while I am there. Reins and harnesses always break and are easy to fix or replace." He was bubbling with excitement. The ideas running through his head were numerous. His dreams would come true. He would see if he could get a wall of glass-fronted drawers filled with all sorts of leather goods and fittings like rolls of rein leather, buckles, and rivets. Also, a small shoe last instead of an anvil and a hammer for small jobs. To have Maryanne nearby was fabulous. Would she let him kiss her at some stage? All he had managed so far was a peck on her cheek. He sighed.

Eddie chuckled. "You are already making a list, aren't you, Rob? I can see your brain working."

Rob nodded, grinning, and said, "You bet. When do I start?"

Charles roared with laughter. He replied, "Hopefully, before Christmas. The foundations are down already. The first few courses are stone, then the rest should go up quickly. That's what the new building is at this end of Parramatta. My four boys have been discussing how it would work best. We've come today, so you have time to jot down some ideas, and we can discuss the project after church. Can we meet around my big table at the inn on Sunday after the service? We'll expect you for luncheon."

The family nodded in unison.

For the next half hour, the discussion focused on the other businesses that could benefit. Rob didn't lose concentration once. This was about something he loved: selling.

As they only made side saddles and lightweight English saddles, George asked, "Charles, could Ben supply a range of full saddles? I could also sell some excess African hides, as well as the usual variety of skins available for sale. I have boxes of off-cuts in various usable sizes for crops and other decorative purposes. Many use these scraps for all sorts of things, like spinning wheel hinges."

Charlotte's eyes were almost dancing with delight. Her gaze had not left Robbie's face. He showed interest in a project for the first time in a long, long time. Milly had shown more interest in the leatherwork than her youngest son did.

After discussing the new store for some time, George saw that Charles had more to reveal.

George frowned. "Spit it out, Charles. Something is on your mind."

His friend gave him a coy smile. "You could say that." He turned to Bertie and said, "This will affect you mostly, Bert. You see, it seems I am Ned's third cousin. We were unaware of any connection. His father and grandfather had no siblings, nor did mine. However, we had a mutual great-grandfather. We realised our similarity, but I had no idea that Ned's real name is Edward Lockley." Charles's gaze returned to his friend. Almost apologetically, he said, "My name and colouring are what drew him to me on the ship. He wondered if his brother Paul could be my twin. The baby supposedly died after two days, and he was named Charles. However, I was born later that month. I had no idea of any connection, George. None at all. Truly! Ned never let on about his family name."

George chuckled. "I wondered if there was something between you. I thought you could be a younger brother under an assumed name."

Charles's head shook. He swallowed somewhat nervously. "After Ned's identity was made public, Bill Miller revealed that he knew Ned's real name the entire time. Jack recently told me he also realised who Ned was as he'd met his father and brother in London. They never said a word to anyone, including Ned." He took a long draw of his tea. "Bill and Molly met David and Ned in London before they were sent out. As they were servants, Ned didn't notice them. Jack was probably the same. I never asked. I have since discovered that the Millers have had their convictions overturned, just like Jennifer Williams. I didn't even know that could occur, but I'm telling you only because Ned has had mine wiped, as well."

The audience gasped.

George frowned as he could see Charles was uncomfortable. What more could he reveal? George said, "And...?"

Charles took a deep breath and added, "And...Bertie, as you know, Ned took some of your saddles home. Most were for his family's use, but he gave the embossed sidesaddle to Her Majesty Queen Victoria. She was well pleased with her present." He opened his mouth and closed it again.

Bertie gasped, as did the rest of the family.

George knew his friend's expressions. He still looked worried. "Charles, go on?"

Charles nodded. "I'm getting there, my friend." He swallowed again and lowered his voice. "However, that is not my biggest news. I came to terms with being a convict years ago. Being Ned's cousin has elevated my role to a somewhat distracting degree. You see, apparently, I am an earl and have been since my father died when I was five. My title is Earl of Coxheath." He swallowed nervously.

Exclamations of awe circled the room.

George gathered his jaw off the floor enough to say, "You're a blooming earl? Really?"

Charles nodded sadly and said, "I'm not sure Papa even knew, as his own father also died quite young. Our house was on the edge of the ducal estate at Coxheath. It's how I know about the castle, but we didn't know there was a connection between the two families. The title carries no land or money. Sadly, word has already spread in Sydney. Unfortunately, I've been given a role in the colony. Last week, the governor summoned us to the official residence, and we had to get togged up." He waved his hand over the new attire. He turned to his son. "By the way, Ed, that will not occur often, do you understand?"

Eddie was grinning so broadly that his dimples were visible. He gave a nod.

Bertie was trying hard not to chuckle. He had a feeling he knew what was following.

Charles said, "Well, dash it, but the governor has asked me to be a sort of Assistant Viceroy for Western Sydney." He released an exasperated groan. "I don't want this! I want to go on being me. The upshot is that Sal and I are moving into Christina's old cottage, which Ned gave us, and Eddie and Jenna are to build a new house up the road. Charlie and Gracie will take over the inn full time, bringing me to my final point." He blew out his cheeks. Looking around the room at his friends, his eyes settled on Bertie again. He said, "You see, Earl's children all get titles. Charlie is an honorary viscount; the other five are all 'The Honourable'. Bert, that means Liza has a title, as all five are 'The Lord' or 'The Lady'." Phew! He'd said it.

Bertie paled. That was not what he was expecting. Money, yes, but a title? Seriously? The most expressive thing he could muster without swearing was, "Cor!"

Charles said, "Liza is The Lady Elizabeth Shannon Ellis. Sadly, you don't get anything, Bert, but she should now be officially addressed as Lady Elizabeth. I let her know before we came out to you. She will join us when she has fed Albie. Unfortunately, only Charlie's children, if he has any, will inherit titles. Otherwise, that will go to Eddie, then to his son, Neddie."

Eddie blanched. He had not thought of that. He repeated Bertie's "Cor! I'll have to hurry him up."

The apologetic look on Charles's face made George start chuckling.

Charlotte soon joined him, and her laugh was infectious.

When Liza joined them a few minutes later, the sitting room was awash with the sound of the group in stitches. From convicts and tanners, they were now in the company of another of England's peers of the realm. She had wondered how her husband and in-laws would accept her elevated status. She had married into the family when she was only a convict's child.

George finally caught his breath. He wiped his eyes and said, "Charles, you looked like a sulky brat. Most people on this land would give their eyeteeth to inherit such a title as you have."

Charles gave a shy smile before replying. "They may, but I was happy living my obscure life, as you well know, my friend. It's like me asking you, 'Why didn't you take to the stage to be paid to play your violin?' You could have made a fortune on the stages of Europe. There are some things I have a choice over, and this is not one of them. My Charlie nearly died when I told him he would one day inherit the title. However, he is already an honorary viscount, and he hates it. He hates being in the limelight even more than I."

Eddie grinned. "I never wanted to be the eldest child; now I'm pleased I'm not. I will insist that Charlie and Gracie have lots of sons. I always wanted to build a full foundry and work with Mr Tindale. This money that I have been given will help me do that. Dar was sent back pay, and he has some ideas of what to use that for. However, I intend to continue Major Ned's work and improve the town. I will start with the emporium, and that's why Rob is vital. However, I intend to do what you have, Mr Ellis. I want to give some of the less fortunate boys a skill, and if we can grow the smithy's forge, we can take on more apprentices from Howard Marlow's orphanage."

Eddie's penetrating gaze turned back to Robbie. "It all hangs on you, Rob. We will need a one-hundred per cent commitment. No woolgathering while you're at work. We're the same age, and I know your likes and dislikes. It's why I thought of you first. Yes, you can do small repairs if you want us to build a small workshop there. That will be another string to our bow and one I had not thought of."

Rob's grin was all the answer Eddie needed. However, it was followed by a nod. He replied, "As I said, I'm in!"

The revelations from this morning still made George reel.

George shook his head to clear his thoughts. Friday, the sixth of January, 1843, is a date he would never forget for as long as he lived. He smiled as he remembered the conversation from that morning.

Robbie came to life after the Lockleys left. After luncheon, when the boys and maids returned to work, George called a family meeting. Rob bubbled with delight at what an amazing turn his life had taken. He intentionally didn't mention his desire to befriend Maryanne, but her working with him was undoubtedly an enticement. Having his own money would also be terrific. Currently, he had no income, as all funds were pooled. To have a regular salary was beyond his wildest dreams. Eddie mentioned that he could even have a small flat at the back if they had enough building material. He felt like dancing a jig and shouting from the rooftop. To keep the news in the family for a while was going to be difficult. However, he would have a reason to seek Maryanne out after church in two days and talk to her. After the family discussion, he returned to salting the fresh hides and started whistling as he worked. Her coy glances stirred his lust. How close would she let him get? Hopefully, very close.

George chuckled. As he walked towards the shed after his friends departed, he lifted his eyes heavenward and gave thanks. Even his father's tannery at home would never have had access to a shop such as this.

~

When Eddie's emporium opened five months later, it stocked coopered barrels, buckets, drums, and ironmongery of all kinds from various businesses in town. Near the front door was an orders desk for taking custom requests. The cash drawer and stock book were also there. Everything was itemised, and Robbie had developed a system to track every sale, ensuring each maker was paid their just dues. Eddie built a workbench for Robbie, and underneath the bench, the shelves held a small anvil, a shoe last, and many other items. Some of Rob's great-grandfather's tools were given to him for repairs.

One of the carpenters wanted to join the project, so there were joinery items, such as slot-together shelving, chairs, beds, and various small household furniture pieces. Larger pieces could be ordered. Having a toll gate on either side of the town meant that some stores on the outskirts found it challenging to sell their wares. Therefore, the emporium shopfront was a raging success from day one. All the craftsmen closed their shops at their homes.

Maryanne set up a tea room in a connected lean-to extension. It also sold fresh produce from various households, which her father mainly grew. Paddy Connor also planted some flowers. His roses were spectacular, and cut flowers were kept in a bucket on the main counter inside the store. Robbie managed to get his kiss the week the store opened. Maryanne gave it willingly, then returned for another, and another.

The Kellow-William's fresh cheeses were also a popular item for sale in Maryanne's store. Although Jennifer and the family had returned to Cornwall, Jennifer's grown son, Kit, came back after completing his education in England and had married on the voyage. Now twenty-two, Kit Kellow ran the family dairy behind the government one and continued the cheesemaking. Most of Kit's unique hard cheeses were returned to Cornwall for sale there. However, the soft and plain hard cheeses were sold locally. Kit reverted to his birth name of Kellow, hence the hyphenated name of the dairy.

The selection of metal items from Eddie and Mr Tindale's forge ranged from nails of all sorts, including sewing pins, to eight-inch bridge nails. There were tools, shears, clamps, callipers, hammers, and more items than you could dream about. Steel posts for fences and tubular ramming tools for them. They stocked fence wire and everything imaginable for a farm. Walker's Loganberry Farm, located along the Hawkesbury River, sent woven baskets and honey in small ceramic jars. Colin Osborne's pottery business had supplied these to the farm for decades. Jonny Osborne now ran the business, but his parents, who were First Fleet convicts, still lived in the house. Maryanne Connor sold fresh produce that her father, Paddy, grew in the vast garden at Eddie's new house. Some of the Connor family had moved into the backyard of Eddie's new home before the building began. The garden was well established before Eddie and Jenna moved in.

The bootmaker placed his boots for sale in the emporium. He had an oversupply of them and decided to move some stock. He did so well that he wished to build his own shoe shop next door, as he was not allocated any more room in the emporium. Other items were oilskin coats for outdoor work, felt hats for the men and straw hats for garden work for the women. Items like whitewash and coloured paints would be added. Bolts of fabric for curtains and furnishings were popular, and dark-dyed cheesecloth was used to cover the windows as an insect barrier.

When Charles Lockley's youngest boys, Wills and Luke, wanted pocket money, he told them they had to earn it. They bagged some aged stable manure to sell for mulch and garden vegetable matter for the town gardens. This was particularly beneficial for small home gardens that lacked access to stables. Many people did not have horses, as they hired nags from the government stables that Charlie ran next to his inn. The manure was a penny a bag and was an affordable fertiliser. Eddie also added a rear loft, which stored stock feed. There was an awning so that they could load wagons in all weathers. The loft had grain, hay, and other fodder supplies required for stables, with a cantilever pulley system for loading heavy items.

George thought they were busy before the emporium's opening, but now they were run off their feet. He had taken on another dozen boys from the orphanage. George sighed. The only fly in the ointment was Robbie.

George watched Bertie scud a cowhide before placing a new hide on his elevated scudding post. George gave a long sigh. He had to arrange a quick wedding. Yesterday morning, Rob confessed that Maryanne was three months gone with his child. He was sure Robbie's ears were still red after he had chewed his youngest son out and all but dragged him over the coals.

George and Charlotte were livid, but after the emporium closed, they visited Maryanne's parents at Eddie's house with Robbie in tow. Eddie's new home was a fantastic residence. The two-story dwelling was bigger than Government House on the hill above it.

Paddy and Cara Connor welcomed them warmly. They were life convicts but had fallen on their feet when they became Eddie's staff. Maryanne had not told them of her condition, so the meeting was decidedly uncomfortable. Paddy's glare at Robbie made George wonder if their son would survive the meeting.

Robbie begged her parents' forgiveness. He had sought permission to court her more than a year ago and had been refused.

Paddy was furious and let Robbie have an earful.

Eddie joined the meeting after overhearing their raised voices. With Eddie's calming presence, Paddy eventually calmed down and listened. The young couple would marry as soon as could be arranged and live in the small residence behind the emporium. The condition was that the emporium be opened for longer hours, including Saturday mornings. Robbie had no choice but to agree. The option was probably being shot by Paddy. He had warned him away from his daughter, and Robbie disobeyed.

George knew yesterday's interview was humiliating, but Eddie and he smoothed things over with Paddy. Their children were to marry in a few days, by a special licence arranged by Charles. This was so that Banns wouldn't need to be read publicly, and there would be no announcement in the paper of when the nuptials occurred.

Rob was living onsite in a small room at the back of the building, and his single bed would be widened. There would be little room for any luxuries. A small wicker baby basket would fit on top of their chest of drawers. Eddie planned to build a manager's cottage behind the store, which would now need to be fast-tracked. George would contribute money so the new couple had somewhere to live when the baby arrived.

He had many new lads making leather, so Bertie could concentrate on making saddles. He had more orders for side saddles than he could handle. Roo hides were no longer sold but kept for Bertie's saddles. Quinn tanned most of them. George focused on the hide he was working on. He sighed in frustration. His body was failing him. These days, his back ached after a day doing this work. He straightened up and removed the cleaned hide. He took the skin to the coopered barrel and dipped it to wash off the remaining hair.

George turned to the boys and said, "I'm done for the day, lads. Keep working and come in for dinner when the sun hits the top of the trees."

Bertie lifted his head and waved. He was composing as he worked. Hopefully, he would remember the tune.

George paused and watched his son work before heading indoors.

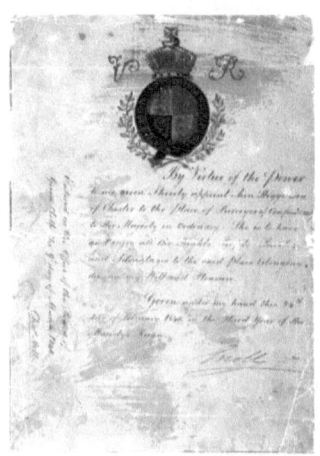

Chapter 21 Unstamped Mail
Late 1843

Word spread quickly that the Duke of Gracemere had presented one of Bertie's saddles to Her Majesty Queen Victoria. People now needed to place orders with Bertie six months in advance. They had come a long way from Paterson and Foveaux's first orders. George turned and looked around him. His folks would have loved it here. Foveaux may have had a fierce reputation, but he had seen the boys' skills and set them up as a business quicker than either lad dreamed.

Initially, Quinn made the wooden trees out of cedar for the side saddles himself. Soon, Bertie had the new apprentices making the parts and assembling them.

Having learned the skill, Quinn's eldest son, Craig, returned home to help his father with their growing business. Young Bryan, another orphan, had taken his place. Quinn's business was also busy. They had officially dissolved that partnership some years earlier, but the friendship remained. Quinn was still George's brother. George was always happy to lend a hand when a large order needed to be filled.

Bertie's apprentices churned out the tree bases and tanned leather almost faster than Bertie could finish the saddles. All were made with the local red cedar. They were light and strong.

George knew that his son's workmanship at finishing and refining the saddle trees surpassed Ben's, but Bertie's skill in the decorative work on the side saddles made them outstanding. Charlotte had taught him well.

George reappeared at the kitchen steps and walked to his son.

With a backlog of orders for saddles, Bertie was relieved of all other work. He needed to concentrate on finishing this order. He pushed the two needles through the punched holes and tied off the thread. He had just completed the last stitches when he stood, stretched his back and realised his father was watching him. "Hello, Papa. Anything I can do for you?"

George nodded and revealed what he was hiding behind his back: two violin cases. "I was wondering if your fingers could do with a bit of a flex? We haven't played together for ages."

Bertie's grin showed that George had chosen a good time. "You bet, sir. I can polish this tonight. They will be here to collect the saddle at noon tomorrow, so I have some time to spare. Can we play that new arrangement of Pachelbel's *Canon in D*? It's much better with two violins."

George grinned.

Bertie washed up, and they walked to the verandah, where they sat in their comfortable cane chairs. With their skill widely known, George no longer played in secret. Many wanted him to play if it was warm enough to be outside, and this afternoon, it was.

Charlotte brought them a tea tray, but it sat forgotten as the two men played the beautiful melodies the town had come to adore.

They had been playing for over half an hour when they saw the postman approach. He brought the late mail.

The afternoon's post nearly always brought a swathe of orders. They were in no hurry to read the letters, as it would mean more work to do.

Their friend, Brad, was the postie, and he always liked to chat. He leaned against the verandah post and listened to the duet. As they finished the piece, the postman handed over their stash of letters.

As Bertie was closer, he reached out for them. "Thanks, Brad."

Bradley put it in his hand and said, "There be an hinterestin' one amongst them, Bertie. Looks like some posh toff is writin' to ya. It's not the Dook 'cause his writing is real distinctive like. This one 'as got gold on it."

Bertie placed his instrument on the table. He flicked through the pile.

The postman showed his toothless grin. "'Tis the one on the bottom, Bert. It's got no stamp, and that's strange."

The letter was found. As Brad said, the envelope bore no stamp, but on the reverse were two crested hand-painted emblems. The envelope was circled in black and gold and did not look like an ordinary letter. He wondered who could post a letter without a stamp other than the monarch.

Mr Albert Ellis was scrawled almost illegibly on the front. The A and E were written with an elaborate flourish.

Bertie was none the wiser. He looked at his father with a cocked eyebrow.

George shrugged, as he was as intrigued as Bertie was.

Bertie flicked his eyes to the postie and then to his father. He slipped his finger under the back seal and opened the letter. He slowly extracted the sheets inside and opened them.

Unfolding a parchment document, he noted a floral single-letter monograph of a capital V with a crown on top. Perspiration beaded on his brow, and he wiped his forehead with his arm.

George noticed the blood draining from his son's face. "Bert, what's wrong?" He saw Bertie glance at the sheet underneath. George could see a crested blue and red diagram on a sheet of parchment, but could not read what it said. He did notice the *V R* on either side of the orb. He saw Bertie's hands start shaking.

George felt like snatching the paper from his son's trembling hands. His instrument joined his son's on the table. "Bert, what the blooming heck does it say? What's wrong?"

Bertie's head shook sideways. His white face lifted to meet his father. "Papa, read this." He held the two sheets out to his father.

The postie hadn't moved. "Is ya gonna tell a poor chap what's in that fancy letter? I is dying to know."

George held up his hand to silence the man. His hands also started shaking. He read the short letter, then glanced at the gold-edged, linen document with a royal monogram. Then he threw his head back and laughed.

At this sound, Charlotte and Liza came to join the men. They had remained further along the verandah as they loved listening to the music.

The ladies nodded a hello to the postman and went to stand near their husbands.

Liza saw Bertie still shaking and bent down beside him. "Bertie, is everything all right?"

He nodded but was still unable to speak.

Charlotte stood behind George and read over his shoulder. Her gasp made her hand fly to cover her mouth.

Liza and the postie both shrugged.

George moved and held out his hand to his son. "Congratulations, Albert Ellis! You have a Royal Warrant to supply her gracious majesty with side saddles for the term of her life."

The postman nearly slid off the verandah post. He stumbled, righted himself, and said, "He's got what, gov?"

George was grinning broadly. "You heard right, Brad! My son will make Queen Victoria's sidesaddles for as long as she remains on the throne." George shook Bertie's hand so hard that the chair moved.

The postie recovered from his shock. "Cor, Bert! First, you married a real lady; sorry, Mrs Ellis, I mean Lady Liza, I mean Lady Elizabeth, but now this."

Liza chuckled. "Bradley, you are a big gossip. We have known each other before you were breeched. We even went to the charity school together, so get off your high horse and congratulate my beloved husband for his good work. Major Ned Grace took one of Bertie's sidesaddles back with him for Her Majesty as a belated coronation gift."

Bradley said, "Ahh, the enigmatic Dook, eh?"

Liza held her finger up angrily to her old friend. "The Duke of Gracemere is my cousin, Brad, so mind your tongue."

Brad chuckled. "Sorry, Lady Liza. I shall mind my tongue and my speech." He made a mock bow to his old friends, followed by a salute and a word of congratulations. With a glance at his childhood friends, he grinned. He left, with a spring in his step, to spread the good news throughout the town.

The four Ellis's watched him leave.

George said, "I think we should have asked him not to say anything."

Liza chuckled. "It wouldn't have made the slightest bit of difference. The fact that Bertie received a letter from Her Majesty will have already spread through the Post Office. The lack of a stamp and emblems on the back gives the sender away. This is big news, not just for us but for the colony! Do you remember how fast the news of Uncle Ned being the Duke of Gracemere spread?" She didn't mention that her father had received a similar letter enclosed with Ned's screed.

The three listeners all nodded. They were all still in awe that Liza called the duke "uncle."

She told them of the night Ned revealed his status to the family. She sighed. "I wasn't there as Bert and I were still on our honeymoon in the cottage, but I heard all about it later. Eddie missed the tale, as bushrangers had attacked him, and he was bedridden. Mama took me aside shortly before Ed's wedding and told me." Liza thought back to that crazy week when bushrangers had nearly killed Ed. Only weeks after their wedding, she realised she was having a baby. Her eyes sought George's. Years before she was born, he, too, had been attacked by a different mob of escaped convicts and nearly died. That danger was still present, as many felons still roamed the scrubby bush.

Swallowing, she continued her saga. "The incident with Eddie brought Ned and his childhood friend Gerry together, and Ned's new status was revealed. Things changed quickly after that." She paused, and after a while, she resumed her story. "Uncle Ned proposed to Aunt Christina that night, and they married a bit over three weeks later. As you know, a month later, when one of Uncle Ned's men married, their new titles were revealed to the town. At this stage, Dar and Uncle Ned still had no idea they were related."

George nodded. Charles had revealed that. The story tallied with what he knew.

Liza reached for her husband's hand and interwove her hand with his. "I love you, Bert. We fell in love before we had anything. I was the child of a felon, and you were the tanner's son. You deserve this honour, so hold your head high."

Bertie leaned over and kissed her. "I love you, sweet cakes."

A thought occurred to George, and he blew his cheeks out and released a long breath. "Ben is not going to like this, nor is Quinn. I hope you realise this, son. The apprentice has surpassed the master in such a way that is beyond comprehension."

Charlotte chuckled. "Kath will love it, though."

George reached out his hand to Bertie. "I really am so proud of you,

Bert! This is the reward for all your hard work." With a grin still on his lips, he took up his beloved instrument. "Feel like playing a celebratory tune to God, I know the perfect one. I call it the saddler's song as it's Ben's favourite. It's from the *Messiah*. As you know, he always asks me to play it. I think that it's a song you can now claim as well."

Charlotte giggled. "Ben claimed it publicly the night you proposed to me at the governor's concert."

With a nod, Bertie grinned. "It's one of my favourites too, Papa. I think playing this song is a perfect way to thank the good Lord for this incredible blessing."

Bertie also tucked his instrument under his chin, and without a word to each other, they struck up the opening bars of *The Hallelujah Chorus*. The glorious and joyous sounds of the music from Handel's Messiah wafted over the air and down the valleys to the town. Many knew this incredible music and the passion that the tanner and saddler had for it. They all knew it as 'The saddler's song,' thanks to Ben.

Thanks to Brad, the town would soon realise what the celebration was tonight. The Ellis family were praising God for their good fortune.

Brad was already spreading the news of the blessing that had come to Bertie and the Ellis family.

*****

When Upon Life's Billows is Crispin and Helena Rosedale's story.
Charles and Ned's history is in *Hands Upon the Anvil*
and *The Lockleys of Parramatta* series.
The prequel, *Unshackled Lives* (Ned's story)
is **free when you sign up for my newsletter.**
The next book in the collection,
Mark and Cathy Duffy's saga - *Tuppence to Pass*
His Majesty's Pageboy is Jack and Martha Turner's saga,
Bound Down in Iron Chains is Howard Marlow's story about the Boy's
Orphanage (2026)

Honest reviews of my books help bring them to the attention of other readers who are more likely to read something from a new-to-them author if it has more reviews. You can quickly and easily leave a brief rating or review on Amazon.

.

Author's note

Bartolomeo Giuseppe Guarneri was an Italian violin maker who equalled, if not surpassed, Stradivarius. His instruments were certainly lauded well before the Stradivarius. Guarneri died aged 46.

Paganini played a Guarneri instrument and composed primarily for the tones of his incredible violin. Fewer than two hundred instruments survive. Some of both makers' instruments are valued at over $20 million USD each. The **Guarneri** violin is more valuable than a **Stradivarius**. There are only about 200 known Guarneri violins and 600 Stradivari violins.

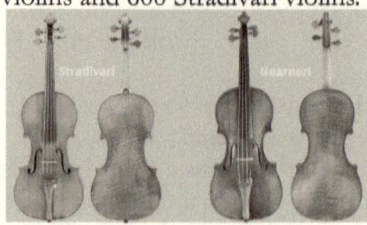

My father, **Norman M. Hunter**, was a very amateur violinist who was given an Austrian instrument by the renowned Sydney instrument maker, A. E. Smith, who taught him to play when he was young. After his first wife died in 1951, Dad would sit on the cliff top at home in Avoca Beach, NSW, and play his violin. He had no idea the sound travelled over the small town where he lived. It took two decades for the community to discover who the mystery violinist was, but when it was eventually revealed, Dad stopped playing the violin. He was never a brilliant violinist, but he played from the heart.

Many similar **concerts**, as I described in this story, would have taken place back in colonial times. Since music was an integral part of everyday life back then, they were rarely noted in the papers. Musical evenings, or later gatherings around the piano, were just a part of everyday life before the era of television and radio.

The history of the **Rum Rebellion** is as accurate as the story requires. Foveaux took command of the colony until Paterson arrived from Van Diemen's Land to command until Lachlan Macquarie arrived. Much has been written about this era, so I have decided to skip over this incident.

The **tanning methods** described in this book, as well as the saddle-making techniques, are historically accurate, including the Zulu shields in Cape Town. (One was sold recently from the Avoca Beach Antique shop, so I was able to see one up close. It still had the fur/hair on it.)

Dog excrement was used to condition the leather. This foul-smelling substance was collected by children called "pure collectors." Urine was also part of the treatment. Those who sold their urine were usually poor, hence the term "Piss poor." Other countries used different processes. Those even poorer folk who "Didn't have a pot to piss in."

Queen Victoria certainly rode side saddle, and some were given to her from Australia, but I have not been able to find a *Royal Warrant* for saddles. It was rumoured that she did have an Australian saddle maker. She issued over 2000 of these Warrants during her reign

Characters

Albert Ellis b 1765 d 1807 typhus
m **Amelia** Attwell 1766 d 1807 typhus

  1 Robert (**Rob**) **Ellis** b 1790 d 1807 typhus

  2 **George Ellis** b 1791 in an outer suburb of London   (on *Lady Sinclair* dept 26/10/07- 28/7/08)

  m 1813 **Charlotte Rosedale** b in Parramatta - of old age.

  Children 4

    1 Albert George (**Bertie**)b 1819- a Sadler/leather goods - in Parramatta

    m 1840 b 1820 Elizabeth (**Liza**) Lockley

      children 1+ Albie

    2 Robert Linus (**Robbie**) b mid 1821

    m 1842 **Maryanne** Connor

      Children 3+ Olivia Cara (**Livvie**) + 2 more

    3 Amelia Agnes (**Milly**) Ellis b 1822

    m Dec 1843 **Marc** Turner

    4 Isabella Charlotte (**Belle**)b 1826

    m 1851, **Sam** Miller

Miles Armstrong bought George's tannery in England.

Ben Parker b 1788 - Arrived with George Ellis, Saddler at Emu Plains

m 1811 Katherine (**Kath**) Rosedale b 1791 in

  See below

Linus Rosedale (ages in 1798) b 1747, d Aug 1811

M 1775 **Agnes** Armstrong b 1750

  Children 16

  1 Gerald (**Gerry**) twin b1776 m 1804 Colleen (eng 1802)

  2 Jeramy (**Jem**) Twin b 1776 m 1804 Erin (eng 1802)

  3 stillborn daughters 1777

  4 **Helena Rosedale** b 1778 - convict on the Surprise 1795 (20)

  M 1795 Private **Crispin Milroy**, Mrs Milroy's nephew & soldier in Gov Hunter's security detail. *Father died in 1792, Aunt in 1793 (dark with dark brown eyes)*

    Children 11

  5 **Mary** 18 m 3/11/99 **Jonas** Thistlethwaite

  6 Phoebe 16 m3/11/99 Arnold Kerr

  7 Nicholas 14 b 1783 m 1804 to a convict girl, Rachel

  8 Tristan 13 b 1784 m 1804 to a convict girl Rebekah (Bek)

  9 Margaret b 86 m 1809 to a soldier, Harry

  10 Patience b 88 m 1809 to a soldier, Algernon Darnley

  11 Victoria b 89 m 1812 Bill Felton b - George Ellis's friend - retired soldier.

  12 Katherine (**Kath**) Rosedale b 91

  m 1811 **Benjamin Parker**, a saddler on Castlereagh Road, Penrith

    4 stillbirths, (3 boys, 1 girl), 2 living children

    1 Mary Kathleen b 1827 m Dec 1847 Alex Turner (eng 1845 - when Mary turned 18)

    2 Violet Agnes b 1829

  13 Charlotte (**Charlie**) 1793 (strawberry blonde, sky blue eyes)

  m 1812 **George** Ellis, a tanner & leatherworker, Parramatta

    Children 4 - see above

  14 Emily b 1794

  15 Rebecca b 1797

  16 Samantha b April 1798 - youngest died in Dec 1798

Quinn, Eric, (orphans stay with George) all b 1796
Pete and Wendell - orphan boys (leave with Ben) b 1797
Captain **Mark** Duffy, 73rd Regiment
m Sept 1809 Cathy Callan née Parks (see *Tuppence to Pass*)
Major **Ned** Grace, aka - Lord Edward Lockley - 6th Duke
    of Gracemere, *see Hands Upon The Anvil*
M Christian Meadows, 25th Dec 1841 (5 children)
Charles Lockley - Earl of Coxheath
M Sarah (**Sal**) McCarthy *see Hands Upon The Anvil*
6 children

    1 Charlie
    m Nov 1842 Gracie Miller (Double wedding with Anna)
    2 Eddie Lockley
    m Dec 1841 Jenna Turner
    3 Liza Lockley
    4 Anna Lockley
    5 Wills Lockley
    6 Luke Lockley
Jack & Martha Turner - at Emu Plains - 7 children. *See His Majesty's PageBoy*
Bill and Molly Miller - 4 children - see *In Defence of Her Honour*
Billy and Jennifer Williams
    Christopher (Kit) Kellow see *Convict Shadows of the Past*
Howard Marlow - ran the boys' orphanage in Sydney. *See Bound Down in Iron Chains*
Captain Guy and Martha Manning, see *Jam or Marmalade for Tea.*
Obadiah Jensen and daughter, Mary

Real People

Lieutenant-Governor Joseph Foveaux
Major George Johnston
Governor Lachlan and Elizabeth Macquarie
Mrs Ovens - Macquarie's Cook at Government House
Captain John Hardy Jackson - Captain of *Lady Madeline Sinclair*
William Hustwick- 3rd Mate – *Lady Madeline Sinclair* of Hull, 600 tons,
Lieutenant Governor Foveaux, with naval stores & 100 troops. (on *Lady Sinclair* dep
    UK 26/10/07- 28/7/08)
Governor Bligh - Rum Rebellion
John and Elizabeth Macarthur
Lieutenant Governor Paterson
Major George Johnston

Bibliography

Leather Tanning
https://en.wikipedia.org/wiki/Tanning_(leather)

Saddle making
https://en.wikipedia.org/wiki/
English_saddle#:~:text=The%20panels%20on%20the%20underside,on%20the%20highest%20
quality%20saddles.

Governor Bligh
https://www2.sl.nsw.gov.au/archive/events/exhibitions/2008/politicspower/docs/
bligh_guide.pdf

Joseph Foveaux
https://en.wikipedia.org/wiki/Joseph_Foveaux

Norfolk Island and Foveaux
https://triffitt1.wordpress.com/overview/
https://historycollection.com/australia-day-secrets-12-incredible-things-never-knew-first-fleet/
12/

Guarneri violin
https://en.wikipedia.org/wiki/Giuseppe_Guarneri
Sound comparison.:- https://youtube.com/watch?v=j3q_VsTfHE4

Darug Dictionary & words
https://dharug.dalang.com.au/language/dictionary?
query=duck&type=English&numeric=Exact&dialect=All#
Corroboree - a tribal dance
yellomundie = storyteller
dadyibalung = good
Buyi = Spirit person, ghost person

The pieces George played... Music - from YouTube
Divertimenti Carnevaleschi, No. 1 by Paganini - https://www.youtube.com/watch?v=4T-ifzpOTz0
Moonlight Sonata by Beethoven -h ttps://www.youtube.com/watch?v=Elswt0QLO5M
Romance No. 2 in F Major by Beethoven - https://www.youtube.com/watch?v=N2rblR3Tmkc
Chaconne by J.S. Bach - https://www.youtube.com/watch?v=wix7vRl3V-E
When I survey the Wondrous Cross- https://www.youtube.com/watch?v=KEp6WKSXYQg&list=PLhkGkd3nKogeZP0brh9l97JH8UyqzWjx3
https://www.youtube.com/watch?v=XPxm1gWL2CI
Romance No. 2 in F Major by Beethoven
Air on the G String" by J.S. Bach
Moonlight Sonata by Beethoven -
Vivaldi's **Four Seasons.** https://classicalmusiconly.com/work/antonio-vivaldi/the-four-seasons-f83i/tv

Royal Warrant from Queen Victoria, 1840 *(she issued over 2000 during her reign)*
https://historical.ha.com/itm/autographs/non-american/royal-warrant-in-the-reign-of-queen-victoria-dated-february-24-1840/a/201537-92021.s

If you loved this book, you may also enjoy these similar titles.
(All are stand-alone stories)

First Fleet Convict Era Trilogy 1788-1800

Gentle Annie Soames

Her dreams lead to unexpected outcomes. An Australian First Fleet story.
*A First Fleet story with the descriptions taken directly from the Journal of
Doctor Arthur Bowes Smith was the doctor on board the* Lady Penrhyn.

Annie Soames is a girl beloved by the community but not afraid to voice her desires. That leads to trouble, illicit love, and a world turned upside down.

Oliver Quilpie, the newly married Marquess, finds his arranged marriage unsatisfactory; he is irresistibly drawn to his wife's companion. Unfortunately, he can't keep his hands off her. In retaliation, Annie copies his every move while riding, dressed as a highwayman. However, she has now fallen in love with him. This ultimately leads to her arrest and banishment to a distant land.

After some years, Oliver's wife dies, and his thoughts turn to Annie. He seeks to find her, but she has vanished. He is horrified to discover she was transported to New South Wales as a convict on the *Lady Penrhyn.* Will Annie want to see him?

ISBN 9780645441574   ISBN ebook 9781923097063   LP ISBN 978-1923097346

Long-listed in the Historical Fiction Company Competition 2024

The Emancipated Potter

Sydney Cove 1788 to Parramatta 1795
Not all felons are convicts, and not all convicts are felons.

Colin Osborne's serene life as a talented potter is crushed by a self-important peer. A single punch sends Colin across to the other side of the globe.

Aggie Gibbs is a young convict girl being hunted by a wayward soldier. The two find themselves in a town of criminals and lecherous men.

Captain John Hunter is Colin's mentor, and he paves the way for a new life for his young friends. Then disaster strikes, and he must leave.

Can Colin keep Aggie safe? Will they fulfil Captain Hunter's wishes to build a decent life for the convicts destined to live out their lives in the penal town? Will John ever return to New South Wales? Paperback ISBN 9781923097476   ISBN ebook 9781923097483

Paternity Unknown

Sydney 1788 - 1800 The Aftermath of the First Fleet landing.
Can forgiveness be that easy?

Connie Waterson is traumatised after she became one of the victims of the attack when the convict women were landed on February 6th, 1788. She finds herself expecting an unwanted child. Along with her friends, she must learn to cope with the challenges of their new environment while protecting the life growing within her.

Nigel Bray is a young convict who almost instantly regrets his carnal actions on the day the prisoners from the *Lady Penrhyn* landed. Knowing that Connie is the unwilling recipient of his base desires, Nigel does what he can to ease her path. He is racked with questions: is the child his? Will she ever forgive him? What must Nigel do to win Connie's trust?

ISBN 9781923097438   ISBN ebook 9781923097445   LP ISBN 978-1923097452

The Hunter to Macquarie Collection 1795-1822

When Upon Life's Billows

Sydney 1795-1821 - Governor John Hunter
Keep your friends close, and your enemies closer.

John Hunter loved life at sea—until a storm wrecked HMS Sirius in 1790. Five years later, as the second governor of the filthy penal colony of New South Wales, he finds himself in the wrong place, trusting the wrong people.

Helena Rosedale, a fierce convict known as "Helena the Hellcat," fights off men who try to abuse her. **Crispin Milroy,** alone in the world, serves on the new governor's security detail—and risks his heart on Helena.

In harsh, disease-ridden Sydney Cove in 1795, food is scarce and survival uncertain. Why does John trust this young couple when others betray him, and what must Helena and Crispin endure to build a life in such an unforgiving town?

ISBN: 9780645783339   ebook ISBN: 9780645783346

The Saddler's Song
London 1790s to Parramatta 1840s
The Strains of Starting Again.

George Ellis is the son of a tanner, living on the outskirts of London. Alone and hurting after a disease takes his family, he seeks a new life, setting up a business in New South Wales. His beloved violin is his most treasured possession, and his talent for making music is hidden from all but a select few. **Ben Parker,** a saddler, is also heading to the colony. Combining their skills to start afresh in a new world, the young men find accommodation with a family. Two of the daughters steal their hearts — but how will the business survive in a stock-starved land where access to leather is limited? What is the saddler's song, and why is it so special?

ISBN: 9780645783353   eISBN: 9780645783360

Tuppence to Pass
London 1800s to Parramatta 1820s
An Unlikely Partnership

Josh Callan never expected much from life—just enough to get by in the gritty backstreets of London. But when he's caught stealing from the very man who murdered his father, Josh finds himself branded worthless by a sneering judge and sentenced to a distant, brutal world: the penal colony of Sydney. Arriving just as **Governor Lachlan Macquarie** takes charge, Josh steps into a colony on the cusp of change—and into opportunities he never dreamed possible. As he earns the powerful governor's respect and becomes a trusted confidante, Josh begins to forge a new path not just for himself but also for his family and his beloved.

Can a boy dismissed as nothing rise to become something more? And what will his unexpected friendship with the governor cost or gain him in the end?

ISBN : 9781923097070   eISBN: 9781923097087   LP 9781923097544

His Majesty's Pageboy
London to Emu Plains, Australia, in the 1800s

Jack Turner, raised in privilege and known as Lord John. However, at age nine, his true identity is revealed. He struggles with society's immorality and shallowness. He finally meets a pure young woman he feels he could love, but because of his chequered background, he is unable to pursue her. Then, his life takes another turn.

Martha Alexander, daughter of a wealthy shipping merchant, met Lord John while at a society ball in London. She is expected to marry well, and she has feelings for John. But her father's drunkenness led to the loss of everything he owned, including Martha, dooming her to a forced marriage. How do these two young people end up as convicts in Australia?

Paperback ISBN 9781923097308 eISBN 978192309792   LP ISBN 9781923097568

A Fist Full of Holey Dollars
Sydney Cove 1810+
The Holey Dollar and Dump Story

Captain Rudi Greenwood is a solitary man, trapped in a pointless job in a colony where alcohol is currency and rules are easily ignored in the pursuit of wealth. He is on the verge of ending his monotonous life.

Bethany Edwards, a grieving widow expecting her late husband's child, slowly begins to change from her grief because of her encounters with the handsome but brooding soldier. As she turns to Rudi for help and support, she must face what she truly feels. Will her faith reach a man who believes in nothing, or will his lack of belief keep them apart?

Drawn to Bethany, Rudi is forced to question his cynicism and imagine a different future. When **Governor Lachlan Macquarie** asks for his help improving the colony's roads, an offhand remark from Rudi sparks an idea that could reshape the settlement: a new currency to challenge the power of alcohol. Will Rudi accept the governor's challenge—and what bold choice will make him despised by both the exclusives and the free settlers?

Paperback ISBN 9781923097407   eISBN 9781923097414

Coming 2026

Far From the Whispering Sheoaks
Set in Australia in 1817+

Fanny Little was in the wrong place doing something she thought was legal. Her actions led to her arrest, trial, and banishment. She was assigned from the female prison to ex-soldier Gordon McKenzie and soon found herself in the despicable and humiliating situation of being sold in the public marketplace.

Phil Bentley is a man running from his jealous uncle. He is seeking safety on a secluded farm half a world away. With the community backing them, can Phil save Fanny from Gordon's vile abuse? Why is their relationship destined to spark controversy? And who is Jas? Why does Gordon wish to harm the child? Will they ever escape the shadows pursuing them?

Paperback ISBN 9781923097315   eISBN9781923097322

Coming 2026

Quest for Survival
Sydney 1798-1810 - Between the Governors

Nell Bywater intentionally gets arrested after hearing that convicts receive free food and clothing. As a twelve-year-old foundling, life is tough. Her options are few, and most of those are distasteful. She gets assigned to Governor Hunter's nephew as a nursemaid for his small children. Then, the Kents leave, and she is left alone in an almost empty house.
Aubrey Grey is a young convict man assigned to convert the Kents' old house into a new girls' orphanage. There, he meets Nell.
Governor and Mrs King oversee the new girls' orphanage and Nell as well. Mrs King ensures Nell is kept safe with Aubrey assigned as caretaker.
As houseparents for over thirty small girls, both find the security they sought. However, there is more to life than a roof over your head and food in your belly. A simple assignment becomes life-changing for both of them when love intervenes.
ISBN   e ISBN

Bound Down in Iron Chains
An Australian Historical Tale, set in the Boys' Orphanage in Sydney in 1818+
Smuggling, Rum and Ructions
A gripping tale of betrayal, courage, and survival in colonial Australia.

When honest London bookkeeper **Howard Marlow** is wrongly convicted and sent to New South Wales, he's assigned to the **Sydney Boys' Orphanage**, where corruption runs deep and the accounts don't add up.
There he meets **Naomi Buckingham**, a convict girl hoping for safety—but facing danger instead. As the two uncover coded ledgers and a smuggling ring tied to the colony's elite, they must risk everything to expose the truth.
In a brutal world built on power and fear, can two convicts bring justice to those who have none?   Paperback ISBN 9781923097353   eISBN9781923097360
Coming 2026

Buddy's Promise
From the Shadows of London to the shade of the gumtrees

Raised on the streets of London, **Obadiah "Buddy" Jensen** hides a fierce loyalty behind a tough facade. When a dying boy begs him to protect his little sister, **Emily Bolt**, Buddy vows to keep her safe—never expecting she'll become the love he can't have.
Exiled to Australia as a convict, Buddy builds a new life, but when Emily reappears years later, everything has changed. He is married with a child.
She was six when he found her. She was lost when he left. Torn between past promises and present choices, can they find their way back to each other—or will fate keep them apart forever? An emotional historical romance of love, loss, and redemption across the seas.
         ISBN 9780645783384   eISBN 9780645783391
Coming 2027

Linen Shirts Aplenty
The first female factory, Parramatta early 1800s.

Biddy Murphy is an Irish girl who caught the eye of an upstart English peer. Convicted and transported as a wanton, she must face the shame of her fallen status.
Major Geoffrey Gilmore is the convict assignment officer in Sydney. His heart goes out to this beautiful but very skilled girl. Can Geoff ease her lot in life, or will their positions in the colony keep them apart? Will the hatred of the Irish mean that Geoff's attraction to this lovely girl be doomed before he can rescue her?
Coming 2027

Unlikely Convict Ladies Trilogy 1792-1840s
Dancing to Her Own Tune
Co-authored by Sheila Hunter and Sara Powter
Sydney 1790s to England 1830s

Annie White is released after serving seven years as a convict in Sydney. She has a visitor who helps her start a baking business. Annie is then asked to assist another ailing man, **Sam Corbett**. She nurses him back to health, and a relationship blossoms between them. They settle into a life together, barely making ends meet, when she realises she's expecting a child. Sam's past is laid bare, and he must come to terms with the revelations. They both must confront their accusers and discover that the answers to their questions are not what they anticipated. Their life experiences seem to cling to them, and, unable to shake them off, they end up back in England. They must face their ghosts and recognise they are not who they think they are. How can they transform their anger and spite into love and forgiveness? The Dance of Life goes on.
         ISBN 9780645110715   ISBN9780645110722
Long-listed for the Historical Fiction Company Competition 2022

Amelia's Tears

Parramatta 1828 – England 1840s
From Tears of Sadness to Tears of Joy.

Amelia Westaweller awaits her assignment in the Parramatta Female Prison. Forced to leave the relative safety of gaol, she is assigned and now faces her worst nightmare. A foul man claims her and makes her life a living hell. Then, her world goes black. A glimmer of hope arises when she hears from her brother, Jim, who has enlisted a friend to help her. She writes to Jim, pouring out her heart and telling him of the horrors of her new life. He encourages her to stay firm in her faith. All she can do is pray. When Major **Ned** Grace, her brother's friend, enters her life in Parramatta, he starts to ease her path. Things have changed, as now she has a child in tow. How can Amelia forge a new life for herself? What man could want her with her background and a child at her side? Who is the gentleman who turns her tears of sadness into tears of great joy?

ISBN: 9780645110739   eISBN: 9780645110746 Hard Cover ISBN 9798420617953

A Lady in Irons

England 1800s - Parramatta 1808+

Katy Harrington is mourning the death of her husband after he died in a shooting accident. Barely coping, she awaits the birth of their child. If it's a girl, she must hand the family home to her husband's brother. The day after giving birth to a daughter, she and her daughter are left on the side of a road. She collapses and is found by someone she thought had died in a fire ten years before. **Perry White** badly scarred himself, nurses her back to health. They marry and move in with Mary, her widowed friend.

After some years, she discovers her husband and friend in each other's arms. Now living in a love triangle, she flees. Grasping the only straw available, she intentionally gets arrested and is sent to a colony far away. By doing this, her marriage can be annulled.

What happens in the Colony is different from what she expects. Governor Macquarie comes to her rescue, but what of Perry and her children?

ISBN: 9780645110784   eISBN:9780645441505

The Convict Birthstain Collection
1820-1840s

NO MORE, MY Love

Hunter Valley, NSW, 1820s

Jess Elkin is distraught when tragedy ravages her family. Now widowed, she becomes the victim of a carriage accident and is nursed back to health by the driver.

Marcus Ryan, a hard-headed woollen mill owner, was not expecting to fall in love. Yet, when Jess's fortunes suddenly turn for the worse, Marcus must decide how far he will go to pursue her. Years after following her to Newcastle, Australia, Marcus vanishes. Jess is left wondering if he will keep his promise to return to her… Will she ever see him again?

ISBN: 9780645441536   eISBN 9780645441581
Long-listed in the Historical Fiction Company Competition 2023

The Vine Weaver

Hawkesbury River area 1820s+
New Beginnings and Old Threats

In the 1820s, **Joel and Hetty Walker** lived on a secluded farm on the Hawkesbury River, which became a haven for the protection of young convict women. A series of events brings **Fran Rea** to Hetty's attention, and she is taken to the farm. Fran and Hetty develop a cottage industry under the compassionate eye of farmhand **Hector Macdougal;** Hector's loving words change lives. It is to him that Fran turns when threatened.

The vines now must draw them close to survive the future revelations, and of those, there are many.

ISBN: 9780645441512   eISBN: 9780645441529
Long-listed in the Historical Fiction Company Competition 2023
The story continues in "Scotch at The Rocks"…

Scotch at The Rocks

Glasgow, Scotland, early 1800s to The Rocks, Sydney 1830s

Orphaned children Brodie Stewart and Heather Anderson live on Glasgow's streets. Although hungry, they somehow manage to survive and stay out of trouble. Heather finds a job and looks to be settled; things go pear-shaped for them both. Eventually, they marry by declaration, but even that gets complicated, and they are both arrested soon after exchanging their vows. In 1838, they were transported to Sydney as convicts. Heather arrives within weeks of Brodie, and they are assigned close to each other. They are now living in the docklands of Sydney, known as The Rocks. They now have to forge a new life halfway across the world from their homeland.

Adventures abound, and Brodie gets press-ganged. While he's away, Heather's life changes and soon, she's officially selling Scotch Whisky at a shop in The Rocks.

You can take a Scot out of Scotland, but where did the Scotch come from?

ISBN 9780645441550 ebook 9781923097001 Large Print 9781923097254

Waiting at the Sliprails

The Bathurst Road 1830s

A Convict's Tale

Bea Dawes's term of conviction nears an end, and she has few options other than marriage to a stranger or going on the street.

Jack Barnes, the hired drover, wants a wife. Bea accepts his offer; then, she discovers that he could be gone for months, leaving her alone with **Billy and Netty**, part of the tribe of an Aboriginal tribe who live on his secluded farm. Bea learns to love her husband and also this wonderful Aboriginal couple. Drought ravages the farm, and Jack must hit the long paddock with the flock. In his absence, a visitor arrives, threatening to destroy everything she has worked so hard for. Can Bea touch her heart? Can she cope? Will the drought ever end? And when will Jack return?

ISBN: 9780645441543   eISBN: 9781923097032

PenCraft Award Winner for Literary Excellence,
Christian Historical Fiction 2024

Convict Shadows of the Past

Two Jennifers, two hundred years apart

The colonial history of cheese in Australia

When she discovers her convict family history, eight-year-old Jenny Kellow learns that she was named after a convict from nearly two hundred years ago. Inspired by her grandfather's stories, she delves into her ancestors' convict past. From him, she hears tales of bushrangers, convicts, and life in the early colony of Parramatta. She embarks on a journey to retrace the footsteps of her convict great-great-great-grandmother to honour her. Jenny's quest begins with microfiche in the 1960s, where she discovers a small tin mining town in Cornwall and the production of a cheese that set London alight. She uncovers that her ancestor, **Jennifer Kellow,** brought her cheese-making skills to Parramatta, where she taught others the craft. Echoes of the past can still be heard if you know where to listen. Who was the first Jennifer, and what does she have to do with cheese? Why is she so elusive? Did Jenny's ancestor, Jennifer, ever see those two small crosses carved into the bricks of the Female Factory? Would Jenny ever uncover her ancestor's story?

ISBN: 9780645783315   ISBN ebook 9780645783322

A NaNoWriMo 2022 book winner

In Defence of Her Honour

London 1800s to Parramatta 1819

Will the real man of quality please stand up?

Bill Miller was raised and educated with the sons of the family. The youngest, Bert Edison-Browne, had been his best friend. However, jealousy intervenes when Bill's excellent schoolwork begins to curtail their friendship. He wins a scholarship and enters Oxford University. When Bill's father dies unexpectedly, Bert insists that Bill take over as butler, but it's more to oppress him. Bert's jealousy grows and festers. He is now looking for a way to rid themselves of their new butler. A ruckus ensues, and Bill is arrested for assaulting Bert.

Molly Ross, the housekeeper's daughter, will vouch for him. It's too late; Bill has been arrested and is soon to be sentenced and transported. With Bill gone, Molly now fights to defend herself from Bert. After hitting him with a pan, she, too, is arrested and sent to Sydney. Bill and Molly arrive with letters of introduction and compensation from Bert's father. Soon, they will be running the best inn in Parramatta with an endorsement from the governor.

ISBN 9780645441567   ISBN ebook 9781923097049

Long-listed in the Historical Fiction Company Competition 2024

I Can't Stop Tomorrow
Irish Famine 1840s to Avoca Beach, Australia

Escaping bigotry and prejudice in Ireland, the O'Shane family lives on a secluded farm on the west coast of Ireland. The potato blight soon decimated their farm. It's always darkest before dawn, and the two remaining girls cling to the hope of a new life. With the kindness of strangers, the eldest girls, **Clare** and **Kerry O'Shane**, head to their cousin, Sal Lockley, in Parramatta, Australia. A new, wonderful life awaits them both. **Shéamus Connor** is the annoying teenage boy who reluctantly draws Clare's affection. However, living in a convict town means ruffians abound.

John Moore is a bad-tempered and troubled Irishman who is content to live alone on another secluded farm until he discovers Clare and two other lads need rescuing.

Can John protect her from the pain inflicted by an evil world?

Can Shéamus find his lost love, who has fled?

ISBN: 9780645441598   ISBN ebook 9781923097056

Madeline's Boy
England 1830s to New South Wales 1840
The race to protect an Orphaned Boy
All is not straightforward when money and titles are involved.

Orphaned, afraid and on the run, Chip must flee.

Madeline was his mother's best friend. Maddie now needs to keep her charge safe and alive. She must give up her life to protect the boy she has loved since birth.

Months after Chip's parents' demise, Maddie sets out to deliver Chip to his Uncle Humphrey, who lives in Sydney. Through him, she meets Chip's uncle's friend, Tim, who falls for Maddie—but will they find happiness?

The menacing presence soon finds Chip, and Maddie needs to hide him again. They are relocated from hidden farms to secret valleys, ultimately ending up in an Aboriginal encampment.

Can Tim find a way to be with Maddie? And if so… Will Chip ever be safe?

ISBN: 9780645783308   ISBN ebook 9781923097094

Long-listed in the Historical Fiction Company Competition 2024

Jam or Marmalade for Tea
England 1820s to New South Wales 1825 (Governor Brisbane Era)

Martha Hamilton is the eldest of four orphans struggling to survive on their own. She is caught stealing, tried, convicted, and transported to New South Wales. With her family gone, she becomes despondent. Life holds no meaning for her, and the ocean waves look inviting.

Captain Guy Manning is a frustrated and injured redcoat soldier returning to Sydney for a new assignment. He notices Martha trying to jump overboard and rescues her. How do two cats bring them together?

A convict ship is no place for romance, and she's far too young anyway, isn't she?

Can Guy save her and forge a life together for them? What connections does he have to try to save her siblings? Why is marmalade important for their future?

Paperback ISBN 9781923097933   eISBN 9781923097285

A NaNoWriMo 2023 book winner

A prequel to 'The Lockleys Parramatta' series
(Free novella with newsletter signup)
Unshackled Lives
Set in England & Australia in the 1800s
Australian historical fiction of early colonial days

Ned Lockley is the second of four sons of the Duke and Duchess of Gracemere. As his mother's favourite, his childhood years were blissful, but he needed to grow up, and quickly.

A whirlwind romance is followed by a loved one's betrayal. The following emotional turmoil is particularly challenging for Ned to cope with, especially amid a collapsing and immoral society. Ned can't stay as his family is falling apart. His mother's words to remain true to himself and his faith make him leave everything he knows. How did Ned end up in New South Wales in charge of placing female convicts? Will he ever find happiness or discover who Charles is?

ISBN 9781923097377   eISBN 9781923097384   LP ISBN: 9781923097391

A 100-year, six-part Australian Colonial series
The Lockleys of Parramatta 1800-1900

Hands upon the Anvil

A blacksmith's life and love are more than work
Parramatta 1830s

Eddie Lockley's parents were transported for their crimes. Can a steadfast lad rise above his origins and guide others to succeed in a land of opportunity?

Ten-year-old Eddie longs to help his mum and dad. Living in a convict town with his family, the keen youngster has been working with the local blacksmith since his sixth birthday. But when a lieutenant doesn't stop abusing his older brother, the young boy yearns for the day when he can stand up and end the torment. Though he's thrilled when his mentor offers to send him off to learn his letters, Eddie fears he won't be around to watch his siblings' backs. But as he takes on the biggest adventure of his life, the brave believer soon discovers that God is looking out for everyone he loves. Does this young man in the making have what it takes to change everything for the better?

ISBN 9780994578235   Ebook ISBN 978-0-9945782-5-9   Hardcover 9798496177368

Out Where The Brolgas Dance

Gold is found, and so is love
Parramatta 1840s
How can a question change so many people?

It's the 1840s, and discoveries across the Blue Mountains continue. Major Mitchell's new road is complete, and towns are planned and being built. Abundant land is available for those who want it. Eighteen-year-old **William "Wills" Lockley** has laid a solid foundation for a respectable career as a blacksmith, but the Lockley lust for adventure flows deeply within his veins. He dreads the monotony of work at the blacksmith's forge and yearns for adventure in a new frontier. Wills meets six Englishmen (*Coping with what is now known as PTSD*) who have the means to make his dreams come true. What they discover changes the Colony and their lives forever. Gold fever ensues. While in the West, Wills must deal with an uncertain romance. Does Cathy even want him?

ISBN 9780994578242   Ebook ISBN 978-0-9945782-6-6 Hardcover ISBN 9798755445504
LP ISBN 9781923097155

Diamonds in the Dirt

Diamonds, love and money… but there is much more to life.
Parramatta 1850s

The youngest Lockley son, **Luke Lockley**, has completed his university education, and his life lacks direction. No job, no money, and no love. Desperately alone, he prays for guidance. How can Luke trust that God has a plan for him if he can't even find a job? He does the only thing he can … he prays. Within a week, life has changed … oh, how it has changed as his brother Wills turns up with a suggestion. Would Luke be interested in joining the expedition with John Evans? **Reverend William Clarke** needs assistance with a government mineral survey. The challenges, adventures and finds are life-changing for many. However, it gives Luke meaning, purpose and direction. The condition of his heart problems also takes a turn. Can he walk away? Will she wait for him?

ISBN: 9780994578273 Ebook ISBN: 978-0-9945782-8-0 Hard cover ISBN 979-8788011141

The Earl's Shadow

Who or what is the 'shadow'? How does it affect so many?
Parramatta 1860s

Charles Lockley, the Earl of Coxheath, spent his youth as a convict in Parramatta, unaware of his noble birth, with limited education and few social skills. Now, after a near-death experience, Charles must decide how to live the rest of his life. He is thrust out of his comfort zone in London. There, Charles discovers his purpose. He delivers a speech in parliament—an action that will reshape the empire.

His eldest son, **Charlie**, shares many of his father's shortcomings. However, the past continues to haunt Charlie.

But how does **Jim Leslie**, the Cobb and Co. coach driver, fit into their story? And what exactly is 'The Earl's Shadow' that he mentions?

ISBN: 9780645110708   Ebook ISBN 978-0-9945782-9-7

Once a Jolly Swagman

An old black Billy Can contains the secrets of an incredible life

An Australian Historical Novel Inspired by the songs of The Seekers

Set in 1870s Parramatta and Kent, UK

Rick Lockley, struggling to escape his family's expectations, runs away to find himself. **Jack**, a jolly swagman, takes him under his care. Even after years together, Rick knows little about the old man.

On his death, Jack leaves Rick his precious billy can; the contents reveal Jack's identity. Stunned, Rick must travel to England to finalise Jack's wishes. There, he uncovers Jack's life of love, betrayal and a link to his own family. Rick also discovers there is much more to learn about this enigmatic man.

ISBN 9780645110753   Ebook ISBN 978-0-6451107-6-0

Jonty's Journey

Gems, Love, Artists and a Golden Lion

Australia and South Africa 1880-1902

Sydney Jeweller **Jonty Evans's** passion for gems takes him to Africa at a volatile time. There, he finds the diamonds he wants and is given a lion cub. However, Jonty is all but kidnapped. His experiences in the Transvaal plunge him into questioning everything he knows about life. Soon, nightmares haunt him. (This is now known as PTSD.)

Upon returning home, he nearly ruins his chance with **Lottie Lockley** before it even begins, and he finds adjusting hard. Lottie's father, **Luke** Lockley from Parramatta, takes him under his wing and directs him to someone who can assist.

Jonty is then called back to Africa as a liaison and reunites with his lion, Chimbu, after saving the life of his security detail. His life journey introduces him to remarkable artists, politicians, poets, rebels, and the scapegoat soldier, Harry Breaker Morant. Can Jonty lay the past to rest and find his lost peace?

ISBN 9780645110777   HC ISBN 9781923097124   Ebook ISBN: 978-0-6451107-9-1

More books are planned for a new trilogy, but they won't be released until 2027

Fools Gold Trilogy

The Breeze Gently Shifts

The Silver Thimble

Knots behind the Tapestry

Co-Winner of 1999 NSW Senior Citizen of the Year, In the Year of the Senior Citizen

Mattie

The Story of an Australian Convict Child
An Australian Historical Story inspired by real Life.

An orphaned child, Mattie, is convicted of petty theft, sentenced to seven years, and sent to Australia. She meets another convict woman who, at her death, gives Mattie a chance for a new life. She makes the most of everything that comes her way, earning her freedom, falling in love, marrying, and becoming a mother. But life is not kind to her. She meets bushrangers, moves to Bathurst's gold fields, and opens a store. Yet, she is the kind of woman who made Australia what it is today. Can she survive alone in a man's world? She is a remarkable woman who breaks down all her barriers.

Her faith is what keeps her strong. Can it sustain her through everything life throws at her? *(Mattie's story continues in The Lockleys of Parramatta - bk 4 & 6)*
Much of this novel draws on family history, including the baptism aboard the convict ship. This occurred to Mary Amelia Harlow on the "Wanstead" in 1814.

ISBN 9781503252370 & ebook ISBN 9781923097018
(The story continues in The Earl's Shadow & Once a Jolly Swagman)

Ricky

A boy in Colonial Australia

Ricky English and his mother immigrated from England to join his father in the new Colony of Sydney. Upon arrival, there was no sign of his father. Ricky's mum uses the tiny amount of money they brought to get lodgings in a run-down building. Things go from bad to worse when his mother dies; he is thrown out of the hired rooms, and the caretakers confiscate all their possessions.

Ricky lives on the streets of Sydney Town as a street waif. Ricky finds safe places to sleep and befriends freed convicts who can help him survive. One day, he encounters a lost child and helps reunite her with her family. These people try to help him, but he insists on doing things his way because of his stubbornness. However, he has found a mentor and confidante. The story follows him through his life. He survives and turns his life around, helping others along the way. Ricky's firm faith keeps him strong, but will his new friends ridicule him because of it?

(Will's story continues in Jonty's Journey)
Paperback ISBN 9781500770570   Kindle ASIN: B00MLYN6IG

The Heather to The Hawkesbury

Four Scottish families brave a new life in a strange land.

Torn from their homeland by starvation, four Scottish families are forced to leave the Isle of Skye and seek a new life in Australia. **Mary Macdonald**, her husband **Murd**, and their family, her brother **Fergus** MacKenzie, sister-in-law **Caro** MacLeod, cousin **Alex** Fraser, and all their loved ones are compelled to emigrate from Scotland because of the Potato famine and Clearances.

The story follows these families as they journey from Scotland to the New South Wales colony in the 1850s. Mary struggles to cope with the changes and losses in the first months of settlement. Although the other women rely on her, she is nearly overwhelmed. Mary can't settle in this fierce land and pines for home.

Together, the families endure hardships such as accidents, loss, floods, and relentless work, ultimately forging a strong bond with their new homeland. Trials, tribulations, and triumphs mark their saga as they establish themselves in Australia.

Will Mary ever find peace and contentment where danger and sickness have taken loved ones? Can her love for Murd sustain her through life's turmoil? Will their faith keep them together? And what becomes of the brooch given to Mary as she leaves her mother?

ISBN 9781503251434   ebook 9781923097025   Large Print ISBN1533473641
Available on Amazon/Kindle & Large Print

Sara's Author Bio

Sara Powter
PACIFIC WANDERLAND PUBLICATIONS

Sheila Hunter and Sara Powter were a passionate mother-and-daughter team of amateur genealogists. As they collaborated on their family tree, they made many fascinating discoveries. Their most significant finding was the discovery of four convicts whose perspectives on colonial life sharply contrasted with those of the military personnel. Transported to Australia between 1792 and 1814, these four felons lived during the peak of the convict transportation era.

Before her passing in 2002, Sheila adapted some of these histories into enchanting stories, later published as her Australian Colonial Trilogy by Sara. Sheila also left a fourth, unfinished story, inspiring Sara to complete it. Before taking on that task, however, Sara first created the 'Lockleys of Parramatta' series to ensure she could honour her mother's work. She completed the first two books in that series before attempting to finish 'Dancing to Her Own Tune'—for which Sheila had written the first 30,000 words.

Vividly evoking the Colonial Era, these books delve deeper into the theme of overcoming adversity in Colonial Australia, exploring how it emerged, the demise of the Convict system, and the discovery of mineral wealth. Sara skilfully intertwines precise archival data with a captivating narrative to craft a collection of stories about faith, love, loss, and redemption.

Two hundred years after her family arrived in Australia, Sara continues the Australian Colonial stories that start with *Gentle Annie Soames,* a saga about the First Fleet. Her *First Fleet Trilogy* is now complete. Following this chronologically are *The Hunter to Macquarie* Collection, the *Unlikely Convict Ladies* Trilogy, and The *Lockleys of Parramatta*. The *Convict Birthstain Collection*, set in the mid-1800s, follows. All the stories are stand-alone novels.

See Sara's web page to keep up to date with more stories.

Amazon Aus QR

Signed copies are available from:-
https://www.sarapowter.com.au
(Australian Postage only)

Email me at
saragpowter@gmail.com

FACEBOOK
https://www.facebook.com/profile.php?id=100063887262514
Would you like*"Unshackled Lives" for free?*
Download from Book Funnel after you sign up.

FREE Newsletter signup
From my web page.